8-99

DATE DUE

NEUROTICA

BANTAM BOOKS

NEW YORK   TORONTO   LONDON

SYDNEY   AUCKLAND

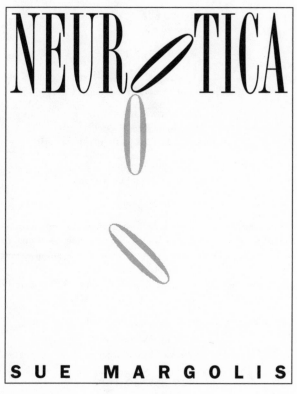

NEUR TICA

SUE MARGOLIS

NEUR O TICA

A Bantam Book / published by arrangement with Headline Book Publishing,
a division of Hodder Headline PLC.

PUBLISHING HISTORY
Headline edition / 1998
Bantam Books edition / July 1999

Book design by Laurie Jewell

Library of Congress Cataloging-in-Publication Data
Margolis, Sue.
Neurotica / Sue Margolis.
p. cm.
ISBN 0-553-10984-7
I. Title.
PR6063.A635N48   1999
823'.914—dc21   98-46978
                          CIP

PRINTED IN THE UNITED STATES OF AMERICA

BVG   10 9 8 7 6 5 4 3 2 1

TO JONATHAN,
WHO NEVER HAS
A HEADACHE

DAN BLOOMFIELD STOOD IN FRONT
of the full-length bathroom mirror,
dropped his boxers to his ankles,
moved his penis to one side to get a better
look and stared hard at the sagging, wrinkled flesh which housed his testicles.
Whenever Dan examined his testicles—
and as a hypochondriac he did this several
times a week—he thought of two things:
the likelihood of his imminent demise; and
the cupboard under the stairs in his
mother's house in Finchley.

It was a consequence of the lamentable
amount of storage space in her un-
modernized fifties kitchenette that Mrs.
Bloomfield had always kept hanging in the
hall cupboard, alongside the overcoats,
macs and umbrellas, one of those long

string shopping bags made pendulous by the weight of her overflow Brussels sprouts. From the age of thirteen, Dan referred to this as his mother's scrotal sac.

These days Dan reckoned his own scrotal sac was a dead ringer for his mother's. His bollocks couldn't get any lower. Dan supposed lower was OK at forty; death on the other hand was not.

By bending his knees ever so slightly, shuffling a little closer to the mirror and pulling up on his scrotum he could get a better view of its underside. It looked perfectly normal. In fact the whole apparatus looked perfectly normal. There was nothing he could see, no sinister lumps, bumps or skin puckering which suggested impending uni-bollockdom, or that his wife should start bulk-buying herrings for his funeral. Then, suddenly, as he squeezed his right testicle gently between his thumb and forefinger, it was there again, the excruciating stabbing pain he had felt as he crossed his legs that morning in the editors' daily conference.

A NNA SHAPIRO, DAN'S WIFE, NEEDED TO PEE RIGHT AWAY. She knew because she had just been woken up by one of those dreams in which she had been sitting on the loo about to let go when suddenly something in her brain kicked in to remind her that this would not be a good idea, since she was, in reality, sprawled across the brand-new pocket-sprung divan on which they hadn't even made the first payment. Looking like one of those mad women on the first day of the Debenhams sale, she bolted towards the bathroom. Here she discovered Dan rolling naked on the floor, clutching his testicles in one hand and his penis in the other with a look of agony on his face which she immediately took for sublime pleasure.

As someone who'd been reading "So you think your husband is a sexual deviant"–type advice columns in women's magazines since she was twelve, Anna knew a calm, caring opening would be best.

"Dan, what the fuck are you up to?" she shrieked. "I mean it, if you've turned into some kind of weirdo, I'm putting my hat and coat on now. I'll tell the whole family and you'll never see the children again and I'll take you for every penny. I can't keep up with you. One minute you're off sex and the next minute I find you wanking yourself stupid at three o'clock in the morning on the bathroom floor. How could you do it on the bathroom floor? What if Amy or Josh had decided to come in here for a wee and caught you?"

"Will you just stop ranting for one second, you stupid fat bitch. Look."

Dan directed Anna's eyes towards his penis, which she had failed to notice was completely flaccid.

"I am not wanking. I think I've got bollock cancer. Anna, I'm really scared."

R ELIEVED? YOU BET I WAS BLOODY RELIEVED. GOD, I MEAN for a moment there last night, when I found him, I actually thought Dan had turned into one of those nutters the police find dead on the kitchen floor with a plastic bag over their head and a ginger tom halfway up their arse. Of course, it was no use reminding him that testicular cancer doesn't hurt. . . . What are you going to have?"

As usual, the Harpo was full of crushed-linen, telly-media types talking Channel 4 proposals, sipping mineral water and swooning over the baked polenta and fashionable bits of offal. Anna was deeply suspicious of trendy food. Take polenta, for example: an Italian au pair who had worked for Dan and Anna a few years ago had said she couldn't understand why it had become so fashionable in England. It was, she said, the Italian equivalent of semolina and that the only time an Italian ate it was when he was in school, hospital or a mental institution.

Neither was Anna, who had cellulite and a crinkly post-childbirth tummy flap which spilled over her bikini briefs when she sat down, overly keen on going for lunch with Gucci-ed and Armani-ed spindle-legged journos like Alison O'Farrell, who always ordered a green salad with no dressing and then self-righteously declared she was too full for pudding.

But as a freelance journalist, Anna knew the importance of sharing these frugal lunches with women's-page editors. These days, she was flogging Alison at least two lengthy pieces a month for the *Daily Mercury*'s "Lifestyles" page, which was boosting her earnings considerably. In fact her last dead-baby story, in which a recovering postnatally depressed mum (who also just happened to be a leggy 38 DD) described in full tabloid gruesomeness how she drowned her three-month-old in the bath, had almost paid for the sundeck Anna was having built on the back of her kitchen.

Dan, of course, as the cerebral financial editor of *The Vanguard*, Dan, who was probably more suited to academia than Fleet Street, called her stuff prurient, ghoulish voyeurism and carried on like some lefty sociology student from the seventies about those sorts of stories being the modern opiate of the masses. Anna couldn't be bothered to argue. She knew perfectly well he was right, but, like a lot of lefties who had not so much lapsed as collapsed into the risotto-breathed embrace of New Labour, she had decided that the equal distribution of wealth starting with herself had its merits. She suspected he was just pissed off that her tabloid opiates earned her double what he brought home in a month.

BUT WHAT ABOUT DAN'S CANCER?" ALISON ASKED, SHOVING a huge mouthful of undressed radicchio into her mouth and pretending to enjoy it.

"Alison, I've been married to Dan for twelve years. He's been like this for yonks. Every week it's something different. First it was weakness in his legs and he diagnoses multiple sclerosis, then he feels dizzy and it's a brain tumor. Last week he decided he had some disease which, it turns out, you only get from fondling sheep. Alison, I can't tell you the extent to which no Jewish man fondles sheep. He's a hypochondriac. He needs therapy. I've been telling him to get help for ages, but he won't. He just sits for hours with his head in the *Home Doctor*."

"Must be doing wonders for your sex life."

"Practically nonexistent. He's too frightened to come in case the strain of it gives him a heart attack, and then if he does manage it he takes off the condom afterwards, looks to see how much semen he has produced—in case he has a blockage somewhere—then examines it for traces of blood."

As a smooth method of changing the subject, Alison got up to go to the loo. Anna suspected she was going to chuck up her salad. When she returned, Anna sniffed for vomit, but only got L'Eau d'Issy. "Listen, Anna," Alison began the instant her bony bottom made contact with the hard Phillipe Starck chair. "I've had an idea for a story I think just might be up your street."

DAN BOUGHT THE FIRST ROUND OF DRINKS IN THE PUB AND then went to the can to feel his testicle. It was less than an hour before his appointment with the specialist. The pain was still there.

Almost passing out with anxiety, he sat on the lavatory, put his head between his knees and did what he always did when he thought he was terminally ill: he began to pray. Of course it wasn't real prayer, it was more like some kind of sacred trade-union negotiation in which the earthly official, Dan, set out his position—i.e., dying—and demanded that celestial management, God, put an acceptable offer on the table—i.e., cure him. By way of compromise, Dan agreed that he would start going to synagogue again—or church, or Quaker meeting house, if God preferred—as soon as he had confirmation he wasn't dying anymore.

MR. ANDREW GOODALL, THE RUDDY-COMPLEXIONED FOR-mer rugby fly-half testicle doctor, leaned back in his leather Harley Street swivel chair, plonked both feet on top of his desk and looked at Dan over half-moon specs.

"Perfectly healthy set of bollocks, old boy," he declared.

Kissed him? Dan could have tongue-wrestled the old bugger.

"But what about all this pain I've been getting?"

"You seemed perfectly all right when I examined you. I strongly suspect this is all psychosomatic, Mr. Bloomfield. I mean, I could chop the little blighter orf if you really want me to, but I suspect that if I did, in six months you'd be back in this office with phantom ball pain. My advice to you would be to have a break. Why not book a few days away in the sun with your good lady? Alternatively, I can prescribe you something to calm you down."

Dan had stopped listening round about "psychosomatic." The next thing he knew he was punching the air and skipping like an overgrown four-year-old down Harley Street towards Cavendish Square. He, Dan Bloomfield, was not dying. He, Dan Bloomfield, was going to live.

With thoughts of going to synagogue entirely forgotten, he went into John Lewis and bought Anna a new blender to celebrate. One can only imagine that God sighed and wondered why he had created a world full of such ungrateful bleeders.

A NNA GOT HOME JUST AFTER FOUR. DENISE, HER BABY-sitter, had taken Josh and Amy swimming after school, so she would be bratless for at least a couple of hours—more if Denise got them sausages and chips at the pool. Anna decided to have a bath and a quick de-fuzz. All through the lunch she had been aware that she was having a bad pubic hair day. The sideburns on her inner thighs were reaching a density that would have done a woolly mammoth proud.

As she turned over Dan's knicker drawer looking for his razor, which he always tried to hide because whenever she used it she left it blunt and clogged up with leg hairs, Anna realized she was getting quite enthused by Alison's feature idea.

She'd said to Alison she wasn't sure if she had time to do it, which was a lie she always told features editors just in case they started taking her for granted. But she thought she probably would. She could never say no to work, in case the Alison O'Farrells of this world forgot who she was and never used her again. But more than that, while Alison was explaining the idea to her, she began to feel rather horny.

Alison had just received a preview copy of Rachel Stern's new book, *The Clitoris-Centered Woman.* Anna despised Rachel Stern almost as much as she despised polenta-eaters. Stern, an American, was one of a gaggle of beautiful Harvard-educated feminist writers, barely old enough to menstruate, who with their pert bosoms, firm arses and live-in personal trainers had the audacity to lecture the sagging, stretch-marked masses on how antiwrinkle creams, Wonderbras and cosmetic Polyfillas were a form of treachery against the sisterhood, or some such rot.

In her last book, *Dermis,* Stern had railed against cosmetic surgery. On the day of publication she had led a massive protest rally outside an LA clinic to launch her "Get a Life Not the Knife" campaign. Hundreds of East and West Coast academics, "educators" and writers—mainly svelte Stern look-alikes, but with a smattering of token uglies—turned up to yell abuse at the women going into the clinic. According to the *LA Times* the protesters even dunked one woman's head in a vat of liposucted fat, thoughtfully provided by a mole at the clinic who was sympathetic to the cause.

"Look, I know you can't stand the bitch," Alison had said, "but I reckon *The Clitoris-Centered Woman* is actually quite sensible. It's about infidelity and why women are more reluctant to be unfaithful than men. She says women don't go in for extramarital shagging because they feel they can only do it if they are actually in love with the guy, and being in love with two men seriously does your brain in, so not doing it in the first place saves all the hassle of whose heart you're going to end up breaking. Anyway, Stern says that all this needing to be in love in order to have an affair is crap and women are just as capable as men of having affairs purely for the sexual pleasure—hence the title. So affairs become no more than a bit of glorified pampering—like going for a manicure or a facial except you get an orgasm instead of your blackheads squeezing. Of course, the most difficult part is keeping it secret and not blurting it out to hubby."

"And don't tell me, she reckons we should all be into extra-curricular rutting because it can really zap up your marriage . . . and what you want me to do is to go out and interview three slappers who make a habit of being unfaithful just for the sex."

"You got it. Two thousand words if you can. You've got loads of time—she's not due over here to launch the book until mid-July, which gives you about eight weeks."

Anna realized she had got so carried away replaying in her mind all this talk of adultery that she had been absentmindedly shaving her pubes for at least ten minutes and had left herself with little more than a Hitler mustache between her legs. As she rinsed Dan's razor in the bathwater and watched her hairs float on top of the white scum, it began to dawn on her that if anybody needed to become a clitoris-centered woman, it was her.

She reckoned the last time she and Dan had done anything which vaguely resembled mind-blowingly filthy sex was at Amy's fifth birthday party, three years ago, before Dan's obsession with his health had started affecting his libido.

It was one of those sweltering summer days when old ladies have funny turns in the Co-op and small boys try to set light to worms with magnifying glasses.

In Anna's back garden poisonous packs of Jessicas, Olivias and Harrys, untroubled by the heat, were rampaging over flowerbeds, hunting the thimble with Smarty Arty, the rented clown, while plump forty-something mummies falling out of their Indian-cotton sundresses made a play for the thirty-something daddies in their white T-shirts and Ray•Bans.

Anna was bustling round the trestle table which she had set up that morning under the apple tree and dutifully covered with matching paper cloth, plates and cups depicting the latest thigh-booted, whip-wielding girlie superhero Amy had been going on about for weeks. She was trying, with little success, to tempt the children with egg mayonnaise sandwiches. They were more interested in tearing around the table blowing raspberries at each other and raucously discussing the similarity between egg smell and fart smell. Dan, sensing she wasn't far off the kind of violence that would have seen her go down for a five stretch, and suddenly fancying her like nobody's business, stopped pouring spritzers for the grown-ups, and made his way towards the table. With a face so straight he could have been saying that her mother had just had a pulmonary embolism and wasn't expected to make it through the night, he whispered in her ear, "I want to fuck you right now."

He handed the Orvieto and the Waitrose fizzy mineral water bottles to a drunken mother, who was so out of it that she didn't bat an eyelid as he dragged a giggling and protesting Anna off towards the house. Nobody else gave them a second glance either, even when Dan put his hand up Anna's silk skirt and kept it there.

Without saying a word he pulled her up the stairs and into their bedroom. He locked the door, unzipped her skirt, then turned and pushed her gently over the pine desk she used as a dressing table. As the grown-ups helped themselves to more booze and Smarty Arty worked the children into a frenzy telling slightly rude knock-knock jokes and producing rabbits from nowhere, Dan pulled her pants down to her ankles, reached for the bottle of baby oil on the table and allowed a few drops of the clear, thick liquid to trickle onto her buttocks. Anna moaned softly as he massaged the oil into her skin. With the lightness of touch he knew she adored he brushed his fingers gently between her wet bottom cheeks and then over her clitoris. She gasped as suddenly, almost violently, he pushed two fingers deep inside her. Anna yelled at him rather too loudly to make her come. For a second she went off the boil, thinking the children might have heard, but Dan, feeling her tense up, started to lick the back of her neck and whisper that it was OK, nobody could hear. Then, while continuing to play with her clitoris, he pushed himself inside her. The exquisite danger and naughtiness of it all made them both come in seconds.

· · ·

FAT CHANCE OF ANYTHING LIKE THAT HAPPENING NOW, ANNA
thought, as she squirted Jif onto the bath and set about the
greasy bath ring with a nonscratch scouring pad.

The most Anna got these days was an occasional wake-up
call in the small of her back from Dan's early-morning erection. In a voice that sounded like a child in Woolworth's trying
to get round its mother for pick-'n'-mix, he would then ask her
if they could do it. She invariably said yes because he looked so
miserable and pathetic and she felt sorry for him. He was also,
if she was objective about it, still as slim, dark and good-
looking as the night she met him. When they had finished their
basic-model, bottom-of-the-range humping, Dan would roll off
her and go back to sleep and Anna would lie there for a minute
before getting up to make tea, thinking how utterly fucking
miserable and lonely she felt.

Then she would go downstairs and slam round the kitchen
getting more and more furious. Furious with Dan for rejecting
her and refusing to see a shrink, and furious with herself because she still loved him and didn't have the heart to walk out
on him.

ANNA BLAMED DAN'S MOTHER FOR HIS HYPOCHONDRIA. AC-
cording to the other Bloomfield children—Gail, Dan's sister, who was married to an architect in Tel Aviv, and Jonathan,
who was a cameraman with CNN in Atlanta—the late Lilly
Bloomfield, who dropped dead from a stroke in Solly's the kosher butcher while delivering some vitriolic rant about the
pitiful size of her briskets, had been something of a tyrant. A
five-foot kosher tigress in Crimplene slacks and strawberry-
blond tint courtesy of Chez Melvin in Hendon, she was one of
those Jewish mothers who was never satisfied by her children's
achievements.

She would stand frying fishballs on a Friday afternoon—a
plastic bag over her new hairdo—waiting for each of them to
come home from school. Then she would start: why had they

only got a B plus that week and not an A plus? Why had they come third in class and not first? Then, over dinner, she would turn on her husband. Stan down the road was earning three times what he got, and just by driving a cab; Morry from the synagogue was taking the family to Rimini twice a year from wet fish. What Lilly wanted was a Lord Sieff, a Baron Rothschild, even Stan down the road. What she had was Lou, who made sixty quid a week selling ties off a stall in Leather Lane market.

Dan used to joke that if Hitler had been given Lilly for a mother she would have turned to him after he had slaughtered six million Jews and said, "Huh, you call that a holocaust?"

Of her three children, it was Dan, the youngest, who had found it particularly hard to cope with his mother's constant undermining. Nevertheless, he was the most successful, academically and professionally. By the time she died in 1981, aged sixty-five, he was making a good living freelancing and doing the odd late-evening shift on the *FT*. But Lilly had almost destroyed him. Not only had she taken away every ounce of his self-confidence, she had also made him fear her wrath at every turn. Eventually, whenever he did anything he believed she might disapprove of, he developed "symptoms" that to him were quite real, even if they were largely invisible to the medical profession.

A S SOON AS THE SEVEN DAYS OF MOURNING FOR LILLY WERE over, Lou sold up and went to live in Marbella with Nora, the shikseh from the post office whom he'd been screwing for years behind Lilly's back.

After thirty years appearing in a marriage without a speaking part, Lou, it seemed, had balls after all—he must have sewn them back on one night when Lilly wasn't looking. For two weeks during that summer, Dan, using his father as a positive role model for the first time ever, decided that now his mother was dead, he could stop living his life trying to please her. She, after all, was now sitting drinking lemon tea on a pink Dralon settee in her celestial through lounge, and couldn't get at him anymore. The time had come for Daniel Bloomfield to rise up, rebel and get the late Mrs. Bloomfield off his back.

He decided that his first act of rebellion would be to go looking for his own Nora and, near as damn it, found her.

In fact Anna found him—at the party his cousin Beany Levine held to celebrate passing his bar exams. It was one of those utterly safe young Jewish singles do's where one's grandmother wouldn't have felt out of place. The venue was the Levine parents' row house in Gants Hill, where, although Beany was twenty-three, he still lived. The boys stood around drinking Coke discussing that day's West Ham versus Tottenham Hotspur game. Beany, who had been a bit of a comedian since childhood, was interrupting with a joke about an ultra-Orthodox kangaroo, a rubber and a box of matzos. All in all, they were the kind of conservative young Jewish men who, when they got married, would invite their mates to a stag coffee morning.

The girls convened in the kitchen, in their velvet jeans with rhinestone studs. They drank lemonade and lime and debated engagement ring settings. A few daredevils had got slightly merry on Beany's parents' advocaat and cherry brandy and were dancing to 10CC in the middle of the lounge.

Anna had come to the party with one of Beany's friends from chambers, who had since deserted her and gone off to meet the rhinestones. She was now standing alone in a corner in her black dungarees, CND T-shirt and short-spiked lefty feminist hair, sifting through Beany's record collection, which seemed to consist mainly of old Monty Python LPs.

Anna noticed Dan sitting at the end of the room in his new denim bomber jacket looking moody and sexy and a dead ringer for Bob Dylan. Sensing a kindred spirit and fellow subversive, not to mention the possibility of sex, she started to make her way over to him.

What Anna took for moodiness, Dan would have described as downright depression. He couldn't work out how, on a Saturday night in his twenty-fifth year, when he should have been defiling his mother's memory by snorting coke in Fulham, he was at his cousin's party on the outskirts of Ilford, drinking it.

He was, at the precise moment of meeting Anna on Beany's mother's tan leatherette sofa, balancing a plate of her cocktail-size gefilte fishballs on his lap. He was pretending one of the fishballs was his mother's head and taking a stab at it with a cocktail stick, when he missed and sent the whole lot flying onto the shag rug. They ended up at Anna's feet. She bent down and picked up two of them.

"Er, I seem to have your balls in my hand," she said.

For many nights afterwards Dan lay awake cursing himself for not being able to come up with a witty reply. The best he could do was an embarrassed smile.

"Hi, I'm Anna Shapiro. Do you fancy making a break for it and finding somewhere to get rat-arsed?" As she spoke she took an Old Holborn tin from a tatty old shoulder bag and offered Dan a roll-up. Realizing he had come face to face with his first-ever Jewish shikseh, he got an instant erection.

It turned out that Anna, who was a postgrad English student at Sussex, had begun life as a nice Jewish girl from Stanmore with a father who was an accountant and a mother who had gold-plated bathroom taps.

As she downed pints of Guinness in the Cocked Hat on Woodford Avenue, she explained how she had rejected the whole neo-bourgeois, crypto-fascist Jewburbia thing by smoking dope in the ladies at synagogue during the Yom Kippur service and turning up to her bubba's Shabbas dinners wearing no knickers.

Dan fell instantly, utterly and overwhelmingly in love.

THE MORNING AFTER DAN AND ANNA FIRST SLEPT TOGETHER, Dan woke up with a pounding head. He'd had a nightmare which involved his mother dressed as one of the Bay City Rollers, in tartan trousers, scarf and red platforms, chasing him round the imitation Louis Quatorze dining room table trying to stab him with the ornate silver scissors she kept in the fruit bowl for cutting grapes.

Two days later, when the headache still hadn't gone, without telling Anna, he took the first of his eleven malignant brain tumors to Harley Street.

SITTING ON THE SIDE OF THE BATH WHILE SHE RUBBED MOIS-turizer into telly-ad-smooth legs, Anna heard Dan's key in the door. He called to her from the bottom of the stairs. The tone of his voice said it all. Anna had no doubt she was about to find yet another electronic juicer, mixer or squeezer on the kitchen table.

CHAPTER TWO

T WAS ENGELBERT HUMPERDINCK THAT finally did it. Anna was standing in her red Cystitis Awareness Week T-shirt that she wore in bed, rubber gloves and Day-Glo-pink nylon slippers, trying to wash up and at the same time fry sausages and eggs for Amy and her two friends who had slept over, when "Release Me" came on the radio.

She knew she had finally scored a personal worst in sexual fantasy, but it was a measure of her frustration when, for a few minutes, she imagined being carted off to some tropical island by Engelbert. She even refused to snap out of her reverie when her rational brain reminded her that sad old medallion-man crooners were much more time-share in Tossa del Mar than beach house in Barbados. But it didn't matter. Dan hadn't made love to her last night—even on electrical appliance night.

Usually when he'd had some good news from some specialist or other, Dan was all over Anna. He would cuddle up to her on the sofa, hold her, hug her and flick her bangs with his fingers. This would be followed by the sorry-I've-been-such-a-bastard-to-you-I-promise-finally-and-forever-that-my-obsession-with-my-health-is-over-and-wouldn't-it-be-great-if-we-put-the-kids-in-kennels-and-got-away-for-a-few-days speech.

Anna would usually respond with her shit-Dan-we've-been-here-a-million-times-before-and-I-can't-live-like-this-any-more-unless-you-see-a-shrink speech. Dan would then assure her that he would definitely get help if she ever found him imagining symptoms again.

Anna always caved in and by ten o'clock they would be in bed, Dan promising her the orgasm of her life. By 10:45 Dan would start whispering in her ear that he was getting carpal tunnel syndrome in his middle finger and could she hurry up. But Anna found it almost impossible to come when she was still so angry. So she held her breath, thrashed her head about a bit, let out a long sigh and said, "Thank you; that was lovely." She then let Dan have his turn. Two minutes later they would both be asleep.

Last night had been the same, up to the children-in-kennels bit, which he'd got to while they were watching *Newsnight*. Some impenetrable European Monetary Union item came on, and Anna got up to make herself a cup of tea. While she was waiting for the kettle to boil, she thought she'd unpack the John Lewis bag, which was still on the kitchen table.

Inside were two boxes, one containing the blender (that made four they now owned), while the other was from a medical supplier in Wigmore Street.

Anna ripped into the bubble wrap with some kitchen scissors and pulled out a square, wallet-sized plastic device. It had a tiny screen at the top, and a round opening at the side. The only instructions were in Spanish or Norwegian, but from what

Anna could make out from the diagrams, this was some kind of newfangled home blood pressure machine. You put your index finger into the anuslike hole, which automatically tightened round it. The electronic sphygmomanometer then gave you a digital readout of your blood pressure.

A few months ago she would have gone screaming into the living room, ranting and raving at Dan as if he were an alcoholic and she had just found three bottles of whiskey hidden in the toilet tank. But last night she had been so bloody worn out with it all, so tired of the pleading and begging, that she simply put the sphygmomanometer back in its box, finished making her mug of tea, yelled goodnight to Dan from halfway up the stairs and climbed into bed.

When Dan came up twenty minutes later she was still sipping her tea and reading. He gave her another hug and told her he loved her, but there was no mention of orgasms. Anna put her book on the bedside table and turned out her light. Dan had his back to her and was pretending to be asleep, but she could sense that under the duvet he was feeling his pulse.

AS SHE GAVE THE SAUSAGES ANOTHER TURN, ANNA DECIDED she had no choice. If she didn't find some fun soon, not to mention some decent sex, she would shrivel up and die. She tore off her rubber gloves, threw down her spatula and dialed Alison O'Farrell's home number.

"Alison, it's Anna. Sorry to ring so early on a Saturday morning, but I just thought I'd let you know, I'll definitely do the Rachel Stern piece."

What she didn't tell Alison was that the stories would be genuine, but instead of belonging to three interviewees, they would all be hers.

Anna Shapiro, thirty-seven-year-old mother of two in desperate need of a tummy tuck, breast lift and open-pore surgery, was about to spend the next eight weeks committing adultery—just for fun.

. . .

BRENDA SWEET, SINGLE MUM FROM PECKHAM TURNED MIL-
lionaire fashion designer, dunked a bit of buttery croissant
into her coffee, and watched as globules of fat started to appear
on the surface.

"But what I don't understand is why you can't make do with
solo sex for the time being? I mean, Dan's bound to recover the
use of 'is pecker eventually."

"First, because 'eventually' might mean forty years from now
when he's got cataracts and incontinence pads, and second,
because when I get up to heaven with all the other Jewish
mothers, St. Peter, or whoever my people's equivalent is, will
read out that summary of what everybody did with their lives.
There will be Naomi Fishman who planted a thousand trees in
Israel, Melanie Greenberg who, despite being blind and having
no arms or legs, stuffed fifteen million chicken necks and won
prizes for her chopped liver sculpture, then there will be me,
Anna Shapiro—who wanked. OK, so I do it when I'm desperate, but believe me, adultery is much more respectable."

Brenda said she took the point and topped up their coffee
cups, which were round and metallic, like sputum bowls with
handles. Apparently they'd cost nearly twenty quid each from
some Japanese shop in Covent Garden, but because Brenda
was her best friend, Anna made allowances for her interesting
taste in crockery.

Brenda's kitchen, on the other hand, went well beyond interesting into the outer suburbs of downright peculiar.

It was situated, stylistically speaking, somewhere between
morgue and sluice room. The cupboard doors were brushed
aluminum, the stainless-steel sink was conical, its metal
U-bend exposed, and the floor was covered in those industrial
nonslip concrete tiles which usually surround public swimming
pools. The only object which bordered on the ornamental was a
six-foot-by-four-foot grainy black-and-white photograph, which
took up most of the space on the wall at the far end. It was of
some poor terrified bastard strapped in the electric chair minutes before his execution.

"Fuck me, Bren," Dan, who could be witty in a sardonic way when he momentarily forgot he was dying, had said the first time they were invited to dinner in the new kitchen. "You certainly do a great line in concentration camp chic. S'pose the Mengeles are just outside parking the car. Hope they've remembered to bring a bottle."

To give Brenda her due, she laughed, but she was obviously a bit put out, because she called Dan "a bleedin' Philistine," whose idea of style didn't extend beyond a matching bread-bin and mug-tree set.

Brenda was very good at putting people in their place. Anna saw her do it the day they met and became friends. It was at the antenatal clinic, ten years ago, when she was expecting Josh and Brenda was expecting Alfie.

The hospital made all the women sit in the waiting room in their maternity dresses, but minus their knickers and pantyhose. These they kept on their laps in wire supermarket baskets. Humiliating as this was, none of them challenged the ruling. These were National Health Service patients, who treated doctors like feudal lords, and in place of a forelock to tug, practically curtsied at the end of their examinations before walking out of the consulting room backwards. The tatty notice on the wall, written in green felt tip, explained that it speeded things up if the doctors had instant access to patients' nether regions.

Anna, however, did make some small effort to assert herself. Along with her wire basket, she always took a copy of *Ulysses* into the consulting room and placed it purposefully on the doctor's desk, like a poker player revealing his hand. This was her way of ensuring that whichever supercilious, patronizing git of an obstetrician she was about to see spoke to her in words of more than two syllables—and didn't refer to her as Mum.

A few weeks before Josh was due, Anna was sitting in the waiting room, wire basket on lap, working her way through a bag of Everton mints, when Brenda walked in, eight months pregnant and a size ten, wearing suede heels and a black Lycra minidress under a biker's jacket. Even her tidy, pert bump looked like a casually calculated fashion statement. Anna took one look at her and was just descending into one of those "Omigod, I look like someone turned the liposuction machine to blow" moments of self-hatred, when Brenda started bellowing at the middle-aged woman on the appointments desk.

"Look 'ere, you daft mare, if you think I'm sitting for two hours with a draft up my jacksy on the off chance some doctor'll decide a poke around my privates is in order, you can bloomin' well think again."

"I'm sorry, it's hospital policy."

"I don't care if it's the soddin' Common Agricultural Policy. It's bloody degrading and I'm not doing it."

With that, Brenda turned on her four-inch stilettos, saw there was an empty seat next to Anna and started to make her way towards it. Anna couldn't help thinking that had this been New York, the whole waiting room would have started whooping, applauding, waving their urine samples in support and queuing up to high-five Brenda. But this being Dulwich, everybody kept their heads buried behind their *Good Housekeeping*s, and the only sound was of embarrassed buttock shuffling.

As Brenda neared her, Anna had the same feeling—without the sex part—she'd had the night she met Dan at Beany Levine's party, of stumbling across a like-minded soul. She knew she was on the point of making a friend.

Brenda was about to plonk herself down onto the empty seat and Anna was about to whisper, "Well done; not many people would have taken on that menopausal old bag" and "Where do you think she gets her tank tops?" when Brenda looked down and murmured:

"Oh fuck. It's curtains for me Manolo Blahniks."

She was standing in a small puddle of broken waters.

Brenda looked at Anna. "Christ, what do I do now? After that performance, I suppose the old bag'll have me down for a triple enema and a shave with a blunt razor."

Anna laughed. "Don't worry, you scared the control pants off her. I'll see if I can find one of the midwives."

A calm, motherly midwife called Iris found Brenda a wheel-chair and took her up to the labor ward. As Brenda hadn't started having contractions yet, she said Anna could stay to keep her company. "Just until we locate your other half."

Brenda said she would rather the hospital contacted her mum.

It turned out that Brenda's other half, Elvis, had done a bunk three weeks ago and was living in Leytonstone with an assistant supervisor from Do It All. Brenda had just moved back to Peckham to be near her mum and dad, and this had been her first appointment at the hospital.

Apparently Elvis, who was a clerk with the Inland Revenue, went off with Dawn who did it all because he felt jealous and threatened when Brenda gave up hairdressing and started making a success of designing and making clothes.

She'd studied fashion design at art school years before, but had never had the confidence to set up in business on her own. After art school, she'd just drifted into hairdressing. From the start, posh clients at the salon in Sloane Street began admiring what she wore and asked her where she bought her clothes. When Brenda said she designed and made them herself—even the Lycra bodies and skirts—she began getting dozens of orders.

The first time she broke the five-hundred-pounds-a-week barrier, Elvis took off.

BRENDA AND ANNA HAD BEEN ON THE LABOR WARD ABOUT an hour when Brenda's mum arrived, all hot flush and eau de cologne. Anna said a quick hello and decided she should leave them to it.

The next day Brenda phoned to say that Alfie had arrived safely with Elvis's ears, but she thought she could learn to love him, and that apart from tits as hard as Contiboard and what felt like a net of satsumas hanging out of her bum, she was fine.

. . .

AFTER JOSH WAS BORN, ANNA AND BRENDA SAW EACH OTHER a couple of times a week. They would sit on the floor in Brenda's living room drinking wine, even though they knew that as breast-feeding mothers they shouldn't because it would get the babies drunk, and would try to work out why they were the only women they knew who thought the joy of watching their babies crawl, walk and talk didn't begin to compare with getting a new head of highlights.

Anna said if Josh didn't stop screaming all day she was going to lock him in his room and he could only come out when he turned twenty-five or did something interesting, like get a record in the Top Ten.

One evening, over a bottle of Chardonnay, they decided to form their own subversive breakaway postnatal support group. In order to join, mothers had to sign an undertaking to feed their children only dehydrated baby food from packets. Anybody found Mouli-ing up organic turnips or avocados would be expelled, as would mothers who were caught coming out of the Early Learning Center with boxes of flash cards about their person. Mothers who were deemed to be the type who would carry on breast-feeding their children until they were old enough to go to Guns N' Roses concerts would be flogged.

They were trying to decide whether they'd get any response if they put postcards in the newsagent's window advertising for people to join when it hit Brenda that Anna had never seen any of the clothes she made.

Anna knew very little about real couture, but she took one look at Brenda's exquisitely cut, hand-finished jackets and trousers and knew this came pretty close.

"Blimey, Bren, I knew you were talented, but I had no idea you were Edina bloody Ronay. I can't understand why you're not making a fortune."

"I'll tell you why. I've got orders coming out of my ears, but I can't keep up, because I've got no staff, one rotten sewing machine in a flat not much bigger than one of Princess Di's clutch bags, not to mention fucking Goering here making twenty-four-hour-a-day territorial demands on my tits."

Anna, being an accountant's daughter, couldn't see the problem. Once Brenda had got Alfie on the bottle and into day care, all she needed to do was form a company, write a business plan, find a backer to put up half the money she needed and her bank would probably lend her the rest.

"God, what planet do you live on? Find a backer? You may not be aware of this but you don't find too many ordinary daddies sticking around in Peckham—let alone sugar ones."

Driving home to Blackheath, with Josh asleep in his carrycot on the backseat and Dire Straits on the cassette player, Anna began running through a list of people who she thought might be able to come up with the kind of cash Brenda needed. In the end she decided the only person she knew who wasn't up to their eyes in mortgage repayments and didn't have the ladies from Barclaycard on the phone every five minutes over late payments was her father. He had the money from his mother's flat in Brighton sitting in a building society. But to convince Harry that investing in Brenda's business would be a sound move, she first had to convince her mother.

A NNA SPENT THE NEXT THREE WEEKS, IN BETWEEN BREAST-feeding Josh, on the phone trying to persuade her mother—directrice of Maison Gloria in Stanmore (Fabulous Fashions For the Fuller Figure)—to take a look at Brenda's work.

Harry had bought Gloria the shop over thirty years ago, when her need to repeatedly clean things—the Maudsley called it obsessive-compulsive syndrome—had reached a particularly worrying phase.

One Saturday lunchtime, he had come home from synagogue expecting a nice bowl of borscht before he went off to see Tottenham. Instead he found Gloria on her knees removing bits of dirt from between the floorboards with a cotton swab while two of his best suits were soaking in a bath full of Parazone.

Her psychiatrist at the hospital suggested to Harry in private that an outside interest would be a good idea.

"Funny you should mention it, Dr. Mittelschmertz. I've been thinking maybe a few gentle rounds of golf now and again would do me good."

Dr. Mittelschmertz grimaced. "I mean for your vife, Mr. Shapiro, for your vife."

Harry began phoning estate agents.

Maison Gloria seemed to have done the trick. Every day, Gloria glided around the shop, black velvet pincushion on her wrist, flogging mauve chiffon evening dresses to size twenty-two mothers-of-the-bar-mitzvah-boy who couldn't lay off the cheesecake.

Anna knew that as far as Harry was concerned, Gloria was northwest London's answer to Coco Chanel. If Gloria thought Brenda was worth backing, he wouldn't hesitate to put his hand in his pocket.

But persuading Gloria wasn't easy. Every time Anna brought the subject up, Gloria told her she was mad and obviously suffering from postnatal depression if she expected her to convince Harry to invest money in a total stranger—a shikseh no less—who at best needed a good elocution teacher and at worst might turn out to be a psychopath, only they wouldn't find out until they woke up one morning dead in their beds.

Anna never quite worked out why—maybe her mother could no longer stand her continual badgering—but finally Gloria caved in and agreed to schlep over to Peckham.

"There'll be dirt and litter and people in Acrilan. What should I wear?"

"Pith helmet and puttees should just about hit the right note."

To placate Anna further she even took a present for Alfie.

Gloria decided that as Brenda had been brought up in public housing and her gene pool probably left a lot to be desired, little Alfie's IQ might need a jump start, and so she bought him a times-tables tape. Furious, Anna made her take it back and exchange it for a furry duck.

EVEN THEN, BRENDA'S TASTE IN INTERIORS WAS UNCONVEN-tional.

"Tell me," Gloria had said on the way home, "what sort of a person keeps her panties in a filing cabinet?"

But, like Anna, she had been bowled over by Brenda's creations.

Anna had never known Gloria to be silent for so long. She was like a little girl gazing at her first party dress in the days when they were pink and frothy with rosebuds and bows.

Gently, she ran her fingers over Brenda's seams. Analytically, she squinted at her buttonholes. Approvingly, she stroked the outside of her sleeves. Anna knew they'd got it sorted when, finally, Gloria took off her glasses and declared that the last time she had seen lapels like these was on her uncle Manny at the end of the war. Apparently, Manny had been a petty East End crook who had once come into possession of a vanload of Savile Row suits. Although he never got nicked for the suits, he went on to do six months in Wormwood Scrubs for black-market onions.

Gloria got home, marched into the kitchen where Harry was munching on a pickled cucumber and reading the Social and Personal column in the *Jewish Chronicle*, and informed him that he was about to invest £30,000 in Brenda's business.

Harry carried on reading.

"Harry, put the paper down, stop making that awful noise and listen to me. You've heard of Christian Lacroix. If you invest in this Brenda Sweet person, I'm telling you, overnight you'll become Yiddishe Lacroix."

Harry did as he was told and even prepared Brenda's business plan for the bank. Three months later Sweet FA-UK was born.

. . .

TEN YEARS ON, BRENDA HAD A PERSONAL FORTUNE OF WELL
over four million, plus an eight-bedroom house in Holland
Park. Harry had made enough money to retire at fifty-five, and
he and Gloria had bought a smart holiday flat in Eilat where
they spent three months every year. Gloria brought in an assistant to help her run Maison Gloria, but refused to sell the shop
because she adored chatting and getting to know her custom-
ers. Over the years the business had become her social life.
Without it she would have been lost.

Brenda always said she would never be able to put into
words how grateful she was to Anna. Anna said she needn't
bother—a couple of free suits a year said it all as far as she was
concerned.

In fact, Brenda did much more than supply Anna with
clothes. When Amy got pneumonia just after she was born, it
was Brenda who phoned one of her clients, who just happened
to be a professor of pediatrics, and persuaded her to have a
look at the baby; when Dan began going peculiar, it was
Brenda she cried to and got drunk with, and Brenda who listened. Now that she was about to cheat on Dan, it was
Brenda she had come to, partly for advice on how to go about
it, and partly because, despite her determination to go through
with it, she realized she still needed somebody to give her
permission.

"God, Anna, you make me feel like the Mother Superior in
The Sound of Music. What do you expect me to do, burst into
song and tell you to climb ev'ry mountain until you find your
dream so that you can waltz out of 'ere in some poxy brown
burlap jacket and silly hat singing to all and sundry down Kensington Church Street that you have confidence in bleedin'
sunshine and rain? I don't think so. Anna, have you any idea
what you'll be risking if you go on this shagathon? I mean, what
if Dan finds out? You could lose the kids."

"But that's the whole point of the exercise," Anna said tetch-
ily, annoyed that she wasn't getting the lavish approval from
Brenda she had hoped for. "According to Rachel Stern, you

can only do it if you know you have the wit not to get found out and the strength not to tell. Perhaps the cow's right."

"And you reckon you've got all that?"

"Yes. Look, I don't want heavy, I'll-show-you-my-angst-if-you-show-me-yours-type relationships and then we fall in love. I just want their bodies."

T HERE WAS A VERY LONG PAUSE. FINALLY, BRENDA LICKED her middle finger and began flicking through a copy of the *Evening Standard* which had been lying on the kitchen table.

"If it really is only the sex you're after, you might find this useful. I noticed it last night."

Brenda stopped flicking and reached for a ballpoint. Anna could see she was ringing one of the personal ads.

"What is it, Bren? If you think I'm going off with some sad creep who has to advertise, you can think again."

"Don't read it now. Wait until you get home."

Brenda tore out the page, folded it over a couple of times and slipped it into Anna's jacket pocket.

G LORIA WAS CONVINCED THAT IF THE LIGHT CAUGHT ANNA'S marble-topped coffee table at a certain angle, she could see a small raised mark. It was either a spot of Superglue, probably spilled by Dan when he was mending one of Josh's Lego men, or a flaw in the marble.

By holding her head slightly to the right she could keep the mark in her sight and move in on it very slowly. The tiniest movement and it would disappear. Then she would have to move back and start again.

It was definitely Superglue. She started alternately spraying it with Pledge and picking at it with her thumbnail. After ten minutes, it still wasn't shifting. The thought of having to leave it filled her with terror.

Desperate for another cleaning fix, she got up from her knees and ran into the kitchen. She opened the cupboard under the sink, took out a bottle of Ajax Liquid and poured nearly half of it into a bucket. As she dipped her J-Cloth into the bucket she could feel her heart rate coming down and the tension easing. Gloria had just begun to wipe down Anna's worktops when she looked up and saw Anna standing staring at her in the doorway.

"My God, Mum, you don't get any better. Am I the only sane one in this bloody family? Would you mind telling me what you are doing? Mrs. Fredericks came in yesterday. The place is spotless."

It turned out Gloria was on her way to her obsessive-compulsive group's annual bazaar, an event which had looked like it was never going to happen. Apparently their group therapist had been forced to postpone it three times because all the obsessive compulsives had been too busy obsessively and compulsively cleaning the hall and checking the wiring to organize the actual event.

Gloria had popped in to see if Amy and Josh had wanted to come, but when she arrived they'd been on their way out to the roller disco with Dan. He'd said she was welcome to stay, as Anna was due back just after one.

"Oh, and there's something else you ought to know," Gloria said to Anna. "I got a phone call last night. Your uncle Henry died yesterday."

"Good Lord. I had no idea he was still alive. He must have been a hundred and six."

"A hundred and two. Just dropped dead out of the blue. The funeral's three o'clock Thursday. They've had to delay it a few days because there has to be a postmortem if you haven't seen a doctor in the past two weeks."

Uncle Henry wasn't Anna's real uncle. In fact, he was no relation at all. In 1901 Henry and Anna's grandma Esther had met and become inseparable on the boat bringing Jewish immigrants from Poland to England. Once the two seven-year-olds had found each other, it wasn't long before their parents became friends too, and when they arrived in the East End, they all lodged together in the same miserable, damp house off the Roman Road.

From then on, the two families never lived more than a couple of streets apart, and Esther and Henry, who were both only children, became like brother and sister. Strangely, as they grew up, there was never any romance between them. As far as both sets of parents were concerned, it wasn't for want of trying.

In the end Henry married a beautiful but half-witted girl called Yetta, and Esther married a young tailor called Saul, who owned three sewing machines and seemed to have above-average prospects. Nevertheless, Henry and Esther remained extremely close into old age. As a child, Anna had always received a ten-shilling note in her birthday card from Uncle Henry and Aunty Yetta, and always thought of them as part of her mother's family.

GLORIA PUT ON HER JACKET, GAVE ANNA'S WORKTOP ANother wipe, took a look in the fridge to check she had enough food in, kissed her and said, "See you Thursday."

ANNA WENT UPSTAIRS TO THE BATHROOM, SAT ON THE TOIlet seat and started to read the small ad Brenda had ringed.

"Are you in a relationship or happily married, but would like a lover? Liaisons Dangereux is a dating agency with a difference." Then there was a telephone number.

Anna refolded the page, rolled it into a small cigar and slipped it inside a box of Tampax.

CHAPTER THREE

WE USED TO BE A HAPPY FAMILY before all this happened,' wept attractive mum of two, Dawn, 40, from the beamed mock-Tudor lounge of her apartment in Barking. 'I used to enjoy going out for a Malibu and Coke with the girls of an evening. Terry used to look forward to a bit of a fight with his mates at the West Ham football matches. These days, all our friends have deserted us. We daren't even walk round the estate without the Rottweilers, because there's always some bastard pointing a finger at us. Sigourney and Keanu are wonderful kids since they came out of the detention center, but they're being bullied so much at school over this, they've been offered counseling.' "

Anna was sitting at the word processor in her bedroom-cum-study, just getting to the end of a piece for the health pages of the *Globe on Sunday* about coping with nits—provisionally headlined "Lousy Mother's Nit Nightmare Shame"—when she looked down at her watch and realized that if she didn't get a move on, she was going to be late for Uncle Henry's funeral.

The article should have taken only a couple of hours to write, but Anna was spending ages on it, because she had passed most of the morning staring out of the window trying to pluck up the courage to phone Liaisons Dangereux, but then decided she couldn't because they were bound to want her to deliver her romantic manifesto in some cringe-makingly embarrassing video. She knew the style, since she had done an article a couple of years ago on women who used dating agencies, and had sat in while some of them performed what one outfit referred to pretentiously as the client's "piece to camera."

The women fell into two groups. First there were the fat middle-aged divorcees with bad perms, who had just started some computer access course or other. Then there were the sad twenty-something lasses with eczema and brains the size of Cadbury's Creme Eggs, who sat in front of the camera and gabbled: "Hi, my name's Nicole and I come from Worcester Park. I work in personnel for a large company which specializes in intimate rubberwear. My ambitions are to meet Noel Edmonds, to find a way to wax my bikini line without getting that embarrassing rash and to end world hunger. At this moment in time I am without a special someone in my life and I'm searching for a soulmate for walks, talks and maybe more. Are you the shining star who can brighten up my lonely nights?"

With the possible exception of receiving a Heart of Gold award from Esther Rantzen, Anna could think of no worse humiliation than making a dating agency video. Nevertheless, she couldn't help fantasizing about what she might say, should the occasion arise. She suspected she would dispense with the introduction and launch straight into: "Look, I live with a fucking lunatic who would rather spend his nights on an Internet

Terminal Illness Forum exchanging information on symptoms and hospice facilities with fellow hypochondriacs in Kentucky than have sex with me. So if you own your own liver, your tap stops dripping after you've had a pee, or better still, you had yet to be weaned onto solids the night Kennedy was shot, I'm all yours."

She typed another couple of sentences and broke off yet again. She didn't know why she was bothering to go to the funeral. She hadn't seen Uncle Henry or Aunty Yetta for donkey's years, but on the phone the day before, Gloria had laid on the guilt, saying that she should go for Bubba's sake. Anna pointed out that Bubba had been dead for eleven years and, as a former person, had forfeited all rights to a sake. Gloria, who was desperate to show Anna off at the funeral and introduce her to Uncle Henry's family, who hadn't seen her for years, as "my daughter the important Fleet Street journalist who once interviewed Maureen Lipman," then instantly changed tack. Suddenly she became an expert on funeral etiquette, a sort of sarcophagal Miss Manners, and warned Anna ominously that if you didn't go to people's funerals, they wouldn't come to yours. Faced with this priceless piece of Gloria-esque logic, Anna gave in.

She wasn't surprised when Dan announced he would not be coming. He'd given her some involved explanation about having to drop off a stool sample at the doctor's surgery and then having to go on to Newport Pagnell for lunch with a trade delegation from Venezuela. As soon as Anna heard the words "stool sample," her eyes glazed over and she stopped listening.

ANNA TOOK ANOTHER LOOK AT HER WATCH. IT WAS JUST AFter one. She bashed out a lackluster final paragraph and faffed irritably with the modem, which, as ever, threw a wobbly and refused to work if she was in a state any more stressful than one of sublime, bucolic repose; indeed, to function properly, the modem would have preferred Anna to be sitting with

her feet on her desk, straw in mouth and humming "One Man
Went to Mow." After fifteen minutes of sending and resending,
roughly as long as it would have taken to dictate the story to an
old-fashioned copytaker, Anna's article was finally ingested by
the *Globe*'s computers.

She took her latest Sweet FA black jacket out of the wardrobe and put it on over a white body and short black skirt. She
decided, even though she was going to a funeral, that the outfit
needed a bit of a lift. She also retained an adolescent urge to
shock at important family do's. So she went to her jewelry box
and took out a brightly colored four-inch-long wooden brooch
she had bought a couple of years ago at a market when she was
on holiday with Dan and the kids in Tobago. It was a carving of
a naked, dreadlocked African painted in ANC colors with a
huge red erection and a joint. She pinned it to her left lapel,
patted it and giggled. Then she grabbed her bag and keys off
the desk, bolted downstairs and out to the car.

DAN THOUGHT A STROLL MIGHT CALM HIM DOWN. AS HE
turned left out of the *Vanguard*'s office and headed down
Kensington High Street towards Holland Park, he realized he
had never been so humiliated in his life. It was nearly four
hours since the incident in the doctor's surgery, but his entire
body was still bright red with embarrassment. Even his internal
organs felt as if they were blushing. He couldn't face lunch. It
was just as well the Venezuelans had canceled.

The day had begun routinely enough. He had dropped in at
the office just after half past eight to check his messages from
the previous night, before popping out to hand in the stool
sample at the surgery round the corner. There was nothing on
the voice mail. All that had come through overnight was the fax
from the Venezuelans postponing lunch until the following
Tuesday, but inviting him to a performance of *Die Mei-
stersinger* at Covent Garden that evening, as they had been
given some free tickets. He sent back a fax confirming the new

lunch date, but politely declining the opera as Wagner always gave him this irresistible urge to annex the Sudetenland.

Ten minutes later he had strolled into the crowded doctor's waiting room. He realized it had been months since he had actually set foot in the surgery because Dr. Harper, the kindly middle-aged lady doctor, had of late taken to discussing his symptoms with him on the phone so that she could dismiss them there and then, rather than waste her time and his with a pointless visit to the surgery.

Last Monday evening, just as Dr. Harper thought she had dealt with her last patient of the day, the receptionist had put a call from Mr. Bloomfield through to her, as she did three or four times a month.

Dan, standing alone at the kitchen phone, began describing his symptoms. This time it was gripping stomach pains, and frequent loose bowel movements, which had a greenish tinge together with reddish streaks which could have been beetroot from the beetroot salad he'd bought from the deli on his way home from work the night before, but then again could have been blood. All this, in his opinion, and he felt sure she would agree, suggested several possibilities:

"Colitis was my first diagnostic port of call, although I'm not sure I've got the characteristic mucus in the blood. I'd have to take another look. Then of course it could be Crohn's disease or diverticulitis. I know that patients bleed with both of those, although I understand people with diverticular disease can remain asymptomatic for years, but certainly severe cramps are a symptom of both. Of course there is an outside chance it could be Whipple's disease—I do have the chronic low-grade fever. Then there is . . ." Dan hesitated before saying the word, ". . . cancer. But of course you'll know better than me," he added as a deferential afterthought.

That afternoon Dr. Harper had dispatched a burst appendix and a suspected ectopic pregnancy to hospital, visited a senile chap who thought his wife was in a coma, but by the look and smell of her she had been dead for at least a fortnight, and had a two-year-old with measles vomit over her new Mansfield suit.

She was tired, irritable and in no mood for malingerers like
Dan Bloomfield.

"Me know better than you, Mr. Bloomfield? You flatter me,"
she spat sarcastically down the phone. "But, with your permission, may I offer just a couple of suggestions? Have you considered Norwalk virus infection or shigella bacillus?"

Dan's heart didn't just skip a beat—it skipped an entire
drum solo. He was about to faint.

Somehow, while still holding the phone under his chin and
maniacally scrambling through the *Home Doctor* index trying
to find N for Norwalk, he managed to get himself onto the
kitchen floor and raise his legs a few feet off the ground. After
a second or two the blood began to return to his head.

"Good God, what the hell are they?"

"What they are, Mr. Bloomfield, are nasty little so-and-sos
which give you an upset tum. You probably have a mild case of
food poisoning, nothing more. Simply take plenty of fluids. If
you insist, you can bring in a stool sample tomorrow morning
and I'll send it off to the lab for analysis. Good-bye, Mr. Bloomfield."

D AN DID INSIST. HOWEVER, IN ALL THE YEARS THAT HE HAD
been one of Dr. Harper's patients, he had never given a
stool sample and wasn't quite sure how one went about it. Dr.
Harper had cut him off without giving him any instructions.
Would the lab want a whole turd, or just a slice of turd, and
what should he put it in?

The first receptacle that sprang to mind as being vaguely the
right shape was the Habitat spaghetti jar standing next to him
on the kitchen worktop. Dan picked up the glass container,
which was full of spinach fusilli, adopted a squatting position
and placed it over his jeans in roughly the right position. He
realized straight away that it was going to be much too tall to fit
between his backside and the bottom of the loo, as well as too
large to go in his briefcase. Crucially, it also had no lid, although he supposed he could cover it with clingfilm.

. . .

THEN, AS HE RIFLED THROUGH THE KITCHEN CUPBOARDS IN search of something expendable, it occurred to him that a pickled cucumber jar might be just the ticket. Once a week, Dan schlepped to Golders Green to buy bagels and a couple of jars of his favorite new green cucumbers. New greens had a distinctive sour taste, which he preferred to the sweet-and-sour taste of ordinary pickles. New greens were also longer and darker. In fact, size and shapewise, they were not dissimilar to the average healthy stool.

Dan reached up and took one of the sturdy screw-top jars down from its cupboard. It was slightly shorter than he'd thought, but he hoped the turd he produced would be of a consistency to curl up and hunker down. He tipped the pickled cucumbers into a Tupperware container and soaked off the Mrs. Elswood label under a hot running tap. He reckoned that pickles were probably pretty sterile, but thought he'd boil up a kettle of water and rinse out the jar just to be on the safe side.

Harvesting the sample was no problem as he still had the trots. He waited until Anna was watching a *Tenko* rerun on UK Gold and then went up to the bathroom to deliver his payload.

Afterwards Dan quickly screwed on the jar lid. He decided that the sample had to be kept fresh until the next morning. He put it at the back of the fridge in a brown paper bag and prayed that Anna wouldn't be overtaken in the night by a desperate yearning for a new green cucumber. For added protection, he ring-fenced the jar with some items he was pretty confident his wife would not be seeking out over the next twelve hours. These included a bottle of infant Calpol, some homemade chutney they'd bought at the school summer fête six months ago and a bottle of the most disgusting no-fat salad dressing.

WHAT DAN HADN'T BEEN ABLE TO SEE THE NEXT DAY AS HE opened the door of the doctor's surgery was a three-year-old boy, with a chesty cough and a stream of green snot hanging down from his nose, careering around the waiting room on a small wooden tricycle. At the exact moment Dan walked in, the child was a few feet away revving his handlebars and making irritating *broom-brooming* noises through his catarrh as he prepared to do a hit-and-run on a baby just old enough to sit up, and who was busy on the floor chewing on a Playmobil pirate. Hours later, Dan still couldn't remember precisely what happened, but in a split second, the baby's mother, sensing imminent danger, had scooped up her child, leaving the speeding toddler a clear path to crash into Dan and send both him and the cucumber jar flying.

IT TOOK DAN A FEW MOMENTS TO GET HIS BREATH BACK AND lift himself into a sitting position, but by that time the little boy had unscrewed the lid and had his nose deep inside the jar. He then proceeded to lift it high above his head and began showing it off like the Jules Rimet cup to everybody in the waiting room.

"Look, man done a great big smelly poo-poo like my do. Why has man done poo in jar and not in va twoilet?"

FOR A FEW SECONDS THERE WAS AN OMINOUS SILENCE. THIS was followed by what can only be described as a universal waiting-room retch-in, after which the little boy's mother started to have hysterics. These involved her climbing up onto her chair, lifting up her skirt and screaming for somebody to remove *that thing*, as if Dan's turd were about to sprout legs and whiskers and start scurrying about the surgery. This led to a widespread panic among the pensioners, who all made a surprisingly aerobic dash for the door, but were forced to a halt when their walking frames, sticks and shopping trolleys ended up logjammed in the narrow hallway.

In a matter of seconds, the receptionist had relieved the toddler of Dan's stool sample, but by that time Dan had es-

caped out of the emergency exit. Five minutes later he was
back at his desk writing an intro to a piece on the effect on the
FTSE-100 of recent profit-taking in Wall Street.

D AN WAS JUST ABOUT TO TURN INTO THE PARK AND WONDER-
ing how one went about changing GPs when he noticed
a 1960 turquoise Ford Zephyr convertible pull into a parking
bay on the other side of the road. A moment later, Brenda
got out, looking as if she had completely lost her sartorial
marbles.

A NNA WAS BEGINNING TO PANIC. THE TRAFFIC ON THE EAST-
bound lane of the North Circular was at a complete standstill. The roads had been clear until just after Hanger Lane
roundabout, but for the best part of ten minutes she had
moved no more than a few feet. She couldn't help thinking that
if they still lived in Blackheath the journey to Manor Park
would have taken no more than half an hour. Not that the
proximity of Blackheath to Manor Park Jewish Cemetery was a
reason for moving back. Anna had loved Blackheath and all the
friends she had there and had been mightily pissed off with
Dan for demanding they move simply because some examination league table or other had insisted that state schools in the
London Borough of Richmond got some of the best General
Certificate of Secondary Education results in the country. So
now they lived on the outskirts of one of the poshest areas of
London, and were struggling every month to pay a whacking
great mortgage on an Edwardian town house, just so Dan
didn't have to send his children to private schools and could
pretend he was still an ideologically sound socialist.

Anna had passed most of the time frantically twiddling the
tuner on the car radio, trying to find the local traffic news, but
kept getting some Talk Radio shrink doing a phone-in. The rest
of the time she had spent staring at the room settings in
Leather Universe, the furniture hypermarket, which was set

back a few yards from the road. A particularly gruesome lounge setting caught her eye. This had, without doubt, been put together from artifacts plundered from Liberace's tomb, because it included a lavender suede three-piece, a zebra-skin hearthrug and a white-and-gold baby grand complete with four-branch candelabra.

Anna took another look at her watch. It was nearly half past two. She was never going to get to the burial ground by three. She decided the best thing to do was to abandon any idea of trying to make it to the cemetery. Instead she would head straight for Uncle Henry's house in Manor Park, where everybody was due to come back for the traditional postinterment tea.

The bugger of it was that because she had missed the actual burial, Gloria had undoubtedly lost important daughter-parading time. Now she would have to make it up to her mother by hanging around until after the rabbi had been to the house to conduct evening prayers. These probably wouldn't start until after seven, which meant she wouldn't be back until ten. Anna reached into the glove compartment for the mobile phone. As she dialed home, she hoped desperately that this wasn't Denise's night for her line dancing, and that the baby-sitter could be bribed with the promise of a few extra quid in her pay packet to stay on until Dan got home.

It took over an hour for the traffic to crawl up to the Brent Cross turnoff, where for no apparent reason it melted away. Anna put her foot firmly on the accelerator. She could see a set of traffic lights a few hundred yards down the road. They had just turned green. She decided if they stayed green until she had gone through them, then she would find a lover within the week and she wouldn't have to phone Liaisons Dangereux and make an awful video. They did.

BRENDA WAS WEARING A SHORT RED-AND-WHITE-CHECKED gingham dress with puffed sleeves, white ankle socks and red sparkly shoes. She'd got her bleached blond hair in two wiry plaits held in place by glittery ribbons, which matched her shoes. A Yorkshire terrier puppy yapping under her arm completed her grits-and-hominy ensemble.

She hadn't seen Dan because she was busy trying to control the puppy, which was wriggling and squirming to get down onto the pavement, probably to cock its leg up a traffic warden. At the same time, Brenda was attempting to rummage through her brown leather school satchel for parking meter money.

Dan, although baffled, had taken one look at Brenda's getup and experienced an immediate lightening of his mood, together with a temporary restoration of his sense of humor. He decided to sneak up and surprise her.

He approached Brenda from behind on what would have been tiptoes had he not been wearing a pair of brand-new Oxford brogues which were still rock hard and almost impossible to bend even when walking normally.

By now, Brenda had put a pound in the meter, but still had her back to him as she stood thumbing through a Nicholson's Streetfinder. Dan tapped her twice on the shoulder.

"What's the problem, Bren? You and Toto having trouble finding the Yellow Brick Road?" To Dan's disappointment and annoyance, Brenda didn't flinch. She'd clearly caught sight of him as he crossed the road.

"Wrong film, stupid," she said, reaching up to kiss him on both cheeks and nearly squashing the dog in the process. "F'your information, this is the prototype for the Sweet FA Pollyanna look I'm gonna be launching in Milan next summer. Me and the team thought it was time we got a bit more cutting edge—more Vivienne Westwood."

DAN COULDN'T HELP THINKING THAT IF BRENDA WASN'T careful, all she would be launching next summer would be a new range of straitjackets together with the latest Sweet FA fragrance, Eau de Largactyl. But for the time being, she sounded fairly sane, even if she didn't look it. She was on her

way to do a home fitting with the actress-model wife of some
worn-out millionaire rock star. She said she had twenty minutes or so to kill, and did Dan fancy a cuppa?

HE HELD THE YAPPING HOUND, WHO WAS CALLED KEITH,
while Brenda hauled up the car's white-canvas hood. She
locked Keith in the Zephyr, and she and Dan headed for a Café
Rouge two or three hundred yards down the road. The young
Aussie waiter couldn't take his eyes off Brenda's outfit. As he
showed them to a table by the window, he seemed unable to
prevent his thoughts becoming words. He pulled out a chair for
Brenda. "You wouldn't prefer a tuffet, I suppose?" he asked.
Brenda pretended not to hear. Dan ordered a decaf cappuccino
(caffeine gave him palpitations) with skimmed milk (full fat
gave him heartburn). Brenda asked for a Perrier with extra
slices of lime.

The waiter went to the bar. "One Perrier, extra lime, one
Why Bother," Dan heard him say.

DAN WATCHED BRENDA CHEW SILENTLY ON HER BITS OF
lime without so much as wincing and then drop the
bright-green crescent skins into the Ricard ashtray. Her mood
seemed to have changed since coming into the restaurant. She
had become very quiet and hadn't said a word for over a minute. In all the years Dan had known Brenda, he had never seen
her looking so nervous and unsure of herself. It was as if she
were trying to pluck up the courage to say something, but
couldn't. Dan decided to help her out.

"C'mon, Bren, speak to me. What's up?"

Brenda looked at him without a trace of a smile or mischief
on her face. She began picking at the lime skins.

The truth was that ever since giving Anna the newspaper ad
for Liaisons Dangereux, she had been tormented by thoughts
of how unspeakably wicked and disloyal she had been to Dan.

Now she had bumped into him out of the blue, she felt she owed it to him to at least give him a vague hint that Anna might be up to something. The problem was that she was frightened of saying too much and spilling all Anna's beans.

"Look, Dan," she began hesitantly, "the last thing in the world I'd want to do is interfere in your marriage, but I don't think you've got the foggiest how much this imaginary illness carry-on of yours has got to Anna. It's driving her seriously off her trolley. I know she still loves you, and she's tried very hard to understand and help, but I'm telling you, Dan, if you don't make a real effort right now, today, to find yourself a shrink, and knock this thing on the head, I'm frightened you might end up losing her."

As Brenda spoke, guilt and shame began to coat Dan's stomach like heavy black treacle. It was the same feeling he'd got as a child the time his mother caught him at the dinner table stuffing her inedibly fatty salt beef into his school trouser pocket.

Dan couldn't look at Brenda. Instead he concentrated on scraping his spoon around the rim of his coffee cup and removing bits of dried-up cappuccino froth. He found himself thinking that if God was meant to be so bloody merciful, why was he inflicting all this emotional pain on him in one day?

He began to realize how the ancient Egyptians must have felt when the Almighty sent down the ten plagues. He was overtaken by an urge to rush back to the *Vanguard* building and smear the main entrance with ram's blood, otherwise there would, he felt sure, be a swarm of locusts hovering over his desk when he got back.

ANNA HAD JUST DRIVEN ROUND GANTS HILL ROUNDABOUT and, glancing at a signpost, realized that not only was she no more than fifteen minutes from Uncle Henry's house, but that the road seemed slightly familiar. It was then she worked out that she must have driven through Gants Hill in her lime-green VW Beetle the night in 1980 when she got off with Dan at Beany Levine's party. But years before that, even, she must have come this way with her parents whenever they went to visit Uncle Henry and Aunty Yetta.

So when was the last time she had seen them? For a few minutes Anna trawled through her mind's Filofax, remembering weddings at the Regal Rooms in Edmonton, Passover meals with Harry's sister in Newbury Park and Harry's sister's son's bar mitzvah at the Manor Hall in Chigwell. Then she got it. The last time she had seen Henry and Yetta was at a particularly poignant Sunday-afternoon tea party at their tiny Victorian terraced house nearly thirty years ago.

The Canadian cousins were over from Montreal, and Yetta had decided to lay on one of her smoked salmon bagel spreads in their honor. Henry had decided to use the occasion to make a dramatic announcement about Sidney. Sidney was Henry and Yetta's only child, whom nobody in the family ever talked about because he was in his forties and appeared to be having a homosexual relationship with a pastry chef he lodged with in Kilburn. The family could never work out what upset Yetta and Henry most—the thought of Sidney living with a man or the fact that he was doing so in Kilburn.

On the day of the tea, about thirty people were crammed into Yetta and Henry's best room. The short, overweight men wore suspenders. These held up trousers which seemed to Anna to come up to their chests. They leaned back in Yetta's faded red moquette armchairs, their chubby fingers looking incongruous gripping the handles of her pretty pink-and-gold bone-china teacups.

Harry was impressing everybody with how well Maison Gloria was doing and what a natural Gloria was for the garment trade:

"I tell you," he said, invoking what Anna now realized was a Jewish joke old enough to have come from the Dead Sea Scrolls, "a man could come up to her in the street these days, open up his raincoat and expose himself, and do you know what her reaction would be? I'll tell you what it would be. All he'd get from my Gloria, God bless her, would be: 'Huh, you call that a lining?' "

Everybody laughed—even the children, who instantly worked out that "expose himself" had something to do with willies. Five of them, including Anna, were sitting bunched up on the settee, the girls in their red Clarks sandals, the boys in their long gray Cubs socks with green Baden-Powell garters. Anna sat on the end, quietly working her way through a plate of her favorite cakes, miniature Danish pastries from Broers the bakers, which were filled with sweet cream cheese and half a dried apricot. She concentrated on finishing her Danish and tried to ignore one of her cousins digging her in the thigh with a sharpened lolly stick, because she knew that if she was good and didn't get into trouble, then Gloria would let her stay up to watch *Sunday Night at the London Palladium* when they got home.

In a lull during a discussion on that brilliant young Yiddishe chap Robert Maxwell and the wonderful things he was doing in business while still being a socialist, Henry chose his moment for the family announcement he had been planning.

He cleared his throat a couple of times, and like some diminutive East End brigadier bringing news from the front to his superiors at the War Office, he announced in an overly loud staccato voice that it was his sad and regretful duty to inform the family that their son Sidney was not, as everybody suspected, a homo—although he had been living a double life. For the last seven years, without their knowledge, Sidney had been married to a Catholic woman and they had two boys. They had now gone to live in Dublin with her family. As far as he and Yetta were concerned, Sidney was no longer their son, and from this time forth they considered him to be dead.

From that afternoon, Sidney-the-one-nobody-talked-about was not talked about even more.

Several years later, when "marrying out" had become more acceptable, Henry finally accepted his son back into the family and used to look forward to his trips to Dublin to visit Sidney,

Maureen and the children. The rest of the family, on the other hand, continued to keep their distance. Yetta's attitude towards her son never changed. The truth was, she hadn't been given much of a chance to change. This was owing to the fact that she choked to death on a nut cluster a few months after the bagel tea incident.

ANNA TURNED RIGHT OFF HIGH STREET NORTH AND INTO Sheringham Avenue. She found Uncle Henry's house easily enough because it was the only one, in a street full of York stone cladding and aluminum window frames, which looked as if it hadn't been painted or the net curtains washed since milk was delivered in churns and one in three infants died from diphtheria before reaching their first birthday.

Anna's timing hadn't been too bad. It was just after five, and there were still relatives, some of whom she vaguely recognized, arriving back from the cemetery and going into the house. She locked the car, dropped her keys into her bag and fell in behind two frail old women who had linked arms to support each other during the arduous journey up the garden path. Despite the warm weather, they were both wearing three-quarter-length camel coats. One of the women had chosen to make hers a touch more funereal by wearing on her head a short black fishnet veil. On top of this there squatted a very large black taffeta rose. From what Anna could hear of their conversation, which was almost everything because they were both stone deaf and needed to shout at each other to get a response, they appeared to be from the old people's day center where Henry had died during a game of kaluki.

"I tell you, Estelle, I saw him lying there dead on the floor. He looked so well. That two weeks in Bournemouth must have really agreed with him."

Finally Anna made it into the lounge, which apart from smelling vaguely of stale wee was just as she remembered it, with its red moquette three-piece and Aunty Yetta's gold-and-onyx serving cart.

The room was seething with arms, hands and elbows pushing and shoving to get to the buffet table, whose white damask
cloth was, for the time being at least, covered with plates, plat-
ters and silver gallery trays, stacked to Kilimanjaro heights with
cakes, bagels, herrings and fishballs. Anna looked round for
Gloria, who had agreed to help with the catering, but couldn't
see her.

Anna was starving, but decided, after the journey she'd had,
that what she needed first was a drink. Various aunts and ladies
from down the road were bringing round cups of tea, but Anna
needed something stronger. As she had come into the room,
she'd noticed there were tiny glass thimbles of whiskey, sweet
sherry and cherry brandy on Aunty Yetta's serving cart. Unlike
the mountains of food, these were remaining, in true Jewish
style, steadfastly untouched.

She reckoned she would need to down at least ten of the
glasses to get a hit and wondered how she could do this without drawing attention to herself and becoming known as Gloria's daughter the dipso.

Finally she decided that everybody was too busy eating to
notice her. She made her way over to the cart and picked up a
glass of whiskey. After about five glasses she was beginning to
feel much calmer, and was just about to go into the kitchen to
find her mother when she became aware of a man's voice behind her. It sounded soft and smooth—as if it spent most of its
life doing Kerrygold butter commercials.

Anna turned round. Every nerve ending in her body capable
of a sexual response, including ones she didn't know about in
her pancreas, suddenly felt as if they were about to take off all
their clothes and step into black silk negligees.

Anna was standing face-to-face with one of the most beautiful men she had ever seen not on the arm of some Hollywood
babe. Her eyes darted quickly to the buffet table to check that
Sharon Stone and Michelle Pfeiffer weren't hovering by the
pickled herrings.

They weren't. The only people lurking by the pickled herrings were wearing man-made fibers, and there wasn't a Nei-

man Marcus carrier bag or an even remotely toned upper body part in sight.

"I was just saying," came the warm Irish accent, "I didn't realize it was the done thing to get plastered at a Jewish wake, but if it is, then I think I'll join you. By the way, I'm Charlie Kaplan. Henry was my grandfather."

D AN WAS GETTING DESPERATE. HE'D DECIDED AFTER SUCH a stressful day to leave work early. As he lay on the sofa going through the ads for counselors in *Time Out,* he felt like a eunuch wandering around an Ann Summers shop. The list of therapies on offer seemed endless. How the hell was he supposed to know if astrological Reichian analysis was any better than Jungian crystal therapy, or if Janovian primal therapy was a safer bet than underwater rebirthing.

What he did know, on the other hand, was that Brenda had frightened the life out of him. It had taken her to convince him, when Anna couldn't, that his health had become an obsession, and that Anna could leave him because of it. Losing her was unthinkable.

Finally he came across a very brief and straightforward-looking ad from a psychotherapist who appeared to be a chartered member of some shrink institute or other. Dan knew psychotherapy only involved talking to a therapist a couple of times a week, and he could get away without buying a snorkel and flippers. He dialed the number and got a calm, reassuring woman's voice on the answer machine: "I hope you won't take it as a personal rejection that I am unable to speak to you just now, but if you feel strong enough to share your feelings, please break down, cry or let go of your anger after the tone."

Dan thought she sounded a caring sort and left a message asking for an appointment.

If Brenda was right, he was, without doubt, on his way to saving his sanity and his marriage. He decided there and then not to mention any of this therapy business to Anna. He wanted to surprise her by coming home one day and announcing he was cured and that he was whisking her off for a holiday in the South Pacific.

What caused his positive and determined mood to evaporate in an instant and made his heart rate shoot up to 155 (he confirmed this using the second hand on his watch) was the thought that Brenda might have got it all wrong. What if this therapist woman started wading into his psyche only to discover that it was too late, that his sanity couldn't be salvaged and that he was, in fact, completely and utterly barking? As he imagined ending his days lying naked on a filthy, piss-soaked mattress in some nuthouse, the strain became too much. He went upstairs to the bathroom and tested his urine for sugar.

CHAPTER FOUR

ANNA KNEW THAT IT DEFINITELY wasn't the done thing to get drunk at Jewish funerals. She assumed God would probably wreak his vengeance on her by making sure the *Globe on Sunday* spiked her piece on nits. What she also knew was that it was even less the done thing for a woman, particularly a married one, to pull at a Jewish funeral. Only after she assured herself that God hadn't turned her into a particularly horny pillar of salt did she pluck up the courage to reply to Charlie Kaplan.

She wanted to say bloody hell if Uncle Henry was your grandfather then that means you're Sidney-the-one-nobody-used-to-talk-about's son, so how come you're so tall and screw-me-quick gorgeous when they always said your father was short and weedy?

But because Charlie was giving Anna the kind of look that would have forced even the most committed lesbian to reassess her position on fellatio, all that she could blurt out was: "Hello, I'm Anna Shapiro. Henry was my uncle."

She paused to take in the understated navy woolen suit. This looked as if it had cost an arm and both legs, plus a certain amount of offal. Underneath he was wearing an equally expensive polo shirt in a slightly darker shade of navy. "Well, not actually my uncle," she continued. "We weren't really related. Sort of adopted uncle. So if I remember right, you must be from Dublin, then?"

"Yes, from a village just a few miles outside. I bought m'self a little cottage there last year, but I'm not home that often. I fly with Aer Hibernia . . . long haul, mainly."

"So you're Captain Kaplan?"

"It is kind of alliterative, but I live with it."

Anna knew it was her turn to say something light and conversational, but she couldn't, because her profound relief that Charlie Kaplan didn't appear to be living with a wife or girlfriend had begun to segue into an exceedingly downmarket, but nevertheless compelling, scenario involving an airline captain, ideally the one in front of her. In her daydream, Captain Kaplan was sitting at the controls with his head turned to face her, wearing nothing but his pilot's cap and a huge erection, while she was sitting opposite him with her legs slightly apart, in a very short black PVC trench coat and no panties.

As Anna came back to the reality of Uncle Henry's living room, she realized Charlie was staring at her and smiling. He couldn't be more than thirty-two or -three. Anna's hand darted from her side to the nonexistent loose skin under her chin and then back to her side again. For the first time she noticed his eyes, which were a deep Irish blue. They looked especially striking against his Semitic olive skin and almost-black hair, which was longish and slightly wavy. He reminded Anna of a very young George Best with overtones of horny Israeli paratrooper.

"Oh, right, good, great," Anna spluttered. She downed another micro-whiskey in one. "Must be fascinating—all that travel."

Charlie agreed, it was.

Then there was a pause which was just slightly too long for social comfort.

"So, Anna, tell me about yourself. What do you do?"

Anna hated telling strangers what she did for a living, especially if they seemed the sort who might look down their noses at the tabloids. It always ended up with her having to spend fifteen minutes justifying her existence as well as the existence of tabloid newspapers. Nevertheless, over the years, she had developed an extremely well argued and erudite case for both, and could deliver it with the force and assurance of a QC on a winning streak at the Old Bailey.

However, in the presence of a man so ravishing he could undoubtedly get Andrea Dworkin rushing out to buy lace open-crotch panties, her intellect and articulacy failed her and she ended up stuttering out something about the tabloids all being crap really, but the money was brilliant.

The conversation would have gone on in this stammering, faltering fashion had Anna not accidentally broken the tension by asking, "So, how's your father?"

In a voice which was pure hormone, Charlie shot back at her with, "Well, I'm down for it if you are, but I'm not sure this is quite the time or place." Then they both burst out laughing, just as Gloria was making a beeline for them carrying a tray of milky tea and looking so anxious even her hair was clenched.

"Good God, Anna, where have you been? We've all been worried sick."

"Don't tell me, everybody's been phoning the police and the hospital, and the Missing Persons Helpline, and the FBI."

"Anna, people worry." Gloria sighed, somehow managing to shrug at the same time as holding on to the tea tray.

"Mum, I've been stuck in the most horrendous traffic on the North Circular." Anna paused to let her irritation at her mother's kvetching subside.

"Oh, and I'd like you to meet Charlie Kaplan," she went on. "Henry was his grandfather."

Anna thought her mother smiled at Charlie for a second or two longer than was decent for a woman of her age. It turned out that the two had already met at the cemetery. Gloria was just saying what a shame it was that Sidney and Maureen weren't able to make it because they were on a Saga holiday in Oslo, when she spotted Aunty Millie at the other side of the room. Gloria looked round for somewhere to put the tea tray and finally handed it over to a passing Kaplan great-niece in red platforms, matching acne and a nose stud. Then she went to fetch Aunty Millie who, before Anna arrived, had been bragging to Gloria about her grandson the top West End accountant.

Gloria wanted to get her own back by introducing Millie to Anna, whose journalistic achievements she had embellished considerably over the last few hours to the extent that Anna had not merely interviewed Maureen Lipman, but they had become best friends and now even shared the same gynecologist.

Anna thought she vaguely recognized the teenager with the acne, who was now letting the tea tray wobble so much as she wandered round the room that the tea was slopping into the saucers. It was Murraine. Family history had it that when the time had come to choose the child's name, Murraine's parents, who owned a unisex hairdresser in Loughton called The Clip Joint, had been determined to put a trendy spin on the name Lorraine. Nobody in the family in possession of a vocabulary had ever had the heart to tell them they had come up with a synonym for pestilence.

AUNTY MILLIE, WHO WAS IN HER EIGHTIES BUT SEEMED TO have been in them for as long as Anna could remember, had, along with an arthritic hip and a mustache, the white powdery lips people get from sucking too many indigestion tablets, as well as traces of lipstick on her teeth. With one arm in

Gloria's and the other leaning heavily on a three-pronged metal walking stick, she maneuvered her way slowly and deliberately across the room towards Anna and Charlie. On her arrival, she gave Charlie the kind of haughty look old Jewish ladies give to the sons of fathers who married out. Charlie's response was to give her a sexy wink, which she pretended to ignore. Millie then squeezed Anna's cheek, gave her a kiss which was all Rennies and mustache, and said she too had begun to put on a little weight round her hips in her late thirties, but made no mention of Anna's relationship with Maureen Lipman. She did, nevertheless, register a modicum of interest in what Anna did for a living:

"Anna, darling, I want to ask you about something that's been troubling me for a while," she said, a tiny bolus of air-borne spittle accompanying her inquiry. "These journalists who work for Sunday newspapers, tell me, so what do they do the rest of the week?"

With that Aunty Millie let out a very lengthy and very noisy fart. Instead of allowing her to stay to hear Anna's reply, Gloria put her arm round the old lady's shoulders and began steering her gently towards Uncle Henry's downstairs bathroom.

A NNA HAD NEVER MET AN AIRLINE PILOT, BUT JUDGING BY that old-fashioned Roger-Wilco-and-over voice the British ones always used to welcome passengers, an accent which invariably sounded like a cross between Kenneth More doing Douglas Bader and the Radio 3 cricket commentary, she had always suspected they fell into one distinct personality type. They were private school chaps on that indefinable cusp between Purley and Prince Andrew, who didn't own an emotion to speak of and were, fundamentally, dull. By rights, they should have been driving company Scorpios back to five-bedroom executive houses with up-and-over garage doors, except that because of some weird genetic fluke, they had been born with an extra derring-do chromosome, and a Ray-Ban Aviator fixation.

As Anna and Charlie sat chatting and nibbling on bagels and fishballs in the corner of Uncle Henry's lounge, as well as working their way through what remained of the thimbles of whiskey, Anna was forced to admit that Captain Kaplan didn't fit her stereotypical image of an airline pilot, although she suspected that should the need arise, he was perfectly capable of assuming full Dambuster mode and landing a sick 747 in a South American jungle clearing no bigger than a squash court while at the same time removing his own appendix. For a start he'd been educated at a public secondary school in Dublin, followed by drama school and some time living on a hippy commune in Cornwall.

"I spent a couple of years helping to run—wait for it—the King Arthur Crystal, Dowsing and Tarot Co-operative in Tintagel. You should have seen me. There I was, this emaciated New Age vegan weed with a ponytail and crushed velvet flares, sitting behind the counter burning joss sticks and reading up on corn circles, then one day in came a gang of shaven-headed Cro-Magnon look-alikes straight off the beach, each of them wearing little more than a chest full of tattoos and a can of Special Brew. Like a fool, I told one of them I could unblock his chakras and did he know that amethyst was traditionally believed to cure drunkenness. His response was to call me a fucking fag. Then he pissed over a box of amethyst I'd just had delivered, after which he and his six mates took it in turns to hit me over the head and generally beat the bejasus out of me with a giant piece of Brazilian quartz."

Charlie had decided finally that, because neither his astrological chart, the tarot nor his palm had predicted the attack in the shop, there was, without doubt, a lot less to life than most people could possibly comprehend. One night in September, he took all his New Age books, crystals and paraphernalia and threw them into the sea. A few weeks later, he began studying for a degree in maths at Trinity. Three years on he came out with an upper second and was accepted immediately by Aer Hibernia for pilot training.

"So, what about your parents?" Anna asked. "The family certainly seems to have given them a rough ride over the years."

"Just a bit, I suppose." He sighed. "But it got better once Grandad started coming over to Dublin for visits. After that a couple of the aunts and cousins began to send Jewish New Year cards, but we never got invited to weddings or bar mitzvahs or any family celebrations. It was strange as a kid, growing up and the truth slowly dawning that you were pariahs. But to be honest, I find it hard to get angry. What could you expect from a Jewish family in the early sixties? The war had been over barely twenty years, and in their eyes Dad going off with a Roman Catholic was simply finishing Hitler's work."

"That's an astonishingly generous attitude," Anna said, feeling anger on his behalf. "I think if I were in your position, I would have found it very hard to come here today and make polite conversation with the family who had ostracized me."

"I needed to do it," he said thoughtfully. "Even if he hadn't been on holiday, Dad would never have had the courage to come, and he wouldn't have considered bringing my mum. Even after forty years of marriage, he still can't bring himself to introduce the shikseh to the family. For me, turning up at Grandad's funeral has been like coming out of the closet. I think it's about time this family started to acknowledge my existence. I'm fed up with hiding in the shadows . . . and to give everyone their due, they've been remarkably friendly today."

Anna had been extremely moved by Charlie's story. As she watched him knock back the last of his whiskey, she realized her eyes were filling with tears. She was desperate not to let Charlie see her cry, which for the woman who sobbed when Pebbles Flintstone went into labor took some doing. It wasn't that she was afraid of showing her emotions, it was just that tears would make her foundation go streaky and she was buggered if she was going to let Charlie Kaplan see her thread veins.

"And the other reason I had to come," Charlie continued,

apparently oblivious to Anna's watering eyes, "was because I felt it was only decent there should be a blood relative here to say a prayer for the old fella."

"Speaking of which . . ." Anna said, nodding her head towards the rabbi who'd just arrived to conduct evening prayers.

As copies of the battered black funeral prayer books were passed round, the atmosphere at once became more somber. Gloria and Murraine, who had now been enlisted as a full-time helper, ran round collecting up the last of the dirty plates, the old people heaved themselves out of their seats and brushed their crumbs onto the carpet, and the men put their hands to their heads to adjust their yarmulkes. Charlie, who up until now hadn't been wearing a yarmulke, produced a brand-new black velvet one from his pocket and placed it self-consciously on his head, just a touch too far forward so that it looked like something he had just pulled out of a rather expensive Christmas cracker.

Rabbi Hirsch cleared his throat a couple of times to indicate that he was ready to begin as soon as he had complete silence.

Anna opened her book at the mourners' prayers, and then handed it to Charlie, who was struggling to find his place, having opened his from the left rather than the right. As was usual on these occasions, the prayers proceeded in breakneck-speed Hebrew, with all the men and a few of the women bent over their books, rocking and swaying and reciting the words out of sync, as if each of them was doing their head in to some totally arse-kicking heavy-metal track which only they could hear. The result was that one person's amen could be as much as three minutes behind or in front of another.

CHARLIE WAS FOLLOWING THE SERVICE FROM THE ENGLISH text which appeared on each opposite page of the prayer book. Anna stood next to him wondering what he looked like naked. She made no attempt to join in the prayers, partly because she was feeling far too sexually aroused to concentrate, and partly because she couldn't read Hebrew.

As a child she had constantly and successfully skipped Sunday-morning religion classes. While most of her Jewish friends had their heads down learning the Hebrew alphabet, Anna could be found sitting in the Wimpy bar stuffing her face with chips, or wandering aimlessly round the local park with her co-skipper Melanie Lukover.

Fearing that people, meaning her mother, might notice if she carried on gazing adoringly at Charlie, Anna turned towards Rabbi Hirsch. He was probably no more than thirty, but with his scholarly pallor and shiny greenish-gray suit, as well as his huge wiry beard which gave the impression that God had stuck the minister's pubic hair on to the wrong end, looked much older. Anna wondered if she might interest the *Jewish Chronicle* in a feature on rabbi makeovers. She was trying hard, but having little luck, to imagine him after a few sessions on a sunbed and a trip to a decent barber, not to mention an introduction to an electric nose-hair trimmer. It was then, from about two feet behind her, that there came the distinct trill of a mobile phone.

On the third ring, Anna, who seemed to be the only person who could hear the phone, swung round to see Bunny Wiener, Aunty Millie's other grandson (the dumb one who had, surprisingly, made a fortune in ladies' separates, as opposed to the one who became a West End accountant), fiddling with his prayer shawl in an attempt to get his hand inside his jacket pocket. Bunny was the only man wearing a prayer shawl, apparently the one male mourner who didn't know that they weren't required at a shiva by any known religious authority or cultural tradition. As if this weren't drawing sufficient attention, Bunny, his hand now in his pocket, was also struggling to remove his mobile, which appeared to have become wedged in by a huge bunch of keys and his wallet. The phone carried on ringing . . . five, six, seven, eight rings now. As Bunny dropped the bunch of keys, which landed with a clunk on the floor, Anna shot him a for-Christ's-sake-get-out-can't-you-see-we're-trying-to-mourn-here look. Bunny, who wore his stupidity with the same kind of pride as his handful of gold signet rings and metallic-turquoise Roller, simply ignored Anna's filthy glance, although he did make one feeble attempt at invisibility. As he began speaking into the mouthpiece he moved to the back of the room and pulled one-half of his prayer shawl over his head, as if he were a bird about to go to sleep under its wing. From this position, looking, Anna thought, like some overgrown ultra-Orthodox sparrow, Bunny began to have a row at only slightly less than normal row volume with a person she took to be one of his wholesale suppliers.

"Monty," he said—although because Bunny suffered from some kind of chronic adenoid condition this came out as Bonty.

"You're a jerk, that's what you are, a jerk. What do you mean, you're sending me eight gross in a size eighteen? Yesterday teatime I spoke to Bildred in the office and she confirmed eighteen gross in a size eight. . . . Go on then, you jerk, go and fetch the bleedin' order form then. I'll hold. . . ."

While Bunny held, the hubbub of the badly choreographed prayers continued like an anarchic Greek chorus. Then, after a couple of minutes, Monty obviously returned with the order form and Bunny started shouting and getting really angry with the poor chap. Anna could hear him bashing his fist on the wall, but mostly he just carried on calling him a jerk.

F ROM WHAT ANNA COULD MAKE OUT, THE BARNEY WAS FInally resolved by what appeared to be an unequivocal climb-down from Monty. This was followed appropriately by a stream of uncoordinated final amens from the mourners.

G LORIA RAN INTO THE KITCHEN WHERE TWO OF THE BORrowed kettles and a stainless-steel urn had come to the boil simultaneously, and Anna turned to Charlie and said in a perfectly calm and casual voice that it had been great meeting him, but it really was time she was getting back to her brats.

As she began looking round the room trying to work out

where she had left her handbag, Anna was aware that she felt a bit sick and that she could feel her heart beating so fast she suspected she was having one of those tachycardia attacks Dan seemed to get every other week, which usually ended up with her calling an ambulance at three in the morning and him in casualty wired up to a heart monitor for hours on end, only to be told there was nothing wrong with his heart and that he had been having a panic attack.

Anna knew that she too was panicking. Only hers was the sort that would only go away when Charlie Kaplan confirmed that he fancied her as much as she fancied him and that they weren't about to say good-bye forever in Uncle Henry's shabby, smelly lounge.

After all, they had spent the last hour or so deep in conversation, maintaining the kind of lengthy eye contact people make when they are attracted to each other. You didn't, Anna thought, have to be Desmond Morris to work out that this behavior was the equivalent of a couple of dating gorillas showing each other that red patch on their bums.

She tried to stretch out the hunt for her bag, which she'd actually spotted immediately, for as long as she could. This, she thought, would give him sufficient time to take her to one side and suggest that, as he was going to be in London for a week or so visiting all his newly discovered aunts and cousins, they might have lunch together.

But he didn't. As Anna picked up her handbag from underneath the drinks cart, she saw that Charlie was now over the other side of the room talking animatedly to Bunny Wiener. With a lump in her throat the size of a honeydew melon, Anna went over to them. She glared at Bunny and then extended her hand formally towards Charlie Kaplan, repeating how much she had enjoyed meeting him.

RODGERS AND HAMSTERSTEIN SAT on the pine kitchen table transfixed as Anna belted out "Surrey with the Fringe on Top" while doing a rising trot round the kitchen and at the same time gripping imaginary reins with one hand and holding Amy's old pram sun canopy over her head with the other.

After a minute or two she segued into "I'm Just a Girl Who Cain't Say No." Twirling the sun canopy over her shoulder like a parasol, she skipped over to the cupboard under the sink and took out a new bag of fluffy white hamster bedding.

Whenever Anna cleaned out the kids' hamster cages—which wasn't very often, as she usually got Denise to do it—she always felt it was somehow appropriate to familiarize them with all those daft the-corn-is-as-high-as-an-elephant's-eye lyrics written by their Hollywood songwriter namesakes.

But there was more to Anna's tone-deaf outburst this morning than a tutorial on mediocre melodies for two rodents who were unlikely ever to hold a tune. The precise reason for all the singing, the gallivanting around the kitchen and the performing of unnecessary domestic tasks was that last night, just as Anna was walking away despondently from Uncle Henry's house, Charlie Kaplan had finally got round to asking if he could see her again. Her impromptu musical celebration, which had begun as soon as Dan and the children left the house at eight o'clock, opened with her leaning on the breakfast bar, pushing an imaginary Stetson to the back of her head and launching into "Oh, What a Beautiful Morning."

Anna was feeling a lightening of her spirits which she hadn't known since a particularly significant Sunday night at a Jewish youth club disco in Edgware when she was fourteen. That night Anna had her first ever French kiss, with a zit-encrusted boy named Stewart Levinson, who smelled of TCP and didn't seem to know how to arrange his teeth when he kissed her. Against all the odds, however, she found herself rather enjoying the experience. At the same moment, her crush on Jane Hickling, who was a prefect in the Upper Sixth, ended; Anna realized that her prayers had been answered, and that God had finally decided she didn't have to be a lesbian after all. Now, more than twenty years later, the Lord had answered another prayer and decided to let Anna sleep with Charlie Kaplan.

After she had shaken hands with Charlie at the end of the prayers for Uncle Henry, Anna knew she had to get out of the house and into her car as fast as she could, because she wasn't sure how much longer she could stop herself from blubbing. She was in no mood for another of Aunty Millie's hairy-lipped kisses, so she waved a quick good-bye to her from across the room. Then she poked her head round the kitchen door and did the same to Gloria, who barely acknowledged her since she was giving Murraine a telling-off for pouring out tea without using a strainer. A moment later Anna was walking down Uncle Henry's garden path. As she turned round to close the little wrought-iron front gate, she could see Charlie was behind her, obviously trying to catch up with her.

"Come on," he said. "I'll walk you to your car."

She felt the melon in her throat disappear in an instant and once again hope began to spring internal throughout her nether regions.

As they walked to the car, Anna could sense Charlie's unease and that he was trying to get up the confidence to ask her something. For a second, she thought she might have to take the upper hand by suggesting they meet up in town one day next week. But she couldn't bring herself to do it. Although in her head she was Gloria Steinem and Germaine Greer rolled into one, in her heart she was the sort of unreconstructed eighteenth-century heroine who dashed around Catherine Cookson novels in a hooped skirt, coyly dropping lace handkerchiefs at the feet of Heathcliff look-alikes. She desperately wanted Charlie to take the lead and make the first move. Finally, after a few more moments' hesitation, he did.

"Listen, Anna, I've really enjoyed your company today. It seems a shame to say good-bye. I thought you might like to have lunch next week. . . . Perhaps Tuesday?"

Anna immediately blurted out, "Yes, great, Tuesday would be brilliant," so nervously and overeffusively that she must have come across like some lust-sick teenager finding herself face-to-face with Liam Gallagher in Boots. But Charlie appeared not to notice. He was too busy giving her another one of his long, sexy looks. Anna felt that if her nipples got any harder or larger they would, in the next few seconds, burst through her bra cups like a pair of horny Scud missiles.

Gently Charlie took her arm and Anna allowed him to lead her a couple of yards down the road so that they were away from the orange streetlamp and couldn't be seen from Uncle Henry's house. Then, very slowly, with his hands holding the sides of her shoulders, he began to bring his face towards hers. His lips had come to within a fraction of a millimeter of touch-

ing Anna's when suddenly there was an almighty shriek from
Uncle Henry's front garden.

Anna and Charlie sprang away from each other to put a
respectable distance between themselves, and then stood
watching the commotion as people came tearing out of the
house. From what they could make out, Aunty Millie, who had
probably been following Bunny Wiener to his Roller in order to
get a lift home, had tripped on a loose piece of crazy paving and
fallen over. She was lying on her back in one of the flowerbeds,
screaming at everybody to phone for an ambulance to get her
to Stoke Mandeville as she was paralyzed from the waist down.
Even goofy Bunny was able to point out that paralyzed people
tend not to be able to wave their legs in the air, and offered her
a glass of cherry brandy, which one of the lady helpers from
down the road had placed in his hand. Aunty Millie knocked it
back and said she thought she could manage another, at which
point she began clutching her chest, and proclaimed so loudly
that she could be heard as far away as Chadwell Heath the
onset of a cardiac arrest.

"Look," Charlie said to Anna, "I'd better go and see if I can
help calm the old biddy down. You get going and I'll see you
Tuesday—one o'clock if that's OK. Let's meet at the hotel. I'm
staying at the Park Royal in Kensington."

At the very mention of the word "hotel," Anna almost fell
into a Victorian swoon and thought she too could do with a
swig of cherry brandy.

Fighting the vapors, she took a deep breath and made an
effort to appear composed. She said that would be fine and
that she was looking forward to it, but Charlie, who was obviously finding it hard to forsake her in favor of Aunty Millie's
hysterics, stayed to watch her as she walked round to the
driver's door and got into her car. She had just started the
engine when he mimed to her to wind down the window.

"By the way, I almost forgot. I found this on the floor in the
hall. At first I thought it might be one of Aunty Millie's sex
toys, then I realized it could only be yours."

Grinning lasciviously, Charlie passed Anna her Tobago

brooch, the carved wooden one of the Rasta with the huge erection. It must have fallen off her jacket somehow when she arrived at Uncle Henry's.

"He's certainly a big fella. Reminds me a bit of m'self."

Anna wasn't sure whether she was about to have an instant bowel movement due to her embarrassment that Charlie had found the brooch, or whether she was feeling even more turned on—if that were possible—by his reference, albeit joking, but then again, maybe not, to the size of his own undercarriage.

There was one thing, though, about which Anna had no further doubts: so long as a state of national emergency wasn't declared between now and next Tuesday lunchtime, and provided the Queen didn't phone her on Monday night to say that she was prepared to give Anna the exclusive on her royal romps with Des O'Connor, she and Charlie Kaplan were going to sleep together.

O N THE JOURNEY HOME ANNA EXPERIENCED NOTHING BUT glorious sexual anticipation and almost frightened herself by the lack of guilt she was feeling, now that she was on the point of cheating on Dan. She realized that she hadn't discussed him with Charlie, other than to mention him fleetingly. She was certain, nevertheless, that when Gloria cornered him at the cemetery, she would have filled him in on everything about her, from the irregularities of her teenage menstrual cycle to her blissfully happy marriage.

What Anna couldn't work out was why, since Charlie must know she was married, he hadn't made some reference to Dan, if only to check that he wasn't a karate black belt or a professional assassin.

She suspected it was nothing more than sheer embarrassment. What had she expected him to say? "I really want to sleep with you. By the way I'd love to hear all about your husband. For instance, has he ever taken a piss sitting down, and where does he stand on the debate about whether those logos on men's polo shirts are tacky."

Anna did, nevertheless, have some misgivings about Charlie Kaplan. It struck her that he might well be one of those men who only had affairs with married women and preferably ones who had children. They, no doubt, fell madly in love with him, were desperate to run away with him and were probably on the phone to him several times a day, "just to hear your voice," no matter what continent or time zone he was in. She suspected that he, on the other hand, always bargained on them never having the courage to leave their husband's Amex Gold card, or risk losing their children. This left the charmingly alliterative Captain Kaplan free to fly round the world screwing a different married woman at every stopover, without having to give the remotest thought to offering them anything approaching a long-term emotional commitment.

Still, she realized, she shouldn't really give a stuff what his motivation was for wanting to get her into the sack. If she was a true believer in the gospel according to Rachel Stern, who might yet, if Anna's plan to commit serial adultery succeeded, become St. Rachel, she had to have faith—and keep reminding herself that for a truly clitoris-centered woman, it was the sex and not a bloke's psyche that mattered.

O VER THE WEEKEND, ANNA HAD CONJURED UP UMPTEEN sexual fantasies about Charlie Kaplan. She'd invented her favorite in the communal changing room at the local swimming pool, where she and the children were getting dressed after their usual Sunday-morning splash-around.

While Josh and Amy fought about whose undershirt was whose, Anna had sat on the wooden bench, pretending to concentrate on rubbing her towel over a particularly stubborn bit of hard skin on the underside of her big toe. What she was really doing was clocking the other women's naked bodies. It wasn't that, in her late thirties, Anna was having fresh doubts about her sexual inclination; it was simply that, as somebody with a rotten body image, she liked, needed even, to play "I spy a woman in worse shape than me." A pelican neck and the kind of tits which could be tucked into the waistband of a pair of panties could set Anna up for a week. Pert turned-up breasts on a mother of four would, on the other hand, have Anna wanting to dive into one of the private changing cubicles to phone the Samaritans on her mobile.

This had been a good morning. In a couple of minutes she had spotted a set of hairy nipples, the kind of flabby underarms from which you could make a set of curtains and have enough left over for tie-backs, as well as a severe case of pubic alopecia.

Slowly, Anna continued to dry herself off. Previous thoughts of having to sneak her ill-fitting skin in through the emergency entrance of some swanky beauty salon before her Tuesday-lunchtime assignation began to recede for the time being, at least. What took their place was a kinky daydream about her, Charlie Kaplan and a length of silk cord.

This involved him making her lie down naked on a bed, turning her onto her stomach and tying her hands behind her back. In her dream, he then forced her to wear a black leather slave collar and led her into the shower, where he covered her whole body in some sensational body foam from Harvey Nicks. Then, while he insisted she stood absolutely still, he gently stroked her clitoris, while using a razor in the other hand to shave off all her pubic hair. By now, with Anna in a state of some frenzy, he made her lie down on the cold, hard bathroom floor tiles, spread her legs open and then came deep inside her with an erection the size of a zebra's.

BUT SITTING AT HER DESK ON MONDAY MORNING, SHE thought that, knowing her luck, the reality would be that Charlie Kaplan suffered from some daft neurosis or other, such as a morbid fear of French onion sellers, and couldn't make love until he'd checked there wasn't one hiding under the bed, or secreted in the chest of drawers. Or he would turn out to have an erection the size of Rodgers and Hamsterstein's.

THIS LATEST FORAY INTO CHARLIE KAPLAN'S PUTATIVE PSY-chological underbelly was interrupted by the phone ringing. It was the familiar gorblimey voice of the *Globe on Sunday*'s features editor, Campbell McKee. Campbell had actually studied politics at Oxford, and been the *Observer*'s social services correspondent for several years before moving to the *Globe* for double the salary and a company Mercedes 190. Desperately anxious that nobody there should think of him as an intellectual middle-class wuss, he affected an almost immediate personality change. The refined chap who used to wear shrunken threadbare Guernseys to work and was the author of the well-received *Dial and Dialectic*, a Marxist analysis of the role of the telephone answering machine in late-twentieth-century culture, ran over his vowels one night with a lawn roller and took himself to a cheap flashy jeweler in Romford to buy a gold signet ring for every finger. These days he had all the manner and charm of a bent East End boxing promoter. By rights Anna should have despised Campbell; most people who knew about his hypocrisy did. Anna, however, thought he represented a perfect paradigm of human frailty and rather liked him for it.

"Anna, Campbell McKee 'ere. Just fought I'd give you a bell to say what a fucking brilliant job you did on that nit piece. We even managed to find the girl on the cooked meat counter at Streatham Niceprice who refused to serve the family, and got a reaction from their priest. Mine jew, 'aving said that, the mother looks like a complete dog in the contacts I just got from the picture desk—plus she's got jugs as flat as last Christmas's Asti Spumante. Still, it's going to make a bollocking good page eighteen. Listen, Anna, I was wondering if you fancied doing another story for us tomorrow evening?"

Anna hesitated for a couple of seconds. She had imagined spending Tuesday evening at home in the tub, immersed in delicious sexual afterglow and Body Shop bath foam—not chasing round every accident and emergency unit in London on behalf of Campbell McKee because some soap star had been caught shagging a vacuum cleaner attachment.

Campbell immediately picked up on her uncertainty and realized a touch of gentle thumbscrew was called for.

"Anna, don't say no before you've heard me out. Believe me, angel, this is a blindin' story . . . sort of tragi-wacky if you get my drift. Listen, just between you and me, I've had Lucinda Fee Plotter coming into my office every half hour since Friday, begging, just begging me to let her do it, but I said, 'Lucinda, you daft tart, get up off your knees, it'll do no good, you're just not up to it. There's only one reporter talented enough to do this piece and that's Anna.' Angel, just listen for a couple of minutes and let me fill you in. . . ."

Anna listened, but not before deciding that she must take Campbell McKee to one side at some stage and point out that if he wished to remain attached to his wedding tackle he really should stop calling her "angel."

The story Campbell outlined sounded pretty so-whattish. Mavis de Mornay, the seventy-something best-selling romantic novelist who wore Lycra boob tubes and black patent thigh boots, was dying of some mystery illness.

De Mornay was famous for her puerile seventeenth-century melodramas. These usually concerned an amply bosomed parlormaid called Agnes who suddenly discovers she was taken into slavery at birth and is really an Italian contessa, but that's OK, because the swarthy stablehand she has the hots for is really the illegitimate son of a French prince.

They were the kind of twaddle devoured by both office juniors from Upminster and dyslexic Sloanes skipping crème brûlée class at Swiss finishing schools.

Throughout her writing career, de Mornay had been a publicity junkie. In interviews she always said that her need to mainline on maximum press attention in order to ensure her books sold not just in their thousands, but in their millions, was linked to an overwhelming fear of reliving the poverty she'd known as a child growing up as plain Mavis Truswell in a Nottinghamshire coal-mining village. Mavis had gone into service in a grand house in Leicestershire, married a footman, Harold Chettle, and spent twenty years observing the ways of the aristocracy before writing her first novel, *Housemaid No More,* and sending it to a London publisher under the pen name she borrowed from a posh soap label. She ditched Harold in 1955, within a month of signing a ten-novel deal, and subsequently married her publisher.

As a consequence of her addiction to publicity, she'd employed umpteen PRs, mainly called Sophie, over the years to pester news desks every time a new de Mornay was about to hit the book shops—which they seemed to do almost every week. This press harassment took the form of incessant phone calls to editors and the mailing of hundreds of press packs, which included black lace garters and ripped scarlet satin bodices. A couple of times a year there were also invitations to champagne receptions chez the de Mornay pile in Chelsea, where the waiters and waitresses would be dressed as her latest hero and heroine and the climax of the evening was always a musical reenactment of the duel in Chapter 8.

Mavis de Mornay was a bore, and as far as journalists were concerned had been one for donkey's years. Where Campbell's story started to get interesting was when he got to the bit about de Mornay deciding that she would turn her own imminent death into some kind of macabre publicity stunt. She had left instructions with her latest PR—a jolly girl called India, which made a change—that as soon as she lapsed into a coma and her death seemed within hours, she was to invite the press and TV cameras to her bedside to witness her departure from this world into the next.

"What we'll do," said Campbell, "is put a picture of her at the moment of death on page one, and then your obit-cum-color-piece about her final moving moments as she loses her brave battle for life, et cetera, across two and three. Goes without saying none of the broadsheets will touch it, and most of the pops seem to have given it the bum's, so it looks like it's

just us, Jennifer's Diary and *Panorama*. What do you say? India, the PR—nice girl, well, fucking dim, ack-shally—says she's
fading fast and tomorrow evening we'll be sure to catch her au
moment juiced, as they say."

Anna thought it was possibly the most prurient, grotesque
and obscene idea she had ever heard.

"OK, Campbell," she heard herself say. "Fax me the address."

CHAPTER SIX

THE PANIC SET IN YET AGAIN THAT morning, in the lift at the Park Royal going up to Charlie's room. In the few seconds it took to reach the fourteenth floor, Anna could feel dots of sweat breaking through her foundation and her mouth filling up with saliva as if she were about to be sick. The moment the lift came to a jerky stop, she decided she had to get to a bathroom. She pressed the button for the ground floor and started taking deep breaths in between swallowing fiercely to get rid of the saliva. Anna wondered what the odds were on Charlie having the hots for women who smelled of vomit.

•   •   •

THE LIFT TOOK AGES TO REACH THE GROUND. IT STOPPED AT the tenth floor to pick up two American businesswomen wearing big hair, eighties power suits and running shoes, and who were deep in discussion about the best way to get to some dump way out in the 'burbs called Wimple-tahn, a place where, apparently, they had some business meeting set up, but that was famous, Anna gathered from listening to the women, for its tennis. The lift stopped again at the eighth. A Japanese family got in, but not before the father insisted on holding open the lift doors with his forearm and foot while the teenage son stood by a small table in the corridor and spent an irritating few seconds videoing a particularly uninspiring oasis arrangement of pink carnations.

By now Anna had trawled through her handbag and found a half-empty packet of tomato-ketchup-flavor Wotsits, which she'd probably confiscated for some reason from one of the children. It might just come in useful, she thought, when she chucked up.

AS THE LIFT REACHED THE GROUND AND THE DOORS opened, Anna barged past the Americans and Japanese, intending to make a bolt for the powder room, but queasy as she felt, she couldn't resist pausing at the doors for a second and turning back towards the Americans. "If you're looking for *Wimbledon,* I think you'll find your best bet is via Ed in Burrow and Saint Al Burns."

THE NEXT MINUTE SHE WAS SITTING ON A KIDNEY-SHAPED lavender Dralon stool which had gold legs. She was thanking God that, firstly, there was no bored lady loo attendant on duty raring to provide her with comfort, not to mention a twenty-minute discourse comparing and contrasting the size and consistency of her fibroids with those of all her friends, and secondly, the nausea was beginning to wear off. Getting angry with the two Anglophobic tarts in the lift had probably helped.

Thinking back over the events of the morning, it wasn't difficult for Anna to work out why she had felt so anxious and sick in the lift.

She had been OK first thing, when she was laying out on the bed clothes which she thought were contenders as outfits in which to commit adultery. Not that she intended to still be wearing them during the actual committing. It was the bit leading up to the committing which concerned her.

She had decided black was definitely out because she'd been wearing it at Uncle Henry's funeral and she didn't want to look as if she only ran at one sartorial speed. However, that excluded most of her wardrobe. She was left with a bright-pink imitation Chanel suit from M&S which had a gob of either snot or aioli down the skirt—she couldn't tell which—and a powder-blue dress and coat which was very sixties, very Jackie Kennedy and which Anna wore with matching low, pointy slingbacks. She had bought it last spring for a wedding. Although she thought it was ideal for her tryst at the Park Royal, it crossed her mind that it might be a bit dressy, a bit Moët and nibbles, for Mavis de Mornay's deathbed vigil afterwards. Still, if de Mornay was in a coma, she wouldn't give a toss what Anna was wearing, and if she was vaguely conscious, it might cheer her up.

So the blue dress and coat it was—along with a brand-new fifty-quid bra, which was sexy but not overly lacy and tarty, and matching cream-colored panties.

Then, just after nine, as Anna was thinking about getting in the shower, she heard Dan, who had left with the children almost an hour earlier, calling to her from the hall and then come charging up the stairs. She just had time to hide the clothes under the duvet and whip an old emery board out of her dressing-gown pocket. As he came panting into the bedroom, Anna was sitting at her desk filing her nails.

"Got halfway to the station and realized I'd forgotten my

bloody briefcase," Dan puffed. Barely looking at Anna, he bent down and picked up the ancient brown leather briefcase which was propping open the bedroom door.

Until two weeks ago, Dan had never taken a briefcase to work. The only thing he ever carried was a notebook and a Psion, which fitted neatly into his jacket pockets. Up to that point, the briefcase, Dan's only surviving bar-mitzvah present, had been used as a filing cabinet. It was stuffed with insurance policies, bank statements and HP agreements for furniture they had thrown out five years ago. Floating around the bottom somewhere was the tiny plastic ring which had been used to push back what remained of Josh's foreskin after he had been circumcised, and which Anna was keeping in order to bring out at his wedding. Now these family ephemera were stuffed into a black bin bag down by the side of the wardrobe.

Anna had no desire to find out what was in the briefcase. She had assumed it was nothing of any journalistic importance and guessed it contained another of Dan's medical contraptions—probably electronic paddles to jump-start his heart, complete with operating instructions. She figured he'd probably paid a fortune to have these translated into a dozen or so languages. His argument for this would have been that as there were so many tourists in London he had to be prepared in case it was a Xhosa tribesman who ended up spotting him in midinfarction.

Anna's guess wasn't that far off the mark. The story of the briefcase contents had begun one afternoon as Dan was walking past Berry Pomeroy's desk at the *Vanguard*. Berry, who had been christened Barry but thought Berry had more élan, was the TV critic, and was renowned for never being about. The reason for this, which was nonchalantly acknowledged by everyone in the *Vanguard* building, was that he spent most of his time suffering from writer's block, which he could only relieve by going to the cans to masturbate.

As usual, Berry was nowhere to be seen. On his desk was a pile of videocassettes, one of which caught Dan's eye. It was a preview copy of a BBC 2 documentary on spontaneous human combustion. He was unable to resist picking up the tape, and felt compelled to slip into the deputy editor's office, which happened to be empty and had a telly and a video. Dan watched the program four times and then immediately rushed out to Halfords.

The reason he had got into such a terrible stew on the way to the station two weeks later was the sudden and frightful realization that he had left home without his handy-sized fire extinguisher.

I T WASN'T JUST THE CERTAINTY THAT DAN'S HYPOCHONDRIA was spinning out of control like some mad, loose flywheel which had disturbed Anna. There was more to it. Something about his manner troubled her. The way, for example, he hadn't looked at her when he came into the bedroom to pick up the briefcase. There was no doubt in Anna's mind: Dan seemed even more distant and self-absorbed than usual. In fact, he'd been a bit strange all weekend. Whenever she had taken a break from one of her wild sexual fantasies about Charlie Kaplan, she had noticed that Dan, instead of slumping in his usual depressive state, had been positively agitated and jumpy, and kept getting up to check his office voice mail. He also had a faraway look on his face, and kept not hearing the children when they spoke to him. Anna had to repeat herself twice when she was explaining about the Mavis de Mornay job for the *Globe,* and that she might be very late home on Tuesday if the old bat didn't die on cue. Even after she had spelled it out again, she wasn't sure how much he had taken in. Finally, she had decided not to rely on Dan to baby-sit. She'd ask Denise to sleep over.

Anna had suspected that Dan's agitation (actually caused by the sluggishness of the shrink he'd found in *Time Out* in returning his call—as well as the fear that he was going mad) was because he was waiting for the result of yet another test. That would explain the obsession with the phone messages. Nevertheless, it was odd he hadn't given the lab or whomever the home number.

By Monday night he had seemed a little calmer. The call he was waiting for had obviously come. Anna was confident another electrical appliance would turn up on the kitchen table, but none appeared, and Dan continued to be hugely preoccupied.

Standing in the shower after Dan had left with his briefcase, it occurred to Anna for the first time in donkey's years that this time he might be genuinely ill—dying even. Here she was about to commit adultery and her husband might only have months—or possibly weeks—to live. Guilt surged through Anna's veins the way anesthetic does before an operation.

She spent the next few minutes repeatedly soaping her armpits and trying to remember the Jewish position on hell and whether it came with or without fire and brimstone. Just so as she'd know what to pack.

A FTER A WHILE, THE HEAT FROM THE SHOWER STARTED TO soothe Anna, and she began reminding herself how much Dan had neglected her, and how desperately she needed this fling with Charlie Kaplan. It didn't mean she had stopped loving or caring for Dan. If he was really ill this time, she would stop seeing Charlie, forget the idea of taking more lovers and doing the newspaper article and start investigating what was new in headstone designs. Her head clearer, but still agitated, Anna finally rinsed her crotch.

She looked down at her pubes to check all the soap was off. The guilt of a few moments ago had nothing on the horror and anguish which were now following in its wake. Anna could not take her eyes off her pubic area. Overnight, possibly even in the space of the morning, Anna had sprouted not one, but at least seven or eight gray hairs. Long, straight ones. They hung there like straggly weeds in her beautifully tended bush.

Anna accepted that decrepitude started to set in around the

mid-to-late thirties. She just didn't want it to start setting in today.

She couldn't comprehend her bad luck. How was it, she thought, that the one day out of three hundred and sixty-five she had set aside to be licked out by a virtual stranger turned out to be the selfsame buggering day nature chose to pop up with a quick reminder that she was, in fact, a crone in waiting, and that it might be worth taking a look at some of the brilliant half-price deals around on commodes?

God help her, wasn't it bad enough that she would have to make sure she only made love to Charlie Kaplan on her back so that her breasts looked vaguely aesthetic and remained in the rough vicinity of her chest, instead of pointing perpendicularly downwards? Even if she remained dorsal, they were bound to make a beeline for her armpits. Why was it that at thirty-seven she had everything she had at twenty, only now it was lower?

ANNA KNEW THE EASIEST THING TO DO WAS TO LEAVE THE hairs be, and accept that at almost forty, a few distinguished-looking pubes was OK. But she couldn't. She had no intention of letting Charlie Kaplan behold any more of her impending crone-hood than was absolutely necessary. She also decided not to pluck them—a) because it would hurt, and b) because her mother had always taught her that if you plucked hairs, they would inevitably grow back thicker and stronger.

It suddenly struck her that Clairol or someone might make a dye for coloring gray pubes. She quickly toweled herself off, put on joggers and a T-shirt and sprinted to Boots, which was only a couple of minutes down the hill in the George Street.

Of course, there were umpteen dyes for coloring gray hair, but nothing for gray pubes, and she was damned if she was going to ask. Then she spied it, alongside a new range of shampoos and conditioners imported from Australia. Next to a conditioner for permed and colored hair, there was a box with a picture of an Aboriginal man on the front, carrying a long pole.

There it was, written in huge letters across the top of the box: "Bush Magic—specially formulated to color gray in your most delicate area." Anna thought the name was a bit feeble for the Aussies, who she would have expected to have gone for something like Minge Tinge, The Better Way to Color Your Cunt, but she was nevertheless beside herself at her sudden change of fortune. She paid the seven ninety-nine for a color called Kanga Rouge, which the leaflet inside promised was more chestnut than red, then walked out of the shop in the full knowledge that the cross-eyed seventeen-year-old boy assistant now knew she had gray pubes.

B ACK HOME, ANNA REENTERED THE SHOWER AND SHAM-pooed in the dye, which, according to the instructions, needed to be left for an hour to ensure the color became permanent. Pushed for time—by now it was gone eleven—she decided to run the hair dryer over her pubes for ten minutes or so, hoping this would make the Bush Magic take faster. She turned the hair dryer to maximum heat and stood in the middle of the bedroom with her legs apart, looking as if she were about to deflower herself with a blast of hot air. After a while there was a slight smell of scorched pubic hair. But Anna didn't notice. She was feeling the anxiety creep over her again.

Her head was filled with an amalgam of profound fear and self-reproach. She didn't know which was worse—the thought that she was about to commit adultery while her possibly terminally ill husband was sending off stamped addressed envelopes for hospice brochures, or the thought that Charlie Kaplan might decide he didn't fancy her after all once he saw her without her clothes.

The anxiety persisted throughout the drive to the Park Royal. Stepping into the lift it had got much worse. Finally it took on a physical manifestation and the sweating and nausea had begun.

.   .   .

A NNA GOT UP FROM THE LAVENDER STOOL AND WENT OVER to the washbasin, which was shaped like an oyster shell. She rinsed her hands, wet with perspiration as they were, and took a small cotton hand towel from the pile next to the soap dish. As she dried her hands, Anna looked at herself in the mirror. Pendulous boobs and her graying bush aside, she had to admit she didn't look half bad. Rupert, he of Patrick and Rupert in South Molton Street, had cut her hair the day before so that it was now slightly longer than chin length. He had also put in some wonderfully subtle dark-blond streaks and given her a trendy side parting. Finally, he had used one of those little curling brushes to flick up the ends. When she pushed her hair behind her ears, which seemed to be the way everybody was wearing it just now, it showed off her high cheekbones and rather excellent jawline. Her elfin face with its huge gray-blue eyes was still a long way off Nora Batty droop.

Anna took a couple of paces back from the mirror. The dress and coat hung beautifully and the blue was an almost perfect match for her eyes. More to the point, she was, at nearly forty, still wearing a size twelve.

She did a half-turn towards the mirror, flicked imaginary dandruff from the back of her shoulders and decided that if Charlie Kaplan turned out to be the kind of shallow, superficial git who couldn't see beyond a Pamela Anderson cleavage then that was his problem. She had no idea where this sudden surge of right-on thinking and self-assurance had sprung from, but for the time being, at least, she was feeling much better about herself. Even the guilt about cheating on her possibly dying husband was beginning to recede.

Anna fiddled with her hair one last time. Then she took a deep, calming breath. A moment later she was dashing out of the powder room, almost knocking over the nice lady loo attendant, who was on the way back from her lunch break.

•   •   •

CHARLIE, THIS REALLY HAS TO BE ONE OF THE MOST MAG-
nificent views in London. You can see right into Kensington Palace and straight across the river to Battersea. Must be
glorious at night."

Charlie trickled champagne into two glasses and carried
them over towards Anna. She was standing with her back to
him, gazing out of the enormous floor-to-ceiling window which
ran the length of the living-room part of Charlie's hotel suite.
She wondered whether he was normally this extravagant, or
had taken the suite specially to impress her.

"Anna, how's about we try and forget the view for a minute?"
he laughed. "We've talked about nothing else since you arrived.
Come on and have some of this. It'll calm you down."

Anna turned round looking a bit sheepish, as Charlie
handed her a champagne flute. Then, in a very gentle voice, he
said, "Look, if you're having second thoughts about being here,
that's OK. Nothing needs to happen, not if you don't want it
to."

Anna took a huge swig of the champagne. Then she looked
at Charlie standing in front of her in his bare feet, faded Levis
and white T-shirt. His hair was still slightly damp from the
shower. This wasn't a man dressed for lunch at a five-star hotel. There was no doubt in Anna's mind about what he wanted
to happen next, and it didn't involve smoked salmon parcels in
a dill sauce.

Once again Anna's body was experiencing the kind of glori-
ous biochemical sexual responses around which Masters and
Johnson could have based an entire symposium. She held
Charlie's gaze in hers for a couple of seconds.

"No, I've thought about it and I want it to. Honest." Charlie's face was now inches from hers. She sensed he was about
to kiss her, but instead of letting him, she allowed her nervous-
ness to overtake her once more. She moved away, leaving him
alone by the window, and began flitting around the room scrutinizing paintings and ornaments like an *Antiques Road Show*
expert with St. Vitus's dance.

Charlie made himself comfortable in a rose-pink velvet armchair with tassels round the bottom and watched her, smiling. She darted all over the room, picking up and examining department-store china figures usually associated with detached houses in Weybridge and peering closely at the bland central-purchasing-department hotel-room watercolors of Tuscan landscapes.

After a minute or so, her eye seemed to be taken by a large and heavy reproduction mahogany desk. She walked over to it briskly, and ran her fingers over the green leather writing top. Then she started opening and closing the dinky drawers and pushed her fingers inside a couple of them as if she were looking for a hidden catch. Finally, muttering and tutting and looking perplexed, but determined—and still holding one of the Weybridge figurines of a crinolined lady carrying a spaniel and a nosegay—she got down on all fours, her hands caressing the carved wooden legs as she went. Then she crawled under the desk and disappeared.

Charlie shifted off the chair, and sat himself cross-legged on the carpet like a rather sexy gnome, his head peeping into Anna's hideout.

"Anna, please stop running away. You know it's all reproduction crap. I think you'll find there are no hidden compartments."

Realizing she had made a complete fool of herself, Anna scrambled out from under the desk. Charlie was already on his feet and offering a hand to help her up.

"Sorry," said Anna. "I guess I'm finding this adultery lark a bit scary after all." Once again she was filled with the need to escape, or at the very least crack a joke.

"My mother's house in Stanmore is full of this kind of repro stuff. She calls it her period furniture. More like menstruation furniture, if you ask me."

Charlie laughed but was beginning to get a bit cross.

"Stop it. Stop trying to change the subject all the time. You haven't even given me the chance to tell you how absolutely gorgeous and stunning you look in that dress. . . . Anna, do you know you are one of the most beautiful, sexy and funny women I have ever met? I want to make love to you right now."

Anna resisted replying, no, you sing it and I'll hum along. Instead she said, "What do you mean, 'one of'?" and this time she let him kiss her.

As they kissed and Anna felt his arms around her, his erection against her, she experienced a luscious quivering deep inside her belly which she hadn't felt for years and had almost forgotten. Breathing in his warm body smell, which was a mixture of newly washed skin with a hint of fresh sweat and washing powder, all the fear and tension she had been feeling began to drain away. Her sexual energy, suppressed for ages living with Dan, was being unleashed with an almighty intensity that was taking her breath away.

"Come on," said Charlie after they had stopped kissing. "I'm taking you to bed." The next moment, he was scooping her up into his arms like some medieval knight and carrying her towards the bedroom, ignoring Anna's mild protestations of fury.

"Charlie, for Christ's sake, put me down. You can't cart me off like some bloody chattel. If anyone finds out, I'll be outed on the *Guardian* women's page."

In the bedroom, they kissed again, but more urgently this time. By now, both of them were breathing like raging buffaloes, and Anna suspected that she alone was giving off enough body heat to keep an average Inuit family going through a particularly chilly winter.

As Charlie started to run his hands over her breasts and then down to her bottom, Anna could feel herself becoming more and more wet. Taking his time, he began to undress her. As he unzipped her dress and ran his tongue over the back of her neck, her head rolled forward and she began to wonder how much longer she would be able to remain upright. Then, almost as if he were reading her mind, Charlie pushed her gently backwards onto the bed, slipped down her bra straps and began biting and nipping her shoulders and the tops of her breasts.

Finally, he unhooked her bra and her breasts spilled out and arranged themselves tidily on the front of her chest. He spent what felt like ages telling her how beautiful they were before he started kissing them and sucking her nipples.

By now Anna's eyes were closed and she was moaning softly while Charlie concentrated on her breasts. After a few minutes he drew her towards him so that she was on her side, and she felt his fingers slide over her pants and penetrate slightly between her buttocks. She was now desperate for him to take off her pants and she let out another moan, but he ignored it. His response was to let her lie back on the bed and begin kissing her on the lips. With his tongue deep inside her mouth she felt his hand push the crotch of her pants to one side and his fingers brush past her bush, but barely touch her labia.

By now, she was begging him to come inside her. To make her point she undid his jeans belt and started to undo his fly buttons.

Charlie stood up by the side of the bed, and Anna watched him as he pulled his T-shirt up over his head. His upper body wasn't exactly six-pack himbo, but nudging in that direction. He clearly lifted weights when he wasn't landing sick aircraft in out-of-the-way bits of Upper Volta.

Anna knelt on the bed and helped him to pull down his jeans and black cotton boxers. As his erection—which was large, but not quite of zebra proportions, she noted with some relief—flopped forward, she began stroking the underside of his balls. Slowly, she moved her hand to the base of his penis. As she held it there, she moved her head forward and began licking his erection in long, slow strokes from the base to the head. As she covered the tip of his penis with her mouth and let her tongue run lazily over it, Charlie's breathing became more shallow and he began digging his fingers into her shoulders. Anna took more of his penis into her mouth and continued to caress it with her tongue.

Charlie closed his eyes and carried on gripping Anna for all he was worth. Anna could tell he was determined not to let himself come. Instead he pushed her head away and told her to lie back down on the bed. Anna whimpered as he finally pulled her pants down to her ankles and slid them over her feet.

As he ran his tongue along the inside of her thighs, Charlie spread her legs apart. He opened her labia and trailed his forefinger along the folds inside. Then he did the same with his tongue—probing and flicking. After a while, Anna felt his tongue on her clitoris, licking and teasing, hard enough to drive her crazy with excitement but not strong enough to make her come. He brought his head between her legs and pushed his tongue inside her. He started to rub her clitoris with his finger. Once again, it felt as if he could read her mind. She didn't have to tell him precisely where to put pressure. He just seemed to know. He tormented her with touches so light she could hardly feel them and cried out with frustration. Never before had she felt so completely out of control.

As she got close to orgasm, it was Charlie who orchestrated it, who slowed her down, speeded her up, kept her on the same plateau for minutes on end. When he finally allowed her to come, a wave of seismic activity of Los Angeles proportions shot through her entire body, for which, it seemed, San Andreas was not merely at fault, but was wholly culpable.

"Blimey, Charlie," Anna gasped as she officially entered postorgasmic glow. "Have you always been this good at it or is there something extra they put in the Guinness across the water that we don't get over here?"

Charlie just cradled her and grinned.

While Anna got her breath back, Charlie stroked her hair and ran his fingers over her face.

"Don't look too closely," she whispered. "Last time I went for a facial, they offered to make me boots for all my crow's-feet."

"You're a daft girl, you know that, don't you?" Charlie said quietly. "How can you not realize how beautiful you are?"

"Maybe I haven't had much reminding lately."

Anna didn't elaborate. Charlie didn't ask. He looked at her for a while and then, kissing one of her breasts, he said very gently:

"Come on, roll over."

Anna plumped up one of the huge hotel pillows and hugged it as she turned onto her stomach. Charlie ran a finger down her backbone as far as her bottom. She let out a deep sigh into the feather pillow as he brushed past her anus.

She pulled herself up onto her hands and knees. She knew what Charlie wanted her to do. In the next second, he pushed himself deep inside her. With each slow, penetrating motion she gave a little cry.

"Anna, it's OK, I won't hurt you. Come on, just relax."

He cupped one of her breasts and with the other hand felt for her clitoris, which he stroked with tiny, tight circular movements. A minute later they had turned over and he was on top of her, kissing her neck and mouth, searching for her tongue. Once again he was teasing her—this time by almost completely withdrawing after each thrust. Five, ten minutes went by and Charlie controlled her in his easy, almost leisurely way, just like before. Anna was feeling exceedingly light-headed and floaty. It was as if her entire consciousness was focused solely on the sensations coming from her vagina and clitoris. She was aware of nothing else, nothing else at all.

They came together, slowly and gradually, in a delicious heap of hot and wet. Afterwards the two of them lay facing each other, smiling in a breathy, comfortable haze. They both felt gloriously and magnificently knackered. Charlie propped himself up on his elbow and trailed a finger down Anna's neck to her breast and told her again how beautiful, wonderful and sexy she was. Anna was about to return the compliment as sexual etiquette demanded and reiterate her sentiments on Charlie's supreme sexual mastery with particular reference to his spectacular tongue and finger work, when she realized she couldn't because somebody had obviously been along and cut her vocal cords while she was thrashing about in midorgasm.

In fact, Anna's vocal cords were perfectly intact. They were merely suffering from a temporary bout of impotence brought on by shock.

As she started to come back down to earth, and her eyes

slowly began to rekindle their relationship with her brain, she concentrated on focusing properly on Charlie's face. For a moment, she thought all this steamy frenzied passion had been too much for him and given him a nosebleed.

The moment at which Anna had lost her voice was the same as the one in which she was overtaken by a flash of horrific realization and insight. The appalling truth had dawned on her: the reddish-brown stuff forming a beard over Charlie Kaplan's mouth and chin, not to mention the tip of his nose, was not, as she thought, dried blood, but something quite different.

How the blue buggering blazes was she going to explain to Charlie that their copious bodily fluids and juices produced during his magnificent cunnilingus had caused her Bush Magic to run?

CHAPTER SEVEN

ANNA LAY WITH HER HEAD ON CHAR-
lie's chest. Every so often she
would take a quick look up at him
and try to prevent her affectionate smile
from becoming a grimace. In between
looks she kept hoping the dye might magi-
cally dissolve or evaporate. It didn't. The
lower half of Charlie's face continued to be
stained bright bloodred.

She decided she couldn't bear the humiliation of relating the grim saga of her
botched attempt to dye her prematurely
graying pubes. Her only option was get the
dye off Charlie's face in such a way that he
wouldn't realize what she was doing. Short
of confessing to a Lassie fetish and licking
his face clean during another bout of frenzied sex, which would no doubt be followed

by her dropping dead as a result of ingesting some toxic aboriginal ingredient in the Bush Magic, her mind was a blank.

Anna's minimal brain activity was interrupted after a few
minutes by the muffled warble of her mobile phone. The phone
was in her handbag, which she'd left on one of the repro occasional tables in the other room. She let out a long, irritated
moan.

"Shit, I thought I'd turned it off."

Reluctantly, she sat up and swung her legs over the side of
the bed.

"Stay where you are," said Charlie. "I'll fetch it."

As Anna allowed herself to sink onto the two huge pillows
Charlie had just vacated, she suddenly remembered the gilt
mirror above the table.

"No, don't," she almost shrieked, and launched herself to
the foot of the bed in an attempt to pull him back. All she
managed to grab was the air. Panic-stricken, she watched as
Charlie's toned rear rippled out of the door.

Two seconds later he was handing her the phone. Judging by
his untroubled expression there was no sign that he had looked
at himself in the mirror.

Anna, who was still lying on her front facing the foot of the
bed, took the phone and propped herself up on one elbow.

"Anna, angel . . . Campbell McKee here, babe." As soon as
she heard who it was she raised her eyes heavenwards, mouth-
ing "jerk" as she did so. Charlie laughed and sat himself on the
bed behind her. He began stroking the inside of Anna's thighs.

"Listen, doll," Campbell went on, "I thought we had the
Mavis de Mornay story pretty much as an exclusive, but it
seems like the whole of bleedin' Fleet Street has suddenly
changed its mind and decided to muscle in. Apparently there's
been a posse of hacks camped out at the de Mornay house
since sparrer's fart. Why the fuck that India girl didn't ring to
tell us the gig was starting early and that we'd 'ave competition,
I've no idea. Anyway, angel, I think you should get over there
postwhatsit. Can't risk you missing the old tart snuffin' it."

By now, Charlie was, with the lightest touch, repeatedly running his fingers between Anna's buttocks. Every so often she would slap his hand and flick it away, but a few seconds later it was back again like some horny mosquito.

"OK, Campbell . . . ummm . . . right . . . I'll be over there . . . in twenty minutes . . . thanks . . . ooh, oooh . . . thanks for letting me know." Anna finally grabbed Charlie's wrist and did her best to hang on to it, but he pulled himself free. Then he made her turn over, forced her legs apart and pushed his tongue inside her.

"Anna, babe, everything OK from up your end? You sound a bit odd—sure you're not feelin' a bit Tom and Dick?"

"No . . . no . . . Campbell, my end's fine. Speak . . . speak to you later."

As Anna dropped the phone onto the bed, Charlie began kissing her on the mouth. Anna knew she had to leave, but she was no match for her hormones, which appeared to have formed themselves into armored battalions and were driving Chieftain tanks through her willpower. It took a full minute, but finally she was able to pull away from Charlie.

"Charlie, I really am so sorry," she said gently, "but I've got to go. That was the features editor at the *Globe*. I promised to do a story for them today, only it's all happening a bit earlier than we thought."

Charlie's crest didn't just fall. It plummeted.

Anna started stroking his red face and kissing his cheek. She couldn't help noticing his mouth had become even redder in the last minute or so.

"Listen," she said, trying to cheer him up, "let's get in the shower." As she said the words, she realized she had cracked the Bush Magic problem and kicked herself for not thinking of it half an hour ago.

Charlie's face brightened considerably at the thought of soapy underwater sex. Anna went into the bathroom and turned on the shower. In a couple of minutes steam was filling the room and the huge mirror over the his-'n'-her basins was becoming more and more opaque.

DAN'S CAB DRIVER WAS AN EXPAN-
sive salt of the earth geezer type
who kept taking both hands off the
wheel to look in the driver's mirror and adjust his ginger hairpiece.

"Wife got me the syrup for me birthday . . . can't get used to it. I gen'rally
buy her slippers and a vibrator. I always tell
'er if she don't like the slippers she can go
fuck 'erself."

The driver gave another burst of wheezy
phlegm-ridden laughter and pulled up at a
crosswalk. As he waited he again craned
his neck towards the mirror. He saw Dan
sitting on the backseat staring blank-faced
out of the window. After ten minutes of
trying to engage his fare in some lighthearted misogynist banter and getting nowhere, the driver decided to give up.

Dan was aware of being rude, but was feeling exceedingly
nervous and apprehensive and was in no mood to be matey. He
was on his way to his first appointment with Virginia
Livermead, the pyschotherapist he had found in *Time Out*. She
had finally phoned him at the office late the previous afternoon
and said she could see him at six the following evening. Her
voice was calm and businesslike. Dan hadn't expected to be
offered an appointment so quickly. The same fear that had
overcome him a few days ago, of Virginia Livermead discover-
ing he was insane and beyond help, had engulfed him once
more and caused him to dither over the phone for a few seconds before accepting. Virginia Livermead then said she
charged fifty pounds for an hour's session and was that going to
be a problem? Dan gulped and dithered again before lying that
this would be absolutely fine. He hoped to God she wasn't
going to insist on seeing him three times a week. He wouldn't
have a hope of hiding that sort of expenditure from Anna.

The rush-hour traffic was particularly heavy. The journey
from the *Vanguard* offices to Virginia Livermead's flat, which
was somewhere behind Sloane Square, shouldn't have taken
more than a few minutes. Dan had been sitting in the cab for
more than half an hour. He was going to be late. Once again
his anxious stomach shot burning gastric juices into his mouth
and he began to cough.

He had spent most of the journey trying to imagine the questions Virginia Livermead would ask him and recoiling at the
thought of her probing endlessly, the way he knew shrinks always did, about his childhood. There were things his mother
had done to him that he had never mentioned to a soul, not
even Anna. He'd read somewhere that successful psychotherapy depended on patients trusting their therapists and keeping
no secrets from them. Did he have the courage to tell a complete stranger about the bucket episode?

This had occurred a couple of weeks before his bar mitzvah.
Dan had been getting a pain in his back passage whenever he
went to the loo and was stupid enough to tell his mother. Mrs.
Bloomfield dragged him to the doctor. Forgetting that she

wasn't speaking to old Dr. Lazarus, who had retired, but to the new doctor from Lahore, his mother explained that her son had a sore tuchas. Dan would never forget the confused expression on Dr. Qureshi's face as he asked, "What please is a tuchas?"

The new GP diagnosed a small tear in Dan's rectum caused, he thought, by constipation, and prescribed a steroid ointment. Mrs. Bloomfield allowed Dan to use the ointment, but she had her own ideas for curing his problem. Mrs. Bloomfield prescribed Jewish penicillin.

The following afternoon when Dan got home from school she decided to administer the first dose. He was sprawled on the sofa in the lounge, eating mashed egg and salad cream sandwiches, when he became aware of his mother rooting around in the cupboard under the stairs and pulling out what sounded like a metal bucket. Curious, and not having the blindest notion of what lay in store, Dan got up and watched her put the bucket on the kitchen floor. Then, using both hands, she heaved a huge saucepan off the gas cooker. Sighing with exertion, she took this over to the bucket, which she then filled almost to the top with hot, steaming chicken soup. That done, she proceeded to balance an ancient wooden lavatory seat on top of the bucket. She carried out these maneuvers while at the same time conducting an animated and involved conversation with Aunty Esther, who had come over for tea to discuss the seating plan for Dan's bar mitzvah. Mrs. Bloomfield broke off from listing her reasons why Maisie and Burt should be excluded from the top table and turned to face her son, who was standing in the doorway looking perplexed.

"Come on, Daniel," she said, putting the saucepan back on the stove and sounding slightly breathy because she was overweight and unused to sudden physical exertion. "Don't let the soup get cold. Pull your trousers and pants down and sit on the bucket. The vapor from the chicken soup is good for you. It will take away the pain you get when you do your business. What are you waiting for? You think your Aunty Esther hasn't seen a schmekel before?"

Dan did as he was told. He had never been able to work out why. At thirteen he stood nearly a foot taller than his mother. Had he refused to obey her, she wouldn't have possessed the strength to force him.

He sat on the bucket with his back to his mother and aunt, tears streaming down his purple face. As the two women continued to stuff great chunks of honey cake into their mouths they concluded their discussion of top-table politics and went on to consider the likelihood of Phil Jaffa and his Jazzmen being available the Sunday after next.

BY THE TIME THE TAXI PULLED UP, DAN WAS SWEATING WITH relived humiliation. The driver turned around and slid back the glass partition.

"Sorry, mate," he shouted at Dan, who didn't seem to have registered their arrival. "Can't get any closer. Bloomin' great television van parked in the way. If I double-park I'll be holding up the traffic. The house you want is just a couple of doors down." The driver lowered his window and stretched his arm back to the passenger-door handle.

Dan came to suddenly as the door swung open. He got out of the cab and handed the driver the fare along with a ridiculously overgenerous tip, partly to apologize for being so silent and rude. In return, when he asked for a receipt, the driver flicked through his pad and tore off half a dozen blanks and passed them to Dan through the window. Dan and the driver nodded to each other in a way that indicated that both their backs had been appropriately scratched.

The cabby sat with his engine running while he clipped his receipt book to the sun visor and took out the notes in his money bag to count them.

Dan began walking down the street, which formed one side of a square of intimidatingly grand creamy-white Victorian villas, a few hundred yards, as the Sloane strides, from Peter Jones. Even the houses which had been converted into flats, or embassies serving little-known African dictatorships, retained an air of dowagerlike haughtiness, almost daring would-be visitors who lacked independent means to approach.

It was a couple of seconds before Dan noticed the television outside-broadcast van. He thought little of it until he saw the group of people standing around on the pavement ten or so yards ahead of him. They were eating pizza out of flat cardboard containers. Dan recognized at least half the hacks and photographers. He was just trying to work out what story they could be on, when, to his complete horror, he caught sight of Anna. She was standing in her best blue dress and coat drinking from a can of Coke, which she then handed back to a girl from the *Mail*. Suddenly the penny dropped. They were all here to cover the Mavis de Mornay story Anna had been going on about. Dan knew the way these sordid occasions worked. De Mornay had probably snuffed it a few minutes ago and the hacks, not content with their gruesome deathbed harvest of snaps and quotes, had decided to hang around for another couple of hours in case her children turned up to pay their respects.

Almost as soon as the first penny had dropped, a second followed as Dan suddenly realized that Mavis de Mornay and his shrink shared virtually the same address. Today, of all days, the coincidence was unspeakably cruel.

Dan began to tremble. Virginia Livermead's flat was in one of the houses a bit farther down the road. To get to it he had no choice but to walk past the press group and, in particular, his wife, and risk being recognized. Anna would ask questions, he would cave in and tell the truth and the promise he had made himself not to tell her he was seeing a shrink would be broken.

It wasn't going to make any difference if he crossed the road because the group had spread to the pavement opposite. His only solution, he realized, was some form of instant disguise. He toyed briefly with the idea of making a mad dash to Peter Jones to see if, by any chance, they sold deerstalkers and false mustaches. Then he remembered. As he got out of the taxi he had noticed a red-and-white hat lying on the dashboard. He swung around. The cab was still there. Dan dashed back and motioned the driver to open his window.

"How much do you want for the hat? I'll give you absolutely anything." The driver's eyelids remained unbatted. He was used to nutters, although in twenty-five years he had never had one make an offer for his clothes. "You're welcome to it, mate," he smiled. "The wife got it for me in one of those souvenir shops on the front at Blackpool. Can't wear it now 'cos when I take it off it takes me syrup off too." He handed the hat to Dan. It had a turned-down brim and was shaped like a cricket hat. Dan put it on. It was slightly too big.

He thanked the driver profusely, pulled up his jacket collar, hunched his shoulders and lowered his head. Then he walked briskly past the group of journalists, who didn't look up from their pizzas. Two minutes later he was waiting outside the shrink's flat.

As she opened the door, Virginia Livermead saw standing in front of her a tall, slightly hesitant young man. He was carrying a briefcase and wearing an expensive gray business suit, a sparkling white shirt and a silk tie. She couldn't see much of his face as it was obscured by the brim of a cheap fairground hat across which was written in large black letters: "Kiss me quick. Fuck me slow."

B Y SIX-THIRTY, THERE WAS STILL NO SIGN OF MAVIS de Mornay's children. The posse of journalists gathered outside the de Mornay house decided to call it a day. A few of them had started to get calls on their mobiles from agitated news editors ringing to remind them that unless they got their fucking arses in gear the story would be too late to make the Guernsey and Outer Hebrides editions.

As people offered each other lifts or headed off to the main road to hail taxis, Anna stood trying to decide if she wanted to go home or for a swift drink with a couple of people from the *Sunday Times.* As they were all working for Sundays they could file as late as Friday or Saturday.

In the end, she decided to pop round to Brenda's. Her nanny
was off sick so she would be at home, probably cooking supper
for Alfie. What Anna fancied, she decided, was a girlie chat
over a glass of wine, during which she could pick at the remains of Alfie's Tesco pizza and give Brenda a blow-by–blow
job account of her blissful couple of hours with Charlie. Plus,
she had a posh dinner party to go to the following week and she
wanted to cadge something to wear from the sample rail
Brenda always kept in her bedroom.

Anna arrived at Brenda's to find her alone. Alfie was staying
at her mother's in Peckham for a few days. Anna was about to
say wasn't that odd as it was term time, but as Brenda seemed a
bit tense she thought it best not to pry until they'd loosened up
over a couple of drinks. Anna followed Brenda into the kitchen
and Brenda pulled out a bottle of a fashionable new Brazilian
Soave from the wine rack.

"So," she said, pushing down the chrome arms on the corkscrew man, " 'ow's it going with this pilot geezer you met at the
funeral? S'pose you've been and done it, you daft mare?" Anna
thought Brenda sounded a bit more cheery.

"Yes, I have. Today, as it happens. Yes, it was brilliant. Yes, it
was the best sex I've had in years, probably ever in fact. And no,
I'm not going to fall in love with him." Anna wasn't about to
give Brenda the upper hand by confessing that the affair was
being slightly marred by her worrying herself sick over whether
Dan was terminally ill. Instead she went even more on the
attack.

"Look, Brenda, I know you don't approve, but I'm not prepared to carry on living with little or no sex for the next ten
years, until I wake up one dark menopausal morning and discover it's too late to have any fun because my genitals have
shriveled up, packed their bags and booked themselves into
sheltered accommodation in Eastbourne."

Brenda finished pouring wine into Anna's glass and poured
herself a glass of Perrier. She had barely smiled at Anna's face-
tious outburst.

"Bren', what the bloody hell is going on? You look and sound completely knackered, your hair's got enough grease on it to take the lead in a fifties musical, your son is staying at your mother's and you appear to be on the wagon."

Brenda pushed her face into her hands. When she released them it took a few seconds for her features to rearrange themselves.

"I'm up the spout."

"What, you mean the business is bankrupt?"

"No, not yet—although the way things are going that could be on the cards pretty soon. . . . No, it's me. I'm pregnant. Some miserable git went and knocked me up at a party."

Brenda bit her bottom lip and then began to cry loud, red-faced sobs full of saliva and snot. Anna got up from the table and put both arms round her. She rocked her back and forth the way she rocked Josh and Amy when life in the school playground got too much and their lives seemed utterly wretched.

It turned out the "miserable git" was Giles Hardacre, the Tory MP for Lymeswold, who was also the Opposition frontbench spokesman on agriculture. Brenda explained that one of her clients who spent a fortune at Sweet FA every year had invited her to her house in Wiltshire for the weekend. Brenda had thought it was going to be just her, the client and the client's husband, but it turned out to be a full-blown house party full of chinless uppers. Brenda had been bored witless. To relieve the tedium she got completely smashed over dinner and then somehow ended up in bed with Hardacre, who had, conveniently, come to the party wifeless.

"And condomless, by the sounds of it."

"Anna, don't start. I know it sounds ridiculous, but I never imagined that I'd get pregnant. It took nearly a year with Alfie."

Anna tried to think of something helpful to say.

"So, is he good-looking, then, this right horrible gentleman?" She knew she must have seen Hardacre on TV, but she couldn't for the life of her remember what he looked like.

"I guess so, in a sort of nobby, foppish, Michael Heseltine kinda way."

Anna said this didn't really help, as it probably described at least half of the Tory party.

"Anyway," Brenda went on, slowly rubbing her finger round the rim of her glass, "I left doing a pregnancy test until Saturday. I'd had my suspicions for a couple of months, but I suppose I was trying to put it to the back of my mind. Once I found out I thought it best to tell him, just out of politeness really. I assumed he wouldn't want anything to do with the baby, but I didn't see that as a problem. I'm not exactly skint and I'm used to being a single parent. When I told him, he was furious and went on and on about 'is reputation being destroyed and 'aving to resign from the shadow cabinet if it leaked out. He insisted I get rid of it.

"But I couldn't even consider an abortion. As soon as I'd got over the shock I couldn't wait to tell Alfie he was going to have a baby brother or sister. I told Giles I was keeping it. I didn't hear a word from him all through Sunday and Monday. Then this morning he phones. The stupid bleeder has only been and told 'is wife. He said he couldn't live with the guilt of it all, or the thought that she might read about it in the papers if I started kicking up, demanding maintenance for the baby. Now she's turfed 'im out, says she'll name me in the divorce. And if that isn't enough, she's threatening to sell her story."

Brenda put down her glass and wiped her nose on a hard ball of scrunched-up kitchen paper.

"Look, I know I should be feeling sorry for the cow. If I were in her shoes, I'd probably do the same, but if Lavender Hardacre goes to the papers my reputation will be down the can. Half of what I sell goes to rich Tory women like her, and the point is, they all know each other. The moment she accuses me publicly of being a husband-stealing slapper, every Caroline in London will come out in sympathy and the first thing they'll do is stop buying my clothes. Anna, she has the power to organize a virtual boycott of Sweet FA. I stand to lose a fucking packet."

Anna reached into her bag. Down among the dead ballpoints

and furry, crisp-covered tampons, she found a cleanish handkerchief. She handed it to Brenda.

"Brenda, please, please don't panic. I'll talk to Dan. We'll
work something out. I promise."

Anna had absolutely no idea what Dan could do. What was
more, she couldn't bring herself to mention borrowing a dress
for the dinner party. She'd have to buy something and Dan
would be furious.

Bugger him, she thought. She had bigger things on her mind
just now than the price of a goddamned dress. Dan would just
have to get unfurious again.

WITH A FORCE JUST A FRACTION
greater than good manners required, Anna stabbed her fork
into another piece of olive-paste-covered
bruscetta. For the last ten minutes some
boorish South African architect, too used,
thought Anna, to bossing black servants
around, had been setting everybody straight
on the reasons for the spread of AIDS in
Africa. It was one of those intellectually
competitive Hampstead dinner parties at
which Dan excelled, but which Anna
feared because they always made her feel
she should have taken the previous week
off work to mug up on the latest opera
crits, the works of Pliny and heaps of hard
vocab.

During the predinner drinks, while Dan

had been on the other side of the room chatting to a couple of people from the *Observer,* Anna, wearing the new black Ghost dress Dan was still livid with her for buying, found herself collared by a chap who, she thought, had to be in his late sixties.

He had come and sat beside her on the sofa. His gray hair was cut into a trendy crop so that his head looked almost as if it had been shaved. He was wearing a high-buttoned burlap waistcoat, a collarless white shirt and tiny oblong steel-rimmed specs. Anna wasn't in the least bit surprised to discover he was a shrink. Taking Anna's eyes in his, he declared he only had to look at a person for a minute before he understood almost everything about their psyche. Sensing that she could cope with him because he was obviously nothing more than a randy old goat, Anna began to relax. It was only when he asked her whether she agreed that Eric Cantona, on the evidence of the latest film he had directed, was the new Claude Berri that she began to panic. In an instant her palms were soaked in sweat and she lost her grip on her champagne flute. This fell onto the coffee table and smashed into tiny pieces. Red-faced and flustered, she began dabbing ineffectually at the mess with a tissue. She gave the shrink a feeble smile and mumbled something about never being at her best among the shattering glasses.

The dinner party was being given by Rebecca Jameson, the social affairs correspondent at the *Vanguard,* and her husband, Bill Hutchinson, who was the London bureau chief of *Lifenews Magazine.* Anna hadn't met Bill before, but she'd spoken to Rebecca a few times at various *Vanguard* drinks do's. She was in her mid-forties, fearsomely bright and confrontational, and according to Dan behaved in conference like a cross between some intellectual Rottweiler and a boot-camp leader. If she thought somebody had said something stupid she would rip them apart for minutes at a time, until, in the end, she almost had them volunteering to make amends by doing one-armed press-ups on the floor.

Anna was expecting Bill to be a stooped, ineffectual, balding

American with a beard and no mustache, but in fact he was a clean-shaven Ivy League American with thick blond hair and he stood remarkably upright. When Dan and Anna arrived he was in the middle of sounding off at Rebecca, in front of several guests, that her understanding of the ramifications of a single European currency were positively junior high. She simply stood there gazing at him the way Julie Andrews looks at Christopher Plummer in the gazebo scene in *The Sound of Music* when he asks her to marry him.

Anna had gradually become less intimidated by Rebecca and had even grown to like her once she realized the woman lacked any humor of her own and that it was pitifully easy to make her laugh. Rebecca had also become less threatening the moment Anna noticed she had a bosom which looked as if it would benefit no end from the cantilever properties of a decent underwired bra.

HAVING DEALT WITH AIDS TO HIS OWN ENORMOUS SATIS-faction, the South African architect paused to swallow a mouthful of the chilled coriander and lemongrass vichyssoise, then led seamlessly into a monologue on suburban design. Anna was thinking of asking whether Le Corbusier had actually invented brandy too, but thought better of it.

"What everybody needs to understand," he insisted in his curt, imperious tone, "about the hierophancy—if you will—of the patio door in the British outer suburbs is that it has its roots in a thesis promulgated in the early twenties by Alvar Aalto. It was Aalto who said that man, even from within his brick-built shelter, needs to preserve his contact with living nature if he is to safeguard his physical and mental well-being. Of course, given our climate and countryside, that's something we have been aware of in South Africa for many, many years."

"Particularly when it came to constructing shelters in black townships," Anna murmured through a stiff ventriloquist's smile. Dan, who was sitting opposite Anna, had been watching her fidget and sigh as she became increasingly bored and irritated by the South African. He hadn't caught the precise contents of her murmur, but he knew Anna well enough to be concerned that they might represent the beginning of an increasingly violent continuum which could end with her suddenly producing a brick from her cleavage. Casually Dan leaned back in his chair, slid his bottom to the edge of the seat and just managed to reach her shin under the table and kick it.

Anna didn't flinch. He'd only managed to tap her. She gave him a childish, mischievous grin, but at the same time decided that her best bet would be to keep any more contentious thoughts to herself until home time.

A S THE SOUTH AFRICAN CONTINUED TO SOUND OFF LIKE some polysyllablic pedant on *Kaleidoscope,* Anna allowed her mind to wander. Inevitably, her thoughts drifted towards Charlie, and in particular to their slightly bizarre final meeting.

This had taken place a couple of days after their rendezvous at the Park Royal. Assuming that Dan had left for work, Charlie had phoned her early that morning to check if she was free for a late lunch around one-thirty.

At the moment the phone rang Anna was sitting at her desk in a pair of Dan's tatty old pajamas, alternating between picking at her cuticles until they bled and peering into the tiny antique mirror she kept on the desk to squeeze the blackheads round her nose. She looked and felt completely drained.

For a start, she'd had Campbell McKee on the phone just after eight and had ended up having to grovel to him. He had called, full of excitement, to give her the news about Mavis de Mornay still being alive and her death being nothing but a fiendishly elaborate stunt within a stunt to get publicity for her latest book, *They Parted at the Altar.* Anna had kicked herself for not having realized what the old bag was up to. Subconsciously she had known there was something dodgy about the entire de Mornay escapade.

For a start, she had looked nothing like Anna's vision of an old person on the verge of death. She had expected to see her looking thin and wasted, her taut white skin stretched over a skeletal face, as she struggled for every breath.

Instead, lying on her priceless carved oak four-poster death-bed, Mavis de Mornay had looked like an aged tart taking a rest between clients. She was wearing a ginger Mary Quant wig, and her sagging features were plastered in thick foundation in an almost identical shade of ginger. Her trademark Cleopatra eye makeup and purple frosted lipstick were as vividly applied as ever, and she was breathing easily as if she were in a deep sleep.

What was more, shortly before the "end," she had suddenly opened her eyes, slipped her hand out from under the tea-rose-pink counterpane and produced a hardback copy of *They Parted at the Altar*. Looking as if she were summoning her very last ounce of strength, she had held it shakily towards the cameras. Anna had been convinced she'd seen a satisfied smile form briefly on the old lady's lips. After a few seconds de Mornay's hand had flopped down onto the bed, and she was, supposedly, gone, the Cleopatra eyes still staring beseechingly into the cameras.

The reason she hadn't seen through the performance, she consoled herself, was that she had still been in a bit of a daze after seeing Charlie. How on earth the other hacks had been hoodwinked she had no idea. But for her part, Anna felt the need to apologize for not being more on the ball.

"No, angel, it wasn't your fault, just one o' them things," he said magnanimously. He went on to explain triumphantly that de Mornay had been caught out by pure chance. A few hours after rigor mortis should have set in, she and India, her PA, were photographed boarding a Concorde flight to New York by some freelance photographer who had been sent to Heathrow by one of the tabloids to get a run-of-the-mill "Joan Collins Flies Out" snap.

The *Globe on Sunday* had paid a fortune for the exclusive rights to the Mavis de Mornay airport pictures. Campbell was beside himself with what a blinding joke it was that the dailies had made complete tossers of themselves by filling their pages with masses of melodramatic hype describing de Mornay's final moments. The *Globe* would now humiliate the lot of them by appearing on Sunday with what Campbell referred to as "the real badger."

"So, what we're talking about in terms of your piece, angel," Campbell concluded, "is a slight shift in spin, if you get my drift. But don't worry about it. I'll tweak it up a bit."

Anna blanched at the thought of what would appear under her byline: when it actually came to tabloid writing, Campbell, like a lot of posh boys slumming it, was dreadful. Indeed, he may well have been the worst writer since McGonagall. But she was immensely grateful to Campbell for relieving her of at least some of the pressure she was feeling.

Despite Dan's continuing chirpiness, she was still being plagued by wave after wave of guilt about cheating on a possibly dying husband. She knew she ought to come straight out with it and ask him if he really was ill, but she kept chickening out. While there was an element of doubt, she reasoned, it was just about OK for her to carry on doing her "research" for the Rachel Stern piece. The moment she was certain he had some dreadful disease, her sense of decency would have to kick in and that would mean an end to any more extracurricular sex.

Then there was the question of what to do about the Brenda situation. Anna reckoned it could only be a matter of days before Brenda had fifty hacks camping on her doorstep. She'd discussed it with Dan several times. At first she was cross with him for being so dismissive, but ended up being forced to agree with him. He was right; in a free country there was no legal way of preventing Giles Hardacre's wife from going to the papers. Brenda might be able to sue for libel if the paper printed anything which wasn't true, but by then she would have been named and the damage done. As the days went by Brenda seemed to be getting herself into even more of a stew. She wasn't eating properly or going to work. Anna couldn't countenance breaking her promise to her best mate. She had to come up with something. It occurred to her that maybe there was some illegal scheme they might consider to put the frighteners on Lavender Hardacre. It didn't have to be very illegal, thought Anna, just slightly immoral, if necessary.

Another thing troubling her was that she'd barely glanced at the copy of *The Clitoris-Centered Woman* she had hidden from Dan in her sweater drawer. Alison O'Farrell had biked it over soon after their lunch at the Harpo. In her naiveté, Anna had been expecting a reasonably slim book. After all, Rachel Stern's thesis on why women should commit adultery wasn't exactly Wittgenstein. But being both American and an academic, Stern had managed to produce a thousand-page, close-typed treatise, packed with overblown rhetoric and impenetrable mazes of meandering sociological argument. Like most journos Anna was a past master at skimming a book in an hour and lifting all the relevant bits, but even skimming this lot was going to take forever.

She knew virtually all her stress was of her own selfish making. She knew too that she could put an end to it in two phone calls—one to Charlie and the other to Alison O'Farrell. Maybe it was time to tell both of them she was having second thoughts. She decided to go back to bed with some Night Nurse, which always knocked her out, and sleep on it. Then suddenly there was Charlie on the line asking her to lunch, his voice sounding as if she could pour it over profiteroles. Miraculously the color returned to her cheeks, her energy level soared and she had no doubt that as soon as she got up out of her chair, there would be a spring in her step.

"Are we talking lunch with food," she said, chuckling, "or naked lunch?"

"Well, I thought maybe proper lunch with clothes on would be nice for a change. Then afterwards we can make up our minds how to spend the afternoon."

Anna's insides turned several glorious anticipatory somersaults.

"I think it might be the last opportunity we get for a while," he went on. "The airline has been brilliant about extending my leave. I've caught up with all the family over here I wanted to.

But I really do have to get back. They've put me on the rota for the Dublin–LA run beginning next week."

ANNA HADN'T FELT UP TO GOING THROUGH THE RIGMAROLE of getting dressed up for lunch in the hotel restaurant, so she suggested a small French place round the corner. They chatted away easily about nothing in particular: Dublin, films, Charlie's cure for jet lag. Anna entertained him with the tale of Amy and Josh's latest head-lice infestation which had got so bad she reckoned the lice were wearing T-shirts with "Bloomfields '98" written across them.

Charlie had got some idea from Anna that things weren't right between her and Dan, but she had given him only the vaguest outline of the situation. She decided against revealing any more details because she felt it would be betraying Dan even further. She resolved that if she were to have any moral guideline in this whole exercise, it would be to protect Dan as best she could.

Charlie also seemed pretty reluctant to talk about his personal life, although Anna had worked out from a few things he had said that there were a couple of women—one in Sydney and another in San Diego—that he was clearly screwing around with. Whether or not he felt anything for them she had no idea.

Anna understood, and she suspected Charlie did too, that the moment they became emotionally intimate, they were, in a sense, done for. Their casual fling would turn into something far heavier.

So they spent lunch being flippant and frivolous. Occasionally curiosity would force one of them to hover dangerously around the other's emotional boundaries, but neither dared do more than hover.

Both of them felt too full after lunch to have sex, so they decided to take a walk down to the Serpentine. They'd just turned into Hyde Park when an early-summer shower material-

ized from nowhere. Anna said she thought their best bet would
be to take refuge in the Culpepper Gallery if it was open. She
knew it had been closed for months while the building was
being renovated. Deciding it was worth taking a look, they left
the winding footpath and started running across the grass towards the white Palladian gallery.

The Culpepper was renowned for exhibiting the kind of
rhinoceros-placenta-in-formaldehyde art guaranteed to outrage
anyone who owned a car coat, while at the same time forcing
those who owned bleached cropped hair, black roots and
Buddy Holly specs to invent new superlatives to describe it.
The gallery's last major exhibit, entitled *Eliminate the Negative,*
had involved a surgeon performing real live plastic surgery inside an enormous sterile Perspex cube. There had been a new
operation to watch every day. They included face-lifts, tummy
tucks, liposuction and breast implants. The day after a woman
had collagen injected into the outer lips of her vagina, there
was a huge squabble in the House of Commons about the
misuse of public money. The *Guardian* headlined its report on
the debate "Tax Spending Under Labia."

Anna and Charlie stood beneath the gallery's decorative
porch wiping their faces with some Kleenex Anna found in her
bag. Charlie told her she looked particularly sweet and vulnerable with mascara running down her face. Anna punched him
playfully. He responded by pushing her gently against one of
the white Grecian columns and kissing her.

"You know, I reckon, given another time and place," he said
when they had finished, "the two of us could have got it together."

Anna was cross that Charlie was suddenly mounting an as-
sault on one of their mutually agreed no-go areas. She decided
to try and keep the conversation lighthearted.

"Cut it out, Charlie, or everything'll start going black and
white and we'll end up in *Brief Encounter.* What's wrong with
what we've got? We've had great sex. We can meet whenever
you're in London and you're free to carry on jetting off to all
your foreign floozies."

"What foreign floozies?" Charlie gave her a look of mock hurt, but she could sense that he was relieved she had let him off the hook and wasn't about to make things awkward by sobbing and begging him not to go.

Anna couldn't get over how cool and matter-of-fact she had sounded. It flashed through her mind that her words had been nothing more than an elaborate act and that really she had fallen in love with Charlie. But she was pretty sure she hadn't. She didn't feel overwhelmed by that clingy I-can't-live-without-you sensation she always got when she was falling in love. She suddenly remembered what she had said to Brenda about it being sex and not a full-blown relationship that she needed. Nothing had changed. She still felt the same. Although they'd only done it once, she'd had a taste of great sex for the first time in years, and it was that she was going to miss when Charlie went home.

"Come on," she said, determined to sound cheerful. "Let's see if this place is open."

Charlie pushed the heavy paneled door and stepped inside. Anna held back for a couple of seconds to get her makeup mirror out of her bag. She was still concentrating on rubbing away at her mascara streaks as she followed Charlie inside and almost tripped on the tiny stone step into the gallery.

It was a long, thin, airy room with tall white walls and a polished beechwood floor. It was also completely deserted. There wasn't a uniformed attendant or even one other visitor to be seen. The reason was clear. Everywhere they looked there was evidence that the place was still in the throes of being redecorated. Around the perimeter of the room there were, perhaps, ten or fifteen aluminum stepladders as well as a couple of huge bits of scaffolding which reached the ceiling. The central area was filled with what appeared to be living-room furniture. Although everything was covered in dust sheets, it was perfectly easy to make out armchairs, a dining-room suite, a couple of sofas and a coffee table. Anna thought this was a bit strange but Charlie said it had probably been removed from the curator's office while that was being decorated.

Anna found it even stranger that there were swatches of Liberty-print curtain fabric lying on top of the coffee table. Next to these was a half-empty gallon tin of paint labeled Egg-shell Magnolia and a roll of Laura Ashley wallpaper border covered in a dark-blue seashell design. Anna thought about the incongruity of the Liberty prints and the Laura Ashley in a place like the Culpepper, but came to the conclusion it was probably OK, *de rigueur,* even, for the curator of a gallery like this to have an office decorated like a suburban row house because it probably represented some kind of tacky chic, an-timinimalist rebellion.

The floor was littered with more pots of Eggshell Magnolia, huge industrial paint rollers, ashtrays overflowing with ciga-rette butts and mugs half filled with tea.

By the *Marie Celeste* feel of the place, the painters had ei-ther done a bunk because the Culpepper was refusing to pay them for some reason, or, more likely, they were still on their lunch break.

Anna turned to Charlie and said as the gallery was closed why didn't they either carry on with their walk or, if it was still raining, go to the café down by the lake for a cuppa.

"Or perhaps we could go back to the hotel for an hour or two." She pulled gently on the lapels of Charlie's jacket, mak-ing him lower his head to kiss her again. They kissed for a second or two before Charlie pulled away, mischief on his face.

"Come over here," he said, smiling. He took hold of Anna's wrist and began pulling her into the middle of the room. Con-fused, Anna tried to pull back, but Charlie yanked her even harder and she lurched forward like a car in the wrong gear.

"Do you mind telling me what the bloody hell you're up to?" she demanded.

The very next moment she had her answer.

"Christ all bleeding mighty. You cannot be serious. Charlie, you're behaving like a total bloody lunatic. What the fuck hap-pens if we get caught?"

Charlie ignored her and continued to drag her over to a sofa draped in an enormous paint-splattered dust sheet. By now

Anna was red in the face as she leaned back tug-of-war style, still trying to pull herself away.

The next thing she knew he had got her onto the sofa and she was lying under the dust sheet with Charlie half on top of her.

"Come on, relax," he said, stroking her cheek. "With nobody here to keep track of them, the decorators'll be in the pub for hours." Very slowly he began kissing her. As his hand slid down under her tights and pants, Anna's anxiety melted into ecstasy and she felt herself sinking into a sublime, almost transcendental, sexual trance which she later described to Brenda as being very sixties, very psychedelic. Brenda said she made it sound less like brilliant sex and more like an elderly tie-dye.

Anna's state was made only fractionally less sublime and transcendental by the almost deafening pounding of rain on the skylight above them.

The noise of the rain, combined with an all-out concentration on their fast-approaching orgasms, meant that Charlie and Anna failed to hear the advance of a small group of art students. They had come to the Culpepper to see the latest Frank Kennedy exhibit, entitled *Anaglypta People*, which, according to the blurb on the wall outside, was "a magnificent example of neofunctional postsurrealism, transgressing traditional perceptions and capturing the essence of the middle-class suburban obsession with design concepts which are primarily conservative and safe."

B UT WHAT I DON'T UNDERSTAND, REBECCA," SAID THE South African, his pomposity and jingoism, unbelievably, having increased still further with the passing courses, "is why on earth the *Vanguard on Sunday* would be concerned about such a story. I just find it disgraceful how your gutter press latches on to these trivial matters. In South Efrica nothing like that would be considered a metter of the remotest interest to cultured people."

"Oh, François," said Rebecca, "you are such a dry old stick

sometimes." Anna kept silent. It was not so much that she was enjoying seeing Rebecca have to defend her newspaper's penchant for the occasional up-market tabloid-style scandal, such as the one she had revealed to her guests was going to be in the *Vanguard on Sunday* the next morning; Anna's stomach was churning more than she could ever remember. She considered pretending to pass out as a diversion. Dan, unaware, of course, of the panic consuming his wife, couldn't be bothered to get involved, having decided the architect was too thick even to engage with.

"The Culpepper Gallery story will be a complete hoot to British people," Rebecca continued indignantly. Anna now put her hands involuntarily over her face, only to remove them smartish. "Once they'd taken the picture the *VoS* is using, the students even approached the couple to double-check they weren't part of the exhibit, but they refused to come out until everybody had left the building. They escaped ten minutes later with jackets over their heads and made a dash to Kensington Road, where they hailed separate cabs. Nobody got a look at them, so we'll never know who they were. It's a marvelous story."

Everybody agreed that it was, indeed, a hoot of Olympian proportions, and a perfectly valid story for the *Vanguard on Sunday* to carry.

Everybody, that is, apart from François, who snorted and shook his head; and Anna, who continued to stare grim-faced into the beady eye of the grilled red mullet lying on her plate, and wish like François that the *Vanguard on Sunday* could only be a bit more serious these days.

IT TOOK FIVE OR SIX WORDS IN ENGLISH to describe Gerald Brownstein. In Yiddish it took one. Gerald Brownstein was a schmo. It wasn't that he was stupid—his IQ probably hovered round the hundred mark—it was just that he looked stupid and sounded stupid. He also insisted on ending every meal with soup.

Gerald came from a long line of schmos. When his grandparents arrived in Britain they decided that in order to become assimilated they needed to anglicize their surname. While most people would have opted for Brown or possibly Steen, the Braunsteins went for Brownstein. They could never get over how people always guessed they were Jewish.

Despite his high-pitched voice, permanently open mouth and indifferent intelligence, Gerald Brownstein had managed to notch up some impressive achievements in his sixty-odd years. The most remarkable of these was his marriage, in 1960, to the beautiful, public-school-educated Kitty Wax. They had met at a synagogue dance. Gerald fell for her long legs and sharp mind. As he so rightly said, "What schmo wouldn't?" She saw in him a chap without a brash or arrogant bone in his body who would worship her and be kind to her.

A couple of years later Shelley was born. She was beautiful like her mother and by the age of five could belt out word-perfect, albeit tone-deaf, renditions of Dusty Springfield's entire oeuvre. Gerald took this as a sign of great intelligence.

In 1970 Kitty's father died. With the money he left them, Kitty and Gerald moved to Stanmore and bought an old newsagent's shop which they turned into a kosher delicatessen. Within five years, the combination of Kitty's business sense, her ferocious drive and dogged determination to own a detached mock-Georgian house with fiberglass pillars had made it the best deli in northwest London.

When Kitty's arteries finally gave out a couple of years ago, as a result of her constant bingeing on fried potato latkes, nobody was surprised. She would bring them home from the deli for supper, along with piles of other fattening leftovers. Gerald had always warned her that potato latkes killed more Jews than Hitler, but she never listened.

At the funeral people remarked on how well Gerald was bearing up. Throughout the seven days of mourning, when he had a constant stream of visitors bearing food and company, he managed to appear almost cheerful. It was only when everybody stopped coming and empty day began to follow empty day that he began to appreciate the extent of his misery. He had no heart to run the deli without Kitty. Without her there to scream orders at him all day long, the business meant nothing. Three months after Kitty died he sold the shop. Shortly afterwards the obsessions began.

At first he kept getting worried and anxious about running

out of food. Every few minutes he would put down the newspaper and go into the kitchen to check the contents of the kitchen cupboards and the fridge. As the months went by he began doing mammoth shops in Sainsbury's. Every few days he would stock up on enough food to keep a family of five going for a month. By the time Shelley, who was living in sin in Temple Fortune with an estate agent called Elton Goldberg, discovered what he was doing, the huge chest freezer was packed with hundreds of packets of fish fingers and potato pieces shaped like letters of the alphabet and the fridge was bursting with chicken legs so out of date they could have walked to the dustbin.

Gerald's most frequent purchase was Bloom's salami. He spent much of his time driving round northwest London from one deli to another, chatting to his former rivals about the iniquities of the Inland Revenue—and buying up all their salami, the kind without garlic. He never asked for it to be sliced. He preferred to buy the whole thing. Because he had run out of fridge space, he decided to keep his salami collection in the bath, which he kept refilling with cold water so that the meat wouldn't go off. When Shelley walked into the bathroom one day to go for a pee, she discovered dozens of thick foot-long salamis in their bright-red Bloom's skins bobbing about in the water like little kosher torpedoes.

Realizing that her father wasn't so much going to Sainsbury's as going insane-sbury's, she sat him down and insisted he go to the doctor and get some psychological help. To his credit Gerald recognized this was what he needed and when the GP suggested he join a support group where people with similar obsessions met to talk over their problems, Gerald needed no persuading.

If nothing else, he reasoned, it would be a way of getting out of the house and meeting new people.

There were ten or twelve regulars who came to the group. Most of them were women, which for a widower, thought Gerald, couldn't be a bad thing. At his first session he had to stand up and announce, "My name is Gerald Brownstein and I am obsessed with buying food." Then everybody clapped and in unison yelled, "Welcome, Gerald."

Each week, members of the group confessed how many times they had washed their hands, checked the gas was switched off or cleaned the kitchen floor. At the end of every session they were given homework by the group therapist. The obsessive cleaners were usually asked to do something like empty the contents of an ashtray onto the carpet and see how long they could walk past the mess without cleaning it up. They then had to report back.

One of the compulsive cleaners was a woman who had been going to the group for years and had still to make the slightest progress. She didn't own an ashtray, refused to buy one and had never got further with the homework than neatly arranging a couple of previously rinsed and ironed Quality Street toffee wrappers in a Waterford crystal sweet dish and leaving the dish and its contents on the floor for two minutes before feeling compelled to clear it up. One week, her face beaming, she announced her best time yet. She had managed to leave the sweet dish for three minutes nineteen seconds, after which, she explained to the group, she had been overtaken by feelings of extreme anxiety and had to rush back into the room, pick up the sweet dish and sponge the area it had occupied on the carpet with 1001.

The woman's name was Gloria Shapiro. She was slim and expensively dressed, with beautifully coiffed blond hair and long red nails. Gerald knew she was married, but he was smitten.

In fact he was more than smitten. As the months went by she became his second obsession. Every evening about six he would pour himself a sweet sherry, put on one of his Joe Loss records and imagine what it would be like to go out with the glorious Gloria. In no time his mind was full of romantic trysts, gentle fox-trots and lingering goodnight kisses.

It didn't take long before Gerald wanted to turn his fantasy into reality. When she happened to mention to the group that

her husband was in Israel for six weeks supervising the redeco-
ration of their flat in Eilat, he saw the perfect opportunity to
ask her out. But knowing full well she would turn him down,
and suspecting he wasn't strong enough to cope with the rejection, he formulated an alternative plan. He decided it would be
sufficient to just catch a glimpse of her every day. Overnight
Gerald Brownstein became a stalker.

G LORIA KISSED MARTIN SOLOMONS GOOD-BYE. EVEN
though he was her dentist and had just finished the last of
her root canal work, she didn't feel she was overstepping
patient–practitioner boundaries by giving her best friend's son,
whom she had known since the day he was circumcised nearly
forty years ago, a quick peck on the cheek. Besides, she adored
Martin. Not only was he, in Gloria's opinion, the best dentist in
northwest London, but he was also one of the gentlest, kindest
men she knew. She put this down to him being gay.

Gloria still had her doubts about whether God had meant to
put homosexuals on the earth. If he had, wouldn't he have
created Adam and Steve? Still, she had to admit that like a lot
of women she felt very much at ease in the company of gay
men and she looked forward to her appointments with Martin
because he chatted away over the amalgam about his boyfriend
troubles and always asked for her advice, which she gave will-
ingly, albeit in fits and starts, every time he allowed her a break
for a mouth rinse.

Today's session had lasted nearly an hour. Afterwards Gloria
wrote out the check at reception and then ran back briefly to
remind Martin in front of his new patient and within earshot of
a waiting room full of people, several of whom were bound to
have been raving homophobes, that in her opinion, lack of
communication was the reason most relationships broke down
and had he and Rob considered counseling?

It was then that she planted the good-bye kiss on his
cheek—and it crossed her mind how embarrassing it would be

if Martin knew that she always referred to him at home as the Tooth Fairy.

With that thought ringing in her ears, along with Martin's reminder not to chew on her left side for the next couple of hours, she closed the surgery door behind her and walked down the steps and onto the pavement.

As both sides of the main road were painted with double yellow lines, Gloria had left the car round the corner in Sainsbury's parking lot. She decided she would pop into the supermarket and get a few bits and pieces for Anna. She'd had a surreptitious stock-take of her daughter's cupboards a few days ago and was horrified to discover that Anna was down to her last half-dozen tins of red salmon.

Gloria was a firm believer in tinned fish. She frequently made the point to Anna that if anybody popped round unexpectedly, it was the most versatile standby. Gloria herself was never to be found without cupboards groaning with food. Although she only had to cook for herself and Harry these days, and despite a full-time job, she retained a profound maternal need, not uncommon in Jewish women, to provide food in abundance.

This afternoon Gloria's assistant, Sylvia, was minding Maison Gloria, which meant she could take the rest of the day off. She would spend an hour or so wandering round Sainsbury's, piling up her cart with treats for Amy and Josh, and then pop over to see Anna and dispense goodies to the children. Anna had said she would be home by four because she had to pick the children up from school. Denise, the baby-sitter, had sprained her ankle line dancing and had taken the day off.

Thanks for Gloria's food-buying efforts would be bestowed in two ways. The children's would come in the form of exuberant hugs, kisses and whoops of "Wow, Gran, thanks. You're the best gran in the world. Mum never lets us have Mars Bar ice creams." For a second or two, Gloria would bask in the nourishing warmth of conditional love. Then Anna would spoil the moment with her usual speech about how undermined as a mother she felt every time Gloria went against her express wishes by feeding the children the kind of crap she and Dan had banned except for Saturday-mornings treats.

Gloria was incapable of mending her ways. She walked towards one of the snakes of supermarket carts outside the main doors. As she struggled to remove the first cart, something caught her eye. She focused on the inside of a midnight blue Jaguar parked ten or fifteen yards away.

A trilby hat appeared to be bobbing up and down behind the steering wheel. For a second or two, Gloria thought it was simply somebody with their head down, searching through the glove compartment. Then a pair of horn-rimmed spectacles came level with the dashboard, bringing with them an over-sized nose and a thick gray mustache.

"Oh, Gawd," Gloria heard herself mutter. "It's that bloody schmo from the group."

All the obsessive compulsives agreed that even by their standards, Gerald Brownstein was a bit odd. Gloria, however, was having particular problems with him. At the end of each meeting he would make a beeline for her. Just as she was getting her coat, she would look up to find him standing beside her. The first couple of times this happened he said nothing. He simply stood there breathing through his half-open mouth, making soft snoring sounds. She smiled politely, said good-bye and disappeared. Lately he seemed to have plucked up the courage to speak to her. The last couple of times he had made conversation, it had lasted over half an hour. In his silly high-pitched voice he had gone on and on about how much the group was helping him tackle his food-shopping compulsion, how lonely he was since his wife died and how he could really do with some female company. This final sentence was always followed by a long, heavy silence, during which Gerald's eyes widened and his tongue protruded slightly from his open mouth.

A few weeks ago, Gloria had spoken in private to Julian, the group's therapist. She suggested it might be better for everyone if Gerald left the obsessive compulsives and joined the neurotics downstairs, but Julian had said that in his opinion Gerald was making excellent progress and should stay where he was.

He went on to suggest, much to Gloria's irritation, that he didn't like members of the group being turned into scapegoats and that maybe it was Gloria who had the problem, not Gerald.

In an effort to give Gerald the impression that she hadn't noticed him, Gloria opened her handbag and began rifling through it as if she had lost something. Every so often she would glance surreptitiously towards the blue Jag. One minute Gerald's face was above the dashboard, the next it had disappeared and all she could see was the trilby. Then Gerald became bolder. The next time he looked up, he took off his glasses and leaned forward. Then he pressed his face against the windshield the way children do on buses. She took one look at the straining myopic eyes, the squashed outsize nose and flattened clownlike grin, and felt sick. There was no doubt in Gloria's mind that she was being watched. Julian had got it all wrong. Gerald Brownstein had developed a new obsession. Her.

Gloria suddenly became aware that he could have been following her since she left home that morning to go to the Tooth Fairy, and that their simultaneous arrival in Sainsbury's parking lot was no coincidence.

She was more furious than scared. Nobody in the group thought for one minute that Gerald, at sixty-something and a shambling five foot seven, would do anybody any harm.

Gloria decided she could either go over to the car, scream at him and threaten to call the police, or she could remain dignified and aloof and get on with her shopping. She was determined not to give him the satisfaction of seeing that she was disturbed by his behavior. She decided she would do her best to ignore him and confront him only if he followed her round the supermarket.

In an effort to look fearless and bold, Gloria lifted her chin and stuck out her plentiful chest. In one easy motion she pulled a cart from the cart line and guided it round to face the automatic doors. She stood still for a second or two and with one hand pulled down on the hem of her short jacket. Then she tried to make the first of what she intended to be huge, fearless strides into the supermarket. Unfortunately she was wearing a tight pencil skirt and four-inch heels.

Gerald Brownstein's eyes were getting tired without his glasses. He took his face away from the windshield, picked up his thick-lensed spectacles and positioned them on their usual spot, a good inch down from the bridge of his nose. As his eyes refocused, his mouth opened even wider than usual. There was a small but unmistakable stirring inside his Aertex Y-fronts as he watched Gloria wiggle and totter into Sainsbury's, looking about as fearless and bold as a geisha girl.

Gloria pushed her cart towards the fruit and veg, trying hard to force her mind away from Gerald Brownstein and back towards Anna's shopping. As she picked up a bunch of seedless grapes and stuffed a couple into her mouth to test them for flavor, she decided she had to make some effort to stop annoying Anna by bringing the children so many sweets. She decided the grapes would do and put four bunches into the cart. To these she added a couple of Ogen melons, several pineapples, two dozen nectarines, some plums, a large bag of Granny Smiths, another of Cox's and three nets of Jaffa oranges. She then moved on to the exotic fruits, to the phylasses, the custard apples and kumquats.

After five minutes she had loaded her cart with enough vitamin C to keep an entire shipload of eighteenth-century sailors free of scurvy for six months. She knew she should make her way to the checkout. Amy and Josh wouldn't love her any less, she reasoned, if she bought them Cox's instead of Coke. But suddenly Gloria was reminded of their gleeful little faces, their wide eyes looking up at her as she handed out the jumbo bars of Galaxy and six-packs of Crunchies. She forced the heavy cart left into pastas and flour, wheeled it past the cook-in sauces and headed for her usual stamping ground among the cans of Fanta, high-fat yogurts with sprinkles on top and tubes of Refreshers.

A few minutes later, she was bending down into a huge deep freeze to take out three or four banoffee pies when she sensed somebody behind her. She knew exactly who it was. She could hear the familiar soft snoring sound. Gloria straightened up, but didn't turn round. For a while she stood facing the ketchup and salad creams on the shelf above the freezer and took a couple of deep breaths. Then she began to turn slowly.

First she saw the trilby hat, then the thick lenses and unkempt mustache. Finally she noticed the cheap Man at C&A trench coat and even took time to wonder why people with money were so often too mean to buy decent quality clothes. It must have been several seconds before Gloria noticed that the front of the trench coat was being held wide open to reveal two puny bare legs and a pair of baggy Aertex underpants. Stuffed inside Gerald Brownstein's underpants and exiting from the right leg as far as his knee was a very thick and very red Bloom's salami—without garlic.

MUM, I CAN'T BELIEVE I'M HEARING THIS.'' ANNA TURNED away from her mother for a second or two as she stretched across the kitchen table and took out a couple of kumquats from one of the Sainsbury's carrier bags.

"What do you mean," she continued, shivering with revulsion at the bitterness of the kumquat, "by saying there's no need to involve the police. This Brownstein creep has been stalking you, for Christ's sake. Heaven knows for how long. There you are standing with a banoffee pie in each hand and an old Jewish man comes up to you and starts playing with his salami. Brenda, would you please tell my mother she is completely barking."

Brenda, who was staying with Anna and Dan for a few days in order to escape the reporters she assumed would be camping outside the Holland Park house any minute over the Giles Hardacre business, said that as far as she was concerned not going to the police went beyond Barking and was, in fact, getting on for Dagenham and even Upminster. With that she put a slice of custard apple into her mouth, decided she couldn't swallow it and got up to look for some paper towels while at the same time mumbling something about it being no mistake that the conquistadors brought back oranges from the tropics and not custard apples.

"Look, he ran off sobbing his heart out. I'm convinced he felt terribly ashamed. Maybe I'll have a word with him next week at the group. I can't go to the police. They'll charge him with indecency and throw him into a cell. He could even end up spending months on remand. Anna, people commit suicide on remand. What if he killed himself? How would I feel? And think of the headlines in the *Jewish Chronicle*."

"Yeah," said Anna, suddenly seeing the funny side. " 'Salami Stalker Found Sliced in Cell.' "

Then the three of them broke into giggles and began making up dafter and dafter headlines, culminating in "Salami Madman Goes from Bad to Wurst." When Dan, who had spent the day working at home, came into the kitchen five minutes later to get a cup of coffee, they were all sitting round the kitchen table laughing their heads off like anally obsessed seven-year-olds in the grip of the latest turd howler.

Dan asked who was for coffee, but nobody took any notice because they were all still having hysterics. Anna took even less notice because she was laughing and at the same time trying to yell at Amy and Josh. For the last half hour they had been charging round the kitchen demanding to know where Anna had hidden the Hula Hoops and Twixes and going yuk, puuuke, when she suggested they help themselves to some of the wonderful fruit Grandma had brought.

Dan filled the kettle to the top anyway. While he waited for the water to boil he propped himself against one of the kitchen units, and started to smile. He couldn't remember the last time he'd seen Anna laugh. He thought how beautiful she looked and how much he loved her. Dan knew that after everything he'd put her through in the last couple of years she had every right to leave him. As quickly as it had appeared, the smile vanished.

He'd spent ages in his first session with Virginia Livermead telling her how scared he was of Anna leaving him, and how he really had tried his best to stop himself worrying about getting ill and dying. In fact, he had been so nervous when he arrived at Virginia's flat that he had started to blurt it all out while standing in her hallway wearing that ridiculous hat the cabby had given him. She had simply smiled briefly, nodded and started to lead him into her consulting room. It was only when he caught sight of himself in the hall mirror that he realized he was still wearing the hat. He did an emergency stop in mid-sentence and ripped the thing from his head. It was then that he saw what was written across it. In an instant he was hit by the full humiliating horror of turning up to see his shrink wearing a kiss-me-quick hat. For a split second he thought of running away. Then he looked up. Virginia appeared utterly composed and unruffled as she stood holding open the door of her consulting room waiting for Dan to go through. He decided the reason she seemed so relaxed was either because she was used to dealing with loonies and could tell he wasn't violent, or because the flat was fitted with umpteen panic buttons connected to the local jail, and she knew an armored police van was already on its way.

He glanced sheepishly at Virginia Livermead, who was in her late fifties and wore her gray hair in a severe crop. He mumbled an apology for the hat and said it was a long story. Then he stuffed it into his pocket.

The room was small and bright. The off-white walls were covered in paintings, mainly abstracts done in vivid reds and greens or brilliant purples slashed by black. French doors overlooked a pretty and well-tended walled garden and let in the early-evening sunlight. In the middle of the room, two black leather high-backed armchairs stood facing each other about six feet apart. At the side of one of the chairs was a small, square aluminum-and-glass table. On this stood a thin white vase containing half a dozen yellow freesias. Next to the vase was a box of tissues and a small digital clock.

Virginia indicated that Dan should take the chair nearer to the table.

They both sat down. Virginia sat bolt upright in her chair, her feet placed precisely together in front of her. Dan noticed she was wearing brown lace-up walking shoes. She placed her hands neatly in her lap, but remained silent. It was clear she was waiting for him to start. After his initial clumsy outpouring in the hall, Dan couldn't think of a thing to say. Virginia sat patiently. As a therapist, she was perfectly at ease with long silences. As a neurotic, Dan was not.

"So," his blustering began, "you're partly Freudian then, but I bet you're still Jung at heart." Dan laughed nervously at his own weak joke. Virginia's hard, chiseled features showed no emotion. When she spoke her tone was quiet and solemn.

"Sometimes people spend their lives making jokes so that they don't have to confront their emotional pain," she began. "If they are too busy laughing they don't have time to cry or get angry. Perhaps the reason you have come here is because you have reached a point in your life where you feel strong enough to face your pain and begin to deal with it."

Dan decided this was therapist speak for shit or get off the pot. He took a deep breath and began.

For the next hour he told Virginia Livermead everything about his imaginary illnesses, his umpteen visits to Harley Street specialists, his nonexistent sex drive and how scared he was that Anna might leave him.

Virginia made the occasional note on a foolscap pad as she listened to his story. After a while she began, as Dan had predicted, to ask him questions about his childhood. He told her how terrified he had been of his mother, how desperate he had always been for her approval and how she had never given it, but instead had done everything she could to humiliate him. He found himself telling Virginia about how she made him sit on the bucket of chicken soup.

"You must be feeling such anger towards your mother," she said when he had finished. Her voice was full of empathy and caring.

Dan said he occasionally got furious with her, but he never allowed the feeling to last very long. Getting angry, he said, seemed pointless. She was dead. It was too late to tell her how he felt.

Before Virginia had a chance to reply, another dreadful incident involving his mother, one that Dan had probably kept buried deep inside him for well over twenty years, leaped into his mind.

It must have happened, he said, when he was about twelve. He'd just experienced his first wet dream. The next day when his mother was stripping his bed she found the evidence of her son's spilled seed. She stopped dead in her tracks, pulled off the bottom sheet and sat staring excitedly at the semen stain.

She remembered reading an account somewhere of how the servants of the young Louis XIV found his semen-stained sheet and realized the stain was shaped like the map of France. They decided this was a sign from God that he would become a great and powerful king. The sheet was put on public display and great rejoicing and jubilation followed.

When Lilly looked more closely at Dan's stain, there was no doubt that she could see a map of the Middle East with the Negev and the Dead Sea quite clearly outlined. Was it possible that she too was being sent a sign from the Almighty and that Daniel, her Daniel, who with his B pluses and A minuses was never going to be the academic genius she craved, was actually destined for great things? Could it be that she, Lilly Bloomfield, had given life to a future prime minister of Israel?

DAN TOOK HIS HANDKERCHIEF FROM HIS TROUSER POCKET and blew his nose. Virginia Livermead reached across and touched his hand. Behind her severe silver-rimmed granny glasses, her eyes were nearly bulging with excitement.

"I can feel so much repressed rage coming from you," she said, clenching both fists in front of her bosom. Her voice was deep and trembling, making her sound like some third-rate Shakespearean thesp. "I think over the next few months we need to start working towards bringing this to the surface."

With that she glanced at the clock and said that unfortunately their time was up. She went on to say she would be happy to see Dan at the same time next week so long as he felt sure they could work together. Dan said next week would be fine. As he got up he handed her the fifty-quid check in a white envelope.

DAN PUSHED THE PLUNGER TO THE BOTTOM OF THE CAFE-tière and poured his coffee. He had his second appointment with Virginia Livermead in just over an hour. He'd told Anna he was going off to interview the chairman of the Bank of Bolivia in town and would be back just before nine in time to read to the kids. He picked up his mug and went upstairs to e-mail the piece he had just finished writing and get changed.

As he did up the cuffs on his denim shirt, Dan realized he was looking forward to his next session with Virginia. He had to admit she was a bit earnest and seemed to lack even the slightest vestige of humor. He also wasn't sure he trusted her when she put on her caring, full-of-empathy face. Nevertheless, she was easy to talk to, she listened and she'd reassured him that he wasn't going insane.

Dan dropped his keys into his jacket pocket and went downstairs. He yelled good-bye to the children, who were in the living room glued to Cartoon Network, promised them he would be back in time to read them a story, then poked his head round the kitchen door. Anna and Brenda were still sitting at the kitchen table talking Tory bastards. Gloria appeared to have volunteered to stay and make supper. She was busy chopping onions for a bolognese sauce, and managing at the same time to go through the fridge checking the dates on all the packets and throwing almost everything she picked up into a black dustbin liner. Anna hadn't noticed because she was on to her third glass of red wine. Dan said his good-byes and asked Anna to leave him some spag bol and he'd heat it up in the microwave when he got home.

·   ·   ·

DAN GOT BACK JUST AFTER NINE. HE BARELY SPOKE TO Anna—Brenda was already in bed—simply said goodnight and went straight upstairs. Once again Anna could see the tense, preoccupied look on his face. She wondered whether perhaps Dan hadn't been off doing an interview and instead had been seeing some specialist who had just given him bad news.

In fact Dan's facial expression owed more to physical and mental exhaustion than anything else. He had spent most of his hour with Virginia in tears as he revealed more and more excruciating stories about his mother. By the time he put his key in the door, his brain was still swimming with emotion. All he wanted was a glass of Scotch and sleep.

The children, who had been sitting in bed waiting for him to get back so that they could have the story he had promised, heard him come upstairs, go to the loo and put himself to bed. He hadn't even come into their rooms to give them a goodnight kiss.

Both Bloomfield children possessed a highly developed sense of justice and fairness. That very evening Amy had gone to bed crying because Anna had refused to buy her a Spice Girls Union Jack minidress with a halter neck. She had taken her mother's decision particularly hard as she was still trying to come to terms with not being allowed to have her ears pierced.

"Look, Amy," Anna had said re the ear-piercing, realizing, but suddenly not giving a damn, that she was about to sound like so many of the other snotty middle-class mothers in Richmond, "the kind of girls who have their ears pierced at your age live in public housing where the Alsatians drink Special Brew and the streets are full of Y-registered Sierras with Confederate flag bumper stickers."

Amy, being eight, had got lost round about "Special Brew." She gathered, nevertheless, that her pierced-ears application had been denied.

Josh took gripes with his parents particularly seriously, and kept scrupulous mental records, going back years, of all the crimes they had committed against him. These included still, even though he was ten, being bought Marks and Spencer tracksuits with pictures of Disney characters on the front, and being forced to eat from the children's menu in restaurants. The last time a waiter had asked him whether he would prefer mermaid or nuclear-submarine-shaped fish nuggets, he had jumped up from the table in disgust and sat out the rest of the meal in the gents.

His worst grievance also involved food. It went back to an evening just before Christmas, when Anna had insisted he eat lamb casserole, which he detested.

Josh had invited a friend over for tea. Anna had said that in return for him agreeing to finish everything on his plate, she would allow the two boys to eat sitting on the floor in Josh's bedroom. They leaped at the offer because this meant they didn't have to break off from building Lego antipersonnel mines. This, in turn, gave them a brilliant excuse to destroy Amy's pink plastic Barbie and Ken trailer.

Several weeks later, the man from Rentokil came to investigate the nasty smell in Josh's room and discovered a mound of putrefying lamb casserole behind Josh's wardrobe. As a consequence, Dan stopped his pocket money for three weeks. Josh's reaction was to thump his father repeatedly on the back and scream all the swear words he knew.

"Mum knows I think lamb's puke," he'd howled in between throwing punches at Dan. "If I'd eaten it I would've thrown up and *she'd* have punished me. I only hid it so's not to make myself ill and not to get into trouble for getting sick all over my room."

He then accused Dan and Anna of being wicked and evil for stopping his pocket money. They refused to listen, concerned only with their son's dishonesty, the Rentokil man's call-out fee and the cost of new wallpaper and carpet for Josh's bedroom.

Tonight, Josh was almost as angry as he had been over the casserole fiasco. It wasn't simply that he was annoyed with his father for breaking his promise about reading them a story; the truth was he felt Dan was severely neglecting him and Amy.

His father never seemed to make time for them anymore. He

was either too tired, too miserable or too ill. His mother was behaving strangely too. Sometimes she seemed very happy, almost in a sort of dream. Then she would suddenly get snappy and irritable. She also seemed to be working more than usual. He couldn't remember the last time she'd cooked a roast dinner. All they got lately were microwave packets or supermarket pizza.

Josh toyed with the idea of waking his father and demanding an explanation for the broken promise, but decided against it as it carried a significant risk of attracting one of his father's rare, but heavy-duty, bawling-outs. He decided it would be safer to remonstrate with his mother.

Josh pushed back his Manchester United duvet with his feet, heard his *Thousand Best Jokes for Kids* thump onto the floor and then went charging downstairs into the kitchen, where Anna was stacking the dishwasher.

"I hate you," Josh shouted at her from the doorway. "You two are the worst parents in the world. You are bloody bastards and I don't want to be your son anymore."

Anna turned round, looking more startled than annoyed. "Josh, calm down. What on earth is the matter?"

"You know what the matter is. You and Dad have never got any time for us anymore. You never do anything with us. You're always too busy and *he's* always too ill. I hate you. I hate you. I don't want you for parents anymore."

By now, Josh had got himself so worked up that he was red-faced and sobbing. Anna put down the dirty plate she was holding and walked over to him. She tried to put her arm round him, but he punched it away.

Anna was barely aware of the blow. All she could feel was the familiar sensation of descending guilt. Nevertheless she managed to retain a semblance of parental authority.

"Look, Josh, I'm not prepared to speak to you while you are being so foul. You either calm down and we have a proper discussion or I am simply going to ignore you."

Threatening to ignore Josh usually calmed him down in an

instant. The thing he hated more than anything was losing his audience.

Anna was about to suggest making them both some hot chocolate when she heard Amy thumping down the stairs.

"Christ, now the other one's here," Anna hissed to herself.

The next moment a drowsy-looking Amy was standing next to them in her ancient, faded Pocahontas nightie.

"Mummy, shut Josh up," she whined. "I was almost asleep. Why didn't Daddy come and say goodnight? I wanted to tell him about how me and Thomas Cooling snobbed in the playground."

"It's snogged not snobbed, you baby," said Josh in a nerna-nerna ner ner voice. "See, even Amy hates *him*."

"I don't hate Daddy. I love my daddy and he loves me. You're just a big fat poo. And Mummy does do things with us. She takes us swimming, and Daddy takes us to the roller disco."

Before Anna had a chance to intervene, Josh was shouting again.

"Everybody else I know has parents who do proper things with them like camping trips and going mountain-biking together. It's abuse, that's what it is, not spending time with your children. You and Dad are bloody child abusers, that's what you are, and I hate your bloody guts. I want to be adopted. Bloody child abusers. I'm phoning Childline."

With that Josh picked up the cordless phone from the worktop and stomped out of the kitchen, heading upstairs.

"Right, you do that. You bloody do that," Anna screamed after him. "Arrogant little jerk."

Anna couldn't decide whom she wanted to thrash more, Josh or Esther fucking Rantzen. Every time she and Dan told him off, Josh ended up phoning Childline for a second opinion. Josh had become such a regular caller that he even had a counselor he asked for. Claire.

Anna always listened in on the extension to Josh's conversations with Claire, who, thank the Lord, was a frightfully sensible young woman. From the moment Josh had started phoning

Childline, which he clearly perceived as grievance procedure for when he couldn't get his own way, a sort of junior ACAS, Claire had somehow grasped immediately that he wasn't being buggered, beaten or emotionally violated. Although she always listened to everything he had to say, she invariably managed to make him see that he had been a naughty boy and that maybe his parents had a right to be annoyed with him.

Deciding to leave Josh to his own mad devices and hoping Claire would calm him down as usual, Anna took Amy back to bed and read her a few pages of Roald Dahl. This was followed by a frantic search for Amy's favorite Polly Pocket toy, without which she could not possibly go to sleep. They eventually found it wedged between the bed and the wall. Finally, clutching the Polly Pocket, Amy gave Peter Andre, who was Blu-Tacked to her headboard, a long, lingering snob, before sliding down under the duvet. As Anna plumped it round her, she gave her a goodnight kiss and a hug. She found it almost impossible to believe that the three-year-old who had once asked her if fish fingers could swim was now puckering up to repulsive pop stars with hooped earrings in both ears.

Anna switched off the light, said a final "Night, night" and gently closed Amy's door. As she walked along the landing towards Josh's room, she expected to hear her son on the phone to Claire at Childline, going through a litany of Bloomfield parental misdemeanors. Instead, there were two voices: Josh's and Dan's.

The bedroom door was open a crack. Anna stood outside and listened.

"So, Dad, do you absolutely promise, cross your heart and hope to die in a cellar full of rats, that you aren't going to die?"

Dan ignored the internal paradox of Josh's request. "Josh," he began gently, "you're old enough to understand that nobody can make those kind of promises. But I promise I'll do my best." He sounded truly regretful; as if it had come as a shock to him that his hypochondria had even been affecting the children.

"And will you promise to at least try to stop feeling ill all the time, and when the weather gets a bit warmer can we buy a two-man tent from Milletts and go camping for a few nights, without Amy . . . just you and me?"

"I promise."

"And next time Mum gets one of her big checks from the *Sun* or the *Mirror,* can I have a Sony Play Station?"

"Josh, you've got a lot of apologizing to do to Mum before we even think about buying presents. . . ."

"But will you think about it?"

"Yes."

"And if I say sorry for the things I said to Mum and am really good from now on, will I probably get it?"

Dan sighed. He knew Josh had the energy to go on nagging all night. "Probably. Now go to sleep." He bent down and kissed him.

Josh fell asleep thinking that for child abusers his parents were, nevertheless, total pushovers.

T HANKS FOR CALMING HIM DOWN," ANNA SAID AS SHE AND Dan got into bed.

" 'S OK. When I heard him having a tantrum downstairs, I realized I'd messed up. It wouldn't have killed me to have at least gone in and said goodnight to the kids."

"Don't beat yourself up over it. We all break promises to kids now and then."

"S'pose. At least I dealt with it rather than letting that Claire woman do it. God knows what she must make of us. . . . I've gotta go to sleep. Turn off the light when you've finished reading."

Dan turned over, his back towards Anna.

Anna propped herself up on her elbow. She decided the time had come to confront Dan and find out what was worrying him.

"Dan, don't go to sleep yet," she said, poking him between the shoulder blades. "There's something I want to talk to you about."

Dan grunted and made a swiping motion with his hand, but didn't turn to face her. Anna poked him again.

"Dan, come on, turn over. Please, I need to talk to you."

Dan didn't move.

"Right then," she said, getting irritated, "I'll talk to your back. I've been getting really worried about you. You've been behaving strangely for over a week and I'm beginning to think that maybe this time you're really ill only you're too frightened to tell me because you think I won't be able to handle it or else I won't take you seriously. Dan, if you're ill I must know, otherwise I can't help you. . . ."

WHILE ANNA CARRIED ON SPEAKING DAN DIDN'T MOVE A muscle. For a few seconds he was concerned that she had found out he was seeing Virginia Livermead. Once he realized this was not the case, he turned over to face her.

"Anna, I'm fine, really." His voice was gentle and soothing. "I promise I'm not ill. It's, it's just that I've been making a real effort lately to stop imagining symptoms. The thing is, I think the strain of trying not to worry is really getting to me and that's why I've been a bit odd. Do you think worrying about trying not to worry can actually make you ill?"

"Christ, you need a bloody shrink, you know that, don't you?"

Dan turned over and grunted.

Anna was no fool. She knew there was something Dan was keeping from her. Nevertheless, she sensed he was telling the truth when he said he wasn't ill.

She picked up her book, read a few paragraphs and then put it down. She couldn't concentrate. In the space of a couple of minutes all the fear she had been bottling up for days had turned to relief, and then to elation. Dan wasn't dying. That meant she was free to carry on with her "research."

The sex with Charlie had been sublime. Just knowing that he fancied her had made her feel more beautiful and more alive than she'd felt in years. She knew she was behaving like some soppy heroine in a Mavis de Mornay novel. She also knew that truly liberated women didn't have to depend on men fancying them in order to feel good about themselves. Over the last few days, Anna had come to the conclusion that edicts such as this were nothing more than the crazed rantings of a bunch of jealous bull dykes.

Even though she had been worried sick about Dan's health, Charlie Kaplan had brought some old-fashioned fun and joy into her life which had been long overdue. Anna wanted to feel that again. Soon.

Charlie had phoned her a couple of times from Los Angeles to apologize for the dreadful way their final meeting had ended, how distraught he'd been that there hadn't been time to say good-bye and to tell her how much he missed her. He also added that he had no idea when he would be in London next.

Anna closed her book. She calculated she had just over five weeks before she would have to sit down and write her article on clitoris-centered women. She realized she was unlikely to see Charlie in the near future; her short affair with him was probably as good as over. It was time to move on. Excitement at the prospect of her next exploit shot through her like steam from a cappuccino machine; this, she was almost ashamed to admit, was fun.

Anna jumped out of bed and went into the bathroom. She opened the door under the basin. Reaching over the deodorant cans and shampoo bottles, she picked up the box of Tampax which contained the telephone number for Liaisons Dangereux.

CHAPTER ELEVEN

R ONNIE, REGGIE! MUMMY WON'T tolerate any more of this fraightful racket!" Reenie Theydon-Bois, director of Liaisons Dangereux, had broken off momentarily from her telephone conversation with Anna.

"Sorry about that, may deeah, my little shih tzus can be such naughty boys sometimes."

The woman's voice, full of high-pitched social pretension, had definite overtones of John Cleese doing the parrot sketch.

"Now then, where were we?" Reenie Theydon-Bois paused. Anna sensed she was drawing deeply on a cigarette.

"Ah, yes . . . Ay tell you what to do, my deeah. You give me your Visa number and then I'll fax you a list of all the male clients

Ay've got on may books. I guarantee you won't be disappointed with the service I offer. I think it would be fair to say that in the fayve years Ay 'ave been presaiding over Liaisons Dangereux, none of may ladies or gentlemen 'as hever once got the 'ump."

Anna decided Reenie Theydon-Bois was, without doubt, an ex-tart, probably from Ilford or Romford, who had struck it lucky and been set up in a mews house in the West End by a wealthy client. She pictured her as plump, probably in her mid-fifties, wearing a bright-yellow Versace suit with too many gold buttons, heavy lip liner and a sunbed tan. Anna could almost smell the Coco.

Liaisons Dangereux, Reenie explained, catered exclusively to respectable married people who, as she put it, felt a bit ne-glected in the bedroom department, and who were looking for someone to make them feel pampered and special. She kept on stressing that none of her clients had any intentions of divorc-ing their husbands or wives and thus discretion was of the "hutmost." So if Anna understood all that and had no more questions all Reenie needed from her now was her seventy-five-pound initial joining fee.

Anna took her Barclaycard out of her wallet. As she read the number down the phone, it struck her for the second or third time in the last few minutes that Reenie Theydon-Bois, with her daft accent and ridiculous surname, was a phoney, that Liaisons Dangereux didn't exist and that the whole thing was simply a way of extorting money from gullible people in celi-bate marriages. The likelihood was, thought Anna, that she would pay her joining fee and never hear another word from Reenie Theydon-Bois.

It wasn't losing the money that bothered her. Joining Liai-sons Dangereux counted as research for her newspaper piece and she would simply add the fee to her list of expenses. What she really hated was the thought of being duped.

She finished reading out the Barclaycard number. Reenie said she would fax over the client list in the next few minutes or so and Anna should give her a call when she had two or three prospective gentlemen in mind.

Five minutes later, as she sipped her coffee and munched on a low-cal rice cake, she heard the faint creaking sound of the fax machine as it spewed out paper onto the bedroom floor. Reenie Theydon-Bois had not scarpered after all.

DAN LEANED BACK IN HIS OFFICE CHAIR AND PUT BOTH FEET up on his desk. The *Vanguard* newsroom was almost empty. Everybody had disappeared to the pub over the road for lunch. Dan had decided to give it a miss because even though he always promised himself he would stick to mineral water, he inevitably ended up having a couple of beers and spending the afternoon fighting to stay awake. Instead, he had popped into Tony's, the sandwich bar next door to the *Vanguard* building.

As he finished chewing on another piece of bacon bagel and took a suck of thick chocolate milk shake, Dan began thinking about his therapy sessions with Virginia Livermead. He had to admit that despite his misgivings about the woman, he had been feeling much better since he'd started seeing her.

Slowly, Dan was beginning to make the connection between his mother and his hypochondria. Virginia explained what Anna had been trying to get through to him for years, that even though his mother was dead, she still had such a hold on him that each time he tried to rebel or break away from her, he experienced feelings of profound guilt. As a consequence he punished himself by developing imaginary illnesses which he believed were going to kill him.

MAKING LOUD, CHILDISH SUCKY NOISES THROUGH HIS straw, Dan drained the last of his milk shake and dropped the cardboard container into the wastepaper bin under his desk. He had eaten only half of his bacon bagel. He stared at the bit he had left and reflected that this was by no means the first time he had deliberately eaten a Jewish roll filled with nonkosher meat and then compounded the heresy by drinking milk at the same time.

If he thought back, he had been consuming forbidden food since his early teens. Instead of shouting and screaming at his mother and telling her precisely what he thought of her whenever she humiliated him, he had invariably dealt with her abuse by disappearing to the greasy spoon down the road and demolishing a bacon-and-egg fry-up.

Dan was aware that this was the first time in his life he had not felt guilty after doing something which he knew his mother would deplore. It further occurred to him that if Virginia Livermead had got it right and his imaginary illnesses were nothing more than a way of punishing himself for upsetting his mother, this might also mean the end of his hypochondria. If he felt no guilt, Dan reasoned, then there was no need to punish himself.

Dan bent down and reached under his desk for his briefcase. Neatly stowed inside were his fire extinguisher, his electronic blood pressure machine, a stethoscope, the little sticks he used to test his urine for sugar and a few sterile essentials necessary for draining a collapsed lung. These included a yard of plastic tubing, a couple of kidney-shaped bowls made of gray eggbox card and a scalpel.

Looking round to check that nobody had come back into the office, Dan took each piece of his medical paraphernalia out of the briefcase and placed them on his desk. Slowly he ran his hands over every item. He lingered over the fire extinguisher, caressing and stroking its smooth, curved body as if it were a lover. Then he placed his finger inside the small opening on the side of the blood pressure machine and felt the familiar tightening.

For the first time in years Dan dared to believe he might be fit and well. If that were the case he didn't need to keep monitoring his health. He didn't need this apparatus. The thought of losing his beloved crutches and failsafes filled him with terror.

He reminded himself of what Virginia had said as he got up to leave at the end of their last session: "You know you're not ill, Dan. You are simply angry and guilty—and perhaps a little confused."

Dan rammed everything back into the briefcase as fast as he could. He felt his pulse quicken. He took a deep breath. He decided he must have the courage of his confusion. He would ditch the lot. Right now. He realized he was probably cruising for a psychotherapeutic bruising from Virginia, who would doubtless have preferred him to take fifteen years gently building up to this moment, but he didn't care.

A NNA LOOPED THE YARD OF FAX PAPER OVER HER ARM. AS she took the scissors from her desk drawer she cursed herself for being such a cheapskate and not paying the extra fifty quid for a fax machine with a built-in cutter.

Finally she stapled the pages together. There had to be at least a hundred men on Reenie's client list. None of them gave their names. Instead they used a reference number. This was followed by a seven- or eight-line personal résumé and a description of the kind of woman they were hoping to find.

Anna scanned the first twenty or so ads and got bored after a minute. There appeared to be a standard form of words which she found dull, smug and predictable: "Professional male, late forties, some gains round waistline, compensating with losses round hairline, good sense of humor, married but physical side dead, seeks sensuous slender (size 12 max) twenty-something lady with firm, voluptuous bosom, to lift him from his despair and share uncomplicated passionate meetings and occasional overnights. Total discretion assured. Photograph appreciated."

Just then Anna heard the front door open. Brenda yelled a "Hi, I'm back" and came plodding up the stairs. She'd been to a meeting with Alfie's head teacher who was anxious to know where Alfie was and why he was missing so much school.

Brenda plonked herself down on the edge of the double bed. Anna turned to face her. Brenda looked dreadful.

"I'd forgotten," she said, bending over to pull off her heavy-duty CAT boots, " 'ow bad this morning sickness lark gets. Coming back from the school, I had to stop the car three times to puke. I think I might feel better if I knew when that bloody Hardacre woman was intending to make her move—I mean, it's been days since she threatened to sell her story. What's she playing at?"

"Well," said Anna, "I'm pretty sure she hasn't spoken to any of the papers yet. Dan and I still haven't heard even the faintest rumor that anybody's about to run it. That could mean she's got cold feet about dobbing you in. Alternatively she's a sadistic cow who is simply enjoying the thought of you sweating it out waiting for the shit to hit. Whatever the reason for her taking her time, it's allowing us some grace. What we really need to do is rake up some scandalous muck from the old bag's past which nobody knows about. Then you simply threaten to use it against her unless she backs off."

"Yeah, right. Easy. Listen, Anna, I'm barely coping with feeling sick all the time. I could do without the threat of being sent down for a five stretch for blackmail and giving birth in Holloway shackled to a couple of twenty-stone female screws." Brenda had kicked off her boots and was on the point of going down to the kitchen to get a glass of Perrier to relieve the nausea when she caught sight of the fax lying on Anna's desk.

"Christ, you don't waste much time," she said, picking up the sheets of shiny paper. "That Charlie geezer's only been gone five minutes and you're already planning your next campaign. If you ask me, I reckon there should always be a decent period of mourning between one lover and the next. You know, three months when you live in the same pink velour tracksuit and gray saggy bra, don't wash your hair, and eat nothing but Twinkies and peanut butter from the jar. I used to do that years ago before I had Alfie and the business. I always found it helped me get my head together, even if I'd been the one who'd done the chucking."

Anna said that although it didn't look like it, she was missing Charlie. She was certainly missing his body, but he was commuting between Dublin and LA, and she was here. What was more, she continued, she was still living with a man who lacked any semblance of a sex drive, and added to this, there was the small matter of needing to get started on her piece for Alison O'Farrell, which was due in a few weeks.

Brenda decided she was in no position to argue with Anna and get holier-than-thou, bearing in mind she'd got herself in the club after a one-night stand and had also been the one who'd introduced Anna to Liaisons Dangereux in the first place. She began looking down the list.

" 'Ere, look at this one. He reckons he drives a Testarossa. That means he's probably got a winkle the size of an oven chip. . . . Mind you, what about the next one down?"

Keeping her finger on the ad, Brenda leaned forward and passed the list to Anna.

"Sounds like he might be the business," she went on. "Not that I approve, mind you. I still think you're playing with fire. Or in your case, shagging with it."

With that Brenda ran to the bathroom, her hand over her mouth. Ignoring the dreadful sounds of retching and heaving coming from inside the lavatory bowl, Anna started reading the ad.

" 'Frustrated Quasimodo look-alike seeks his Esmeralda. Small fat ugly guy with hairpiece and own hump, drives brown Datsun Cherry, wife finds him sexually repulsive due to ongoing psoriasis, wants to make bells ring with any woman brave enough to reply to this ad. Use of beach hut in Shoeburyness.' "

Anna giggled, read the ad again and wondered how on earth she'd missed it. By the time she'd finished reading it for the second time, she'd come to the conclusion that Quasimodo was either a regular bloke with an excellent sense of humor and a huge amount of self-confidence who had decided to write an eye-catching ad, or a deformed weirdo with scabs and an anorak who kept a selection of kitchen knives and nylon rope in the trunk of his Datsun Cherry.

Ignoring the continuing retching sounds coming from next

door, Anna picked up the phone, hesitated for a moment and dialed.

DAN CAME TEARING OUT OF THE OFFICE AND STOOD HOVER-ing by the lifts for a few seconds. He knew if he hung around too long he might change his mind about dumping his medical equipment. He decided to take the stairs. Once outside, he crossed the road to the Oxfam shop. He dashed in and without even pausing to acknowledge the blue-rinse lady in a floral shirtwaist who was stacking shelves, dumped the briefcase on the counter and darted back out into Kensington High Street. As he strolled back to the office, he hoped his treasured brood would find a good home with a caring couple of hypochondriacs in the country.

IT HAD TAKEN ANNA OVER AN HOUR TO GET THROUGH TO Reenie Theydon-Bois because Reenie's line had been constantly engaged. When Anna finally managed to speak to her and said she might be interested in meeting Quasimodo, Reenie almost choked on her cigarette. It was clear to Anna he wasn't the most popular client on Reenie's books.

Anna immediately confessed her doubts about Quasimodo. She said that for all Reenie knew he could be some homicidal maniac taking a correspondence course in garotting studies. Reenie, whose concerns were centered entirely on the substantial amount of folding money she raked in each time she set up a meeting between two clients, went in search of her sincere, reassuring voice, and found it in a trice.

"You ab-so-lutely must not worry, my deeah. Ay vet all my clients person'ly. 'Ee does 'ave a somewhat idiosyncratic sense of humor, I admit. I keep telling 'im it puts the ladies off, but he refuses to listen.

"Look, Ay shouldn't be revealing this so early on without having obtained his say-so, but he is actually a medical gentleman. As a matter of fact, he's a Harley Street consultant."

Anna's first thought on receiving this information was that if she agreed to meet him, she would at least know to address him as Mr. Modo and not Dr. Modo.

Her second thought was entirely sexual. She had always half believed that because doctors knew so much about human anatomy it followed that they had to be brilliant in the sack. She'd never told a soul, not even Brenda, that the majority of her sexual fantasies involved groups of wondrously handsome male doctors in white coats undressing her, strapping her onto an examination couch, forcing her legs into stirrups and taking it in turns to do unspeakably perverted things to her with their speculums.

She knew that this was a particularly outrageous fantasy, not because it was depraved, but because in her experience most medics were imperious, bombastic idiots, whose Godlike position in society rested almost solely on having got an A in A-level chemistry, who lacked both humor and compassion and whose sex appeal would barely cover the bottom of a specimen bottle.

Nevertheless, like many women, Anna tended to develop crushes on her gynecologists, especially the odd chap who flirted with her. She remembered one in particular. She had gone to him for her postnatal checkup, six weeks after having Amy. What felt like his entire hand had been deep inside her for a full five minutes. Finally he looked up from between her legs and told her in a voice which, in this case, was definitely soft and sexy that for a woman who had delivered two very large babies, she possessed particularly tight vaginal muscles. When he added the bit about this being vital to good sex because the muscles needed to support the shaft of a man's penis, Anna knew this was more than mere medical observation. She didn't know whether to jump on him or report him to the BMA for gross misconduct.

In the end she did neither. She simply said that he was obviously fond of tinkling the ovaries, but if he'd finished tinkling hers, she wouldn't mind having them back. He withdrew his hand as if he had touched scalding water.

· · ·

WHAT I'LL DO THEN, IF IT'S ALL RIGHT WITH YOU," REENIE continued, "is fax the gentleman your details, and then if he is agreeable we should think about arranging an initial tayte-a-tayte for the two of you. Does that sound acceptable to yourself?"

Anna was miles away. She was imagining surgeons in gowns and masks taking it in turns to massage her inner thighs with K-Y jelly.

"Are you still there, Anna deah? . . . Ay was just wondering if that arrangement would be acceptable?"

Anna confirmed that indeed, it would be.

CHAPTER TWELVE

FOR THE FOURTH TIME THAT DAY, Dan sat in one of the cubicles in the *Vanguard* gents breathing rapidly and heavily into a Pret à Manger brown paper bag. Once again the desperate urge to take his blood pressure, combined with the knowledge that he no longer possessed his electronic sphygmomanometer, had caused him to hyperventilate.

As his blood oxygen levels gradually returned to normal and his head stopped swimming, he took his face out of the bag. At the same time he reassured himself that although he was experiencing the odd setback, he had over the last couple of days made excellent progress in his attempts to live without his medical appliances. His panics about not being able to take his blood pressure or test his urine for sugar were undoubtedly becoming less frequent.

Dan also noticed he was developing fewer symptoms than usual. In fact, apart from the malignant melanoma on the back of his hand, which the helpful lady pharmacist in Boots had diagnosed as a liver spot, he had in the last forty-eight hours experienced no worrying symptoms at all.

He smiled a triumphant smile. Then he folded up the Pret à Manger bag and slipped it inside his jacket pocket, just in case he needed to use it again.

DAN SAUNTERED BACK TO HIS DESK, PICKED UP THE PHONE to check his voice mail and at the same time downed the last inch of his decaf, which had become lukewarm while he was in the gents. There was one message. This was from a mate at the *Standard* offering to buy him lunch the following week. He put down the phone and screwed up his face, not as a reaction to the taste of tepid coffee, or because he didn't want to have lunch with his mate from the *Standard,* but because he was suddenly despondent. Derek Foster should have got back to him by now.

DEREK WAS IN HIS SEVENTIES, AND ALTHOUGH HE HAD OF- ficially retired from journalism, he still knocked out a couple of thrillers a year, mainly whodunits based round the Stock Exchange. A few months ago he began submitting a small investor column to the *Vanguard.* Dan had been so impressed that he had commissioned it as a regular feature.

Dan had taken to him from their first meeting. He found it almost impossible to believe that this easygoing piss artist was once the most feared news editor in Fleet Street.

In the sixties, when he ran the newsdesk at the *Courier,* it was said that no other news editor in the country was capable of keeping a check on the whereabouts of his reporters like

Derek Foster. No matter where they were, or what time of day it was, Foster could root them out.

This was due to him invariably having about his person his battered red exercise book. This contained every number of every public phone in every journalist's haunt from Costello's Bar in New York to the Plaka Taverna in Nicosia. Fleet Street legend had it that the night the Six-Day War ended in Israel in 1967, Derek knew exactly where in Tel Aviv the reporters would go to get pissed and laid, and roughly what time they would leave and what time they would be passing a particular public phone box on the beachfront. At two-fifteen in the morning he rang the number and let it ring continuously. A very drunk but curious *Courier* reporter answered the phone and was told by Derek to sober up and get his arse to LA by the next day because Spencer Tracy had been found dead at his kitchen table by Katharine Hepburn and she might be available for an interview.

DAN HAD LAST SPOKEN TO DEREK A DAY AGO. THEY HAD spent five minutes or so discussing what Derek was planning to put in that week's column, and then, for no reason in particular, Dan found himself telling Derek about Brenda's night with Giles Hardacre, and how Lavender Hardacre was threatening to go to the papers.

Dan had barely got to the end of the tale when Derek burst into a long and very wicked Sid James–style cackle.

"No need to go on. I get the picture. If it's dirt you're looking for, look no further."

Derek said he was almost positive his son had been at university with Lavender. He remembered being told the story of how, in her final year, she got rolling drunk at the rugby club dinner and did a striptease on the dance floor. The MC had joined in and the pair of them ended up shagging in front of two hundred people.

"What's more, she continued to put it about after marrying Giles Hardacre. She's been known secretly amongst the Demp-

ster lot for years as Shagger Hardacre. Christ only knows why
no newspaper's ever done her over. You'd think it was right up
the *Mirror*'s street."

Derek said he would double-check with his son, but he was
pretty sure he'd got the rugby club dinner story right because
you didn't get too many girlies to the pound called Lavender.

Dan hadn't been in the slightest bit surprised to discover
Derek's connection with Lavender Hardacre. Over the years
there had been umpteen occasions when he'd got to the bottom of some financial scandal or other after receiving a piece
of priceless information from an improbable source. It was
Murphy's Law that this kind of luck only occurred, if it occurred at all, after weeks and weeks of fruitless, bollock-
breaking phone bashing. What knocked Dan for six was that
this was the first time in his career he had achieved such an
astonishing result on the first phone call.

Dan's amazement and self-congratulation were short-lived.
Derek had promised to phone his son and get back to Dan in
an hour or so. That was yesterday lunchtime. Dan had heard
nothing since. By now he was pretty sure Derek had been
thinking about a different woman.

Dan, who had really been looking forward to impressing
Brenda with his sleuthing powers, decided he would console
himself, instead, with a large slice of the canteen's disgustingly
commercial chocolate cake which always came topped with a
collapsed hillock of spray-on cream.

He stood up and checked that his wallet was in his back
pocket. He'd walked across the newsroom, and had almost
reached the door, when he heard his phone go. Something
about the ring, which of course was no different from usual,
told him precisely who was calling. He shot back to his desk.

"Dan, it's Derek here. Sorry to have taken so long to get back
to you, mate, but my son has been away for a few days. Only
got back last night. Look, this is just to confirm that your lady
and mine are one and the same. I reckon that's a very large
lunch you owe me. . . ."

.   .   .

ANNA AND BRENDA STOOD ON THE PAVEMENT, THEIR NOSES pressed up against the restaurant window.

"I can't see a tall fair-haired bloke sitting on his own. Everybody's in twos or fours," Brenda said, wiping condensation from the glass with the end of her sleeve.

Anna said she couldn't either. She then announced that she had no intention of hanging around for hours in the dark until he decided to turn up. Reenie Theydon-Bois had promised that Quasimodo would be waiting for her at the Bhaji on the Bush in the Goldhawk Road, just before eight. It was now two minutes past. Anna stood back from the restaurant window and said that if he didn't show up in the next five minutes they might as well go for a drink in the pub opposite and then head off home. She sounded cross and irritated, but Brenda suspected it was just nerves.

She was right. Anna was still petrified that Quasimodo might be a paranoid schizophrenic. The last time she spoke to Reenie Theydon-Bois she had asked if she could have his telephone number—she was desperate to check him out before meeting him—but Reenie had refused. She was also only prepared to give Anna a vague idea of what he looked like. Anna assumed this was because Reenie was desperate for her fee and probably never gave much information away because she didn't want to risk putting clients off. All Anna knew about Quasimodo was that he was forty-two, very tall, exceedingly distinguished-looking and blond.

EARLIER THAT EVENING, ANNA HAD PHONED DAN AT THE OF-fice to tell him that she and Brenda were going out for a girlie dinner and would be back late. Dan decided to save the pleasure of telling them both his good news on the Hardacre front until later.

By seven o'clock Anna was getting dressed. She was determined not to get too glammed up as she didn't want to give a potential rapist the impression she was gagging to get laid. She decided on jeans and a smart jacket. She had got one leg into her Levis and was just about to hobble onto the landing to call down to Denise and remind her it was Josh and Amy's hairwash night, when Brenda, who had agreed to come on Mission Quasimodo with Anna, came into the room to show off her outfit for the evening.

Brenda had promised—not before she had raised several objections about how disloyal she felt she was being to Dan—to wait round the corner from the Bhaji on the Bush in her car, mobile phone at the ready, so that Anna could ring for help if Quasimodo proved troublesome. To mark the undercover nature of the mission, Brenda was wearing combat fatigues and had applied a touch of camouflage paint to her face.

"You know me," she said, giving Anna a quick twirl. "I couldn't go out on night maneuvers without getting into the spirit of the occasion."

A NNA WAS ON THE POINT OF DECLARING THAT QUASIMODO'S time was up and they should go for a drink across the road when she noticed a very tall chap with a mass of thick fair hair walking alone towards the restaurant.

"That has to be him," she said in a screeched whisper. "Start walking. Look casual. Don't attract his attention."

The two of them began strolling down the road. After a minute they turned back and resumed their position in front of the restaurant window.

"Blimey, Brenda," Anna said, staring in through the glass. "That is one very tall, very blond man."

"Yeah, he is gor-geous," Brenda said, virtually salivating. "Looks exactly like Johnny Weissmuller in those Tarzan films. You can just see 'im in one of those leopardskin miniskirt things."

"Brenda, the only thing I can see this guy in is a brown shirt and a swastika armband. He is far too Aryan for my taste. Definitely not my type. Bren, I think I'm going to give this one a miss."

"Oh, no you don't!" Brenda's tone was full of command as

she found herself warming to her military persona. She was certain Anna was just looking for an excuse to duck out of the meeting. In an instant she had frog-marched her the few paces to the restaurant door.

"Phone me," she said, "if he starts goose-stepping around the restaurant, claiming he's only following orders."

With that she opened the restaurant door and almost threw Anna inside.

A NNA REGAINED HER BALANCE AND TOOK A DEEP, CALMING breath. The air was the usual popadam palace mix of cumin and cigarettes. She'd eaten at the Bhaji on the Bush a couple of times with Dan. Looking round she noticed it had been redecorated since her last visit. The red flock wallpaper was now a deep petrol blue. Everything else was just as she remembered it: battered chairs covered in burgundy Dralon, a single carnation in a slim white vase on every table, pale-pink linen and, in one corner of the restaurant, underneath a giant, gaudy print of the Taj Mahal at dawn, a cart loaded with stainless-steel pickle pots.

The tables near the window were taken. The chap Anna assumed to be Quasimodo was sitting at the back of the restaurant, near the bar. Anna adjusted her bag strap on her shoulder and pushed her hair behind her ears. Squeezing past a waiter who was taking an order for six chicken vindaloos with extra chilis from a group of lagered-up blokes in Lacoste shirts and hooped earrings, Anna started walking towards the blond man's table.

She could see him dunking a piece of popadom into some pale-green yogurt and bringing it towards his mouth. En route, the yogurt began to drizzle down his fingers and drip onto his purple-and-gold silk tie. In a couple of seconds two long milky rivulets were coursing down his front. Realizing what he had done, he began rubbing at the tie with a pink napkin. His mass of straight fair hair was without a trace of gray. It made him look far younger than forty-two. Anna would have said he wasn't a day over thirty-four. She stood next to the table, watching him. He hadn't noticed her.

"You'll ruin the silk if you carry on like that," she said by way of announcing herself. She sounded far more assured than she felt. "Quasimodo, I presume. Hi, I'm Anna." Smiling, she held out her hand.

"Oh, right, Christ," he said, clearly flustered, but managing to return Anna's smile. His look of confusion had turned, almost immediately, into one of delight. For a longish moment he surveyed her face. His eyes gazed into hers. They remained there just a moment too long. Finally he appeared to sense her discomfort. His eyes shot down towards the pink napkin, which he was still holding. Then he stood up too quickly, jogging the table as he went. This sent several pieces of cutlery flying onto the floor. He was slim, broad-shouldered and towered over her. Blushing, he leaned across the table and shook her hand.

"I seem to have got myself into a bit of a pickle." He chuckled, pushing back some of his hair, which had flopped into his face, and indicating the huge greasy stain. His voice, which was a touch Gordonstoun and the Guards, confirmed Anna's suspicion that it was a Gieves and Hawkes tie.

"Do sit down. I'm Alex. Alex Pemberton." He waved his hand towards the chair in front of her. Anna spotted a gold signet ring on his little finger. She also noticed his nails were buffed and manicured. There wasn't a loose end of dried-up cuticle in sight. She lowered herself into the chair. For a paranoid schizophrenic, she thought, Alex Pemberton was certainly very well groomed.

Anna decided that her first impression of him, outside the restaurant, had been spot on. The man looked like a Nazi. There was no doubt in her mind that the six-foot-three frame, the square jaw, pale-blue eyes and flaxen hair belonged at a Nuremberg rally.

His was the look she had been brought up to fear and revile. She had been out with twenty or thirty boys before she met Dan. They had all been dark. Even the non-Jewish ones looked vaguely Mediterranean. None of them had been more than five foot ten. Despite Anna's youthful defiance, she had found it hard to shake off her parents' prejudices about all things German. As late as two years ago, when she and Dan had bought a Bosch fridge-freezer, she had felt like a traitor. It had taken her a fortnight to pluck up the courage to tell her father what she'd done.

The likelihood was, Alex Pemberton had no German blood in his veins whatsoever—and so what if he had?—but this logic made no indentation on Anna's emotions. As far as she was concerned, tonight she would be eating with the enemy.

While they waited for their drinks, they finished the popadoms and compared notes about Reenie Theydon-Bois. Alex had met her a couple of times and said she was a mercenary old baggage, but otherwise quite straight.

"So what made you place the Quasimodo ad?" Anna asked. "I mean, it was very funny, but it did occur to me to come armed with a posse of social workers, in case you went barmy during the coffee and After Eights and needed to be sectioned."

Alex laughed and explained that he'd placed traditional ads in the past and had ended up with one miserable, lonely woman after another. Nearly all of them, he explained, were the type who'd spent years being martyrs to their husband's infidelities and had finally decided they wanted to get their own back by sleeping with other men.

"But when it came to it, they just wanted to talk about their husbands' affairs, have a good cry and give me detailed accounts of how they'd tried to top themselves."

Anna imagined a long line of sour-faced middle-aged women with perms, calf-length skirts and day returns from Bexleyheath.

"So you placed the wacky ad in the hope of attracting someone a bit more upbeat."

"Something like that," he said, grinning and pushing back his hair again, as the waiter delivered two cold Cobras. "Plus writing it reminded me that, hopefully at least, I still possess a sense of humor. I get seriously fed up playing the sober-suited consultant." He began to fiddle repeatedly with his leather watch strap, twisting it nervously round his wrist in short, sharp half-turns.

Anna drank some of her beer. Instead of the arrogance she had anticipated in a consultant surgeon, there was a diffidence and charm about Alex which she liked. She eyed his exquisitely tailored charcoal-gray pinstripe with its hand-stitched lapels. The conservative Savile Row suit, the posh tie and gold signet ring gave him a gentlemanly, almost aristocratic air. Old-fashioned words like "dashing" and "debonair" sprang to Anna's mind. She was beginning to see what Brenda was getting at when she said he was gorgeous.

Although she was still hoping Alex might darken up and shrink a little as the evening wore on, Anna could feel herself slowly letting go of her prejudices.

She was daring to imagine what it would be like allowing herself to be pounced on by this perfect example of Aryan manhood. Even two years ago such a thought would have appalled her. Now the wickedness excited her. Lust and guilt fought a brief duel in her body. It was no contest. Guilt forgot to bring bullets. There was little doubt left in her mind that she and her rebellious streak were about to boldly go and explore their final sexual frontier. She had a brief image of him giving her an orgasm and then leaping out of bed to click his heels. But it was only brief.

ALEX SMILED AT ANNA. HE LOOKED AS IF HE HAD JUST opened a mail order parcel and realized to his joy and utter surprise that the company had sent him precisely what he'd ordered.

Anna smiled back.

"So what branch of medicine are you in?" she asked.

"Good Lord, I'm surprised Reenie didn't tell you. She usually can't wait. She seems to be under the impression that what I do is terribly glamorous. Of course, it's not really. I'm a plastic surgeon." His hand went to his watch strap once more.

Had there been any beer left in Anna's mouth, she would have choked on it. Instead, in one immediate reflex action her hands shot up from the table to her breasts, and down again.

Although she disapproved of cosmetic surgery for all the usual women-aren't-meant-to-have-bodies-like-Barbie-dolls, and aging-isn't-a-crime reasons, she wasn't sufficiently confident of her feminist stance to take off her clothes, fling a breast insouciantly over either shoulder and jump into bed with a cosmetic surgeon.

Her body could never be good enough for this man. He would always be trying to change her. Instead of flowers he would bring her implants. Instead of foreplay he would produce a protractor, calipers and scientific calculator to assess her droop and sag quotient. Anna saw them in their tender postcoital moments, thumbing through nose catalogues.

She decided there was no point spending the evening getting to know Alex. Sleeping with people meant getting naked, and she was about as likely to get naked in front of Alex as her mother was to give up her three-bottles-of-Jif-a-day habit.

She was on the point of making her excuses and leaving, when she came to and realized Alex was speaking to her, apparently oblivious to her horrified state.

". . . So you see it was one of the main reasons," he was saying, "I wanted to meet you."

Anna apologized for appearing distracted and said something feeble about being a bit tired as she'd had a particularly busy day and could he say that last bit again.

Alex seemed quite happy to oblige.

"I was just making the point that when Reenie Theydon-Bois told me you were a journalist and worked for the tabloids, it struck me that we had rather a lot in common. I'm always having to justify why, after the government paid for me to spend seven years learning how to heal the sick, I am now devoting myself to satisfying the vanity of the well heeled. I thought that working for the tabloids you must receive your fair share of flack from the broadsheet brigade."

"You could say that," Anna said with heavy irony. It was as if the flag had gone up at the starting gate. She was off, rabbiting on about how she loathed having to justify what she did for a living. Barely pausing for breath or a sip of beer, she told him how she only worked for the tabloids for the money, but had, nevertheless, worked out this brilliant philosophical justification for the existence of tabloid newspapers, based on the fact that for years they had been the only part of the media which had dared tell the truth about the royal family, had been rubbished by the Establishment for doing so and proved ultimately right down to the finest detail; they had simply outreported, outresearched and outfaced the broadsheets, the BBC and the rest of the pompous media, and should be proud of their muck-raking, not apologetic over it.

When she had finished, Alex said that he still got terribly hurt when people laid into him about what he did for a living. He said there had been two reasons for him becoming a plastic surgeon. The first was that despite what most of the world said, he genuinely believed he was helping people and improving the quality of their lives. He said it wasn't all face-lifts and breast implants. He regularly saw people with striking imperfections which the National Health Service refused to treat.

"Sometimes pinning back a teenage boy's bat ears can cure him overnight of the kind of hang-ups and insecurities it would take a therapist years to cure."

For the sake of politeness Anna decided not to pursue her argument that it was mainly women who had cosmetic surgery and that in her opinion cosmetic surgeons were power-crazed men who wanted to control women by mutilating them.

Instead she played safe.

"So what was the other reason?"

"Same as yours. Money."

To Anna's complete surprise, it turned out that Alex had been brought up by his widowed mother in a thirties row house in Hounslow. His father had died when he was three and his mother, who was a clerical officer at the public housing department, used to eat jam sandwiches for supper and make a tea bag do for three cups, in order to give him steak and piano lessons. When he passed the exams for public school she did extra typing in the evenings in order to pay the fees.

"Sometimes in the winter we would run out of coal. I remember her holding my hand as we walked the streets just to keep warm. From the age of about seven I knew I didn't just want to be well off. I wanted to be very rich indeed."

Anna asked him if he had achieved his aim. He gave a self-mocking chuckle and admitted he was getting there.

She couldn't help wondering why, with all his money, he had brought her on such a cheap date.

Just then the waiter came to take their order. He was extremely matey and called Alex by his first name. They clearly knew each other very well. When the waiter had gone Alex explained that he ate at the Bhaji on the Bush at least four times a week. This was partly because ever since working at a hospital in Bradford years ago, he had become a curry-holic, and partly because he couldn't face going home.

Over chicken spinach, lamb passanda and pilau rice with fluorescent pink bits, Alex told Anna about his miserable marriage and why he had joined Liaisons Dangereux.

His wife, he explained, was American. Her name was Kimberley. She'd kept her maiden name, which was Tadlock. As they hadn't had sex for over a year, Alex had nicknamed her Padlock. He laughed as he said this, but Anna could almost taste the sadness behind the laughter.

Kimberley, he went on, came from the American Deep South. He had met her in 1981 while he was doing a year's internship at a hospital in Birmingham, Alabama. She was a theology student at UAB—the University of Alabama, Birmingham. Kimberley was also a part-time waitress at Vinny's Diner, a famous roadside eatery a few miles out of town.

"We met there one Saturday lunchtime in August. The day was so hot and humid it could have steamed peas." He put down his fork and stared past Anna into the distance.

A group of them, all male doctors at the hospital, had driven out to Vinny's in an open-top fifties Chevy. They had been driving along the same empty stretch of country road for ages, going through one identical village after another. These had names like Nectar and Locust Fork. The small houses on either side of the road were wooden, single-story affairs with white picket fences and porches. Alex and his four mates were beginning to think they must have accidentally driven past Vinny's when one of them noticed the huge 7UP sign ahead. It came towards them, shimmering in the heat haze.

Vinny's turned out to be a huge painted shack with dozens of wood-effect Formica tables and red plastic bench seats. The place was sweltering. The rows of ceiling fans did little more than rearrange the heat.

Alex said that walking into Vinny's felt like walking into a Steinbeck novel. Being a weekend it was full of families, mainly white farming people. Everybody was wearing denim dungarees.

Alex and his friends stood waiting to be seated and watched huge plates of fried catfish or Southern-style chicken with candied yams being set down at the tables. Most of the waitresses were middle-aged, motherly women with thick ankles and rear ends as wide as Mobile Bay. The skirts of their pink nylon waitress uniforms hugged their hips like taut shrink-wrap.

There were two or three young, pretty waitresses. They wore their skirts short and their eyeshadow thick. After a couple of minutes one of them came smiling towards them.

She was about twenty, with freckles, excellent teeth and long red hair tied into a ponytail. She cocked her head to one side and said, "Hi y'all, Ahm Kimberley. I'll be your waitress fur today." Then she turned to Alex and in a voice that was pure Blanche Dubois she whispered, "How're ya doin', sugar?"

There was a wiggle in her walk as she led the group to their table. Alex could see she was undoing a couple of the buttons down the front of her blouse. They sat down, and as she bent over Alex's end of the table to hand them the menu and go through the specials, he could see her huge breasts spilling out of a skimpy flesh-colored bra. In those couple of minutes, he fell in love.

According to Alex, over the weeks that he kept driving out to

Vinny's on his own every Saturday and Sunday, Kimberley fell for his accent, navy blazer and brogues.

So it was that Alex and Kimberley started dating. After four lust-filled months they married in a tiny Baptist church in Locust Fork and came back to England.

They bought a Victorian house in Hammersmith which they did up. Kimberley went a bit overboard by buying four rocking chairs and trying to cover all the available wall space with cross-stitch samplers, but Alex didn't mind because he knew they reminded her of home. She bore him two ginger-haired, freckled children called Brandy and Jim Bob, filled the freezer with Mississippi mud cakes and pumpkin pies, and became a devoted fan of the Queen Mother and cream teas.

When Alex announced that he intended to specialize in cosmetic surgery, Kimberley wasn't sure if she approved.

"Seems downraht un-Christian," she said, "to go meddlin' with what the good Lord dun give us."

Nevertheless, she stood by her man. While Kimberley recreated down-home domestic bliss in Hammersmith, Alex pursued nips, tucks and large checks in Harley Street.

They had been happy until two years ago, when Kimberley started to put on a huge amount of weight. Alex would stand outside the kitchen and watch her stuffing her face with chips, pizza and Coke.

At first he thought his wife was trying to make a political or moral statement about how he earned his living. As the months went by and she became truly obese, he realized there was more to it than feminist ideology.

She now wore her long hair in a cheap corkscrew perm. She had also taken to wearing voluminous pink shorts which she asked her mother to buy for her at the local Wal-Mart back home. Kimberley's sister would buy them in packs of six and they would arrive in huge padded envelopes. Kimberley would team the shorts with glitzy T-shirts which had shoulder pads, white cotton socks with pom-poms and a mint-green eyeshade.

Kimberley, he realized, was turning herself into a caricature of a middle-aged working-class Southern woman. The reason for this was that she had become unspeakably homesick. Getting fat and wearing clothes from Wal-Mart put her back in touch with her roots.

Very soon she decided she wanted to rediscover Southern-style Christianity. She located a few expats in west London and together they set up their own Baptist chapter which they called the Evangelical Women of Salem in Hammersmith and Barnes.

Alex packed her off to Alabama one summer with the children, but it made no difference.

In fact it made things worse. When she got back she would only cook Southern-style food and began trying to locate possum suppliers in west London. Breakfasts became unbearable. Brandy and Jim Bob made it clear they preferred Coco Pops to grits, but she wouldn't listen. Nothing changed. Every morning they got up to find grits bubbling on the stove and Kimberley standing by the kitchen table holding a Bible, waiting to conduct morning prayers.

Every day she filled the children's lunchboxes with mountains of cold fried chicken, umpteen slices of pumpkin pie and great chunks of cornbread. What Brandy and Jim Bob couldn't eat they distributed like Red Cross parcels to their classmates. The other children, most of whom were on low-fat, low-salt, low-sugar diets, wolfed it down.

One mother phoned Kimberley and said that her little Anastasia was putting on weight eating all this Southern fried food. Her child, she explained, was used to live yogurt and pieces of sushi in her lunchbox. Kimberley got quite angry, saying they had sushi in Alabama too, but there it was called bait.

Her latest attempts to turn their bit of Hammersmith into rural Dixie included trying to get planning permission to build a stoop on the front of their house and insisting that because she took the children on so many camping trips they should invest in a thirty-foot Winnebago.

"When I asked her where we were going to park it, she said the Lord would provide. . . . I try to get home as late as I can each evening. If I get home too early she's either having a prayer meeting at the house or she and her good-old-girl friends are sitting on rocking chairs whittling and making patchwork quilts. I think the reason she refuses to have sex is because she feels trapped here with the children and blames me."

Alex offered Anna some more lamb passanda. She smiled, said the food was lovely, but she was full and couldn't manage another bite. She watched him take some for himself.

She wasn't sure what to make of his tragicomic saga. He was either the most incorrigible joker, or his tale of Southern discomfort was genuine. Working for the tabloids, she was no stranger to the bizarre-but-true. She knew Brenda would call her a gullible tart, but she decided to give Alex and his story the benefit of the doubt.

"So," Alex said, putting the stainless-steel lamb passanda dish back on the hotplate, "that's my story. What's yours? What made you phone Reenie Theydon-Bois?"

It was Anna's turn to put down her fork and stare into the distance. She had been dreading him asking that. She still had no intention of compounding her betrayal of Dan by discussing the problems in their marriage. Nor was she about to confess to Alex that one of the reasons she had contacted Liaisons Dangereux was because she needed another subject for her unorthodox journalistic experiment.

She was about to deliver a pre-prepared anodyne speech about twelve-year itches when all of a sudden her mobile phone started to ring. She picked up her bag from the floor and reached inside. She put the phone to her ear, but before she could say anything, the voice came at her, low, breathless and full of panic.

"Hello, Anna, is that you? It's me. Please don't be cross, but I need you to come over now, right away. Something dreadful has happened. I'm hiding in the airing cupboard. Anna, be quick, I'm terrified for my life." Then the phone went dead.

The voice belonged to her mother.

CHAPTER THIRTEEN

BRENDA!'' ANNA YELLED. ''FOR Chrissake take it easy. Did you ever have proper driving lessons or did you just take the correspondence course?"

Anna and Brenda were steaming towards Gloria's house in Stanmore. Anna couldn't believe Brenda was managing to get nearly eighty out of her ancient Zephyr.

Still in battle dress, she was flashing and hooting at anything which got in her way and then saluting her thanks as she careered past. Anna kept making the point that nobody could see her saluting in the dark, but she carried on doing it anyway.

Ignoring Anna's plea to take it easy, Brenda pulled out to overtake a lorry. In the process she cut off a Porsche which was careering down the outside lane. Anna winced, clutched her seat belt with one hand and shielded her face with the other.

"Brenda, for crying out loud . . . will you slow down and bloody listen?" she bawled. "There is absolutely no reason to get us killed. My mother has pulled stunts like this before. Whenever my father goes away her obsessions get worse. She's probably having a panic attack because she's run out of Flash liquid."

For the umpteenth time, she leaned forward, picked the phone up off the dashboard and stabbed the redial button.

"Still engaged," she spat, slamming the phone back on the dashboard. "My mother is a woman clearly so terrified for her life that she can't resist sharing her terror with all one hundred and twenty-six members of the synagogue ladies' guild."

Brenda said nothing. Anna folded her arms, looked out of the window and sulked.

She was irritated not only with her mother, but with Brenda too. Anna had given her a brief outline of the Kimberley and Alex story. As she had predicted, Brenda had called her a gull-ible tart.

"What you have to understand," Brenda had said in a pa-tronizing tone which got right up Anna's nose, "is that blokes like him tend to marry Sloane Rangers called Annabel— women who have amazing grace rather than sing it. Then, what usually 'appens is that during the week while she is safely stowed away in the country with the kids and the dogs, he's safe to bonk around in London. In 'is case I would guess it's mainly grateful face-lift patients. I'll bet you a tenner 'e's got the use of a flat over his Harley Street practice."

"And what you have to understand," Anna had replied coldly, refusing to allow Brenda to undermine her judgment, "is that I have spent my entire working life pursuing stories which sound like hoaxes and then turn out to be true. What about that tip-off I got last year about the woman in Shanklin who heard voices coming from inside her washing machine and called in a priest to get it exorcized, only to find a four-foot midget who'd hidden inside the drum when he was disturbed burgling the house?"

Brenda had grunted to indicate her partial submission.

"Just because you have a nose for a good story doesn't mean this bloke's genuine. I still think 'e sounds like a smarmy upper-class git."

SUDDENLY THE ZEPHYR LURCHED FORWARD ALONG ITS chassis as Brenda screeched to a tire-scorching, Disney-style halt outside the five-bedroom mock-Georgian house.

Getting out of the car, Anna could see all the curtains were drawn. She could hear nothing but the hum of traffic in the distance.

"It all looks perfectly normal," she whispered. "She's probably got over her panic and gone to bed. I tell you, we are going to scare her witless if we just march in."

Brenda agreed they should ring the bell and give Gloria a chance to answer the door. Anna pressed the button. The chimes played three choruses of "Hello, Dolly!" There was no answer. Anna took out the set of keys to her mother's house she always carried. Gloria had given them to her just after she and Harry had moved to the house, in case of an emergency. She turned the key in the lock. The paneled door, which was guarded on the outside by two miniature stone lions, opened.

The hall lights were on, illuminating Gloria's newly painted mural depicting a Venetian street scene. It covered three walls. Anna had first seen the mural a couple of weeks ago and told Gloria that cute didn't begin to describe it. Gloria's hall, she said, resembled the interior of a motorway cafeteria with ideas above its service station.

The walls were covered with rows of charmingly dilapidated Italian houses with peeling terra-cotta paint. Each one had been given a wrought-iron balcony from which there trailed nonspecific purple and orange flowers. There were several small arched bridges crossing canals, as well as three gondolas complete with gondoliers and courting couples. There was even a sickeningly cute mouse poking its nose and whiskers out of a hole in one of the charmingly dilapidated bits of wall.

There was, however, no sign of Gloria.

Anna stood at the foot of the staircase and called to her mother. Silence. Brenda said she was going upstairs. They ran up, passing a doe-eyed Italian beauty hanging washing from her balcony, still calling. Gingerly they opened Gloria's bedroom door. The light was on, but the bed hadn't been slept in. For the first time Anna began to feel frightened. Brenda was almost hysterical.

"Right, that's it. I'm phoning the police."

"No, Brenda." Anna caught hold of her arm as she reached into her pocket for the phone. "Don't. Wait."

She walked along the landing to the airing cupboard and opened the door. Gloria was sitting cowering and shaking at the foot of the oversized hot-water tank. She was wearing her peach velour dressing gown and slippers and clutching her cordless phone. Her face was covered in a thick layer of night cream. This made the rims of her eyes, which were red and swollen from crying, look particularly hideous.

"Mum!" Anna screamed. She put her arm round her mother and gently helped her stand up.

"He's down there! He's down there!" Gloria sobbed. "I've been trying to reach your father in Tel Aviv, but the line's been permanently engaged." Anna's arm was still round her mother's shoulders. Gloria was shaking like a water diviner's hazel twig.

"Mrs. S., if there's somebody in the house," Brenda was standing next to them now, "you should have phoned 999."

"No, you don't understand . . . I wanted to ask Harry's advice first." Gloria took a deep, shuddery breath. "Now you two are here it'll be all right."

"Mum," Anna said, looking confused, "what in God's name has been going on?"

Gloria said nothing. She put the phone into her dressing-gown pocket and took hold of Anna's arm. She led her towards the staircase. Brenda followed. The three of them crept down the stairs, backs close to the wall, clutching each other like Enid Blyton children exploring a haunted castle. They tiptoed along the marble floor tiles as Gloria led them through the hall towards the downstairs loo. They stopped. Gloria stood in front of Anna and Brenda and gripped the brass doorknob. She paused and closed her eyes for a few seconds as if summoning strength. Then, very slowly, her eyes still closed, she opened the door a crack, reached in and turned on the light. Coming from inside was the sound of soft snoring. This was punctuated every couple of seconds by bouts of desperate wheezing and gasping. It was as if somebody was fighting for breath. The door finished opening. Brenda's and Anna's eyes shot towards the loo window.

S O THERE'S ME AND ANNA, QUAKING AND BLOODY TERRI-fied—it's just like that bit in *Close Encounters* when they watch the spaceship land—thinking there's some maniac standing in the lavvy with 'is axe poised." Brenda broke off to slurp some of her cocoa. "And the first thing we see is a great huge bunch of red roses and a box of Milk Tray which appear to have come in through the window and seem to be thrashing around in midair just above the loo seat. Then we see the horn-rimmed specs, the trilby and the half-open mouth and we realize there's a bloke stuck half in and half out of the window. Finally we work out that the sash must have broken, sending the frame careering down onto his back and trapping him."

By now it was nearly two in the morning. Anna had dragged Dan out of bed and made him come and sit with them in the kitchen, drink cocoa and listen to this latest installment in the Gloria and Gerald Brownstein saga.

"So, I take it he is now safely tucked up in the nick," Dan said, rubbing his face, which was creased and puffy with sleep.

Anna and Brenda exchanged glances. Anna shifted from buttock to buttock on her chair.

"Not as such," she said, concentrating on dunking a Jaffa Cake into her mug and watching the chocolate melt and leave a trail in the cocoa.

Dan yanked at the belt of his toweling dressing gown and tightened it. Anna thought he suddenly looked like a particularly gruff bank manager, albeit a very unusual one who attended his overdrawn clients in his dressing gown. Glowering, he sat waiting for her explanation.

Anna said that it was Gloria, who, yet again, had refused point-blank to let them call the police. Once she had calmed down she had begged Anna and Brenda to let him go. She kept saying over and over that he was an old, ill man who needed psychiatry, not incarceration.

Apparently, before he had got stuck in the window, Gerald had spent nearly an hour ringing on Gloria's doorbell and calling through the letter box, begging her to open the door because he was in love with her and wanted to give her some flowers and chocolates. She had kept shouting at him to leave them on the porch and go away.

Finally everything had gone quiet. Gloria thought he had driven off, so she got ready for bed. Then, after a few minutes, she came downstairs to make a drink and heard him trying to break in through the loo window.

By the time Anna and Brenda got to him, he was white with fear and fighting for air because the window had trapped him so tight he could hardly breathe. Seeing Brenda in her fatigues and because he was old, frightened and a bit confused, he assumed she was a policewoman and that Anna was a plain-clothes detective.

He spent the next five minutes, still half in and half out of the window, weeping and begging for mercy. He implored them to take pity on him as he was having a lot of trouble with his bowels and had to be at outpatients on Tuesday afternoon to get the result of his barium enema and Dr. Mednik, the nice Jewish gut doctor, had said his intestines were looking none too promising. According to Gerald, the doctor said he'd seen frankfurter skins with more life in them.

Their anger beginning to subside, Brenda and Anna forced the window up a few inches and the three of them managed, without too much difficulty, to haul Gerald down onto the loo seat. He sat there for a few minutes trying to stop shaking and then, summoning up his last ounce of pathos, held out the roses and the chocolates towards Gloria. Gloria managed a half smile, helped him into the kitchen and made him a cup of tea.

While he was drinking it she took Brenda and Anna into the living room and pleaded with them not to call the police. She said that if they let him go she would have another word with Julian at her obsessive-compulsive group and see what could be done to help Gerald.

"Gerald, of course, still thinks we're real cops," Anna went on. "So Brenda and I, having caved in and agreed not to call the police, decide the old boy should, nevertheless, be taught a lesson. So we march him out to his car, where Brenda screams at him to lean over the hood and spread 'em. Then she reads him his rights, frisks him, screams at him as if she's on some parade ground, telling him he's an abominable, vile and depraved piece of humanity who deserves to be castrated. Then she lets him go. . . . Come on, Dan, please try and understand. I'm beginning to think my mother is right. I really don't think Gerald is dangerous."

Dan rubbed his face again and said he thought they were crazy, that they were not qualified to make judgments about a person's state of mind and that Gloria could be in serious danger. He then said he wasn't going to argue with them about it anymore, because he had some *really* interesting news vis-à-vis the wife of their honorable friend, the member for Lymeswold.

T HEY GOT TO BED JUST AFTER THREE. BRENDA DIDN'T bother trying to sleep. She was feeling too wired. After Dan had given her the dirt on Lavender Hardacre she had gone whooping and dancing round the kitchen before almost hugging the life out of him. Instantly adopting a new moral stance as well as setting aside her fears about being banged up in

Holloway, she spent the rest of the night lying in bed planning how best to go about blackmailing the old tart.

Dan left the house at seven because he had to be in Birmingham by ten to do an interview with the EC Commissioner for Herrings. As a consequence, Anna was forced to do the school run.

When she got back she had a shower, woke Brenda with some toast and herb tea and then decided she would phone Alex to apologize for running out on him. She couldn't believe she had been so rude to the poor man. She had simply taken the call from Gloria, said that she was sorry she had to leave because her mother wasn't well and got up from the table.

She rang the Harley Street number—Alex had chased after her as she was leaving the restaurant and pressed his card into her hand—but got the answer machine. He wouldn't be in for another half hour.

She decided she would fill the time by making a further attempt to come to grips with Rachel Stern's leaden and incomprehensible introduction to *The Clitoris-Centered Woman.*

The jacket blurb described Stern as a "passionate feminist," and proclaimed that her previous work, "a scorching attack on cosmetic surgery and the women who betray their sex by going under the knife," had "fundamentally changed" the way women saw their bodies. "Now," it continued, "the fearless and outspoken author of *Dermis,* her prose as lucid and accessible as ever, turns her attention to adultery."

Anna flicked to the introduction, which was headed "Beyond the Political Economy—the Clitoris Under Capitalism." She got about four paragraphs in before pronouncing it bollocks and deciding to try phoning Alex again.

SHE EXPECTED TO GET SOME PLUMMY SECRETARY. INSTEAD Alex answered.

"Anna, I am so glad you rang. I was quite convinced you'd done a Lawrence Oates on me last night and I'd never hear from you again."

Anna began explaining what had happened, but Alex interrupted her. Apologizing profusely, he said she had caught him at the worst possible time. He was in between patients and having to manage alone as his secretary was off with flu. He suggested meeting the following afternoon for tea if Anna wasn't too busy.

"A couple of patients have phoned to cancel their appointments, so I should be free just after four."

Anna said she was pretty sure she could get away and she'd look forward to it.

They agreed to meet at Whittaker's Hotel just off Bond Street.

O FF FOR ANOTHER BIT OF 'ORIZONTAL HOLD THEN?'' Anna swung round on her chair to see Brenda standing in the bedroom doorway managing to grin and crunch Marmite toast at the same time.

"I dunno if you realized," she went on, as she waved her half-eaten slice of toast in the air, "but there wasn't even a trace of hesitation or guilt in your voice. I'm beginning to think you've found a new vocation. You should think about jacking in newspapers and teaching evening classes in practical adultery."

With that Brenda's grin faded, her face turned white and she ran into the loo on the landing to chuck up her breakfast.

A NNA CAME OUT OF THE TUBE STATION, WALKED ALONG OXford Street for a few yards and then turned right. Walking down New Bond Street towards Whittaker's, she began thinking again about what Brenda had said. She knew she hadn't been serious, but she did have a point. Anna had to admit, she had become almost blasé about cheating on Dan. Now she knew he wasn't dying, the periodic guilt she had felt about deceiving him had disappeared.

She had also proved to herself that she really could keep a hold on her feelings. Charlie had been gorgeous, intelligent and fun. A weaker woman might have allowed herself to fall in love with him, but she hadn't. She had refused to let their relationship go beyond the purely physical. She knew that even if she had continued seeing Charlie, she would never have allowed him to threaten her marriage. It would be the same with Alex.

She stopped to look in Fenwicks' window. As she ogled a slinky black evening dress which was cut so low at the back it revealed the mannequin's buttock cleavage, her confidence suddenly descended into despair. The skimpy black dress, which called for granite-hard glutes and breasts like grapefruit halves, reminded her for the umpteenth time that day that she, with her bum like a bag of wet porridge and breasts like worn-out pillows in which the feathers had collected at one end, was about to jump into bed with a cosmetic surgeon.

ANNA TURNED RIGHT JUST PAST RUSSELL AND BROMLEY AND crossed the road. Whittaker's was facing her. The hotel, which had only twenty or so rooms, was discreet and unspeakably expensive and was popular with Hollywood actors. They adored the pry-vacy and the "English country house charm." The stars also appreciated the hotel's wonderfully understated touches. The management always saw to it that on every guest's bedside table was a selection of the works of L. Ron Hubbard.

Anna walked into the hotel reception, which was small and cozy. Everywhere there were vases of beautifully arranged flowers and bowls of upmarket potpourri. The place smelled faintly of cinnamon and cloves. There was no reception desk, just a large bowlegged walnut table. Behind it stood a smiling young woman in a piecrust collar and cashmere cardigan. She said that Mr. Pemberton had arrived about five minutes ago, and directed Anna towards the lounge.

Alex was sitting on a chintz sofa in the square bay window, flicking through a house copy of *Tatler*. As soon as he saw her he sprang to his feet. He was wearing another gray suit, lighter this time, over a pale-blue shirt with a buttoned-down collar. The tie was a trendy knitted one with broad navy and cream horizontal stripes. He looked much more fashionable than he had two nights ago. Anna wondered if he had changed his image just for her.

He started coming towards her, beaming. Instead of continuing on across the room to meet him, Anna stood still for a few seconds, watching him. She knew she would never feel the same molten passion for Alex that she had felt for Charlie. Nevertheless sex with Alex, who still looked every bit as Aryan as he had in the Bhaji on the Bush, represented the kind of cultural heresy which Anna found utterly irresistible. Would that he knew it, Alex was about to become a bacon bagel. As she watched him draw closer, she realized that rebellion was up and about inside her belly, and ready for action. Maybe her mutinous urges would conquer her fears about the state of her body.

As Alex reached her, Anna returned the smile and said hello. She stood on tiptoe and they kissed on both cheeks, Alex gently holding her upper arms. She was aware that the second kiss lasted fractionally longer than the regulation peck. For a couple of moments, Alex kept his cheek next to hers and she could feel him breathing in her perfume. He only stopped when his embarrassment intervened.

"Anna, I'm so glad you could make it." Anna detected a hint of nerves and anxiety in his voice. He started to fiddle with his watch strap. She knew he fancied her but suspected it might take ages for him to pluck up the courage to invite her to bed.

"Come and sit down." He motioned to her to go in front of him. She walked across the huge Indian rug towards the pale-turquoise sofa. She sat down and allowed her back to relax into the squashy feather cushions. Alex came and sat close beside her, and stretched his arm along the back of the sofa, just above her shoulders. Then, almost at once, looking to Anna as if he was having second thoughts about the appropriateness of such behavior, he quickly withdrew his arm and shifted himself towards the end of the sofa.

They sat in shy silence for what seemed like ages. Finally, the lady with the piecrust collar came over and asked them if they were ready to order tea. Anna said she could murder a toasted teacake. They ordered toasted teacakes for two and, at Alex's insistence, a selection of cream cakes. The lady then reeled off a list of about ten different teas and said she could recommend the orange pekoe. Alex said it was Anna's choice. She said orange pekoe would be fine. The truth was she detested pretentious teas, but was too embarrassed to ask for PG Tips.

"Anna, you look absolutely stunning," Alex said when the lady had gone. As the June weather had turned chilly again, Anna was wearing her bright-pink imitation Chanel suit. It still had a trace of aioli down the front, but she'd managed to get most of it out with Fairy Liquid.

"Thank you," she said, blushing. Looking down at her lap she began picking off imaginary bobbles of wool from her skirt. After a few seconds her face met his again.

"Listen, Alex, I'd really like to explain about the other night—"

"There really is no need, you know."

"No, I want to."

She began by explaining how Gerald Brownstein had stalked her mother in the supermarket. She was in the middle of telling him the bit about the salami in Gerald's underpants when their tea arrived. Alex, who had thrown back his head and was roaring with laughter, didn't notice the lady with the piecrust collar, who was clearly not used to hearing stories about Jewish flashers being recounted in the hotel lounge, give Anna a look which could have dissolved iron filings.

Anna poured them tea from the silver pot. They spent the next half hour sipping the orange pekoe from pretty bone-china cups as she told the story of how she and Brenda came to find Gerald Brownstein trapped in Gloria's downstairs loo window. She hammed up the climax for even greater effect.

The more Anna made Alex laugh, the more he relaxed. By the time she had finished telling her story, he was almost gasping for breath. Wiping his eyes, he reached for the plate of cream cakes and held it towards Anna. She shook her head.

"Well, I think I shall, even if you won't."

"That must be your fourth," she said in mock horror as he reached for a strawberry tart. "I always assumed doctors were into healthy eating. It seems to me, Alex, that you exist on a diet of curry, cream and Southern fried chicken."

Alex patted his flat stomach and chuckled.

"Work it all off on the squash court. I'm the same weight now as when I was at medical school."

Anna grunted and said she still thought he should watch what he ate. She then laughed as she spread her teacake with thick butter. As she bit into it, some melted butter trickled down her face. Alex reached into his pocket and took out a freshly ironed white handkerchief. He leaned towards Anna and wiped the corner of her mouth. Anna giggled and said thank you. Then, slowly, he moved his hand onto her cheek and kept it there. Anna smiled at him and didn't attempt to move it.

After a moment or two, Alex put his handkerchief back in his pocket and Anna took another sip of tea.

"Listen," he said brightly, a thought suddenly occurring to him, "it's almost time for a real drink. I've got this flat that I use sometimes when I'm working late. It's over my consulting rooms. Do you fancy coming back for a glass of wine?"

Anna started choking and spluttering on the last of her orange pekoe. That was a tenner she owed Brenda.

"Sorry, I didn't mean to put pressure on you. Maybe another time," Alex said, clearly embarrassed and disappointed.

"No, no," she said, still coughing and covering her mouth with a napkin. "Tea went down the wrong way . . . that would be great. I'd love to come back for a, um, glass of wine."

"Or two," said Alex, grinning.

·   ·   ·

THEY'D GOT AS FAR AS CAVENDISH SQUARE BEFORE ALEX GOT round to repeating the question he had asked her in the Bhaji on the Bush.

"You never told me, Anna, about why you decided to join Liaisons Dangereux."

Anna knew there was no getting out of it. Finding it impossible to look him in the eye, she gave him her spiel about boredom and twelve-year itches. She sensed from his expression that he knew she wasn't telling the truth, but he was too polite to push her any further.

ALEX UNLOCKED THE FRONT DOOR TO THE GRAND HARLEY Street house, which had been divided into consulting rooms. He went in first.

"Come on in. Lights are off. It looks like everybody's finished early." He reached for the switch. Anna followed as he made his way towards the stairs.

"I can never get over how these places always look the same," she said, turning her head to look round the hallway. "I reckon there's some central depot where all you posh doctors buy your Regency-striped wallpaper and worn cherry-red carpets. I bet your room has got one of those chandeliers which drip fake wax."

Smiling and raising his eyebrows, Alex put his arm round her shoulders and began marching her away from the mahogany staircase.

"Why don't you come and see? It's down here on the left."

He led her back along the hall towards the entrance. He held open a tall paneled door. Anna walked in. The room was surprisingly bright and modern. The walls had been painted in brilliant white emulsion. Gray fitted carpet covered the floor. All the furniture was black. Alex's huge black ash desk stood in front of the grand Victorian fireplace; the chairs and the sofa along one wall were all made of black leather. Anna looked up to the ceiling. There were several rows of inset spotlights.

"Mmm, why do I get the feeling that eighties style had a really profound effect on you?" she said with just a hint of sarcasm. She bent down towards the smoked-glass coffee table and released two balls of a Newton's cradle, one of those irritating "executive" playthings which people used to buy and then wish for years they hadn't. Looking up she noticed the screen at the far end of the room. It was the only item there which gave a clue that this was a doctor's consulting room.

Feigning hurt at her observation about his taste, Alex picked up a copy of *Elle* from the coffee table, rolled it up and tapped her playfully on the head. Anna stood up and turned towards him. Very softly, without any conviction, she said, "Ouch."

The smile had gone from Alex's face. He dropped the magazine onto the floor and drew her towards him. For a moment they simply looked at each other. Then he cupped her face in his hands and began kissing her on the lips. It was a while before she felt his mouth open and his tongue push gently into her. She kissed him back. Afterwards, Alex reached to stroke Anna's hair, but she pulled away.

"Alex, there's something I need to tell you before we go any further." She turned her back on him and walked over to one of the fireplace alcoves, which was covered with dozens of ten-by-eight black-and-white prints in Perspex clip frames. They were pictures of some of Alex's patients before and after surgery. Anna stood with her back to him, studying a photograph of a woman whose particularly gruesome postchildbirth tummy flap almost reached her knees.

"You see," she said and then hesitated as her eyes alighted on a photograph of a woman with saggy breasts similar to her own. She clenched both fists and turned back towards Alex.

"You see . . . Oh, what the hell, I'm just going to come right out with it." She took a deep breath. "The point is, I've had two children. I breast-fed both of them and, well . . . I look a bit like her." She pointed to the picture behind her.

"And you're frightened," Alex said kindly as he moved towards her, "that because of what I do, I will judge you and humiliate you."

Anna nodded. He took her hand and led her to the sofa. He sat her down.

"I promise I would never, ever do such a thing." As he kissed her, his hand reached under her short pink suit jacket and moved up to her breasts. Anna could feel her anxiety beginning to melt.

"You know," she said when they'd finished and she was resting her head on Alex's shoulder, "I've never told anybody in the world—not even my husband—but I sometimes have these really depraved sexual fantasies about doctors." No sooner had she said the words than her hand shot over her mouth. "Oh, God, I'm sorry . . . I have absolutely no idea what made me say that."

Alex burst out laughing. He was clearly unperturbed by her revelation.

"What, being tied down by men in white coats, legs in stirrups, that kind of stuff? Loads of women do. It's quite common."

They were quiet for a while. Alex spoke first.

"I've got an idea." His voice was brimming over with sexual promise.

Anna had thought several times since they first met that Alex, with his conservative gray suits and polite, diffident manner, might not be the most imaginative of lovers. She sensed she was on the point of being proved wrong. Not only was she about to be taken to rebellion's very pinnacle by committing adultery with a man who looked like a Nazi, but it appeared that he was going to insist they took a scenic detour round debauchery heights. Excitement gushed through her like millions of gallons of water filling a dam. She got the feeling the glass of wine he'd suggested in Whittaker's was never going to materialize.

"Stand up," Alex ordered. There was an almost harsh edge to his voice. Without asking why, she did as she was told.

"Take off all your clothes. I want to take a look at you."

Anna took off her jacket and stood in front of him in her white sleeveless body and short skirt. She could feel her face going red, humiliation beginning to overtake her. At the same time she was feeling indescribably horny.

Realizing she was wetter than a rainy Sunday in Frinton, she unzipped her skirt and stepped out of it. Alex didn't move from the sofa. His eyes were on her legs and crotch. There wasn't a trace of emotion on his face.

As she stepped out of her shoes and rolled down her pantyhose, Alex yanked at his tie and undid the top button of his shirt. Anna pulled the body over her head and then stood there in her creamy lace bra and panties. She unhooked the bra and pulled it away. Finally she pulled down her panties and stepped out of them.

Alex still said nothing. He just stared at her dispassionately. After what seemed like ages he got up and came towards her, but didn't touch her. He began walking over to the surgical screens. Anna followed him, feeling that her legs were about to give way. He folded back the screen to reveal an examination couch.

"Climb up." His voice was cold and matter-of-fact. Once again Anna did as she was told. As she lay on the couch, her head on a pillow, he caressed her belly. Then, taking his time, he stroked each of her breasts in turn. Anna could feel moisture seeping from between her legs.

Brushing past her pubic hair, he moved his hand down to the insides of her thighs.

"Please, please, touch me," she begged.

"Ssh, relax. What I want you to do now is bend your knees and bring them onto your chest." She did as he asked.

Alex picked up a doctor's rubber glove from a small cart next to the couch. He pushed his hand into it. Anna heard it snap round his wrist. Then he reached for a tube.

Christ, she thought. It's K-Y jelly. What the fuck does a cosmetic surgeon want with K-Y jelly? He must make a habit of this. She didn't have time to pursue the thought. Slowly, Alex was running his finger back and forth from her bottom to her clitoris.

"You know, Alex," she said, gasping through the ecstasy,

"you are a power-crazed pervert. And I'll kill you if you say 'Yes, but you're loving every minute of it.' "

A brief shadow of a smile crossed Alex's face. He turned back towards the cart and from the bottom shelf produced two lengths of what looked like washing-line cord.

"Lift your hands above your head," he ordered. She moved her hands.

"That's good," he said. "Very good." He moved to the head end of the couch. She whimpered as he began gently twisting the cord round one wrist. He wound the last six or seven inches of each piece of cord tightly round the top of the couch leg so that she couldn't move her arms.

Finally he pulled out some kind of extension at the end of the couch. Anna realized the couch was now Y-shaped. This meant there was a gap at the bottom where Alex could stand and have easier access to her. From nowhere he produced a pair of stirrups. For a second or two Anna found herself losing concentration.

"Christ, you're like bloomin' Mary Poppins. I suppose you've got a lamp stand and a mirror stashed away down there as well."

Ignoring her, he began pushing her feet into the stirrups. Spread-eagled now, she was completely helpless. Then he picked up the tube and put some more jelly on his fingers. By now Anna was arching her back and writhing with the sheer wantonness of it all.

"Just let your legs flop open."

"I haven't got much choice in these bloody things." But she made a conscious effort to relax the muscles in her vagina. She felt him gently prise open her inner labia. As he slipped two fingers up inside her she cried out.

"Good. That's excellent," he said, pushing into her a little harder and turning his fingers.

Rhythmically he moved his fingers inside her vagina. With his other hand he went back to stroking her anus and clitoris in turn. She begged him to put more pressure on her clitoris, but he ignored her.

Anna moaned in protest. Then Alex produced two metal phallic-shaped objects. One was much thicker than the other. The thicker one he inserted expertly into her vagina. With extreme gentleness and care he pushed the second one a centimeter or so into her anus.

By now Anna's eyes were closed and she was taking sharp, shallow breaths. Slowly, almost imperceptibly, he increased the pressure on her clitoris. Anna felt herself floating. Alex continued to stroke her. Then, as she felt she was about to lose consciousness, she felt the first tiny tremor inside her. She opened her eyes for a few seconds and focused on Alex's blue eyes and flaxen hair, the continuing cold indifference in his Aryan face. She heard herself cry out:

"Liebchen, liebchen, oh . . . oh . . . das ist so wunderbar, mein liebchen. Du hast ein Blitzkrieg between mein thighs gemacht."

She came in short, electrified jerks which made her whole body go rigid. For a few minutes, as she lay there warm and relaxed, Alex stroked her hair. Then he took her feet from the stirrups and began untying her hands. Finally he covered her in a pale-blue sheet, kissed her on the mouth and whispered:

"Anna, you're the first woman I've met who can come in a foreign language."

"German's nothing. . . . In Latvian I really let rip."

Anna reached for his hand and pulled him towards her. As they kissed, she moved her hand down between his legs and traced the outline of his erection.

She sat herself up and let the sheet fall. She undid his belt, but he stopped her.

"Let's go over to the sofa. There's a bit more room."

As they stood in front of the sofa, Anna helped him off with his jacket and shirt. Then she unzipped his fly and lowered the front of his pants. Kneeling down, she took his penis in her hand and brought her mouth down towards it. As she ran her tongue over the length and tip of his penis, he let out a series of long, slow moans.

All of a sudden his voice became urgent. "I want to feel you again. Now. Sit on the sofa."

She sat down while he pulled off his trousers and underpants.

"Bend your knees and bring your feet onto the sofa. That's it. Now open yourself wide with your fingers."

Anna spread open her labia. He knelt down and made her lean onto the back of the sofa. Bringing his head between her legs, he began flicking her clitoris with his tongue. Then he turned her round so that she was lying along the length of the sofa and pulled himself on top of her.

Anna reached for his penis and rubbed it over the entrance to her vagina. Urgently he kissed her face, pushed his tongue into her mouth and pleaded with her to let him come inside her. This time it was her turn to make him wait. Finally she relented. He let out a long sigh as he entered her. His thrusts were long and hard.

After a few minutes Anna insisted they change positions. She eased herself from under him. On top now, she rose and fell on him he while he cupped her breasts. His breathing became faster and faster. Anna watched him as he finally held his breath and his body quivered and shook. His orgasm seemed to last for ages. Finally he half opened his eyes and kissed her.

They lay with Anna still on top of him for several minutes. Then he moved himself to one side.

"Open your legs again." He ran his fingers over the moisture on the insides of her thighs and then parted her. She came in seconds. Afterwards Alex covered her face and breasts in kisses.

"You are very, very beautiful. Promise me you won't ever try and change your body. It's perfect just as it is."

Anna was about to quote from *Shirley Valentine* and declare that "men are so full of shit," but she thought it might be ungracious. Instead she smiled, promised and pulled herself back on top of him, as she was about to fall off the edge of the sofa. For a while they lay there saying nothing. Anna rested her head on Alex's chest and he stroked her hair. After a while her gaze was drawn back to the before-and-after pictures on the wall. She began studying the face-lifts. She couldn't quite put her finger on why, but the surgery seemed to have given the women a strange, timeless quality. Anna decided there was something unnatural, even mutantlike, about their faces. Lacking both the character of middle age and the filled-out plumpness of youth, it was as if they existed in some kind of strange, ageless limbo.

She turned her head back towards Alex. She couldn't help noticing he looked a bit pale.

"You OK? You look like the excitement's been a bit too much."

"No, I'm fine." Alex was rubbing the center of his chest with his fist. "I think I may have a bit of indigestion from all those cream cakes."

Anna thought it best to climb off him. She stood up and walked across the room to pick up the sheet she'd dropped on the floor next to the examination couch. She wrapped it round her. She found another one folded on a chair next to the couch. Perching on the edge of the sofa, she covered Alex with it. He was still rubbing his chest.

"So," she said, "have you operated on anyone famous? Are there any soap star secrets a tabloid hack should know about?"

"Even if there were, you know full well I'm not allowed to tell you." He tapped the end of her nose with his forefinger.

"Anyway, to tell you the truth, I haven't really done anyone famous," he went on. "The nearest I got was last year. An American writer, some sort of feminist academic I think she is, came to see me and ended up having a whole load of work done. If I remember she had breast, cheek and chin implants, a bottom lift, liposuction, the lot. Why she didn't have the work done in the States, I've no idea."

As her brain suddenly lurched into top gear, Anna leaped up from the sofa. Her mind and heart were racing. It couldn't be. Then again it just fucking might be.

"This woman," she said, trying to sound as casual as she possibly could, "I think I might know who she is. Alex, I know you can't tell me her name, but if I say who I think it is, do you think you could just wink at me if I'm right?"

"Can't imagine why you're so interested in some obscure Harvard academic. She's not exactly tabloid material."

"Alex, if this is who I think it is, she writes these shrill, severely holier-than-thou books denouncing women who've had cosmetic surgery and calling them traitors to the feminist sisterhood. She's due over here soon to publicize her latest book, which is on adultery. Alex, please, please, this is really important for me to know. Just blink if I'm right. . . . Is her name Rachel Stern?"

He blinked.

"Hang on, was that a blink blink or a yes-it-was-Rachel-Stern blink?"

Alex blinked both eyes like Benny Hill, making a funny face at the same time.

Anna hugged him tightly and kissed him on the forehead. "Gotcha, you hypocritical bitch," she muttered, punching the air. Running her fingers through his hair, she began turning over in her mind how and when she would release the story. Curiously, Alex had said nothing; she was expecting him at any moment to start blustering about patient confidentiality.

It was as her mind was running amok that she noticed he seemed to be reacting rather worse to having revealed a patient's identity than she had thought.

His face was turning white, then whiter. Beads of sweat were beginning to appear on his forehead.

"It's OK, Alex, don't panic. I won't let you get struck off. There's bound to be a way of writing the story without actually naming you. I promise that once I've written it, I'll speak to the newspaper's lawyers."

"No, no, Anna, it's not that. I don't seem to be feeling very well. I feel sick and a bit light-headed and the pain in my chest is beginning to shoot down my arm." He grabbed the top of his left arm and grimaced.

The next moment he sat up, his hand gripping his chest. His face was contorted. He was clearly in a great deal of pain.

"Anna, I think I'm having a heart attack." His voice was surprisingly calm and even. "Please, go to my desk and dial 999."

It didn't occur to Anna to question or challenge his self-diagnosis. She immediately shot to the desk, picked up the phone and called an ambulance, reading the address from a sheet of Alex's letterhead. Tightening the sheet round her, she then ran out into the hall, opened the front door and left it ajar for the paramedics. By now, she could feel herself shaking with fear.

When she got back Alex was lying down. His expression had changed. He had a vacant, lost look in his eyes. Anna watched as his hands, which were still clutching his chest, began to turn as white as his face.

She took one of his hands and gripped it. He gripped her back. His hand felt cold and clammy. She leaned over him and dabbed at his forehead with the edge of his sheet.

"Just hang on, Alex. I'm here," she said, fighting to stay calm. "The operator promised the ambulance would be here in five minutes." She could barely watch as his face became more distorted and he cried out in pain. He was beginning to gasp for air.

Tears streamed down Anna's cheeks.

"Christ, I feel so fucking useless. . . . Alex, please, please, just hang on." Her mouth was full of saliva, snot was running down her nose. "Hang on, just a few more minutes and they'll be here."

As she gripped his hand tighter, practical questions started flying into her mind: should she ring Alex's wife? If she did, what the fuck would she say to her? How on earth could she pick up the phone and announce, "I've just been shagging your husband, and by the way he's had a coronary"?

Realizing that she had no choice but to phone Kimberley, Anna asked Alex for his home number. But the pain was so great he couldn't get the words out. Then, slowly, his eyelids flickered and closed.

"No, no, Alex, don't do this. Alex, speak to me," she ordered, her voice frantic. She leaned over him and began tapping his cheeks. "For Christ's sake, say something." She shook his shoulders and gave his face a final hard slap. Nothing. Instinctively, she grabbed his wrist. His pulse was fast, weak and irregular. He was still alive. Just.

"Where the fuck is the ambulance?" she screamed. She was sure Alex couldn't keep going much longer. She had only the faintest notion, gleaned through watching umpteen episodes of *ER* and *Casualty,* of how she might save him. As adrenaline took over, she pulled the sheet off him and straddled his upper body. She made a fist, raised her arm to shoulder height and brought it down onto his chest in a blunt thud. After punching him five or six times, she lifted his head with a hand under his chin and took a huge breath. She managed to prise open his mouth. Then she brought her head down towards his and breathed into his mouth. She carried on like this for a couple of minutes, alternating between pounding his chest and performing her version of the kiss of life. Tears were still streaming down her face.

DAYS LATER, WOEFULLY ASHAMED OF HERSELF, SHE WOULD confess to Brenda that by this stage her tears weren't simply tied up with her feelings of helplessness and her fear of seeing Alex die. In the final minutes before the ambulance arrived it passed through Anna's mind that if she lost Alex, she would also lose her scoop.

As the two paramedics came running into Alex's office they were met by the rear view of a hysterical half-naked woman straddling an unconscious naked man. She was thumping and punching his chest like some kind of maniacal naturist. Over and over she screamed, "Alex, for Chrissake, don't go. Please don't go. I need you to go on the record. I need times. I need dates. I need fucking details."

CHAPTER FOURTEEN

FUCKING FREUDIAN FUCKING BITCH.''
Dan took the tin opener from the
cutlery drawer, slammed it on the
worktop and went in search of a tin of
Heinz spaghetti. He bent down and opened
the kitchen cupboard. One tin remained,
at the back, hiding behind the cans of to-
matoes and the children's baked beans
with minisausages. He reached into the
cupboard, grabbed the can and stood up.

"She'll get this right up her fucking anal
phase if she's not careful," Dan fumed as
he brought the tin crashing down beside the
tin opener. He clamped the opener to the
tin and, using the kind of force most people
would reserve to inflict a multiple wound-
ing, began to turn the handle. The can
open, he reached across to the bread bin.

Dan was alone in the kitchen. He had just returned from another session with Virginia Livermead in which she had informed him in that quiet, arrogant way of hers that, because of his childhood experiences, his personality was so flawed, so badly put together, that the only solution was for him to allow her to demolish it and then rebuild it.

Dan rolled back the bread bin lid.

"Supercilious, self-satisfied cow . . ." He took out a loaf. "Why is there never any sodding white bread in this house? Anna knows brown bread makes me ill." His anger with Virginia Livermead was momentarily relieved by the combination of his exasperation with Anna and his colostomy fantasy.

Dan took a plate from the drainer. He slapped two slices of wholemeal bread on it and held the can over one of them. The spaghetti came sliding out quickly in one tangled, glistening mass. Dan's head was suddenly taken over by the image of a filling colostomy bag.

He spread Marmite on the second slice of bread and placed it on top of the spaghetti. He then flicked the switch on the kettle. While he waited for the water to boil, he checked the messages on the answering machine. There was just one from Anna reminding him that Brenda had taken the children to see Alfie at Brenda's mother's and that she was going to join them later. As it was Friday and the children didn't have to get up for school, they were planning to stay the night.

Dan was relieved. That meant he wouldn't have to explain his foul mood to Anna.

He rewound the answer machine tape and picked up a couple of unopened envelopes lying next to the phone. One was clearly from the bank. He flicked it back onto the worktop unopened. He was in no mood for dealing with complaints about their overdraft. The other was from Barclaycard.

Dan ripped into the envelope and pulled out the statement. His eyes went straight to the total-amount-owed box. It was just over four hundred pounds—far less than he had bargained for. He began scanning the list of purchases. It was only when he saw cosmetics and underwear from Dickins and Jones in

Richmond that Dan realized he'd opened Anna's statement by mistake. He was about to stuff it back in its envelope when one particular item caught his eye. Anna appeared to have paid £75 to something called Liaisons Dangereux.

"What the fuck is Liaisons Dangereux when it's at home?" he muttered. He stared at the printout for a few seconds, went over to the kettle and poured boiling water onto his tea bag. His first thought was that Liaisons Dangereux sounded like some squalid suburban escort agency. He spooned the tea bag halfway out of the mug and dropped it back in. Brenda had warned him that Anna was on the point of cracking up over his hypochondria. For a few hideous moments it had occurred to him that Anna had either flipped or was now so angry with him and so frustrated over their nonexistent sex life that she had been seeing male prostitutes. Dan noticed his tea was turning the color of Guinness. Slowly his heart rate began to come down. The idea was preposterous. Even if Anna hated him, there was no way she would get back at him by doing something as odious and vile as paying men to sleep with her. The likelihood was that Liaisons Dangereux was a new nightclub or the latest themed restaurant. Anna was probably writing a piece on it for one of the tabloids.

Nevertheless, the bill still troubled him. Instead of leaving it on the worktop for Anna to find, he threw the envelope in the bin, folded the bill into quarters and stuffed it into his back pocket.

Doing his best to forget about the Barclaycard statement, Dan went into the living room, dropped onto the sofa and put his mug of tea on the coffee table. As he bit into his sandwich, several spaghetti ends oozed out from between the bread and dripped tomato sauce onto the plate.

H E PRESSED THE TV REMOTE. REALIZING HE'D MISSED THE nine o'clock news, he began surfing the channels. He found an ancient episode of *Cheers* on Paramount, but could only stay with it for a couple of minutes. Having pushed Liaisons Dangereux to the back of his mind, his thoughts kept returning to the therapy session.

When, a couple of sessions ago, Virginia had first suggested leveling his personality, he had nodded eagerly. Chewing on his sandwich, he cringed at the memory of his initial enthusiasm. He had behaved the way he imagined trusting, confused old ladies behave when smooth-talking conmen try to flog them unnecessary double glazing.

His naive assumption that Virginia was the expert and knew best, combined with his determination to consider doing anything which might make him better, meant that he did not immediately question her judgment. It was only towards the end of today's session, when he had been in the middle of telling Virginia about the imaginary friend he'd had when he was six and how his mother had preferred the imaginary friend to him, that he was suddenly struck by the sheer arrogance and downright pomposity of her suggestion.

His mind might not have been in the healthiest of states, Dan thought, but then whose was? And who the hell was she to declare his only fit for the bulldozer? Sitting opposite her, he had been possessed by the overwhelming urge to get up and hit her. Instead he'd said: "Virginia, getting back to what you were saying about demolishing my personality . . . what would this actually look like? I mean, do you bring in the psychotherapeutic equivalent of Fred Dibnah and get him to scale the outside of my body and attach a whole load of plastic explosive to my head and detonate me in front of a crowd and a BBC film crew, or what?"

Virginia sat looking at him, expressionless. Her feet were together, her hands were in her lap, as usual.

"I wonder who it was in your family, Dan," she said, employing her even, unemotional tone, "who couldn't face pain and taught you to turn everything into a joke."

"Virginia, this has got nothing to do with my family," Dan said, trying to match her tone, but finding it hard. "I think you will agree, it's a pretty major step, allowing somebody to destroy your personality. I've had it for forty years. We don't always get along, I admit—I like Chekhov . . . it prefers to go and see West Ham even when they get slaughtered, but it's the only personality I've ever had and I was merely trying to find out exactly how you are proposing to flatten it."

"Dan, I detect some hostility. . . . I think there may be some unresolved issues around for you, to do with trust. Perhaps in the past it has been hard for you to have faith in people."

"Look." Dan was beginning to get tight-lipped and cross. "I just want to make an informed decision before we pack my personality off to the knacker's. I wouldn't buy a secondhand car from somebody without asking to see the logbook and checking out its service history. As far as I'm concerned, it doesn't matter whether I am buying a car or trying to make up my mind about which direction my therapy should be heading, I need some facts."

"So, is that how you see me, Dan . . . like some crooked secondhand car dealer . . . a trickster, somebody who is out to get you? What do you think I might be hiding from you—a twisted chassis, perhaps, a faulty braking system . . . or perhaps something far worse. Could I be about to destroy you?"

"Virginia, I'm getting sick and tired of this. Are you going to answer my question or not?"

"Dan, I hear what you say, but I think the important issue for us both is why you feel the need to ask the question."

Dan, overtaken by utter fury and outrage, sat clenching and unclenching his fists and glaring at her. He knew that if he opened his mouth he would start swearing and that Virginia would simply use his abuse as more ammunition against him. Virginia, who, as always, refused to be intimidated by silence, sat perfectly still and at ease. She was happy for him to take his time before he started speaking again.

After a couple of minutes, which Dan perceived as a silent deadlock, he got up from the black leather chair, marched over to the door and walked out, making sure to slam it behind him.

Had he looked back, he would have seen Virginia still sitting upright in her chair with her feet together and her hands in her lap. Not even the faintest trace of emotion crossed her face.

Driving home, feeling as if green steam was shooting out of all his orifices, Dan began to realize that Virginia's arrogance and persistent refusal to countenance being challenged wasn't the only thing about her which was infuriating him.

For a start, whenever he was late for a session, she always insisted on what she called "exploring" the reasons for this. Dan always explained that there was no deep underlying motive for his lateness. The only reason for it was the rush-hour traffic. Her response was always the same.

"I think your conscious mind believes it is the traffic which delays you, but if we could summon up your unconscious voice, then I think we would discover the truth. You arrive late because there are issues in therapy that you find painful and want to avoid."

Dan always protested. Virginia simply looked at him and smiled a smile which said she understood the workings of Dan's mind far better than he did.

After a while, whenever Dan arrived late he would invent a childhood trauma and confess to Virginia that he had been trying to avoid talking about it because he found it so harrowing. Each time he did this Virginia's face would fill with joy and delight and she would lean forward, take off her glasses and say:

"Good, Dan. That is very, very good. I feel honored that you felt able to share your pain with me. I think at last we are making some progress." At this point he was always overtaken by the urge to confess he'd just made up the story to get her off his back. For some reason he never acted on the urge. Dan frequently disagreed with Virginia's analysis of his feelings. Occasionally he got angry with her if he felt she was off beam. If this happened during a Friday session, she would say he was angry because the weekend was coming up and there would be two days during which she would not be available for him. If he got annoyed on a Monday it was because he was cross with her for abandoning him over the weekend.

When Dan explained that he was an adult and, despite his dodgy mental state, could actually cope without her for a couple of days, she simply ignored him and suggested he was suppressing painful memories of maternal rejection.

As the sessions wore on, feelings of bewilderment and frustration kept welling up inside him. Virginia rarely accepted his explanation for anything. She had clearly been furious with him for getting rid of his medical appliances. He could tell because when he told her, one side of her face and one nostril began to twitch. She made it clear that he should have discussed this with her and that she would have helped him build up slowly to getting rid of his emotional crutches. Dan said that might have taken fifteen years. Virginia said nothing, refusing to be drawn into an argument. There was no doubt in Dan's mind that she was determined to make him emotionally dependent upon her.

D AN TOOK A FINAL BITE OUT OF HIS COLD SPAGHETTI-AND-Marmite sandwich. He hadn't touched the crusts. These he left, as he had done since childhood, on his plate, in two neat angular smiles. He wasn't sure how one went about formally breaking up with one's therapist. He lay back on the sofa, his hands behind his head, and thought about it for a while. Finally he decided to send her a handwritten note. He would give Virginia the same sort of spiel he used to give girlfriends when he got fed up with them. He would explain that he wasn't ready to make a long-term commitment to one person and wanted to be free to see other therapists.

This did, of course, leave him with the problem of what to do about all his pent-up, unresolved feelings of anger towards his mother. On one occasion Virginia had brought a third chair into the room and asked him to imagine his mother was sitting in it.

"Speak to her," Virginia had said. "Let her know how she made you feel when you were a child. Allow yourself to get angry with her."

Dan stared at the chair. He opened his mouth a couple of times and looked as if he was about to say something, but each time he stopped himself. Finally he told Virginia that he felt ridiculous attempting to speak to an empty chair and he couldn't do it.

AS DAN TRUDGED UPSTAIRS TO BED CARRYING AN APPLE and that week's *Economist*, he was still desperately searching his mind for a way to rid himself of his anger and of the hold his mother still had on him.

He fell asleep an hour later, and began dreaming almost at once. It was night. In the moonlight, he could see a shimmering gossamer image of his mother floating up from behind her tombstone. For the purposes of the dream, this was shaped like a giant boiling fowl. She was naked except for a pair of spats and a rolled-up umbrella. Dan yelled at her to cover herself up, but she ignored him and began floating towards him, waving the umbrella. She was crying out to him, repeating something over and over again in a long, melancholy wail. It sounded like "Dan, Qantas has a leak." Even in his dreaming state, Dan could feel the desperate frustration of having one irritated Australian airline executive after another hang up on him as he pleaded with them to ground their aircraft because his mad Jewish mother had come to him from beyond the grave to prophesy a midair disaster due to fuel seepage.

As his mother floated closer, he could hear that she was actually saying, "Dan, I want us to speak." In his sleep, Dan breathed a heavy sigh of relief.

"Please, Dan, make contact." She moaned a long, echoing moan. By now her naked, shriveled body was hovering just above his head. Then, like a genie being sucked into its bottle, she was whisked back towards the marble boiling fowl. In a second she had disappeared.

.   .   .

THREE DAYS LATER DAN WOULD PHONE ADA BRACEGIRDLE, the well-known spiritual healer and medium from Dagenham.

BRENDA OPENED HER MOTHER'S FRONT DOOR IN PECKHAM, munching on a spring roll. She stood staring at Anna's white, mascara-streaked face and bright-pink suit covered in red stains.

"Christ, Anna, you look like you've come straight from the JFK motorcade."

Anna pretended to ignore the remark. Blowing her nose noisily on a tissue, she pushed past Brenda, slumped into Brenda's mum's lounge and threw herself facedown on the leatherette settee.

Brenda followed her into the room and switched off Trevor McDonald. "OK, I'm a perceptive woman," she said. "There's definitely something up. What's 'appened? Don't tell me, you had a fight with Hermann Goering and he came at you with a ketchup bottle?"

A muffled sob came from deep within a brushed-nylon cushion. "Anna, what is it?" Brenda demanded, the cheerful expression starting to leave her face. She sat down on the sofa next to her.

"We didn't have a fight," Anna said, sitting up. "We made love and it was absolutely wonderful, and then . . . and then Alex had a heart attack."

Brenda managed to look gobsmacked for about thirty seconds before resuming flippant mode.

"Bet 'e had a smile on 'is face, though."

"Brenda, will you cut it out," Anna hissed. "I thought he was going to die. Then, if that wasn't enough, while he was being examined at the hospital, I went to the coffee machine and some sixteen-stone yob who'd been stabbed in the arm came into casualty, passed out over me and bled onto my skirt."

"Christ, Anna, I'm so sorry." Brenda cuddled Anna. Anna sniffed loudly and wiped her nose on Brenda's shoulder.

"So, 'e's gonna make it then, Quasimodo?" asked Brenda.

"I think so," Anna said, pulling away. "I stayed at the hospital for a couple of hours and pretended I was his secretary. I spoke to the consultant and he said they would have to do a whole load of tests, but his first instinct was that the attack was fairly mild. . . . Didn't look mild to me, though. The paramedics gave him oxygen in the ambulance, but he kept turning blue. Brenda, I was so scared."

"What about his wife? Has anybody phoned her?"

"I asked the sister on casualty to do it, but the answer machine was on. She came over to me twice to check I'd given her the right number. Apparently she kept getting this finger-picking music and a woman's voice singing 'I Come from Alabama with My Banjo on My Knee.' . . . So it looks like Kimberley Tadlock exists after all. . . . Brenda, I could really do with a drink."

"You'll be lucky . . . you know my mum doesn't keep booze in the house. She's probably got some Emva Cream left over from Christmas, but I can't imagine you'd want that. How about I heat you up some Chinese?" She jerked her head towards the glass-topped coffee table. It was covered in a mess of dirty plates and virtually empty foil containers left over from the takeaway Brenda had ordered as a treat for her mum and the children.

Anna shook her head, "Don't think I could keep it down," then immediately changed her mind. "Oh, go on, then," she said. "Maybe I could manage a couple of duck pancakes and a bit of sweet-and-sour pork."

"Stay there, I'll do it." Carefully, Brenda separated the last two pancakes and laid them on an unused plate. Anna watched as she sprinkled the pancakes with bits of shredded cucumber and spring onion.

"Listen, Brenda, there's something else I need to tell you, something Alex told me before he had the heart attack."

Brenda could sense the excitement in Anna's voice.

She handed Anna the plate. "Sure you don't want me to heat it up?"

Anna shook her head.

"So what was it Alex told you?"

Brenda listened wide-eyed and unblinking as Anna explained about Rachel Stern's cosmetic surgery. Anna lost count of how many times Brenda said, "Would you fucking Adam and Eve it?"

When Anna had finished, Brenda chuckled, put her hand into one of the takeaway containers, pulled out a cold, sticky sweet-and-sour pork ball and raised it like a glass. "Right, then, here's to old Hermann living to tell the tale." She popped the pork ball into her mouth.

They sat in silence for a few moments while Anna polished off the food. Finally Brenda asked her if she was up to coping with another bit of news.

"Fuck it," Anna shrieked. "Lavender's sold her story?"

"No, not yet." Brenda stretched out on the floor and propped her head up on her hand. She told Anna that she'd been back to the Holland Park house to collect her mail and found two extremely abusive and threatening letters from Lavender as well as a dozen or so similar messages on the answer phone.

"In the letters—I've given them to my solicitor—she calls me every sodding name under the sun—'baggage' was her favorite—and promises it will be a matter of days before her story appears in the papers and my business is finished."

"Christ," Anna exclaimed. "Why haven't you got up off your arse and phoned the cow to let her know what we've got on her?"

Brenda smiled.

" 'Cos I thought this might be more fun." She pulled a piece of paper from her jeans pocket. "I tore it out of this month's *Country Life*." She handed the paper to Anna.

It was an advertisement inviting women to come on a one-day course to learn how to become the Perfect Company Wife.

Anna scanned it and then began reading it aloud in a mocking, high-pitched upper-class voice:

" 'Are you desperate to get it right, anxious for your husband's praise, but uncertain about what to wear for that all-important company dinner? Are you hopeless at making conversation with your husband's colleagues? Does organizing a cocktail party for twenty high-powered executives fill you with dread? If you are committed to becoming the consummate corporate consort, but need some help to achieve your goal, then this course is for you.' Brenda, what is all this crap?"

"Look at the name of the woman organizing the course."

Anna read the name. It was Lavender Hardacre.

"Can you believe the woman's cheek?" Brenda said indignantly. "Spends 'er entire marriage cheating on 'er husband and then has the aw-bleedin'-dacity to lecture women on how to be perfect wives."

Anna stared hard at Brenda. Brenda turned away, unable to meet her eyes.

"Tell me you haven't," Anna growled. "Brenda, please, tell me you haven't. Please tell me you haven't enrolled us on this course. If you want to go and have some fun confronting Lavender Hardacre, then go. Don't drag me into it. No. The answer is no."

Brenda gave her a pleading look.

A MILE OR SO FROM THE HARDACRES' PILE, LOVEGROVE Hall, Brenda slowed down to read a signpost and then turned towards Anna, who was retracting the aerial of her mobile phone.

"So, when did you say they're letting Alex out?" she asked.

"In two or three days, so long as he gets the all-clear," Anna replied. "The consultant saw him yesterday. He's really pleased with his progress. Poor jerk's got about ten different drugs to take and has been told to drastically alter his diet. Plus he's got to take things really easy for a while."

"So that puts the mockers on any more shagging, then?"

"For the time being, I guess. To be quite honest, I don't give a stuff about the sex, I'm just grateful he's alive and I won't have to live out the rest of my life thinking I was responsible for killing him." She put her mobile in her handbag and reached for the road map, which was on the dashboard.

"I think that's the entrance up ahead," she said, looking up from the map, moving her head towards the windshield and squinting. Brenda braked, gently for a change, and turned in through the huge black iron gates. Leading up to the house was a long gravel drive with trees on either side. Like folk dancers, the trees had joined hands with their branches and formed an arch, so that the drive became the floor of a long, dark tunnel. Through the gaps in the trees Anna and Brenda glimpsed what looked like hundreds of acres of Hardacre parkland.

Brenda drew up a few yards from the front door, alongside a selection of Mercedes estates, Volvos and Jeep Cherokees. She pulled on the hand brake.

"S'pose this is what you call unmock-Tudor," she said, unwinding her window, sticking her head out and eyeing the huge five-hundred-year-old house with its black beams and red herringbone brickwork.

"Christ knows what it's worth," Anna said, leaning across Brenda to get a better look and counting the first-floor mullioned windows. "Must have at least ten bedrooms." She imagined there being a huge oak four-poster in one of them, with Elizabeth and Essex carved on either side of the headboard and a furry nosegay hanging from the middle. Brenda turned off the ignition and adjusted the curly red wig she'd insisted on wearing.

"I want Lavender to find out who I am, but not until I'm ready. . . . You don't think she'll recognize me, do you? I mean, my face is pretty well known."

"Brenda, she won't have the foggiest," Anna reassured her. "Just remember, don't go losing your temper with the woman. She'll only call the police and it'll be all over the papers in a matter of hours."

"I'm not going to lose my temper." Brenda grinned, reaching onto the backseat for her bag.

"When I nail the fucking tart's 'ead to the floor, I shall make sure I'm perfectly calm."

THEY WALKED UP TO THE FRONT OF THE HOUSE AND BASHED the heavy iron door knocker. They could hear footsteps and loud barking coming from inside the house.

"Christ!" Anna whispered. "I take it you gave Lavender a false name."

"Oh, God, yes. I'm Begonia Cockington. You're you."

Before Anna could gasp at the ridiculousness of Brenda's choice of pseudonym, a beaming Lavender Hardacre opened the front door.

In their discussions about her, Anna and Brenda had decided she would be tall, glamorous and haughty. The woman who greeted them was short, tending towards plump, with Angela Rippon eyebrows and thinning, overlacquered blond hair. She was wearing a chain-store calf-length navy pleated skirt and a matching short boxy jacket. She looked red and flustered as she struggled to keep her grip on the collar of an overexcited liver-colored Labrador.

"Oh, how lovely. You must be Anna and Begonia," she gushed breathlessly. "You're the last of my ladies to arrive. Do come in, do come in." Her voice was plummy and jolly. There appeared to be nothing remotely haughty about her.

Her entire body listing to one side as she continued to do battle with the Labrador, Lavender held open the door.

As Brenda stepped forward, her arm extended to shake hands, the dog finally broke away from its mistress's grip and leaped up at Brenda, leaving muddy paw prints over her skirt.

"Oh, dear, I'm most dreadfully sorry," Lavender said, clearly distressed. "Your poor skirt . . . Ochre, bad girl. Get down." She managed to grab the dog's collar and pull her off. Brenda flicked the mud with her hand and said not to worry, but Lavender had already turned her back on the two women and was dragging the dog, its claws scraping, along the parquet floor.

"Do excuse me," she said, turning her head back towards

them. "Be with you in a jiffy. I must get rid of this frightful hound." She left Anna and Brenda standing in the oak-paneled hall beside a wooden hat stand. There must have been three or four different items of headgear on each hook. Anna counted several deerstalkers and velvet hard hats, a couple of Panamas, an ancient cricket cap and a couple of floppy tweedy things covered in brightly colored fishing flies. She turned to Brenda.

"Why is it," she said in a whisper, "the British upper classes can't perform any activity without wearing a bloody hat?"

"Dunno, s'pose they're just copying the royals. . . . I bet Lavender's got one she wears on the can. . . . What d'you make of her?"

"She's got a voice that sounds like it's spent its life organizing village gymkhanas, but apart from that, I think she seems really nice. I can't believe this is the woman who's been threatening you."

"Course it's 'er," Brenda shot back, her voice loud and indignant. "She's just a bleeding two-faced cow, that's all."

Suddenly hearing Lavender's footsteps, they wheeled round. She was coming towards them almost at a trot, still flushed and beaming.

"Now then, I'm certain you must be in dire need of some refreshment. I'll go into the kitchen and rustle up some more coffee. All my other ladies are in the drawing room." She indicated an open door on the right. "Do go in and say hello." With that she turned her back on them once again and continued down the hall.

A dozen or so women, mostly in their thirties, were standing round the sunny, comfortable room braying at one another and drinking coffee from translucent china. There were a number of Hermés scarves and umpteen strings of pearls. One woman stood out from the rest because she was wearing expensive black Lycra trousers, a Moschino belt and Chanel earrings, but it turned out her name was Cheryl, which explained it.

While Brenda wandered round the room examining the portraits of grim-faced Hardacre ancestors and looking down her nose at Lavender's floral linen loose covers and needlepoint cushions, Anna went over and introduced herself to a group of three women who seemed to be getting fiercely competitive about their respective husbands' company perks.

The husband of a woman in Armani jeans and a navy blazer appeared to have the edge. She broke off briefly from telling the other two women how many pairs of Gucci mules she packed for her holiday at the company villa on Mustique to find out what Anna's husband did for a living. Deeply unimpressed that Dan was a newspaper executive, they turned away from her and the blazer reclaimed center stage.

"So, when we got back from the Caribbean and the company delivered a Mercedes in the wrong color, I insisted that Jeremy fax the MD, ASAP. Jeremy protested and said he didn't want to bother him, and anyway, the MD had abandoned ship for three weeks and gone off to an interim target forecast conference in Kansas City. In the end I thought, to hell with it, and I faxed him myself. And do you know what? There was an olive-green Mercedes sitting in our drive at eight o'clock the next morning. I tell you, darlings"—she lowered her voice as a preface to the indispensable counsel which was to follow—"strictly *entre nous,* it definitely pays to let the MD squeeze your breast at the Christmas bash."

The other women guffawed. Just then Anna noticed Lavender come into the room carrying a tray. She made her way towards the group. Smiling and saying thank you, Anna took the two cups and saucers off the tray.

"Right, as everybody's here," Lavender said heartily, "I think it's just about time to bully off."

She stood in front of the inglenook fireplace, gave a dainty clap of her hands and raised her voice to a polite rallying cry.

"Do, please, gather round, ladies. . . . Squat wherever you can. That's it. Budge up . . . room for a little 'un there, I think. And there are a couple of ancient pouffes down here if anybody fancies them. . . . Good-o . . . Right, first of all I would like to welcome you all on to the How to Be the Perfect Company Wife course. . . ."

.   .   .

THE WOMEN TOOK NOTEBOOKS FROM THEIR HANDBAGS. Anna and Brenda sat next to each other on a sofa, sipping their coffee. Lavender cleared her throat and announced that the first part of her lecture was entitled "Company Don'ts for the Company Do." Everybody chortled. The woman on the other side of Anna wrote down the title in what looked like her best handwriting and underlined it with a Perspex ruler.

"When it comes to making conversation at that all-important company dinner," Lavender began, "the perfect company consort *doesn't ever* talk about herself. It is vital that she is an excellent listener. She must be endlessly fascinated not only by the intimate details of her husband's career, but also by those of his colleagues."

The women scribbled. Lavender followed this advice with instructions on the appropriate dress for the annual company jaunt to Glyndebourne, an excellent tip about using salt to remove menstrual flow from a white cocktail frock and the importance of keeping a hostess book when entertaining company executives and their wives. "In it you must write down the names of your guests and the date they came to dinner, what you cooked, what you wore. By keeping a record you will never cook the same thing twice for the same people, or, heaven forbid, commit the ultimate social faux pas of letting them see you in the same dress."

She then went on to explain how the perfect company wife is always prepared for the unexpected and has no problem knocking up a quick suprême de volaille and a dozen meringue swans covered in spun sugar and floating on a sea of chocolate cream when hubby phones from the station at seven o'clock and announces he's bringing home nine Japanese for dinner.

At that point one woman put up her hand to ask if, once she had served dinner to her husband and his colleagues, it was her place to stay and eat with them. Lavender frowned slightly as she paused to consider her reply.

"Christ," Brenda muttered to Anna, "some of this lot are seriously off their hostess carts. They'd need years of assertiveness training just to become doormats."

Having considered her response to the woman's question, Lavender started to speak.

"Not an easy one, this, but I think one's best bet under these circumstances would be to retire discreetly to the kitchen and catch up with some of those annoying odd jobs one never seems to have time for—like cleaning out the lint filter on the tumble dryer or relining the cutlery drawer with sticky-backed paper."

Brenda decided she'd heard enough. Lavender wasn't just evil, she was also a moron. Brenda was about to seize the moment. She put up her hand. Lavender smiled at her.

"Yes, Begonia?"

"Lavender, I was just thinking . . . what d'you reckon to company wives who go in for a bit of extramural how's-yer-father?"

Lavender gawped at Brenda in horrified silence. Anna couldn't decide if this was due to the content of Brenda's question, or her inelegant use of English. There were muffled giggles from around the room.

After a few moments, Lavender took a deep breath and spoke. "If she were found out," she said in a clipped tone, "it would most certainly affect her husband's promotion prospects. . . . Now then, where had I got to. . . ?"

Brenda had the bit between her teeth.

"Say," she went on, devilment all over her face, "she had some kind of dodgy past . . . I dunno, s'pose for instance that as a student she shagged a bloke in front of two hundred people at the university rugby club dinner. I mean, if that came to light, don't you think that might be a teensy bit problematic?"

Lavender's expression turned to flint. She could smell enough rats to fill an entire sewer. In a pitiful effort to appear uninterested in what was being said, the other women lowered their heads and began pushing back their cuticles. "I . . . I have absolutely no idea what you are talking about," Lavender stammered, close to tears.

"Bollocks," declared Brenda.

There were umpteen sharp intakes of breath.

"I think you know precisely what I'm talking about," Brenda said evenly. "I'm talking about the woman known as Shagger Hardacre who leaves threatening messages on answer machines and sends abusive letters."

Lavender gave a tiny, horrified yelp. She produced a lace handkerchief from her sleeve, brought it to one eye, paused for a moment and then shot out of the room.

Brenda and Anna got up and ran after her. They followed her to the kitchen.

They stood in the doorway. Lavender was sitting sobbing at the far end of a long pine refectory table. The end nearer to Brenda and Anna was covered with pale-green-and-gold dessert plates. Each contained a white meringue swan covered in spun sugar and floating on a sea of chocolate cream. A heavenly roasting chicken smell was coming from the Aga. Lavender had clearly spent ages preparing lunch for the group. Despite the woman's abominable behavior, slight pangs of guilt began to prick Brenda and Anna.

The two women stood watching her shoulders heave as she sobbed into the handkerchief. Having prepared themselves for a fearless tirade rather than tears, they exchanged what-the-fuck-do-we-do-now glances. As luck would have it, Lavender spared them from having to do anything. She looked up.

"Brenda . . . I presume you are Brenda Sweet," she began, doing her best to speak calmly through involuntary sobs. "You will probably never realize how desperately sorry and ashamed I am. Threatening you was the most ghastly, wicked thing I have ever done in my life. But, you see, I was at my tether's end. Giles's affair with you was the final straw."

"That's rich coming from an old slapper like you," Brenda said, marching into the kitchen, leaving Anna hovering by the door. "You've been cheating on Giles since you got married."

Lavender stared hard at Brenda. In the distance they could hear engines starting up and the sound of tires on gravel.

"That just isn't true." Her tone was almost desperate. "I have never once been unfaithful to my husband. I have spent the last fifteen years raising four children and running this house single-handed, while he carved out an exceedingly successful career in politics, and bedded anything over the age of consent. He always promises each affair will be his last and that he loves me. Then he begs me to stand by him. I always do and I suppose, despite everything I've said about divorcing him, I always will. He's so hopeless, you see. I know he couldn't manage without me here to organize him. The thing is, I know they're only flings because they're always with common types and I'm certain he'd never leave me for a floozie."

Anna, who had now come into the room and was standing next to Brenda, watched her friend clench her fists and turn purple with rage at this final remark.

"Leave it," she hissed. "Just leave it."

'So," she said to Lavender, "how did we manage to get the story so wrong?"

"You got it wrong because you listened to Fleet Street gossip. One night, eight or nine years ago, Giles and I had a flaming row. I'd just found out about another of his affairs and I said I would sell my story to the papers. He then shot off back to town and got legless with a chap on the *Express* and gave him this sob story about *me* being unfaithful. The journalist phoned me. I told him it was all lies and begged him not to run it. Thank the Lord, he was a decent chap. He took pity on me and Giles's story never appeared. Nevertheless, a huge amount of whispering went on and the dirt stuck."

"What about the rugby club dinner. Is that true?"

"Yes, but I was twenty and high as a kite on coke and booze. Surely you weren't planning to use that against me?"

Brenda could feel another wave of guilt descending. She looked at Anna.

"Only to stop you going to the newspapers about me and Giles. Have you any idea the harm you could do my reputation and my business?"

Lavender stared down at the table.

"Please, please forgive me. I couldn't think what else to do to make him stop. I know I'm supposed to be divorcing him, but you see, I still love him. I just can't put up with his women any longer. I'm so tired."

With that Lavender got up, went over to the wine rack next to the Aga and opened a bottle of red wine. The bottle in one hand and three long stems in the other, she came back to the table and poured them each a glass. Brenda realized it was the first time in weeks that she had fancied alcohol.

Lavender knocked back half a glass of wine in one go and began crying again. Brenda got up, hesitated for a moment and then put her arms round her.

"Ssh, ssh, 's OK," she said, realizing she had absolutely no doubts as to the truth of Lavender's story. "You're forgiven."

Lavender looked up at her meekly, through red pug eyes. "Thank you. Thank you so much."

"Don't thank me too soon. I mean, my outburst in there can't have done much for your reputation as the perfect company wife. I thought you were out to destroy my career and now I've managed to destroy yours. I s'pose you'll have to give up running the courses."

For a moment Lavender said nothing. Anna and Brenda could sense she was turning over ideas in her head. Then she wiped her eyes one last time, shoved her handkerchief firmly up her sleeve and banged on the table.

"Give up? Never!" she boomed, sounding like a memsahib determined not to relinquish her bit of India. "I know exactly what I shall do. I shall write to all the people who came today and, with your permission, make up a story about you and Anna being members of the gutter press sent on a muckraking mission, the object of which was to discredit me. I shall lie magnificently about how I outwitted you and sent you packing. What's more, I will announce that I am running a company wife course next month devoted to coping with press harassment. To accompany the course, I will, naturally, provide a glossy handbook outlining my utterly brilliant and infallible ten-point plan for keeping journalists at bay when hubby is discovered tethered to a dog kennel in some tart's flat wearing nothing but a leather muzzle and harness. For this I will charge a fiver on top of the usual course fee. Won't take me more than a couple of hours to write. Truth to tell, the women who come to these things are such morons, they wouldn't know the difference between a manual on dealing with press harassment and a list of Girl Guide instructions for tying knots."

Lavender drained her glass and placed it triumphantly on the table. "What do you reckon, chaps? Is that damage limitation or what?"

Gobsmacked by the sheer energy and enthusiasm of Lavender's comeback, Anna and Brenda could only smile and nod their agreement.

A gleeful Lavender topped up their glasses and then, probably due to the onset of squiffiness, began talking nineteen to the dozen about her rotten marriage.

They finished the bottle of wine and started on a second. It wasn't long before Brenda took her wig off and was telling Lavender about Elvis and how he had abandoned her while she was pregnant and how she'd been a single parent for the last ten years. Finally, Anna decided to throw caution and loyalty to the wind and tell the story of her sexless life with a hypochondriac.

Gradually the atmosphere lightened. The more drunk they became, the funnier everything seemed.

"D'you know," Anna said, sweeping her glass through the air as if she were making a grand toast, "if Dan did actually . . . you know, snuff it . . . as it were, I would get the life assurance money and the mortgage paid off. I'd be worth over a million quid. Christ. Makes you think. . . ."

All three of them cracked up.

When Anna and Brenda discussed it a few days later, Anna said she couldn't remember who started singing first. Brenda insisted it was Lavender who, after five glasses of wine, ended up standing on the table to deliver what she insisted was a purely ironic version of "Stand By Your Man." This was followed by Anna and Brenda climbing up to join her and the three of them attempting, and failing, to do "I'm Gonna Wash That Man Right Outa My Hair," in a round.

They were seen later that afternoon, by the woman in the blazer, who had decided to hang around in the hope of gathering gossip, kneeling at the side of the lake in Lavender's garden, trying to race her meringue swans.

CHAPTER FIFTEEN

DAN FINISHED CLEARING HIS UPPER respiratory tract by pronouncing an especially throaty version of the German first person singular. He'd arrived twenty minutes early for his psychic consultation with the world-renowned Ada Bracegirdle and was sitting in the car, which, in order not to be noticed, he'd parked a few doors up from her house. He was passing the time listening to *Woman's Hour* and trying to cough up phlegm. As Jenni Murray introduced an item on a Guatemalan lesbian crocheting cooperative's struggle for survival, Dan took his handkerchief away from his mouth and looked inside. He expected to find a small puddle of yellow gluey gob streaked with blood. Instead, all he found was clear, healthy-looking mucus.

Dan's cough had started at the weekend. Nearly a week later it was still nothing more than a persistent and irritating tickle at the back of his throat. The new Dan, who had thrown away his medical appliances and had taken to thinking of himself as a recovering hypochondriac, was trying to convince the old Dan that his condition was nothing more than a minor infection. Old Dan, on the other hand, was preparing himself for the imminent onset of silicosis. As a consequence of his fear, Old Dan thought it wise to keep a half-hourly check on the consistency and color of his pulmonary secretions.

Dan scrunched up his handkerchief and put it back in his trouser pocket. On the radio, the Guatemalan feature had ended with the lesbians announcing their plans to go on hunger strike unless the European Union provided them with free crochet hooks out of its overseas aid budget, and Jenni Murray was announcing a twenty-four-hour BBC hotline number which would enable listeners to donate money to the cause.

Dan looked at his watch. His appointment wasn't until eleven. It was still only ten to. He reached into his pocket for his snotty handkerchief and began wiping the dust off the dashboard. This took about fifteen seconds. Playing around with the position of the car shoulder mirror with the electric button on the inside of the driver's door took another ten. Dan looked at his watch again and decided he could either spend the next nine minutes going round the outside of the car touching up chipped bits of bodywork with the can of spray paint he always kept in the glove compartment, or be early for his appointment. He decided to be early.

He locked the car and turned round to face the outside of Ada Bracegirdle's row house.

He'd been so taken up with his phlegm that he had failed to notice the B-registered brown Bentley sitting majestically on the narrow concrete drive looking down its long nose like faded gentry at a redneck barbecue.

The Bentley, albeit old and bubbling with rust, was the only immediate evidence of Ada Bracegirdle's countrywide fame and success. She'd certainly lavished no money on the house. All the other row houses in the small cul-de-sac had been tarted up. They had frilly Austrian blinds at their windows, brass stagecoach lights on either side of their storm porches, and wrought-iron Spanish guitars nailed to the brickwork. Mrs. Bracegirdle's house, on the other hand, was exceedingly run-down. The window frames were balding and rotting, most of the guttering was loose and tall weeds had pushed through the cracks in the concreted-over front garden. The bell wasn't working, so Dan tapped on the frosted-glass door with his knuckle. As he waited for Ada Bracegirdle to answer the door, he felt an overwhelming sense that his decision to see a medium had been the right one.

Despite a lifelong cynicism about anything "supernatural," Dan had been convinced right away that his dream wasn't simply another of his occasional nightmares about his mother. He was in no doubt that her spirit had come to him that night and that she wanted him to make contact with her.

As he woke the next morning his mind had been filled with a sense of eagerness and excitement. There were two reasons for this. He was profoundly curious about what she had to tell him, but more than that, he knew that it would be the perfect opportunity to confront her and tell her how angry he was with her. Speaking to his mother's spirit would be almost like having a conversation with a living person. Infinitely preferable, thought Dan, to Virginia Livermead's empty chair.

Lying in bed, he realized it wasn't simply eagerness and excitement he was feeling. Something about him had undergone a transformation. He began patting his upper body and head to check nothing Kafkaesque had happened while he was asleep. His bits felt pretty much the same as they always had. Suddenly he realized the transformation wasn't physical, but emotional. His self-confidence appeared to have surged overnight. He felt brave, bullish even. Suddenly, he didn't give a toss if his mother's spirit flew round the room swearing at him in Yiddish and shaking an accusing ladle. For the first time in his life he was ready to confront her. The thought even passed through his mind that maybe psychotherapy had done him some good after all.

It had taken him no more than a couple of hours to track down Ada Bracegirdle the morning after his dream. Being a Saturday, the *Vanguard*'s cuttings library was pretty quiet. Dan had asked the librarian to find him all the cuts on psychics and spiritualists. In the time it took for him to drink a cup of stewed caffeinated coffee in the canteen and develop palpitations, the librarian produced a thick pile of photocopied newspaper cuttings which he took back to his desk to read. The name which kept coming up over again was Mrs. Bracegirdle's. The articles went back to 1968. Over the last thirty years, it appeared that Ada Bracegirdle had led the police to an assortment of mutilated murder victims, and had correctly predicted dozens of earthquakes and plane crashes. She was now in her sixties, and still traveled round the country lecturing and giving demonstrations of her psychic powers. In addition she also held private sittings at her house in Dagenham.

Dan had found her number in the phone book, and had made an appointment to see her the following Thursday.

THE ANAGLYPTA WALLS INSIDE ADA BRACEGIRDLE'S HOUSE were yellow with age and nicotine. The place reeked of cats. Dan followed her into the living room. She was just over five feet tall, and fat. She also had bandy legs and the beginnings of a dowager's hump. He couldn't help noticing that her size and shape were almost identical to his mother's.

Mrs. Bracegirdle gave Dan a huge purple-frosted smile and showed him to a worn moquette armchair with an embroidered antimacassar on the back. She threw a scrawny tortoiseshell cat off the armchair opposite. As she lowered herself into the chair she adjusted a bra strap through her imitation chiffon blouse. Her bust, like his mother's, was immense. As a child he used to wonder if his mother's tits were long enough to tuck in her knicker elastic. The same thought was occurring to him now.

Ada Bracegirdle picked up a packet of Silk Cut from the coffee table.

" 'Ope you don't mind, my darlin'," she said cheerily, "only I find I can make contact with the other side much quicker once I've lit up . . . 'elps me concentrate." She began scraping her finger across a crusty dried-up stain on the arm of her chair.

Dan waved his hand and said it was fine with him. She had a face like a Gypsy. The skin was excessively wrinkled. The eyes were piercing and, despite her age, still very blue.

Ada Bracegirdle stared into the barrel of the cannon-shaped table lighter and lit her cigarette. Just then a man poked his head round the door and offered them tea. He was about forty, with a moon face and cropped hair. Partly concealed behind the door was a zeppelin-sized beer gut. He wore this under a grubby white T-shirt.

Dan strongly suspected that Ada Bracegirdle's kitchen was a rich source of E. coli and politely declined the offer of tea. Ada said she wouldn't have any either as she'd had five cups this morning and another one might mean going to spend a penny while she was in a trance. The head disappeared.

"That's my Anthony." She pronounced the "th." "He's my eldest, bless 'is heart. He's been living with me ever since his wife ran off to Tilbury with a tattoo artist. I don't know where I'd be without 'im. He chauffeurs me all over the country in the Bentley." She emphasized the make of car and waved her cigarette towards the bay window. The Bentley was just visible through the filthy net curtains.

A look of impatience must have crossed Dan's face because Ada Bracegirdle suddenly sat very upright against the back of the chair and took several deep breaths.

"Right, my darlin' . . . I can feel there's a loved one on the other side who is very anxious to come through." She took a long drag on her cigarette and closed her eyes. "It's a woman. I'm getting the initial G. I think Gertie wants to speak to you. Is there a Gertie who passed recently with her kidneys?"

"Sorry," Dan said, "the name means nothing."

"What about V for Vera?"

"Nope."

"S?"

"No."

"W?"

"No."

Ada Bracegirdle put her cigarette-free hand to her forehead and frowned.

"I think I must have a bad line today, my darlin'. . . . No, wait. . . . I'm getting it. . . . It's definitely N. I've got Aunty Nellie here for you with a message. She says your sister made the right decision to take holy orders. That brickie was never going to make an honest woman of her."

" 'Fraid not . . . there's nobody in my family called Nellie, and we're Jewish."

Dan shuffled in his chair. He was beginning to get irritated. According to the newspaper cuttings, Ada Bracegirdle was the most gifted medium in Britain. He was already fascinated by the idea of what a consultation would be like with the least gifted.

But suddenly, Ada Bracegirdle began turning her head in a slow circular motion. Once again her breathing became noisy and deep. Keeping her eyes closed, she felt along the chair arm for the ashtray and stubbed out her cigarette. Then her entire upper body joined in the circular movement. This gradually became faster and faster.

Dan looked up. The faint sound of music and singing was coming from the ceiling. He felt a tremor go through him. The slow, melodic singing got louder. The voice was unmistakable. It was Sophie Tucker. She was singing "My Yiddishe Mama"— his mother's favorite song.

The singing seemed to be all around him now. Dan's eyes darted round the room, looking for a stereo and speakers. There was nothing. He was beginning to feel frightened. The singing continued. Dan looked at Ada Bracegirdle. She had stopped turning her head and body and was now sitting completely still and ramrod straight. Her eyes were still closed. She began to moan quietly. The moans possessed an almost melodic quality. They seemed to quiver and vibrate—almost as if they were trying to follow the music. Then, in the space of a few seconds, it happened.

Dan could only blink in childlike disbelief as the features on Ada Bracegirdle's face started to change. He could almost hear the blood pumping round his head. Any minute he would require a change of underpants.

It was her skin which began to change first. The wrinkles disappeared and were replaced by dark, leathery skin. This had huge open pores and sagged bloodhoundlike at the jaw. Her blue eyes turned dark brown. In place of her small pointed nose, there appeared a rubbery, bulbous 747 hooter. Her bubble perm seemed to dissolve. A moment later she was sporting a strawberry-blond, heavily backcombed Chez Melvin of Hendon special.

Dan, icy and trembling, was staring into the face of his dead mother. Only she wasn't dead. Her eyes were open and she was staring back at him. There was nothing remotely phantomlike about her appearance. "My Yiddishe mama . . . I need her more than ever now. . . ." Sophie Tucker's voice was still floating in the background, but Dan barely heard it. The only thing he needed more than ever now was a stiff drink. He gripped the arms of his chair so hard that his knuckles turned white.

In the midst of his fear, he remembered that a couple of the newspaper cuttings had mentioned Ada Bracegirdle's rare psychic ability to take on the face of a dead person. They'd referred to the phenomenon as transfiguration. Dan had dismissed it as hysterical nonsense.

Finally the moaning stopped and the singing faded.

Lilly Bloomfield began looking her son up and down.

"Daniel, stop slouching." The fierce haranguing tone he hadn't heard for seventeen years hit him like a thunderbolt. "You want to turn into a hunchback like your uncle Barnet in Westcliff?"

Instinctively, Dan straightened.

"So, you've got a kiss, maybe, for the dead mother you haven't seen in seventeen years?"

Dan looked down at his hands, which were still gripping the arms of the chair. Slowly, he relaxed them. As his heart began to leave his mouth he got up. His mother turned her cheek towards him. Dan leaned over, gave her a nervous peck and returned to his seat.

She grunted as if to say, "Is that the best you can do?"

"And look at you, Daniel." She pointed an accusing forefinger. "You're nothing but skin and bone."

"Mum, don't start," Dan heard himself say. "I'm just over twelve stone, which is ideal for my height."

"Height, schmeight. . . . He turns forty and he's an expert all of a sudden. Daniel, believe me, a mother knows. Just one look at you and I can tell you're not eating enough. A sparrow with a terminal disease would eat more. Doesn't she cook for you, this shikseh you married?"

"Anna is not a shikseh. She's as Jewish as you are . . . were. And we both work, so we both cook."

"Huh."

Dan couldn't believe it. He'd been in his mother's company for less than three minutes and he was already on the point of losing his temper. They sat in silence for a few moments while Lilly continued to inspect her son.

"Why is your suit so creased? You look like a bottom."

"You mean bum . . . and this suit happens to be the height of fashion. It's made of linen. It's meant to look crushed."

"By you it's crushed, by me it's demolished. Believe me, if you sent it to Oxfam, the starving children would send it back. . . . Take it off."

"What?"

"You heard me, Daniel. I said take it off. There's an iron and ironing board by the window. I'll give it a quick press."

Daniel said nothing. He sat staring at his mother in utter disbelief.

"What's the matter? Daniel, I'm your mother. I wiped your

little tuchas. Now suddenly you're too shy to let me see you in your underpants. Now then, do as you're told. Take it off."

To his absolute horror and disgust Dan found himself taking off his jacket. He then undid his trouser belt and unzipped his fly.

A few seconds later he was sitting in his shirttails and boxers watching his mother cross the room on Ada Bracegirdle's bandy legs. On the upright chair next to the ironing board was a pile of Anthony Bracegirdle's grayish shirts. A couple of them had been ironed and were hanging from the picture rail on wire coat hangers. Lilly picked up the iron and spat onto its underside. The iron fizzed. She held up Dan's trousers, making a center fold along one of the legs, and laid it on the ironing board.

"So, the shikseh you call a wife can't even do your ironing. I'm a dead woman and still I can manage to iron your clothes. . . . Still, you wouldn't expect a woman who carries on like she's been carrying on recently to have any energy left over for ironing."

There was a rasp of steam as the iron glided along Dan's trouser leg. The name Liaisons Dangereux was suddenly lit up in neon inside Dan's head.

"What do you mean, 'like she's been carrying on'?"

There was panic in his voice. There was something important Lilly wanted to tell him. This had to be the reason she'd asked him to make contact.

"I'm not saying another word," she said, turning the trouser leg over to iron the other side. "I'm no marriage wrecker, but don't say I didn't come from beyond the grave to warn you."

Dan came towards his mother and stood towering above her.

"Warn me of what? Come on, you called this meeting. What is it?"

"I just know what I know. You need to keep your wits about you, Daniel."

"About what?" He was becoming exceedingly frustrated.

She smiled a smug smile.

"There's nothing, is there? It's just you making fucking mischief, isn't it? You can't resist making me miserable, can you? You've been back from beyond the grave for five minutes and already you've managed to pick holes in my body, my clothes and now my wife. For fuck's sake, Mother, why is it that in my entire forty years I have never once done anything which meets with your approval?"

She stood the iron on its end and looked up at Dan, hands on hips.

"Tell me, what sort of son swears at his dead mother?"

"This one, you stupid, overbearing fat cow."

Lilly let out a long sigh and clamped her hand to her chest.

"And there's no point having a heart attack, because you're already dead."

Dan realized he was nearly screaming. He snatched his trousers from the ironing board. As he stood putting them on, furious words came tumbling out of him like marbles from a tin. Lilly made her way back to her armchair. Along the way she clutched the furniture for support. Dan followed her, still shouting.

For the next fifteen minutes he stood in front of his mother and, barely pausing for breath, told her precisely what he thought of her. He called her wicked, cruel and insensitive. He reminded her in detail of each of his childhood humiliations.

"Christ al-fucking-mighty, what sort of woman in her right mind constantly pulls her child to pieces and refuses to give praise or recognize his achievements? I always got brilliant marks at school, but you were never even remotely impressed. Do you know, I don't remember you once saying you loved me or were proud of me."

"So," she said, turning away from him, "this is how he thanks the mother who, every Friday night, nibbled on a chicken wing so that her son should have breast. This is how he treats the woman who used to schlep home every day weighed down by six bags of groceries and then stand on swollen ankles to cook for him. This is the thanks I get for sewing on buttons with used dental floss for five years so that the money I saved on cotton could be put towards your first record player."

"But Mum, are you proud of me?"

She turned her head towards him.

"You're an editor on a national newspaper already. Tell me, what's not to be proud of?"

"And do you love me?"

"You're my son. What's there not to love?"

The closest Lilly had ever got to an affectionate smile flitted across her face.

Dan looked at her. Alive or dead, he knew there was no changing his mother. She was never going to acknowledge how she'd damaged him while he was growing up, and that she had been responsible for his hypochondria. He suspected that the pain of doing so would be too much for her to bear. But suddenly it didn't seem to matter anymore. For the first time in his life Dan had been able to get angry with her. He had stood up to her. He had changed. The transformation which had begun the day he ate a guilt-free bacon sandwich and ditched his medical appliances was now complete.

As he stood watching Lilly, he realized it had been enough just to tell her what he felt about her. He didn't need her to say sorry, and he was more certain than ever that he didn't need her approval anymore. He got up, put his arm round her shoulders and kissed her. She looked up at him and grunted. Then, without saying anything, she took his hands in both of hers. Just for a second or two, Dan could see there were tears in her eyes.

He picked up his jacket from on top of the pile of Anthony Bracegirdle's shirts, sat down opposite his mother and watched the slow return of Ada Bracegirdle's small pointed nose, wrinkled skin and bright-blue eyes.

"Remember"—Lilly's voice was hovering somewhere in the distance now—"it was me who went without lunches for a month in 1974 and fainted from low blood sugar, in order to save a few pennies so that you could go to that Andy Stewart concert at the Oval."

"Rod Stewart, Mum."

"Whatever."

CHAPTER SIXTEEN

ANNA WAS TEARING ROUND THE BED-
room, naked except for a pair of
flesh-colored knee-highs, flinging
clothes into a black leather holdall. She
opened her knicker drawer and paused for
a few moments in order to work out how
many pairs of panties she should pack,
bearing in mind she would only be one
night in Dorset on the hen-party feature
Campbell McKee had commissioned her to
write for the *Globe on Sunday*.

The logical side of her brain could see
no reason to pack more than one pair of
knickers. The other side, anticipating umpteen personal hygiene emergencies, including groinal sweating, copious vaginal
leakage and loss of bladder control, wanted
to pack half a dozen.

She compromised. She took four pairs of panties from the drawer and stuffed them into the bag. She considered taking out a couple of pairs of shoes to make room for a box of panty shields, but decided against it because the shoes matched the outfits she'd already packed. Making room for the panty shields would involve rethinking her entire wardrobe for the next twenty-four hours. Not that she imagined for one minute that she would wear more than one of the three outfits she'd packed. It was just that she liked to have a choice.

She tugged the zip across the bag and left it on the bed while she started to dress. She was just doing up the cuff buttons on her cream silk blouse when the doorbell and phone rang simultaneously. Ignoring the phone Anna flew onto the landing and yelled down the stairs to Denise.

"If that's my cab, tell him I'll be down in five minutes." The phone was still ringing. Anna shot back to the bedroom. She picked up the receiver, held it under her chin and carried on doing up her shirt buttons.

"Anna, angel . . . thought I'd give you a quick bell just to check that you're all monkeyed up for tonight."

It was Campbell in old-style Fleet Street vernacular mood, checking she'd been assigned a photographer—a monkey—for her assignment.

"Yeah, Campbell, it's all sorted," she said. "The picture desk rang me at lunchtime. I'm going with Monalisa Blake. Look, Campbell, I'm in a tearing hurry . . . there's a taxi waiting. I arranged to meet up with Monalisa at the *Globe*—we're driving down to Poole in her car—so I can pop in and see you before we leave if you want to chat about the piece."

"No, angel, I'll leave it to you. I always trust you to bring home the badger. Just do me a favor, that's all. Remind that barmy artsy-fartsy Monalisa bint that this is not the *Independent* and I shall not be requiring any of 'er snaps of miserable lone gits standing in the middle of bleak housing developments under canopies of menacing black clouds. We're talking hen parties here. I want to see gangs of pissed tarts with 'appy

smiley faces and wobbly jugs. She can shove anything else right
up her aperture. You get my drift, don't you, angel?"

Anna assured him she did.

DAN SAT IN THE X-RAY DEPARTMENT WAITING ROOM, PLAN-
ning his funeral.

He'd considered it fleetingly as he'd watched Dr. Harper
slowly remove her stethoscope earpieces from her ears and
look at him in a way that indicated he might be better off
buying day returns to the office rather than monthly seasons,
but had only begun to give it serious attention on the way over
from the surgery to the hospital.

Dr. Harper's look had coincided with a slow shake of her
head.

"I never thought I would hear myself say this, Mr. Bloomfield," she said, putting the stethoscope down on her desk, "but
your symptoms are giving me cause for concern. That is a nasty
little cough you've got there and I do not like the color of your
phlegm." She picked up Dan's balsamic vinegar bottle from her
desk. The bottle was empty of balsamic vinegar, and a quarter
full of Dan's catarrh, which, in the few days since his appointment with Ada Bracegirdle, had turned bright green and was
the reason he had changed his mind about seeing Dr. Harper.

"I think the wisest course of action," she went on, "would be
to have your chest X-rayed—today, if possible. In fact I think
you should get yourself along to the hospital as soon as you
leave here."

Dr. Harper began filling out the X-ray request form.

"You don't need an outpatients appointment," she said
briskly. "Just hand this in at reception. You may have a bit of a
wait, but I'm sure they'll fit you in."

She stood up and handed Dan the form, indicating that his
appointment with her was at an end. Dan took the piece of
paper. He noticed she'd written "Urgent please" across the top.
He made no attempt to leave his seat. He sat clutching the
form.

"So," he said, looking up at her, "you really think I could have something serious then?" Panic was beginning to rise in his voice. "I mean, it must be, if you think it's important I have the X ray right away."

Dr. Harper sat down. She reached for her spectacles, which were on her desk. Holding them by one arm, she swung them gently.

"Mr. Bloomfield, we will know nothing until we have the result of your chest X ray. I am not in the habit of making diagnoses without being in full possession of the facts."

"But you suspect this could be more than just an infection?"

She put down her glasses and brought her hands together as if she were at prayer. Then she rested her hands on her chin.

"It could be. . . ." For a moment her tone had become uncharacteristically gentle. "As I say, we will know more when we have your X-ray results. Please try not to worry."

I T COULD BE. . . .'' WALKING BACK TO THE CAR, DAN HAD repeated Dr. Harper's words out loud, over again. Each time he managed a perfect imitation of her slow, measured delivery and the way her voice had dipped at the end of the sentence. "It could be" usually meant the speaker was in some doubt. There had been no doubt in Dr. Harper's voice. The tender tone of her "It could be" said it all. She meant "It definitely is." Dr. Harper knew precisely what was wrong with him, and so did Dan. He'd read enough medical books in his time to know that a persistent irritating cough was one of the first symptoms of lung cancer. So that was it. He was dying. The X ray was merely a formality.

Dan felt strangely calm. He had spent years imagining what it would feel like to be told he was terminally ill. He had spent nights awake in bed picturing himself shaking and hysterical as he knelt in front of some anonymous consultant, clutching his trouser leg, begging and pleading with him to say he'd made a mistake.

Now that it had happened, or as good as, all he could think

about was what it was his death would mean to Amy and Josh. He was going to leave them forever. They were about to lose their daddy . . . the daddy who had taught them to swim and ride their bikes, the daddy who used to read them *The Very Hungry Caterpillar* when they were tiny and couldn't sleep.

It suddenly hit him that he wouldn't be around to check the tires on Amy's boyfriends' cars before they took her out on dates, or to have shouting matches with Josh about whether or not he was old enough to go to Glastonbury. He also remembered the promise he had made to Josh about the two of them going on a camping trip that summer. The thought of explaining to that little boy why he was breaking his promise was the most painful Dan had ever experienced.

He stuck his key in the ignition, gripped the steering wheel and wept.

The tears were still coming ten minutes later. Finally he blew his nose loudly and started the engine. As he set off for the hospital, he realized that his feelings towards Anna were, to say the least, exceedingly confused. If he combined his suspicions about her Barclaycard bill with the hints his mother had given him, they clearly added up to her having an affair.

He could barely take in the enormity of what seemed to be happening. Here he was, dying, probably with only weeks to live, and his wife, whom he loved and adored, was cheating on him. But more than anything else, he couldn't believe how all this could have befallen him now, after he'd worked so fucking hard to kick his hypochondria. For weeks he'd been planning the glorious moment when he would put his arms round Anna's waist, swing her round in the air and announce that he was cured. He'd even picked up some holiday brochures from Thomas Cook.

As he drove, he realized that at least one positive thing would come from his death. Anna would feel indescribably guilty for the rest of her life. That, at least, gave him some satisfaction.

It was passing an undertaker's that made him start thinking once more about his funeral. The thought of a traditional Jewish burial added more misery to his despair. The no-flowers tradition made them such bleak, colorless affairs.

The bit before the interment was the worst. The mourners stood facing each other, women on one side of the cemetery chapel, men on the other, watching the coffin, draped in black velvet, being wheeled in on a battered wooden handcart. It had often occurred to Dan that this contraption looked like something Jewish cemeteries had bought as a job lot after the Great Plague. The chap pushing the cart was usually some elderly, rabbinical-looking type wearing a top hat, a long, navy gabardine raincoat and mud-caked Wellington boots.

Over the years, Dan had observed that as a consequence of having never met the deceased, the majority of rabbis conducting funerals operated a system of one eulogy fits all. At his mother's funeral, the rabbi had spent the first two minutes of his tribute referring to "our dear departed Lionel."

S ITTING WAITING FOR HIS CHEST X RAY, HE WAS BEGINNING to think about his funeral tea. He was determined this should be a grand affair with musicians and posh caterers. He imagined three long, willowy girl cellists in black taffeta playing Handel while waitresses came round with trays of sushi, deep-fried baby squid and fingers of mozzarella wrapped in Parma ham. He was aware that his choice of menu might not go down too well with some of his elderly Orthodox relatives. It would, he decided, be necessary to provide some traditional Jewish food. This would come in the form of the buffet table centerpiece. He could see it now—his death mask molded in chopped liver. The picture of his gluttonous aunts and uncles gathered round the buffet table gouging out bits of his head and spreading him on tea matzos made Dan feel almost lighthearted.

He was toying with the idea of having himself stuffed rather than buried, and wondering whom he should phone to get a quote, when he heard a young female voice call his name.

Turning his head towards the voice, he saw a nurse smiling

at him. She was holding open the door to the X-ray room. Dan stood up and wiped his palms down the front of his hospital dressing gown. He hesitated a moment longer and then started walking towards her.

THE MINICAB DRIVER TURNED ROUND TO ASK ANNA IF SHE minded him playing a tape of northern Turkish folk music. The sound of goat herders playing their pipes, he said, reminded him of the village where he grew up. Hoping that this would mean he wasn't going to make conversation, Anna said she didn't mind at all.

As the goat herders began their atonal piping, Anna folded a stick of Wrigley's into her mouth. She found herself wishing for the umpteenth time that afternoon that she hadn't agreed to do the hen-party feature. She still hadn't got over the trauma of Alex's heart attack and the last thing she needed was an overnight in some seedy B and B with Monalisa Blake.

Monalisa was acknowledged as one of the best newspaper photographers in the country, but the woman gave Anna the creeps. She wore black lipstick, thirties hats with veils and white goatskin gloves. She also talked incessantly, loudly, and usually over dinner, about her passion for photographing human cadavers. What Monalisa didn't know about lighting a corpse's face in order to eliminate shadow and create a flat monotone effect wasn't worth knowing.

When Campbell had first suggested doing a three-parter on hen nights, Anna had immediately assumed that, as a reward for all her hard work on the Mavis de Mornay piece, she would be accompanying the yuppie contingent, which she imagined would be heading off to the Gritti Palace in Venice or the Royalton in New York. It turned out that this wasn't what Campbell had in mind for her.

"Sorry, angel," he'd said, "I've got Tiara Bulmer-Pilkington covering the posh leg of the story. 'Er and a gang of Sloanes are jetting off to some steak house in Tirana. Apparently cuisine chunder is the latest fad with the uppers. They have competi-

tions to see who can chuck up the food first and then, totally
slaughtered on the local cognac, they go lurching through the
streets singing 'Jerusalem' and taking the piss out of Albanian
haircuts. . . . No, angel, I thought you would appreciate going
off on something a bit more challenging, something with a bit
more—what's the word?—depth. Yeah, that's it, depth. Angel, I
can see your piece now, and believe me I'm thinking poignant
social critique here, a piercing indictment of life as she is lived
in rural England . . . sort of *Panorama* meets *Emmerdale.*"

It was then that Campbell outlined his plan for Anna to
accompany a butter churner from Dorset on her hen night.
Apparently the butter churner, who was called Kelly, and
twenty of her mates had booked to see the Lover Boys at the
Starlight Club just outside Poole. The Lover Boys, he explained, were the West Country's answer to the Chippendales.

T HE CAB CROSSED KEW BRIDGE AND PULLED UP AT THE
Chiswick roundabout traffic lights.

Anna took the gum out of her mouth and began rolling it
contemplatively into a ball. God only knew what a group of
Dorset butter churners would make of Monalisa, particularly if
she started passing round her photo album of corpses.

Still, a night in the company of Monalisa Blake was the least
of Anna's worries. There were other, far more important issues
troubling her. First, she was feeling exceedingly guilty because
she hadn't been to see Alex in hospital. Alex had forbidden her
to visit in case she came face-to-face with Kimberley, who had
been at his bedside almost round the clock since the heart
attack.

As soon as Kimberley had found out that Alex's heart attack
had been caused by his bad diet, she'd gone out and bought a
cookery book full of low-fat recipes. Every day she would come
onto the ward carrying a wicker basket. It contained a low-
cholesterol treat for Alex and cakes and pies wrapped in red-
and-white-check gingham for the staff. While Alex munched
on a malted oat finger, Kimberley would stand at the end of the

ward cutting up slices of Hummingbird cake topped with extra-thick cheese frosting and urging the doctors and nurses to sample her corn pones.

As Anna couldn't visit Alex in hospital, she had insisted he phone her a couple of times each day. Over and over again he thanked her for saving his life and over and over again Anna said she'd done nothing other than call an ambulance. He said he felt terribly guilty for frightening her and she said she felt guilty because she thought she was to blame for his heart attack.

"In what possible way?" he asked.

"You know . . . the sex. It clearly put a strain on your heart. If we hadn't made love the attack would never have happened."

"Don't be so daft." Alex chuckled. "According to my consultant, it was a heart attack simply waiting to happen. I was just lucky you were there. I could have been on my own somewhere and dropped dead. Anna, I owe you so much. I promise, as soon as I'm up and about, we'll have dinner and I shall say thank you properly."

It was the "I owe you so much" bit which was still doing circuits inside Anna's head. It would have been unspeakably selfish of her to put Alex under pressure by asking him if he'd had any more thoughts about dishing the dirt on Rachel Stern's cosmetic surgery. Nevertheless, she had barely slept in over a week, so desperate was she to get a decision from him. If he agreed to the interview and she got her timing just right, she could even ensure that the story appeared on the same day that Rachel Stern was due to give her keynote address at the League of British Feminists' annual lunch.

Today was Friday. Alex was due out of hospital tomorrow. Anna decided to leave it until Tuesday and then she would phone him.

As she wrapped the ball of gum in a Kleenex, Anna found herself thinking about Dan.

The feeling she'd had a couple of weeks ago as they lay in bed that he was keeping something from her hadn't gone away. If anything, it had grown stronger. She had even wondered whether he was having an affair. She'd dismissed the possibility almost immediately, on the grounds that the irony was too ridiculous for words, and it made her feel like a creature in an Aesop fable who was about to get its comeuppance.

Added to Dan's air of secrecy was his latest neurotic symptom: he had started interrogating Anna about her movements. Every evening when he came home, he demanded to know precisely how she had spent her day. When she told him that the hen-night story would involve a night away he had spent half an hour quizzing her about where she was staying, which photographer she was going with and what time she would be home on Saturday. Anna, supremely confident that she had furnished him with not even the slightest evidence of her adultery, had simply smiled patiently and answered all his questions calmly and without fuss.

She had wondered if his hypochondria was becoming so severe that he was transferring his anxiety onto her. Could it be, she'd thought, that he was now petrified that she was going to get ill while she was away from him? This had made sense until it began to dawn on her that Dan appeared to be becoming a little more relaxed about his health. Last week when she'd suggested he see the doctor about his cough, he had shrugged and said he was sure it would clear up on its own. Barely looking up from the West Ham game he was watching on Sky, he said he might go to the doctor about it "sometime."

She realized he could be starting to overcome his hypochondria. She supposed she should have been delighted. Instead she'd been horrified. If Dan got better that meant he would want to have sex with her—not that she wouldn't welcome that, but it meant that she would have no justification for her adultery apart from the rather flimsy one of a piece she had to write for a newspaper. Despite Alex's heart attack and despite Charlie disappearing and only ever sending her one chewed-up postcard from New York in which he hinted heavily at a burgeoning romance with a nursery nurse from Cork called Fidelma, Anna had got into the swing of extramarital sex. She had no intention of stopping.

Not, at least, until she'd scored her hat trick.

The cab pulled up outside the *Globe on Sunday* office. As Anna reached into her bag for her wallet she sensed there was something a bit different about the music coming from the car cassette player. Although the northern Turkish goat herders were still playing their pipes, they appeared to have completed their repertoire of northern Turkish folk music. They had segued into "Ferry Cross the Mersey."

CHAPTER SEVENTEEN

ANNA LOOKED AT HER WATCH.
She'd been sitting in reception at
the *Globe on Sunday* for nearly half
an hour. There was still no sign of Monalisa Blake. After twenty minutes, she'd
asked the girl on reception if she could use
the phone.

Anna thought she'd ring the picture desk
first to see if they had any idea where Monalisa was. The temp who answered the
phone said she'd never heard of her. When
Anna said she'd try Campbell, the girl said
not to bother as Campbell and his PA had
gone tearing out of the office an hour ago.
When she asked her if she knew when they
were due back, the temp had said she
couldn't say, but she wouldn't be at all surprised if they were gone for the rest of the
day.

Apparently a crisis had arisen on the photo shoot for Campbell's "Who Really Bonks Big Girls?" supplement. The twenty-stone mother of seven from Ipswich whom Campbell had conned into being photographed naked wrapped in the trunk of a male elephant had become hysterical and was threatening to walk out because every time she went near the animal he either dropped a colossal heap of steaming dung or tried to mount her.

Anna thought it unlikely Campbell would need all afternoon to calm the woman. If she knew Campbell, he would put a comforting arm round her, toss her a large box of Ferrero Rocher along with a couple of tickets for *Cats* and the promise of a free nosh-up for her and the family at the Harvester of their choice and she'd be, to quote one of Campbell's favorite phrases, "sweet as a dipstick coated in sherbet" in three minutes flat.

Although Anna anticipated Campbell's imminent return, she knew she couldn't depend on it. She and Monalisa should have left by now. It was essential she speak to Campbell right away.

She opened her handbag and took out her Filofax. She found Campbell's mobile number in a matter of seconds, then went back to the reception desk and dialed. All she got was the answering service.

"Fuck." Anna slammed down the receiver and picked up her Filofax from the desk. As she turned to go back to her seat she noticed the automatic doors part and a man come running in, a canvas camera bag slung over his shoulder. She recognized the breathless, puffing chap at once. It was Ed Brzezinski, one of the *Globe*'s staff photographers.

"Anna . . ." He was coming towards her, his hand raised in recognition.

In the newspaper world, Ed Brzezinski was a superstar. In the ten years before he joined the *Globe,* he had made a name for himself throughout Europe and America as a brilliant and gifted war photographer. Several severe bouts of malaria he first picked up in Rwanda had finally forced him back to

London and into taking a less intrepid newspaper job on the *Globe*.

Although he was almost forty, he was tall and slim with a bum like two nectarines. The sight of Brzezinski, hard-bitten and chain-smoking in his tatty Levis, beaten-up tan suede jacket and heavy stubble, had most women in the *Globe* office crossing their legs with frustration.

And for a lucky few, the frustration was relieved. Ed was known throughout the *Globe on Sunday* as the Steeplejack. "On account," Campbell had explained to Anna when she inquired about the nickname soon after she'd started writing for the *Globe*, "of 'im always bein' up something, if you get my drift."

Anna had only ever worked with Ed once. That was almost two years ago. Although they bumped into each other occasionally in the corridor, or by the coffee machine, for no reason in particular their professional paths hadn't crossed since.

The job they had worked on together had entailed going to Isleworth to doorstep a King Charles spaniel who could howl "Don't Cry for Me Argentina."

Ed had driven them to Isleworth in his clapped-out Mini. It had been an uncomfortable journey, due partly to the Mini's decrepitude and partly to Ed looking angry and sullen and doing little more than grunt in response to Anna's attempts at conversation. There had been no doubt in Anna's mind that he considered the singing-dog story to be beneath him. It wasn't until they were almost there that Ed finally allowed his anger to erupt. He called Campbell, on whose orders the pair had been dispatched to Isleworth, a buffoon and tabloid tosser. He began spluttering and taking his hands off the steering wheel to wave his arms around, saying that he had no idea how the man could even consider demanding that someone with his experience and talent go on such a tacky story.

Anna had to bite into the side of her cheek in order to stop herself saying that Ed could always bugger off to the nearest war and with a bit of luck he might step on a land mine.

By the time they arrived in Isleworth, she had come to the

conclusion that although Ed Brzezinski was, with his swept-back brownish-auburn hair and face full of boyish freckles, severely fanciable, he was a precious git with a grossly inflated ego.

Suddenly, all the office gossip about him made sense. The Steeplejack had a preference for nineteen-year-old girls, usually nineteen-year-old Japanese girls. This was a man, Anna realized, who couldn't abide being contradicted or challenged—particularly by women.

During Ed's outburst on the way to Isleworth, Anna decided she would rather eat a pile of her toenail clippings than give him even the vaguest hint that she found him intimidating or attractive. She was determined to assert herself and stand up to him.

She began almost at once. As they walked towards the small group of reporters and photographers standing outside the small terraced house which was home to the King Charles spaniel, Anna noticed that Ed appeared to have brought only one camera with him. It was an old Leica, most of its black enamel chipped off, which she'd noticed him stuff crossly into his jacket pocket as he got out of the car. She pointed out all the other photographers with their Nikons and Canons strung round their necks and informed Ed curtly that compared to his colleagues, he wasn't very well hung.

Ed ignored the remark, but there was little doubt in Anna's mind that he had been furious with her. On the way back to the office he did his best to pick an argument with her. First he tried goading her by suggesting that a reporter's life was much easier than a photographer's.

"If the story doesn't pan out, or the interviewee does a bunk, you lot can bugger off back to the office and make it up. If I come back empty-handed, there's a dirty great hole on page seven and I'm dog food."

Anna refused to be drawn. She simply smiled and said he probably had a point.

Ed said nothing for a minute. He was clearly considering his next move in his campaign to get some response from her to his teasing. Finally he announced that he was going to his Jewish godson's circumcision the next day. For the next ten minutes he didn't stop sounding off about how barbaric it was that in this day and age, Jews were still mutilating their baby boys. Finally he had turned to Anna and demanded to know how she could possibly justify it.

The truth was that Anna couldn't justify it. If she was honest, she thought circumcision was horrific. Like many Jews, she and Dan had circumcised their son out of some irrational atavistic tribal calling rather than religious conviction. Nevertheless, Ed had touched a nerve. She was buggered if she was going to let him win the argument, but was still determined not to lose her temper. Remembering that his parents were Polish Catholics, because she'd heard Campbell refer to him at a drunken leaving do as a Catholic Polak, Anna looked at Ed, and in a calm, self-assured tone which belied her galloping pulse said:

"Ed, please don't lecture me about barbarism. There are religious reasons as well as sound medical reasons for circumcision. On the other hand, your Polish ancestors had no motive other than hatred for carrying out pogroms against the Jews."

Ed didn't say another word on the matter. Anna knew this wasn't as a consequence of her having shot down his argument about circumcision being barbaric. She knew she hadn't. She suspected Ed had shut up because he was in shock. He simply wasn't used to being with a female who fought her corner. There was no doubt in her mind that this was the first time a woman had put him in his place.

That moment of sweet victory became one Anna would recall time and again over the next two years.

ED REACHED THE RECEPTION DESK WHERE ANNA WAS STANDing. He was still panting heavily from his sprint.

"Ed . . . hi. What's going on?" Anna inquired. "And correct

me if I'm wrong, but would I be right in thinking the Gonzalez family has a long-lost English branch, and that you are it?"

Ed was still too puffed to speak, or even smile. Instead he held up his index finger to indicate that he would explain everything, but he needed a minute to get his breath back. He put his camera bag on the floor, placed his hands on the desk and lowered his head between his outstretched arms.

Anna looked across to where she had been sitting and noticed some small bottles of Evian water standing next to the coffeemaker. As she walked across to fetch one for Ed, for a second her mind went back to the minicab and to her thoughts about not giving up on adultery until she'd scored her hat trick. . . .

As she picked up a bottle of water, she turned her head to look at Ed. He looked smarter than usual. His Levis were less faded and his well-cut woolen jacket looked brand-new. As he leaned against the reception desk, she could see the jeans pulling ever so slightly across his behind. It was even more compact than she remembered.

She went back to the reception desk, unscrewed the cap on the water bottle and handed it to him.

"Here, this'll cool you down." Ed lifted his head up from between his arms and smiled his thanks. The dark-navy jacket looked stunning against his gray-blue eyes and amber freckles. Anna had to admit that although Ed Brzezinski was the most arrogant and conceited man she had ever met, he was also one of the most beautiful—second only to Charlie Kaplan.

As she watched him put the bottle to his lips and lean his head back, a large flock of sexually aroused butterflies materialized in Anna's belly, only to disappear in a matter of moments. It was all very well having the hots for Ed Brzezinski, she thought, but if he was still the unpleasant, egotistical fool he was two years ago, she couldn't even consider sleeping with him. She wasn't about to do an impression of a simpering nineteen-year-old geisha. She was desperate to find the third man for her article, but not that desperate.

What was more, Ed was unlikely to have forgotten her pogroms outburst. She was still proud of her speech and didn't have the faintest regret about making it. Nevertheless, she had to acknowledge that because of it, he probably thought her an aggressive, argumentative cow and hated her. There was very little chance he would speak to her in anything other than curt monosyllables, let alone go to bed with her.

"Anna, I am so dreadfully sorry I'm late," he said as he put the bottle down on the reception desk. Anna looked at him in utter disbelief. Not only was Ed speaking to her, using several polysyllabic words, he was actually apologizing for something. Could it mean, Anna wondered, that he had changed his tune and thought of her as his equal, as someone worthy of his respect and consideration?

Wet tails of tawny hair were stuck to his forehead. As the butterflies took up residence once more inside her, Anna wondered if people with auburn hair had auburn pubes.

"I've been at the High Court in the Strand all morning," he went on. That explained his smart clothes and absence of stubble.

"I left ages ago, but the traffic was murder round Trafalgar Square. . . . Then when I got here I couldn't park. I finally found a meter a mile or so down the road and I sprinted all the way back. I was frightened you'd set off for Poole without me."

Anna looked at him, a mixture of confusion and irritation on her face.

"But the picture desk said I was going with Monalisa Blake. When did they change their minds? And why didn't somebody leave me a message to let me know what was going on?"

"I don't think there was time," Ed said, running his fingers through his hair to get rid of the wet bangs. "Monalisa phoned Campbell just as he was about to dash off to a photo shoot. Apparently the dozy cow got confused about where the two of you were going and forgot she was supposed to meet up with you first. To cut a long story short, she left home at nine this morning and instead of driving to Poole, she went to Goole in Yorkshire."

Anna frowned. "I don't believe it. No one's that daft. I reckon she's playing hooky. I bet some pathologist mate of hers invited her along to some juicy postmortem. She's probably bouncing a flash off some poor bugger's liver as we speak."

Ed Brzezinski said that Anna was probably right.

"Anyway . . . you've got me instead of Monalisa." He bent down and picked up his camera bag. "Campbell bleeped just as I was leaving court and asked me to take her place on the hen-party job."

"Great." Anna beamed insincerely. She paused, assuming Ed was about to explode and deliver another diatribe on the indignity of being asked to cover such a down-market story. When, after several seconds he hadn't detonated, she decided it was safe to continue making conversation.

"I can't say I was looking forward to an evening with Monalisa. I swear the woman dabs formaldehyde behind her ears."

Ed grinned. She couldn't remember ever seeing his face in anything other than a scowl.

"So what were you doing in court?" she asked cheerily, buoyed up by his expression. "Tom Cruise had you up for harassment?"

His smile disappeared at once.

"Not exactly. I'll explain on the way."

T HEY GOT A CAB BACK TO ED'S CAR, WHICH WAS PARKED in a side street. Ed paid the driver and, seeing Anna struggling to get her holdall out of the taxi, went to help her.

"Jesus, Anna," he said, heaving the overstuffed bag across the floor of the taxi. "Don't tell me, you've just pulled a one-woman bullion heist and the real reason we're going to Poole is to meet up with your fence?"

He hadn't lost his aptitude for sarcasm, but at least today it had come with a side order of humor. Anna giggled. Ed turned to face her and let the bag drop with a thud at her feet. Anna said thank you and watched Ed rearrange the bank notes in his wallet. He looked pale and exhausted, as if he hadn't slept for days. She couldn't believe she hadn't noticed it when she first saw him in reception. He stuffed his wallet into his back pocket.

"You know, what with my stuff, I'm not sure your bag's going to fit in the trunk."

He nodded in the direction of the car parked a couple of yards down the road. Anna's face fell. He was still driving the clapped-out Mini.

"And if you dare call it a pile of crap like you did that time we went on that singing spaniel story," he said in mock anger, "I'll drive down to Dorset on my own and you can cart this thing on the train." He kneed Anna's bag along the pavement towards the 1966 dark-green Mini Cooper S.

"This car is a classic," he said, getting out his keys. "Cost me twenty grand three years ago. Bugger of it is, the classic market collapsed and she's only worth about fifteen now."

Anna said she failed to see why anyone in their right mind should want to pay even fifteen thousand pounds for a thirty-odd-year-old Mini.

"Ed, I've ridden on seaside donkeys with better suspension than this car possesses."

She waited for him to come back at her with some cutting remark. She watched him open his mouth and then close it. It was as if the fight had suddenly gone out of him. Could it be that Ed Brzezinski had mellowed? She remembered one of Brenda's favorite sayings: "A leopard can never change his spots unless he's kept the receipt." Perhaps Ed had kept his.

Saying nothing, he turned away from her, pushed the front seat forward, maneuvered the holdall into the back and set it down alongside his camera bag.

Being elderly, it was legal for the pile of crap to have no seat belts. As they bumped and lurched along the Westway, the Mini's engine sounding as if there were a thousand angry bees trapped under the hood, Anna found herself clutching the plastic handle above the passenger window for support.

They'd talked a bit about the hen-party story and the kind of pictures Campbell had in mind, but Ed seemed to be finding it immensely difficult to carry on being cheerful and enthusiastic, and after a while the conversation dried up.

Anna stared out the window and watched the city relinquish its hold on the landscape. Every so often she turned to glance at Ed. Even from his profile she could see the pain on his face. She assumed it had something to do with the court case. Finally she plucked up the courage to ask him about it.

"So, Ed . . ." she said gently, "you still haven't told me why you were in court."

He didn't take his eyes off the road. It was a moment before he spoke.

"I wasn't exactly on trial. Although I certainly felt like a criminal by the time I left. My wife and I divorced a couple of months ago. We were in court for the child custody hearing. As of today I have been denied all contact with my kids."

"Ed, I am so sorry." She put her hand on his shoulder and kept it there for a few seconds. "I thought I kept up with all the gossip at the *Globe,* but I had no idea you'd got married, let alone had children."

"We had a couple . . . twin boys. They're a year old now."

"But what on earth happened? I don't understand. . . . How could you be left with no contact whatsoever?"

"Simple. My wife bribed the au pair. She gave her a grand to say in court that she'd seen me beat her up and that I got drunk whenever I looked after the babies. What gets me is I've barely had more than a nightly glass of wine since the twins were born. I even gave up the cigarettes. Anyway, the judge, who was some crusty old fart, decided to believe her. He then described me as a violent and abusive husband, and an unfit father. Apparently I can appeal, but God knows how long that'll take. Even if I win, there's a good chance the court will insist my visits are supervised."

As his voice trailed off, Ed turned towards her briefly. For a second or two their eyes met. Anna had no trouble imagining Ed being a narcissistic pain in the arse to live with. She certainly had no trouble believing he had been unfaithful, but seeing his wretched, broken expression, she found it impossible to accept he was a violent man.

She searched her brain for something constructive to say, but could think of nothing that wasn't a ridiculous palliative. The only useful thing she could do was listen. She decided to sit quietly and wait until he was ready to carry on speaking. She glanced out of the window. They were about to join the M3. They would be in Poole in an hour or so.

After a couple of minutes Ed began speaking again. The words were suddenly pouring out of him. He seemed desperate to talk.

Ed had met his ex, Tilda Hasselquist, a tree surgeon from Sweden, while he was covering a Christmas charity event in Scotland. Along with half a dozen other tree surgeons Tilda had agreed to help cut down fir trees which were going to be distributed to needy children.

Campbell McKee had been tipped off about the story from a mate who worked for BBC Scotland. He'd been distinctly underwhelmed by it until the mate got to the bit about one of the tree surgeons being some six-foot Swedish girl with waist-length butter-colored hair, Bambi eyes and breasts like a couple of honeydews.

Immediately Campbell had summoned Ed into his office and instructed him to get his arse on a plane to Edinburgh.

"What I'm after is a snap of the tart up a tree . . . starkers except for a Father Christmas cloak. I'm relying on you to come back with the business. Ed . . . I'm talking stiff nipples, wet, pouting lips . . . and for fuck's sake make sure she looks like she's really caressing her bleedin' chainsaw."

Needless to say, Ed had been up in arms about being sent on such a prurient assignment. Campbell's reaction had been to throw him a bundle of rolled-up tenners "to keep the mare sweet" and make the point that as the highest-paid newspaper photographer in the country, Ed shouldn't be so fucking picky.

"Oh, and by the way," Campbell shouted to Ed as he was about to walk out of Campbell's office and slam the door behind him, "I'm not bothering to send a reporter with you. I thought, seeing as you're so intelligent, you could ask her a few questions. What I'm after are tales of saucy sauna romps, her thoughts on whether British men keep it up longer than Swedes, which of course she'll say they do . . . and find out which is her favorite ABBA hit. . . ."

Although Tilda Hasselquist was, as Campbell's mate had described, tall, blond and big-chested, she also had an IQ of 180 and a Ph.D. in arboriculture from Edinburgh University, not to mention a highly developed fiscal sense.

Ed, who'd fallen madly in lust with her in about three nano-seconds despite her high intelligence, did everything he could to persuade her that posing nude for a tabloid newspaper was as good as prostituting herself. Tilda laughed, accused him of being a prude and said there was nothing wrong with people admiring a beautiful body like hers. She was determined to go ahead with the picture, so long as she received an appropriate fee.

There was nothing he wouldn't do for Tilda, so he spent hours on the phone to Campbell negotiating her fee. Campbell finally agreed to pay her two thousand pounds.

The Sunday before that Christmas, the picture of Tilda, batting her thick eyelashes and naked except for a Father Christmas cloak and her chainsaw, appeared on page five of the *Globe on Sunday*. The headline accompanying it, which Campbell had composed in a matter of seconds, was "Xmas Chainsaw Mascara."

WE DATED FOR A FEW MONTHS," ED CONTINUED. "I would fly up to Scotland at weekends or Tilda would come down to London. Then we found out she was pregnant. By that time we both knew we were in love and we didn't think twice about getting married."

One of the reasons Ed's lust for Tilda had turned to love was that she had seen a loving, caring man beneath his inflated ego and bad temper. She forced him to confront his anger and made him understand that it had only come about because he had been forced to give up war photography.

With Tilda by his side and the babies on the way, Ed was able to develop a new sense of self-worth and, for the first time in years, become a likable human being.

He stopped taking himself so seriously and developed a sense of humor. He made his peace with Campbell and even found he enjoyed going on some of Campbell's ridiculous capers.

After a while, he became less emotionally dependent on Tilda. It was then that he started to find fault with her and become bored.

He accepted that many Swedes got depressed during the dark winter months and took her seasonal suicide attempts in his stride. What he found harder to accept was that even in the spring, when she cheered up, she was an unspeakably dull companion.

Tilda's idea of fun was an evening spent reading aloud to Ed from the works of the Greek philosopher Theophrastus. She considered Theophrastus' *On the History of Plants,* in particular his section on the treatment of tree wounds, to be the most significant contribution to the development of modern arboriculture. Afterwards she would attempt to engage Ed in a heated debate on the pros and cons of bare-root transplanting of deciduous trees.

It was at these moments that Ed found himself looking back fondly on their trips to casualty to have Tilda's stomach pumped.

He wasn't sure which he found more tedious—Tilda reading aloud from her tree books, or going out for a meal with her. Her favorite eatery was the self-service canteen at IKEA on the North Circular road. She insisted they go there for lunch every Saturday. While Ed toyed with his gravadlax, Tilda listened to a

Strindberg play on her Walkman and tucked into a huge plate of Swedish meatballs with lingonberry sauce. This was accompanied by an even huger portion of Janssons' Temptation, a creamy potato dish designed to keep the daily calorie count of Swedes in the frozen north as close as possible to the annual food intake of the average African tribesman.

After lunch Tilda would drag him round the store looking at roller blinds or light fittings for the new house. All their furniture came from IKEA. She must have been the only customer who referred to each item of furniture by the cutesy Swedish names IKEA assigned them. "Have you had a new delivery of Bjorns?" she would ask the salespeople. "How are they comparing in empirical functional utility with the old Stig?" Ed only realized that Tilda's passion for the place had turned into an obsession when he came home one evening to discover a huge wire basket sitting next to the fireplace. It was filled to the brim with miniature garden rakes called Sven.

AS ED CONTINUED TO POUR OUT HIS STORY, ANNA NOTICED A "motorway ends" sign. They were almost in the New Forest. She reached into her bag and started to unfold a sheet of shiny fax paper. On it were the directions to the Starlight Club which Campbell's PA had faxed to her that morning.

"We carry on the A31 from here almost all the way," she said. "So what made you finally decide to divorce?"

"It got to a stage where I felt she had no place in her life for me. First came trees, which were all that mattered to her, and then after a while it was the twins. I'm afraid I slipped back into my old ways and ended up having an affair with a woman who worked on the subs desk at the *Globe*. It only lasted a few weeks, but some evil bitch in the office wrote to Tilda and told her about it and that was it. She chucked me out and we were finished. I know having an affair just after she'd had the babies was a wicked and cruel thing to do, and I know she has every right to despise me, but I never thought she'd punish me like this."

Anna said that divorces were always messy, but what Tilda had done with the au pair was the most callous act of cruelty she'd ever come across. What was so wrong with having the odd affair if someone wasn't satisfied with their marriage? she said indignantly. "I know lots of people who do." It was the furthest she dared go.

Ed looked at her briefly and managed a weak smile. Anna wasn't sure; perhaps his look conveyed nothing more than gratitude at hearing somebody else confirm his thoughts about Tilda's treatment of him. It was hard for her to tell whether he was in the least bit interested in her.

Anna turned away from him and looked down at the fax. She realized that for the second time today, somebody had cocked up. The club was, in fact, miles from Poole, out at Bere Regis. She stared at the small map at the bottom of the page.

"Christ, I don't believe this. Campbell said this place was in Poole. It looks to me like it's twenty miles farther on."

Ed asked if he could take a look at the directions. Anna handed him the sheet of paper. Ed then proceeded to study the directions while at the same time negotiating a very large roundabout.

"Well, funnily enough, I know exactly where it is. A mate of mine in New York owns a cottage not far from there. In fact, I often spend weekends there when he's away. I keep the key in the car. Funny spot for a club, though. It's right in the depths of the countryside. I'd say it's about half an hour from here . . . tops."

Anna looked at her watch. She'd asked the butter churner and her mates to get to the club by seven-thirty so that she could do a brief interview with them before the Lover Boys came on. If Ed stepped on it, they should just about make it.

Relieved that she could leave it to Ed to navigate them through the center of Poole, she let the conversation drift back to his divorce and the child custody hearing.

After fifteen minutes or so the divided highway turned into a narrow, winding road with hedges on either side. As they discussed Ed's plans to appeal against the judge's decision, Anna couldn't help thinking how glorious the Dorset countryside looked in the early-evening sunlight.

They realized almost simultaneously that the car was beginning to lose power.

"Ed, speak to me. What the fuck is going on?" Anna's tone was on the cusp of anger. "I always said this car was a junk heap, but I made the mistake of believing that, bearing in mind how much traveling your job involves, it was a reasonably well maintained junk heap."

"It is, it is," he said, almost squealing his disbelief. "I haven't got the vaguest notion what is going on."

With that the Mini slowed to a crawl. Ed just managed to direct it into a farm gate entrance before the engine died completely.

They spent the next five minutes with their heads under the Mini's hood. Knowing nothing about car mechanics, Anna had nothing useful to offer. She did, however, occupy herself by saying "I knew this would happen" over and over again. It was only when she realized that she sounded exactly like her mother when her father got lost trying to find a bar-mitzvah venue that she stopped.

Ed, fraught, and still none the wiser, took his head out from under the bonnet and said there was nothing for it but to phone the AA. He got back into the car and rummaged through his camera bag for his mobile.

"Shitting bollocking buggery . . . it's fully charged, but there's no fucking service."

Anna reached into the car and found her phone. It wasn't working either. Leaning against the car, she looked at her watch. It was nearly seven. In all her years as a newspaper reporter she had never been sent on a job and come back empty-handed. She wasn't about to start now; as Ed had so perceptively explained to her that time on the way back from

Isleworth, she could make up her story if necessary. He would have to make his own photographic arrangements.

"Look, why don't we cross this stile and see where the path leads. Perhaps there's a farmhouse at the end of it and we can call the AA from there."

Ed agreed that it seemed the most sensible thing to do. He took his camera bag from the car, locked both doors and turned towards Anna, who was standing in front of the stile.

"After you." He took her hand as she climbed up onto the narrow wooden platform and maneuvered herself onto the other side.

Neither of them was able to explain the reason for what happened next. It could have been that an earlier shower had left the stile greasy and slippery. It could have been that Anna wasn't concentrating and lost her step. Whatever the cause, two seconds later, she found herself lying facedown in a wet, muddy ditch.

Ed was over the stile and crouching by her side in an instant. He put down his camera bag and helped her to her feet. Anna was coughing and spluttering. She tried to wipe the mud off her jacket, but succeeded only in rearranging it. Her beige Sweet FA suit and matching silk blouse were ruined. She could feel pieces of straw in her hair.

Ed took out a clean white handkerchief. As he wiped her face and pulled a long piece of straw out of her hair, he looked into her eyes and smiled.

"Anna, has anyone ever told you, the yokel look is very you."

Managing to hold back a smile, she raised her arm to thump him, but he grabbed her wrist before she could do him any harm. He kept his grip on her arm, forcing it to remain in midair. They looked at each other, neither of them saying a word. The silence seemed to go on forever. Finally, he let go of her arm and drew her towards him. "I remember wanting to do this two years ago," he said, cupping her face in his hands, "when you got furious and accused me of being an anti-Semitic Pole."

"Ed, I never said anything remotely like that," Anna protested. "All I said was—"

She didn't have a chance to finish because Ed was kissing her, very slowly, on the mouth.

"Come on," he said when they'd finished. "Let's carry on walking for a bit and see what's round the next bend."

CHAPTER EIGHTEEN

WHEN THEY DISCOVERED THERE was nothing round the bend except another bend, Anna and Ed decided to return to the car. They tramped back, dodging the muddy puddles, in embarrassed silence. Anna couldn't help thinking that, although she had enjoyed it immensely, the likelihood was that the kiss meant nothing to Ed. The man was exhausted. His emotions were all over the place. He'd probably wanted nothing more than to be close to another human being for a few seconds. He was bound to regret it now. The reason he wasn't speaking was that he didn't know how to tell her. Anna decided that the easiest and most diplomatic way of dealing with the incident would be to say nothing, pretend it hadn't happened—and hope it did again.

Ed unlocked the car, opened the glove compartment and took out a packet of prawn-cocktail-flavored crisps. He offered some to Anna. She shook her head. She thought the flavor of synthetic prawn combined with the shock she was still feeling from falling in the mud, not to mention Ed's kiss and her anxiety about them missing the Lover Boys' show, might make her throw up.

"I think the best thing we can do," Ed said, putting a handful of crisps in his mouth, "is flag down the next car that comes along and see if we can cadge a lift. I'll sort the car out tomorrow."

A FEW MINUTES LATER THEY WERE ACCEPTING A LIFT FROM A jolly middle-aged couple in cricket hats, who were towing a tiny two-berth trailer with their Morris Marina. They were heading for a trailer site near Dorchester, and reckoned the village where the club was would only be a couple of miles out of their way.

The chap got out of the Marina and insisted on helping them move their luggage. He also suggested Anna might like to use the trailer to change her clothes.

"By the way," he said, extending a hand, "we're the Meatyards. We hail from Orpington." His voice had the kind of irritating nasal quality which Anna always associated with bought ledger clerks. "I'm Terry and this," he said, waving a hand towards the woman in the passenger seat, who was working her way through a pile of dainty sandwiches which she was taking from a Tupperware container, "is my wife, Elaine. I call her the hand brake." He slapped Ed matily on the back. "You know, doesn't let you go anywhere." With that he burst into a laugh which sounded like a donkey having very fast and exceedingly energetic sex.

As Terry slapped Ed on the back for a second time, Elaine stuck her head out of the window, and, by way of greeting, waved a half-eaten crustless sandwich.

Anna and Ed exchanged a surreptitious glance which, although fleeting, successfully communicated their mutual distaste for Terry Meatyard. Ed explained that they were Anna and Ed and hailed from the *Globe on Sunday*, but Terry wasn't a listening type, and was off again.

"So," he said, "what brings you and your lady wife to this glorious neck of the woods? I know, don't tell me . . . you've got rid of the ankle biters and you've come away for some long-overdue you-know-what—"

"No, no . . . we're not married." Anna almost shrieked her interruption. "Well, what I mean is . . . I am, but not to Ed."

"Say no more, little lady. Say no more. My lips are sealed." Terry turned away from Anna and dug Ed conspiratorially in the ribs. "You're a long time pushing up the daisies, mate. Get it while you can, that's my motto. If I had my time again . . ." He looked back at Elaine, who had put the Tupperware on the dashboard and was now cleaning the wax from her ears with a cotton swab.

"I'm afraid it's not what you think," Ed said. "Anna and I are colleagues. Anna is a reporter and I am a photographer. We work for the *Globe on Sunday*." He then went on to explain about the hen-night story.

"D'you hear that, Elaine?" Terry shouted. "These people are from the *Globe on Sunday*." But she didn't hear him because she was too busy inspecting the lumpy orange tip of her cotton swab.

"Elaine was in the papers once. She won a bravery award about ten years ago. Our next-door neighbor's house was on fire and Elaine went in and rescued the goldfish. When she came out with the bowl, the poor blighter looked like it was a goner. Totally unfazed by its seemingly terminal state, Elaine, who, I should add, had just finished her St. John's ambulance training, insisted on giving it the kiss of life. Needless to say she brought it back from the dead. I kid you not, there were reporters on our doorstep within the hour. The story made a huge splash in our local free sheet. Maybe you saw it?"

Ed and Anna apologized profusely for having missed it.

"Do you have a trailer?" Terry asked.

"Not really, no," Ed said. "I don't know about Anna, but I do camp quite a lot."

"Don't worry about us, old boy. You won't find any prejudice chez Meatyard against our tented friends. Live and let live, that's what I say. You can always work your way up to a trailer."

"Yes," said Ed, warming to his theme. "I spent six months under canvas when I was in Chechnya covering the siege of Grozny for *Time* magazine."

"Oh, right," Terry replied. "Nice site, was it?"

"Yes, quite pleasant other than when we were under intensive artillery bombardment by the Red Army."

"Oh, noisy then."

"A little."

FIFTEEN MINUTES LATER ANNA EMERGED FROM THE MEAT-yards' trailer wearing jeans, a black jacket and fresh makeup. She put her dirty things in the trunk of the Marina, with the rest of their bags. Terry shut the lid.

"Elaine's moved into the back. Why don't you sit next to her and then you girls can have a good old chinwag about your ovaries and whatnot, and I'll sit with Ed in the front and point out some of the points of interest. Although I says it myself and shouldn't, we've been motoring in these parts for more than thirty years and I am somewhat conversant with the locale."

It was only when Anna got into the car that she realized that Elaine was wearing the identical royal blue polo shirt and baggy red shorts as her husband. With the white cricket hats, they looked like a pair of French flags.

As Terry started the engine, Elaine began offering round violet creams. Realizing she was hungry and beginning to feel a bit light-headed, Anna took two.

Elaine turned out to be just as voluble as her husband. In the twenty minutes it took to get to the Starlight Club, Anna heard about Terry's run-in with Homebase over some dodgy window putty, her recurring eczema which she was prone to

develop "in all those moist places" and the tarnish—"Well, it's
more of a speckled effect, really"—on their new bath taps. Every so often she would break off to demolish another violet
cream. During one of these pit stops, Anna caught a snatch of
Terry's tour commentary.

"Now, Ed, that church up ahead is really ancient. I believe
they started it around 1245 . . . and finished it at half past
four." He gave another burst of horny donkey.

While Ed rubbed his shoulder, which, after several of Terry's
slaps, was beginning to feel quite sore, Elaine started telling
Anna about the wavy hem on the navy two-piece she'd just
bought for her son's wedding. By now, Anna was barely listening. This was due partly to boredom and partly because she had
noticed that the narrow country lane had turned into a divided
highway and that coming up on the left was a low modern
building, set back from the road. Huge pink neon letters announcing the Starlight Club rose up from the flat roof. There
were at least half a dozen coaches in the parking lot. "Brilliant,
we're here." She leaned forward and spoke to the back of
Terry's head. "I think that's the entrance coming up on the
left."

Terry slowed down and pulled off the road. Elaine, totally
unaware that she had lost Anna's attention, had moved on to
the tale of her anorexic sister-in-law who had come round from
her sterilization operation and demanded that her sugar drip be
replaced with Sweetex.

NOW THEN," TERRY SAID TO ED AND ANNA AS HE HEAVED
Anna's holdall out of the boot and placed it on the ground,
"you know where we are. Don't be strangers. Elaine loves visitors. Gives her an excuse to bring out her commemorative
thimble collection."

The three of them shook hands. Terry got back into the car,
started the engine and began towing the trailer slowly towards
the parking-lot exit. Elaine stuck her head out of the car win-

dow. "Anna, maybe we could have lunch one day at the Oxford Street Littlewoods. I still haven't told you about the flaky skin I get between my toes."

"Great," Anna said, waving. "I'll look forward to it."

I NSIDE THE STARLIGHT CLUB, THE MC, WHO WAS WEARING A maroon double-breasted jacket, finished tapping his mike.

"OK, girls," he shouted, accompanied by a piercing howl of electronic feedback, "I want to hear a big 'oooh' from all the virgins in tonight."

The two hundred women who packed the dimly lit dance floor had been in a frenzied state of Lover Boy anticipation since stepping onto their respective coaches at six o'clock. They oohed as one.

Anna and Ed sat at one of the tables on a raised carpeted area which formed a border round the dance floor. Despite Elaine's violet creams, they were both starving and were stuffing themselves with peanuts. Going down less easily was the on-the-house liebfraumilch, presented to them on their arrival by Tony, the Starlight Club manager.

Seeing what a state Anna had got herself into about missing the Lover Boys, Tony had shown them to a table, ordered the bottle of wine and kept reassuring her that all she and Ed had missed was the drag act. The Lover Boys weren't due onstage for over an hour. This gave Anna plenty of time to do her interview with Kelly the butter churner. The problem was, how was she going to find her among all these people? She had popped her head into the bar just to see if Kelly was still there, but it was empty.

"Now I want you to put your hands together," the MC continued, "for Kelly who's marrying her Dave tomorrow, Dawn who's just got divorced and Shirley who's having her tubes tied on Monday."

The crowd, divided by age into crop tops worn over flares and hooped gold earrings worn with black-cherry lip liner, whooped, cheered and clapped as the MC presented each of the women with a bottle of Asti Spumante. At the foot of the stage Kelly, Dawn and Shirley posed for the Sureshots.

The next minute "Like a Virgin" was blaring out of four massive speakers and women from seventeen to seventy were bopping around in their white stilettos, cameras looped over their wrists.

While Ed fiddled with his lenses, Anna watched the dancing. After a few minutes she realized that the music was relaxing her, and that she was beginning to enjoy herself. She poured herself another glass of wine and then picked up the white menu card which was propped up between the salt and pepper pots. She had had no idea the club was serving dinner. They had a choice of grapefruit segments or melon cocktail, followed by chicken croquettes with seasonal vegetables and Black Forest gateau. Anna read the menu to Ed.

"I don't know about you, but I could murder a couple of chicken croquettes, even ones from a cheapo mass catering pack."

Ed looked up from his lenses and grimaced.

"Forget it. . . . I'll cook us something later. Graham, my mate who owns the cottage, always leaves the deep freeze loaded up with M and S packets. He won't mind me nicking a couple."

The words "cook," "us" and "later" ricocheted around Anna's brain like three baffled bullets. Did that mean he had meant to kiss her; that it hadn't been a faux pas? Was he assuming she was going to spend the night with him at this mate's cottage? Anna wasn't sure whether her sudden light-headedness was a result of lust or Liebfraumilch.

Before she had a chance to ask Ed what, precisely, he had in mind for the rest of the evening, he was on his feet, urgently snapping away at everything as if he were back in Grozny.

"Look, Kelly with the bottle of bubbly is probably our Kelly the butter churner. Why don't we go over and grab her now. You can get a quick interview and I'll take some pictures. I'll take some more while they're throwing their knickers at the Lover Boys. I won't need more than half an hour. Then we can be on our way."

From what Anna could tell, Ed was making the arrogant assumption that she was coming back to the cottage with him. Despite having the hots for him she was put out that he hadn't had the courtesy to actually invite her. She realized she was severely pissed off with him and told him so.

"Does that mean you won't be coming?" he said, suddenly looking even more miserable than he had on the drive down.

"I didn't say that," she said, still trying to sound cross, but failing. There was something Anna found intensely appealing about the good-natured way he refused to rise to her anger. As she picked up her notebook and shoulder bag from the table, Ed kissed her very briefly on the back of her neck. He then took her arm and began steering her towards Kelly's table, which was by the fire exit. The drag artist in crimson lamé and big ginger hair had just come onstage to start the second half of his act. Within seconds he was cracking jokes about foreskins, second comings and Chinese restaurants called the Wan Kin.

Anna suspected they could probably hear the laughter as far away as Weymouth.

IT'S LOIKE WE'RE ONLY DOING THE SAME AS BLOKES 'AVE done for years. Oi mean, if it's OK for them to watch women strip, why can't we come and see fellas get their clothes arf? And when you go to a Lover Boy show, it's all girls, so you're not getting felt up by fellas every five minutes . . . and there's no husband or boyfriend looking over your shoulder telling you how to behave. I mean, my Dave, he's great an' all that, an' I really loves 'im, but he's a bit old-fashioned, and he don't roight approve of me getting drunk or swearing. He likes me to be a lady. Comin' to a show like this, you can . . . you know . . . let yer hair down and be a bit filthy. S'all about goin' a bit wild

with yer mates . . . 'specially with this bein' my last night of
freedom an' all. . . ."

While Ed and Anna sat waiting for the Lover Boys to come
on, Anna put on her Walkman headphones and listened to the
tape of her interview with Kelly.

"There's some great stuff here," she said to Ed as she took
off her headphones. "With a bit of tweaking and tidying up I
can get some great quotes out of this."

"Anna, tell me," he said, giving her a sexy grin, "have you
ever written a piece you didn't make up?"

"Ed, change the record. You were going on about tabloid
hacks making it all up when we were on that job two years ago.
Stop being such a fucking wind-up merchant . . . the Lover
Boys are about to come on. Be a good boy and go and snap
something. It's easy, you know."

"I always love watching the way women's nipples go hard
when they're turned on," he said, still smiling.

"Ed," she said, sighing with mock weariness, determined not
to give him the satisfaction of blushing and slapping her hands
to her chest, "the only thing you are doing to my tits right now
is getting on them."

Giving her a look that could have melted frozen Bournville,
Ed stood up and slung his camera bag over his shoulder. As he
walked over to the butter churners, Anna leaned forward and
quickly felt her nipples under the table. They were as hard as
walnuts.

After a couple of minutes, the lights went down and the MC
picked up his mike from the stand, ready to perform one final
act of tantalizing foreplay with the audience.

"They're hunky, they're horny . . . they've got rock-hard
bodies that give off more heat than a lava flow. Lie back and
get ready for an eruption. They're here, and they're available
now. Girls . . . step into your fantasy."

The women went berserk, to the accompaniment of "When
a Man Loves a Woman." It was all bass and drums, the musical
equivalent, Anna decided, of cheap aftershave.

As the stage filled with dry ice, the audience quieted down a little. Then out of the haze came the six dancing Lover Boys, dressed as firemen in yellow helmets, heavy jackets and huge black boots. Each of them was wielding a large plastic axe which looked like something bought in Toys "R" Us.

Somebody yelled, "What a bunch of prats." Then the entire audience joined in, screaming at them to "Get 'em off" and "Show us yer willie."

The Lover Boys' dancing talent was nonexistent. They stomped around in their huge black boots, rhythmically hitting the air, stroking their crotches and thrusting their hips, barely trying, Anna thought, to keep time with the music or each other. Nobody seemed to mind because by now the boys were down to their jockstraps. They'd torn off their firemen uniforms in one flamboyant movement. This maneuver was particularly easy because the uniforms were only held together at the seams with Velcro.

A few women couldn't resist the chiseled tanned torsos and concave stomachs. Four of them ran up on stage for a quick feel of pumped-up baby-oiled pec, but were swiftly removed by the MC.

The Lover Boys ended the routine with some simulated masturbation involving firemen's hoses. After a few minutes of rubbing, massaging and rhythmic hip thrusting, there was a perfectly synchronized ejaculation of fireworks. The audience hysteria was eclipsed minutes later when they repeated the performance using banana skins and suntan cream.

FOR THE NEXT HALF HOUR OR SO, THE LOVER BOYS CAME ON dressed as sailors in white suits, Tarzans in leopardskin jockstraps and Aztec warriors in cardboard masks.

Then the pace slowed down and one Lover Boy, bare-chested except for a dinner jacket and bow tie, stood alone in the center of the stage. Behind him was a small table covered with a white cloth. It was laid for two. In the center of the table was a bottle of champagne and two glasses.

Anna, who had become increasingly bored as the Lover Boys segued from one uninspired dance routine into the next, had put on her Walkman headphones again and was going through her interview with Kelly for the second time and taking notes. She realized she had plenty of material to fill the bulk of the piece, but was struggling to find something which would make a strong final paragraph.

She looked up briefly from her note-taking and realized she recognized the Lover Boy standing on the stage from his picture in the program. His name was Tor. According to the blurb he was never happier than when taking a chick out on the back of his Harley.

As Frank Sinatra sang "It Had to Be You," Tor walked into the audience and told them he was looking for a companion to "take to dinner." He turned and nodded his head towards the table. The audience screamed with delight. Some poor cow was for it.

Anna missed his announcement because she was listening to Kelly on her headphones and still trying to find a decent quote for the final paragraph. It was a good fifteen seconds before she noticed Tor standing in front of her, holding out his hand. Nauseating as she found men with long blond highlights and sunbed tans, she had to admit he was pretty. She took off her headphones and was about to ask him what was going on when he gave her a Persil-white smile, reached down for her hand and gently pulled her to her feet.

The penny finally dropped that Tor wanted her to go with him onto the stage when she saw Ed bounding back towards their table, bashing into people's chairs en route. Once he'd reached it he positioned himself in front of Anna and Tor and began taking pictures. Anna shot him a horrified pleading look which said, "For Chrissake get me out of this," but he ignored it and carried on clicking.

"Ed, you bastard," she hissed. "I'll never fucking forgive you for this."

A couple of seconds later she was on the stage and Tor was opening the bottle of champagne. Naturally, its contents spurted forth with appropriate magnificence and the audience roared. He poured Anna a glass and then began taking off his jacket and bow tie. She stood sipping it, trying desperately to look as if she were game for a laugh, but finding it impossible to do much more than stare down nervously at her feet. In an exaggerated gesture, Tor threw his jacket onto the floor. He then put one arm round Anna's waist and drew her close to him as he slowly unzipped his fly and stepped out of his trousers. The women in the audience were almost making themselves sick with excitement as he rotated his hips and thrust his well-filled crotch towards her. She didn't know where to put her eyes and did her best to focus on a waitress with long greasy hair who was sulking in the corner.

Anna had no idea how he did it, but the next thing she knew, she was on the floor and Tor was kneeling down, pushing her legs apart. Taking his weight on his hands so that their bodies wouldn't actually touch, he then laid himself above her and began moving up and down, in time to the music.

"Come on, sweetheart, relax," he whispered, seeing the look of abject horror on Anna's face. "Just go with it."

Her instinct was to hit him, but at the same time she felt she couldn't disappoint the audience, who, judging by all the whistling and *wurrgh* noises coming from the tables, were lapping it up.

Anna thought this had to be the most degrading thing that had ever happened to her—far worse than when the consultant had come onto the ward with five male students the day after she'd delivered Josh and asked if each of them could take a look at her prolapsed back passage.

By now, Tor had repositioned the pair of them so that his naked rear was facing the audience. He began moving himself along her body until his crotch was over her face, millimeters from her skin. By now her humiliation had turned to fizzing rage. She also felt as if she was about to suffocate.

Tor continued to keep his back to the audience. As a consequence, only he and Anna were privy to what happened next. Anna's anger finally got the better of her and she made a grab for Tor's black leather posing pouch. The amount of adrenaline pumping through her must have given her three or four times her normal strength. The thing simply came away in her hand.

For several seconds, Tor froze and looked helplessly at Anna. Anna froze too, not because she had embarrassed him and felt guilty, but because she couldn't believe her eyes.

Tor, with his huge granitelike torso and thighs which could crush cars, possessed the smallest set of genitals she had ever seen on an adult male. His tiny circumcised penis looked exactly like the top of a roll-on deodorant bottle. She stared at the leather jockstrap. It was stuffed with cotton wool.

IN THOSE FEW SECONDS, ANNA COMPOSED HER FINAL paragraph.

CHAPTER NINETEEN

WHAT DO YOU MEAN, WHY DID I come back with you? . . . 'Cos I thought we could spend the night sitting here in this cottage, sharing insights into Dorset dairy farming. . . . For Chrissake, Ed, why do you think I'm here?"

"No, that's not what I meant." Ed gave the pasta a stir and turned to face her. "I think we both know what we have in mind for tonight. What I'm trying to say is that in my experience, happily married women, particularly happily married Jewish ones, don't usually leap into bed with men who aren't their husbands."

Anna stared into her wineglass and ran her finger round the rim. She said nothing and neither did Ed. She was aware of him backing off, allowing her to get her thoughts together.

She watched him strain the pasta into a red plastic colander. He bent his head into the crook of his arm and wiped the steam off his face with his shirtsleeve.

Anna had assumed that Ed's interest in her didn't extend beyond sleeping with her, so that for a few hours, at least, he could push his pain about his children to the back of his mind. It hadn't entered her mind that he would be curious about her marriage.

"You know you should really rinse the starch off the spaghetti with boiling water—otherwise it goes all glutinous," she said, dodging his question. She couldn't help wondering if he was genuinely interested in finding out about her, or whether he was merely inquiring out of good manners. After all, she'd spent hours listening to his troubles this afternoon. He was probably doing no more than returning the gesture.

"I know what you're thinking," he said, piling the spaghetti into bowls. "I'm not asking out of duty and this is not some kind of cynical verbal foreplay. Look, it doesn't take a genius to see that deep down, underneath all the wisecracks, you're pretty fucking miserable."

Anna looked at him. He had stopped dishing out the pasta and was staring straight into her eyes. Until this minute she had thought she was reasonably happy. After all, she'd had more decent sex in the last few weeks than she'd had in years with Dan. As Ed continued to look at her without saying a word, it struck her for the first time that she had been kidding herself. Ed was right. She was still unhappy. Sleeping with Charlie and Alex hadn't made her problem with Dan go away. How was it possible to fool herself into thinking she was happy, and yet fail to convince somebody she barely knew?

Ed Brzezinski, she realized, not only got inside women's pants, he got inside their minds. She wanted to hump him there and then, until he was nothing but husk.

He walked round to her side of the breakfast bar and stood in front of her.

"Come on. . . ." he said, taking her glass of wine from her hand and putting it on the worktop. "Tell me . . . what is it?"

She sat looking up at him. Her eyes were suddenly glassy with tears.

"You're right . . . I'm not happy." Her tone was flat. She knew that her promise about not discussing Dan with any of her lovers was about to be broken.

Ed pulled her to her feet, put his arms round her and held her. Anna put her head on his shoulder and sobbed like a child.

WHEN SHE'D FINISHED, ED KISSED HER ON THE FOREHEAD and wiped her tear-stained face with his hand.

"Go and sit in the living room. I'll bring supper in and we can eat and talk in front of the fire."

Like all the other rooms in the cottage, the living room was tiny. It had a low, beamed ceiling and uneven white walls. Anna sat down on the rug in front of the fire, leaning her back against the navy linen sofa. Graham had left the fire laid in the grate. Ed had lit it when they arrived and now the room was baking.

After a minute, Ed came in and handed her a plate of spaghetti covered in tomato sauce and Parmesan.

"That looks wonderful. I can't remember the last time I ate so late. It must be after midnight."

"Quarter to," he said, looking at his watch. He went over to the window and threw it open. Anna felt the rush of cool air on the back of her neck.

Ed sat himself down next to her on the floor.

"So . . ." he said, curling spaghetti round his fork.

ANNA TALKED, ALMOST NONSTOP, FOR THREE HOURS. EVERY-thing just spewed out of her. When she began telling him about Dan's hypochondria and his collection of medical appliances, she was expecting Ed to laugh, but he didn't. He just listened and wiped her face whenever she cried. When she told him that she had lived for years with virtually no sex, he put his arm round her shoulders, drew her close to him and kissed the side of her face. She felt his tears on her skin.

It struck her yet again that Ed was playing the role of counselor and confessor merely to get her into bed, but as the hours went by he didn't attempt to make a move on her. He appeared to be genuinely concerned about her unhappiness.

"Come on," he said eventually, looking at his watch. "You're knackered. I think all you need tonight is sleep. The beds in both rooms are made up. Take your pick . . . and there should be a full tank of water by now if you want a shower."

Disappointment went through Anna like a skewer through a kebab. She wanted to run round the room protesting, screaming and proclaiming her wide-awakeness, the way children do when they are ordered up to bed on a bright summer's evening, but she knew he was just being kind. Begging him to make love to her would be too humiliating.

She had a quick shower to get the remains of the muddy ditch out of her hair, put on one of her baggy T-shirts and fell into bed.

She closed her eyes, assuming that sleep would overtake her in a matter of seconds. It didn't. Five minutes later she was lying on her side, propped up on her elbow, gazing out of the tiny bedroom window. It was almost pitch black outside. She could just make out a couple of branches shaking gently in the breeze.

The reason Anna couldn't sleep was because she was remembering standing in Brenda's kitchen the day six weeks ago she had gone to her and pretty much asked for her permission to take a series of lovers. Her words to Brenda kept going round and round her head. What was it she had said? "I don't want heavy, I'll-show-you-my-angst-if-you-show-me-yours-type relationships and then we fall in love. I just want their bodies."

Ed had certainly shown her his angst. She had shown him hers. She knew herself well enough to be certain she would never have done that if she didn't feel something for him.

Ed was a womanizer and a recovering arrogant git, and yet she had invited him into her mind, into her most private part.

In Ed, unlike Charlie, she sensed a genuine desire for closeness. What scared and excited her at the same time was that she sensed precisely the same desire in herself. She wanted to get to know this man. She felt easy and relaxed with him. She loved the way they teased one another, the way he almost seemed to enjoy it when she got stroppy with him. She remembered the way he'd smiled at her in the Starlight Club when she told him he was getting on her tits.

Anna knew they were two vulnerable, searching souls, hungry for comfort. Ed had lost a wife and might be about to lose his children; she felt she had lost Dan to his neuroses. She knew in the end that they might not be right for each other. She also knew that if she began a proper relationship with Ed, not one based simply on sex, she wouldn't be able to keep it from Dan and her marriage would be over.

She turned onto her back and stared at the ceiling. Lying there in the dark, drunk on wine and exhaustion, she suddenly didn't give a monkey's about the dangers of starting a relationship with Ed. The only thing that mattered was that she was falling in love—and what she wanted more than anything at that moment was Ed in bed beside her.

Anna kicked off the duvet. She would run into Ed's room and throw herself on top of him. What stopped her was the sudden fear that maybe she'd got it all wrong, and that the reason Ed had sent her to bed alone was because he had changed his mind and maybe he didn't fancy her after all.

Lying there in the dark, desire seeped through her body like whiskey on a winter's night. She sat up and pulled her T-shirt over her head. The tree branches made a cracking sound in the wind. Lying down again, letting her head sink into the thick feather pillow, she ran her hands slowly over her breasts and belly. She drew up her legs and let them drop to the side and with both hands began stroking the insides of her thighs. After a few moments she parted her labia and felt the wetness flowing out of her. Her belly quivered as she ran her finger over her clitoris. She closed her eyes and felt the muscles tighten in her vagina. Her gentle strokes gradually became harder and faster.

"Why don't you let me do that?"

Anna froze, partly with shock and partly with mortification. How could she not have heard the door handle? Opening her eyes she saw Ed standing just inside the bedroom, watching her, his body backlit by the landing light. He was naked except for a towel round his waist. He'd obviously just got out of the shower.

In a second he was sitting on the edge of the bed and leaning over her. She could feel his breath on her face. Although she hadn't the slightest idea what she was going to say, she opened her mouth to speak. Ed put his finger to her lips.

"Ssh, 's OK. Please don't be embarrassed . . . you looked so beautiful."

He brought his mouth towards her and kissed her. As his tongue entered her mouth, she felt his hand move down over her stomach towards her bush. She put her arms round his neck and breathed in his warm, damp smell.

Ed played with her bush for a few seconds and then pulled away from her. He knelt on the bed and took off his towel. Anna reached out and began running the palm of her hand over the top of his penis. After a while a tiny pearl of semen appeared. She touched it with her forefinger and gently rubbed it away.

"I want to feel you inside me," she whispered.

"In a minute . . . there's plenty of time." Ed moved himself round so that he was sitting up, leaning against the bed's wooden headboard.

"Come here," he said, his arms stretched out towards her.

Anna crawled across the bed and sat herself between his legs, her back against his chest. "But I can't see you," she protested.

"Just let me hold you. Close your eyes."

He held her with one arm while she let her head flop back onto the top of his shoulder.

Gently he opened her legs. A moment later he had found her clitoris. Anna gasped. As his fingers glided over the wetness, she thrust her pelvis up towards his hand. Every so often he nipped the base of her neck and ran his tongue inside her ear. As her body relaxed and melted into his, Anna felt herself swimming in pure pleasure.

Afterwards, Ed carried on holding her. For what seemed like ages, they sat silently in the dark, listening to each other's breathing.

Finally Anna turned round to face him and began running her tongue over his belly. She watched his penis stiffen and turn upwards towards his navel. A moment later he had pulled her on top of him. Their kissing became fierce and urgent. She could feel his fingers almost digging into her buttocks. They rolled across the bed in a tangled, breathy heap like two frenzied creatures attempting to caress and devour each other at the same time.

The next thing Anna knew, Ed was standing on the floor, his hands round her ankles.

"Bring your bottom to the edge of the bed."

Anna obliged. Ed pushed her legs up onto her chest. She felt him run his tongue over her clitoris and put some gentle pressure on her anus. Finally she was aware of his penis rubbing the entrance to her vagina. She winced and let out a tiny whimper as she felt the sensation, which exists somewhere between pain and sublime pleasure, of him pushing himself fractionally too deep inside her. She heard herself beg him to thrust harder.

Anna came first. Then, a few seconds later, Ed let out a huge sigh. Gently, he lowered the top half of his body onto hers. As she held him and stroked his head, she felt the same emotion she used to feel years ago when she and Dan made love. She'd only ever been able to describe it as a feeling of coming home—a sense that she belonged with this person.

. . .

ANNA OPENED HER EYES A FEW HOURS LATER TO SEE THE sun streaming in through the tiny cottage window and Ed standing by the side of the bed. He was bare-chested and wearing yesterday's jeans with the fly buttons half undone.

"For you," he said, putting a mug of tea and a couple of biscuits down on the bedside table. "I nicked the Garibaldis from the stash of crap confectionery Graham keeps behind his jars of cep mushrooms. You could have Jammy Dodgers if you prefer."

Anna laughed and said the Garibaldis would be fine.

"Listen, Anna," Ed said enthusiastically as he climbed over the bed and sat himself down beside her, "I really don't want you to go home. I've got the cottage for the weekend and I thought once I'd got the car sorted out, assuming there's nothing major the matter with it, we could do a bit of sightseeing and go out for dinner tonight. The thing is, even though you're the most stroppy, argumentative tart I've ever met, for some perverted reason I love being with you and I'd really like to spend more time with you. What d'you reckon?"

Anna dipped her Garibaldi into her tea and bit into it. She decided to ignore the stroppy, argumentative tart bit.

"Ed, I feel the same. I have only ever felt like this twice in my life. The first was when I met Dan. I'd like nothing more than to stay here with you, but I must get back to my kids. I promised I'd be home for lunch. Plus I've got some thinking I need to do."

"About us?"

She nodded, then grabbed his wrist to look at the time.

"Christ, it's gone eleven." She watched a bit of sodden biscuit break off and splash into her tea.

"Please stay." His voice was pleading.

"I really can't," she said tenderly. Seeing the look of utter heartbreak on his face, she put her mug down on the bedside table and pushed him down onto the bed. She then began undoing the rest of his fly buttons. Moments later he was lying naked beside her and she was covering his penis with her mouth.

"Christ, Anna," he said between moans, "you don't give blow jobs, you give entire blow careers."

Afterwards he cradled her in his arms.

"Ed, there's something I feel I ought to tell you," she said, playing with the column of thick hairs below his navel.

Ed sat up, clearly alarmed.

"Bloody hell, Anna, I've had enough bad news in the last twenty-four hours. Please don't give me any more."

"It's not bad news, exactly, but you might not want to see me again when I've told you what it is." Anna took a deep breath and told him about the *Clitoris-Centered Woman* article she was writing for the *Daily Mercury*.

When she'd finished, Ed stared at her for a few seconds.

"So you mean you've used me, quite cynically, as part of your research for this piece?"

"Look, I admit that's how it started out. Please don't be angry." There was panic rising in her voice. "The reason I'm telling you this is because, like you, I feel there's something between us which is based on more than just sex, and ₁ . . ."

But Ed didn't let her finish. He burst out laughing.

"I had no idea you took your job so seriously. I promise, never again will I accuse you of making up the stuff you write."

"I don't get it. If I were you, I'd be furious."

"You told me, that's the important thing. Besides, you don't fancy you like I do."

With that he pulled her on top of him and kissed her.

CHAPTER TWENTY

ANNA PUT HER KEYS DOWN ON THE hall table next to the kids' lunchboxes. These were meant to live in the kitchen when they weren't at school. Pretty sure what she would find inside, Anna opened Amy's red plastic box. As she'd suspected, it contained an empty bashed-in apple juice box, a quarter of a stale peanut butter sandwich and a half-eaten nectarine which had grown green fur overnight and was oozing over a letter from the PTA pleading for cakes for the school bring-and-buy sale.

Feeling slightly irritated with Dan for not emptying them, she picked up the lunchboxes.

"Hey, you lot," she shouted in no direction in particular. "I'm back."

There was no reply.

Anna wandered into the living room. Mrs. Fredericks had been in yesterday to clean, but the room was a dump. It also stank of food which had been left out overnight. There were newspapers, empty glasses and a couple of dirty plates on the floor. One of the plates contained the cause of the stink—an untouched chili dog.

With her free hand, Anna picked up an empty bottle of Red Label from the coffee table and held it up. She was certain that yesterday it had been full.

The untidiness annoyed her; the sight of the empty whiskey bottle, on the other hand, worried her. Dan drank an occasional Scotch late at night, but she had never known him to have more than a glass or two. Perhaps he'd had a mate over last night and they'd got pissed? If that had been the case, he would have tidied up this morning. The mess in the living room had all the hallmarks of a man who had spent the night drinking alone.

Anna ran out of the room and shouted up the stairs.

"Amy, Josh, anyone . . . speak to me if you're up there."

Silence. Dan must have taken the kids out.

Anna went into the kitchen. She put the whiskey bottle and the lunchboxes on the worktop and began sifting through the scraps of paper, old envelopes and ends of American legal pads which always lived in a pile next to the bread bin, to see if Dan had left her a note to say when they'd be back. There was nothing. Anna had a feeling, the kind of feeling her late grandmother always referred to as a "presentiment"—because she could never think of the word "premonition"—that something was seriously wrong.

She began pacing up and down the kitchen, trying to decide whom to phone. Each time she reached the hob, she did an about-turn and walked towards the door which led into the hall. On her third or fourth about-turn, she looked up and saw Dan standing in the doorway. She jumped with fright and then bellowed at him.

"Do you mind telling me what the hell has been going on

here?" She picked up the whiskey bottle and thrust it angrily in his face. His eyes peered out at her from puffy hollows. He needed a hairwash and a shave. And he was wearing the same shirt and trousers he'd had on when he'd left the house the previous morning.

"Nothing very much, other than I felt the need to get mightily slaughtered last night. You'll find an empty vodka bottle in the bin if you look."

Anna found the mock joviality in his voice almost menacing. "What have you done with the kids?"

"Brenda's." Dan went to the fridge and took out a carton of orange juice. He closed the door and glared at her.

"Anyway, I think I am the one who should be asking you what's been going on."

Anna felt herself begin to tremble. "What are you talking about?" She had no idea why she had asked such a fatuous question. She knew precisely what he was talking about. She didn't know how he had found out, but the game, her game, was up.

Dan finished pouring juice into a glass.

"What I'm talking about is this." He took a piece of paper from his back pocket and held it towards her. Anna took it and unfolded it. It was her Barclaycard statement. The £75 payment to Liaisons Dangereux jumped out at her.

Dan finished his juice and put the glass down on the worktop. "Oh, I nearly forgot—there's this too."

He handed her a postcard. It was from Charlie. It was one she hadn't seen before. He had sent it from San Diego.

"Where did you get it?" she said almost in a whisper.

"When I took the kids round to Brenda's last night, I saw it lying on the kitchen table. It seemed odd that a postcard clearly meant for you should have Brenda's address on it. So, nosy bastard that I am, I picked it up. I particularly like the bit where he says, 'You're simply the best.' I find it hard to believe you slept with a bloke for whom the pinnacle of literary expression is to quote from Tina Turner.

"Oh, and *then*," he continued, "there's Reenie Theydon-

Bois, but you don't have to explain about her because I know all I need to know. After a little research yesterday, I found the number for Liaisons Dangereux and I spoke to her last night. Charming woman. Says she found you a 'delaytful' doctor to screw."

Anna could feel the color draining from her face.

"What, she told you?" she gasped, holding onto the worktop for support. "She promised everything was confidential."

"It's funny how unconfidential everything can become when you threaten to report her for operating illegally as an escort agency when Liaisons Dangereux is registered at Companies House as a shih tzu breeding establishment.

"How many men have there been, Anna? How many men have you fucked in the last couple of months?" He was shouting at her now, his face almost touching hers. His breath reeked of booze and he was spraying her with saliva. "Two, three, four, a dozen maybe. How many, Anna, how fucking many?" A split second later she felt a sudden and intense burning sensation down one side of her face. Her hand leaped to her cheek. Her head spinning, she caught hold of the worktop to steady herself. Dan stared down at his hand in disbelief. In all the years he had known Anna, he had never laid a violent hand on her.

Anna fought the instinct to back away from him. Instead she stayed put. Dan looked up again.

"Three," she said, staring into his eyes with a forced calmness. "There have been three. I managed to find three men who wanted to make love to me when you wouldn't. Three men who made me feel beautiful and wanted me while you sat at home taking your fucking blood pressure."

Dan scraped a chair noisily along the polished floorboards and sat down at the kitchen table. He put his head in his hands.

Anna sat down opposite him. She reached across and touched his arm. He withdrew from her in an instant. After a couple of minutes he looked up.

"If I'm honest, I think I probably saw it coming. Brenda tried to warn me a few weeks ago that the illness thing was driving you to breaking point. She hinted you might do something like this."

Anna realized she felt no anger towards Brenda for speaking to Dan. She knew it was just her friend's way of trying to help.

"So, did Brenda mention the article I'm supposed to be writing?"

He shook his head. "What article?"

For the second time that day, Anna explained about the *Clitoris-Centered Woman* piece.

"Talk about crap timing." He laughed bitterly. "You decide to get laid at the same time as I try to repair our marriage. After Brenda told me how much my hypochondria was affecting you, I went straight out and found a shrink. I didn't tell you I was seeing her because I had this plan to come home one day, announce that I was cured and whisk you off on some exotic holiday."

"I think at some level I knew you were up to something. I had the feeling you were less obsessed with your health lately. The thing is, Dan, you left it too late. You know as well as I do that you should have gone into therapy years ago."

"Probably."

"Dan, I'm sorry. I'm truly sorry I've hurt you."

"Yeah, right," he said flatly. He paused. "There's something else you need to know." In an almost matter-of-fact tone he told her about his visit to Dr. Harper, the chest X ray and the certainty in his mind that he had lung cancer.

Anna listened in horror-struck silence.

"But you don't know for definite," she said when he'd finished. She was doing her best to sound upbeat. "You haven't had the results of the X ray and then there will be loads of other tests they'll want to do."

"Anna, you weren't there. You didn't hear Dr. Harper, the tone of voice she used when she put down her stethoscope. She's been a doctor for thirty years. Believe me, she recognizes the beginnings of lung cancer when she hears it."

Anna wanted to hug him, hold him, but she knew he would push her away.

"So," she said, "what happens now?"

Dan sat up straight and tapped his palm briskly on the table. "I should have the X-ray results in a few days. In the meantime, I shall go and see a solicitor about a divorce. I suggest you do the same."

"OK," she said wearily. "If that's what you really want."

Dan stood up and glared at her again. "And get this absolutely straight, Anna: if by any chance I am not ill, I will be going for custody of Amy and Josh. In my opinion sluts do not make fit mothers."

Those last words were the most hateful she had ever heard come from his mouth. She would have preferred it if he'd hit her again.

Dan walked to the kitchen door and said he was moving in with his cousin Beany for a couple of weeks. For a few seconds Anna was transported back to Gants Hill and the night she and Dan had met at the party to celebrate Beany passing his bar finals. Dan had always kept in touch with his cousin. It was Beany who dragged Dan to West Ham most Saturday afternoons. He had a lot of time on his hands since his divorce the previous year. These days he lived alone in a flat in Hammersmith. After ten years of marriage, he had been too shellshocked by the split to get swiftly back into the swing of dating women. He would, thought Anna, probably be only too grateful for some blokeish company.

She followed Dan into the hall. She watched him take his jacket from the hat stand and pick up a large canvas bag. It still had the flight tags on the handles from their Tobago holiday.

He opened the front door and paused. After a few seconds he turned round.

"D'you know what? The bugger of it is, I still love you."

After he had gone, Anna sat at the bottom of the stairs. She knew that if she had got down on her knees and begged him to forgive her she might have been able to persuade him to stay. But she couldn't bring herself to do it. Despite what he'd said about being ill, despite his plans to fight her for the children, she couldn't lie to him anymore and pretend she wanted to be with him. She was glad he had left her. She needed to find out if she had a future with Ed.

A NNA, WILL YOU WAKE UP AND SMELL THE DEEP SHIT you've got yourself into?" Anna had gone round to Brenda's a couple of hours later, to pick up Amy and Josh. While the children played upstairs, Brenda was laying into her. "You're an arrogant cow, you know that, don't you? Nearly two months ago, you came round 'ere, you sat on the same chair you're sitting on now and tried to convince me that you were capable of living by Rachel whatserface's rules. Anna Shapiro had it sussed. Anna Shapiro reckoned she was capable of having affairs just for the sex, that Dan would never be any the wiser and that she would never fall in love. Surprise, fucking surprise, she fell arse over tit. Look at what you are doing, Anna. You're about to flush your marriage and two kids down the can, all for the sake of some slimy git with a long lens. I mean, you can't really believe he gave a flying fuck last night about your happiness or your relationship with Dan—God help me, I cannot believe I am having to explain this to a woman of nearly forty. Anna, read my lips, he just wanted to get 'is leg over. For Chrissake, you told me five minutes ago, the man is a serial shagger."

"Brenda, will there ever come a day when you stop telling me how to live my life? At least I haven't got myself up the spout."

"Maybe not, but at the rate you're getting through blokes these days, you might find yourself ending up with a nice dose of the clap."

Furious, Anna got to her feet.

"For the first time in years," she spat, "I've got a chance of some happiness. I agree, it may not work out with Ed, but at least I want to find out. What I could really do with just now is your support, but it seems that's not an offer."

Anna grabbed her car keys from the kitchen table and stormed out of the kitchen. Brenda heard her yell upstairs for Amy and Josh. A minute later the front door slammed.

"Shit, shit, shit." Brenda stood at the kitchen sink and chucked a dripping dishcloth at the window.

CHAPTER TWENTY-ONE

ANNA WASN'T DUE TO SEE ED until Monday night. Barely able to contain her excitement at the thought of being with him again, she filled Sunday with relentless activity. This included writing the hen-party piece, which was scheduled to appear the following Sunday, cleaning out the bathroom medicine cabinet and binning a packet of condoms which had expired in 1994. She also made a dozen chocolate Rice Krispie cakes for the school bring-and-buy sale.

Keeping busy meant that she didn't have to give any thought to what Brenda had said to her on Saturday night. It wasn't until she arrived at Ed's flat in Notting Hill that she began to question the wisdom of letting Dan walk out.

The flat was small and a bit shabby, the kind of place twenty-two-year-olds rent when they get their first job. This didn't bother Anna. She knew Ed was broke. He was paying maintenance as well as the mortgage on the house he'd bought with Tilda. What moved Anna almost to tears was going into the living room and coming across the piles of legal correspondence covering his desk. She picked up a handful of letters. Some appeared to be from his solicitor, others were from Tilda's. Each related to his battle with Tilda over the children. It hit Anna that if she pursued her relationship with Ed, she would find herself being drawn into the battle. She would have to live it with him and support him emotionally, maybe even financially. What hit her even harder was realizing that if she allowed her marriage to end and Dan fought her for Josh and Amy, she would find herself fighting a similar battle. She could face months, if not years, of Dan's vitriol, legal brawling and court appearances. Christ only knew what effect it would have on the children.

"You seem miles away," Ed said, coming in from the kitchen with two glasses of wine.

"Sorry. I'm OK, just a bit knackered. It's only beginning to hit me that Dan has actually gone. I've also been worrying about what to tell the children. I've said he's away on a story, but I can't keep on lying. I keep imagining their little faces when they find out the truth."

"I know, it'll be nasty, but you mustn't do it alone. Dan's their father. He should be there too. Come on," he said, putting his arm round her shoulders, "I've got something that'll cheer you up."

Anna followed him into a tiny, windowless room. A naked bulb mounted on the wall cast a soft red light. She recognized the acrid smell of photographic fixer from school, where she had once dabbled vaguely in photography.

"This used to be a walk-in larder, but I turned it into a darkroom. Take a look in the tray."

Anna took a sip of wine and bent over the white plastic tray. Floating in the colorless chemical were a couple of ten-by-eight

black-and-white prints. They showed Anna, her face swathed
in panic, being led up onstage by Tor the Lover Boy.

"God," she said, putting down her wineglass and picking up
one of the photographs with a pair of tongs, "it's Imelda
Marcos and she's just discovered Freeman Hardy Willis have
gone bust. You really are a bastard, Ed."

"I know," he said softly.

As she continued leaning over Ed's workbench, looking at
the prints, she felt him rub his hand slowly over her bottom.
The weather had turned very warm and she was wearing a
summer dress and no pantyhose. He pulled the straight skirt
up to her hips and began stroking the inside of her thighs. She
inhaled deeply and let go of the tongs as he made her lean even
farther over the bench. He slipped his hand inside her knickers
and began stroking her bare behind. A moment later her panties were round her knees and he was sliding his fingers between her buttocks towards her clitoris.

At the time Anna had no idea what made her do it. All she
knew was that in a split second her feelings towards Ed had
changed. The only person she could think of was Dan. She
reached out and grabbed Ed's wrist, forcing him to stop.

"Ed, I'm sorry. I can't do this just now," she said, turning
round and reorganizing her clothes. "Please forgive me. Suddenly this, us, doesn't feel right. I need to go home."

She barely glanced at Ed's face. She knew it would be full of
shock and anguish. Instead she pushed past him, grabbed her
bag from the living-room floor and tore down the stairs into the
street.

It was only as she sat in the black cab on the way back to
Richmond that the penny dropped and she understood why she
had run out on Ed. She knew she'd started to have doubts
about getting involved with him the moment she saw all the
legal correspondence on his desk, but that was only part of the
reason.

She had run away because, unlikely as it seemed, in that five
minutes in the darkroom, she had begun to recapture her feelings for Dan. As Ed had started to caress her and touch her,

she had suddenly been reminded of the afternoon Dan had dragged her away from Amy's birthday party to make love to her.

She remembered it vividly. The day had been baking, just like today. In her mind she could feel the way Dan had lifted up her skirt, bent her over the desk in the bedroom—just like Ed had forced her over the workbench—and tugged at her pants. She remembered Dan reaching for the baby oil and dripping it onto her buttocks.

Anna swallowed hard, trying to force back the tears. She wished more than anything that she was going home to Dan. She wanted him to hold her, to make love to her. She'd always wanted Dan to make love to her. If it hadn't been Dan she'd wanted, why had she nagged him for so long about going into therapy? He knew as well as she did that she'd only taken lovers out of frustration and desperation. Now it was too late. She'd made the crucial mistake of believing she was in love with Ed. High on romantic euphoria, and virtually ignoring the possibility that Dan could be seriously ill, she'd allowed him to leave. When she should have been offering him her love and rocklike support and trying to share his burden, she was letting him walk out of the door. Anna had never really understood the meaning of self-hatred, but she was coming close.

The taxi continued along the Upper Richmond Road. As they drove through Sheen, Anna stared out of the cab window. She could see couples eating and laughing in the Café Rouge.

She grimaced and made a tight fist. Her agony was turning to fury. There was only one person who had got her into this mess—Rachel fucking Stern.

Anna was ready to write her article for Alison O'Farrell.

Her original plan, eight weeks ago, had been to disguise her personal account of becoming a clitoris-centered woman by inventing three women who committed adultery for fun and pretending to have interviewed them.

Suddenly, Anna had changed her mind. It was fear of losing her professional dignity which had persuaded her in the beginning to fictionalize the article. Two months on, she'd lost her husband and could even lose custody of her children. Her dignity was of no consequence.

Anna was ready to go public. She wanted the whole world to feel her agony and torment. She wanted the whole world to know that Rachel Stern was a liar and evil trickster who was conning women into believing they could spend their lives committing adultery without ever paying the price.

When she got home, she managed to hold back the tears long enough to say cheerio-see-you-in-the-morning to Denise, her baby-sitter. Then, sobbing almost loud enough to wake the children, she went into the kitchen and made a pot of coffee.

She put the coffee down on her desk, switched on the Anglepoise and began to get undressed. Dan's dressing gown was lying on the bed. She picked it up and held the soft, worn cotton to her face. As she breathed in his smell, she realized her entire body was aching for him.

Sitting at her desk wearing the dressing gown, Anna waited for the computer to boot up. Moments later her fingers were darting over the keyboard.

CHAPTER TWENTY-TWO

ANNA PUT DOWN HER KNIFE AND fork. Her amuse-gueules were distinctly unamusing. She'd chewed on dental X-ray plates which possessed more humor.

Alison O'Farrell had insisted on taking Anna out to lunch to cheer her up. She also wanted to discuss the *Clitoris-Centered Woman* article, which Anna had modemed to her at the *Daily Mercury* first thing that morning.

Alison had suggested trying the Bisto Tower, an expensive and oppressively trendy restaurant in South Kensington which had won awards for its ultramodern interior design.

Anna glanced round the crowded room and then back at the remaining bits of chopped charcuterie on her plate. Clearly nobody had pointed out to Mr. Bisto, or whomever, that cold, hard and minimalist didn't work for food.

"This is an absolutely knock-out piece of writing," Alison said, putting down Anna's article and downing the last of her kir royale. "I don't know what to say. This is the third time I've read it and I still think it's outstanding, truly outstanding. I've just got a few teensy thoughts."

Anna always felt bilious when features editors said this. It usually meant they wanted a complete rewrite.

"Look, Anna, I don't want you to take this the wrong way, but although it's brilliant—and it is absolutely brilliant—it's just a tad miserablist."

"Of course it's bloody miserable," Anna exploded. "The bitch has just destroyed my marriage. . . ."

"Anna, please try to calm down . . . I also think it needs toning down a little. The bit about Rachel Stern being a rank pus-filled boil on feminism's rotten underbelly really is a bit OTT. But don't worry, I'll sort it. I think all we need to say there is that, just like the rest of us, she gets the odd pimple at certain times of the month. I'll get somebody to phone her to find out about her beauty routine. Maybe we could include a few of her skin-care tips at the end of the piece—or even better, get someone from Clarins to advise her on concealers. We could do some before-and-after pictures."

Anna nearly choked on her spritzer. She'd always credited Alison with being bright. Suddenly it was like talking to Campbell McKee. Worse: in Campbell's case, buffoonery was an act. Alison didn't seem to realize she was being stupid.

"Alison, we're meant to be exposing Rachel Stern, not exfoliating her. The woman is a quack academic and a cheat. People need to be told."

"Yes, I understand that," Alison said, lighting up, "but what you've given me is so heavy. I was expecting something a bit more racy. Originally you were going to interview three adulterous women and I was going to have an entire page of bonk-and-tell. I have to be honest, Anna, in this piece you sound like one of those angst-ridden middle-class tarts on the *Guardian* women's page debating whether or not to get their kids grief counseling now the gerbil has died."

"So you're not going to use it then?" Anna said curtly.

"Anna . . . Of course I'm going to use it. But I will have to make some changes. You'll just have to trust me."

Realizing that she had no option, Anna shrugged her agreement.

Their gazpacho arrived. It was all ice cubes and virtually no soup.

For a few minutes they ate in awkward silence. Anna was suddenly in a serious quandary.

She hadn't banked on Alison's less-than-euphoric reaction to her piece. Over lunch, she had planned to drop the bombshell about Rachel Stern's cosmetic surgery. It was now occurring to her that Alison might not be particularly interested. She could see her ignoring the feminist hypocrite angle on the grounds that *Mercury* readers wouldn't get it.

"Come on, Anna," she could hear her saying. "The women who read the *Mercury* are uneducated working-class girls with a vocabulary of about two hundred words and most of those are connected with alcohol. They do not understand words like 'feminist' and 'hypocrite.' The only thing they would be interested in reading about would be how Rachel Stern felt about not being able to pull when she was a thirty-two A and how her life changed after her implants."

Anna took a mouthful of soup and crunched one of the pinkish ice cubes.

The thought of Alison not being interested in Rachel Stern's cosmetic surgery was particularly galling to Anna, since she'd spoken to Alex that morning and he had agreed to go on the record and tell his story.

He explained that if Stern complained to the General Medical Council, he could get struck off for breach of doctor–patient confidentiality, but bearing in mind that he had decided to give up medicine because the strain had clearly made him ill, and go back to Alabama with Kimberley to start a cotton farm, he didn't give a monkey's about the GMC, and the two-faced bitch could do what she liked.

ANNA FINALLY DECIDED THAT SHE SHOULD AT LEAST HAVE A go at convincing Alison that Stern's plastic surgery would make a cracking story. She waited for Alison to stub out her cigarette.

"By the way, I discovered an intriguing twist in the Rachel Stern saga which I thought might interest you. . . . It's—"

She got no further. She was interrupted by a terrible din coming from the next table. Anna and Alison turned to see a pretty woman in her early thirties, with a large bust, a mass of shoulder-length coppery curls and the cutest turned-up nose, giving the waiter hell.

"For crying out loud. . . ." The woman's New York accent rose up through a throat full of ball bearings, "I'm only gonna say this one more time, buster." She thumped the table. By now the entire restaurant was watching. The woman's female companion retreated into the huge menu. "I would like some tofu and vegetables gently sautéed in olive oil and garlic, hold the tamari. I would also like a side order of quinoa."

"Quinoa, madam? I don't think—"

"Yeah, you morahn, quinoa. It's a grain. Great for cleansing the spirit. The Mayan Indians cook with it."

"I'll see what I can do, madam."

"Oh, and waiter, one more thing. The olive oil, how do I know it will be extra virgin?"

The waiter, who was tall and had a certain Jeevesian air about him, decided he'd had enough. "Oh, that's easy, madam," he replied. "All our olive oil is submitted to a rigorous vaginal examination before use." With that he walked away.

The American woman's face turned beetroot red, clashing exquisitely with her hair. She looked as if she was about to bust a gut with fury. Sensing this, her companion got out of her seat, put her arm round the woman's shoulders and did her best to calm her down.

"Christ, what a witch," Anna said.

Alison looked at Anna and laughed.

"You don't know who she is, do you? Come on, Anna, look at the hair?"

Anna looked.

"Christ, it's her, isn't it?"

"Yep. And she's three days early. According to the press release she's not meant to be here until the nineteenth. Thank God you've written the article. I'll probably run it tomorrow."

While Alison disappeared, like she always did, to chuck up in the loo, Anna glanced surreptitiously towards Rachel Stern's table. Having been presented with her food, Stern produced a pair of chopsticks from her handbag and began picking up individual snow peas or slices of zucchini, scrutinizing them and then putting them on the side of the plate. Every so often, a piece of vegetable passed muster and made it to her mouth.

After a while, Anna's eyes were drawn towards Stern's taut-expressioned companion. Anna realized she recognized her. It was Bryoney Keen. Anna knew Bryoney from years ago when they were trainees together on the *Hemel Hempstead Gazette*. Bryoney had gone on to the *Guardian,* and left to do a course in television production shortly before Anna went freelance. She now owned her own production company, Keen Productions, which produced a dreary but worthy breakfast show for Channel Six called *At the Crack with Tim and Heather.* It was as plain as the plastic nose on her face that Stern had been invited to appear on the show.

Anna took a huge gulp of her spritzer. In a matter of seconds, she'd made up her mind. Apart from getting her husband back, what she now wanted more than anything else in the world was the chance to confront Rachel Stern face-to-face about her cosmetic surgery—not to mention her position on adultery.

Under normal circumstances the thought of challenging a woman as combative and aggressive as Stern, particularly on live television, would have scared the life out of Anna. Suddenly, buoyed up by fury and adrenaline, the thought thrilled her.

She would give Bryoney a chance to get back to her office after lunch and then phone her.

"So," Alison said when she got back, "what was the other thing you wanted to tell me about . . . ?" She nodded her head discreetly in Stern's direction.

"Oh," Anna said, barely hesitating. "Somebody mentioned she gets all that volume in her hair using Velcro rollers rather than Carmens."

"Now, *that,*" said Alison, "is really fascinating. We haven't done a how-to-achieve-perfect-big-hair feature for weeks. . . ."

CHAPTER TWENTY-THREE

GLORIA, WHO KNEW NOTHING OF HER daughter's present anguish, had spent the evening trying to get a decent shine on Harry's nuts. Harry was due back from Israel on Monday and she thought he would appreciate coming home to a clean and tidy tool chest.

In common with most Jewish men, a combination of snobbery and utter incompetence caused him to shun virtually all aspects of DIY. Whereas his non-Jewish friends were frequently overcome by the impulse to grout, or the desire to own a cordless drill, Harry had never experienced such impulses or desires. Nor had he ever experienced the delights of a Sunday afternoon spent wandering round local DIY superstores in search of that elusive set of premetric Allen keys. For years Harry thought Texas Homecare was some kind of American neighborhood watch scheme.

This lack of interest in manual labor was reflected in the pristine condition of Harry's thirty-year-old tool box. It was also reflected in its contents, most of which were next to useless. As well as the nuts and a few unopened packets of screws and picture hooks, it contained a fifteen-year-old tube of Araldite, a pair of needle-nose pliers which were meant exclusively for fine electrical work, a ball peen hammer with a loose head and a hand drill with no masonry bit.

Gloria had tipped all the screws, nuts and nails into a pair of pantyhose which were brand-new but had turned out to be the wrong shade of oyster, and put them in the dishwasher cutlery container. When she discovered that not even the hottest cycle could make them gleam, she decided to get a duster and some metal polish and buff the lot up by hand.

By nine o'clock her wrists were aching and her hands were caked in a mixture of black metal oxide and dried polish. She decided to have a break. She would take a cup of tea into the living room, sit herself down and read the deaths column in the local paper. The ridiculous "Mum, we are miffed now you are a stiff" rhymes always creased her up.

She took a clean cup from the dishwasher. While she rinsed it in boiling water to remove any residual germs, Gloria found her mind wandering back to the night Gerald Brownstein broke in through the downstairs loo window. An icy shiver ran down her back. She thanked God that after telling Julian, who ran her obsessive-compulsives group, what had happened, he had finally been convinced that Gerald was seriously unhinged. Julian had gone to see Gerald's daughter and persuaded her to put him in an old people's home.

He was now living quite happily in the Sadie and Manny Lever Home in Hendon, and was allowed out only if a member of staff went with him.

Gloria had been to see him once, but hadn't stayed long. This was because she'd made the mistake of arriving at teatime and one of the residents, a toothless woman called Hettie who could only chew soft food, and who believed she could see into the future, kept coming over to where Gloria and Gerald were sitting and insisting on reading Gerald's fortune in her Alphabetti spaghetti.

Gloria went into the living room and put her cup and saucer on top of the nest of tables next to the armchair. Having shoved a cushion into the small of her back, she put her feet up on her pink velvet footstool and began turning the pages of the newspaper. Her journey towards the births, marriages and deaths was interrupted by an article highlighting a debate between a handful of Stanmore residents and the council over the fate of six sycamore trees. The huge trees grew in a park which backed onto the residents' gardens. They had no objection to the trees, only to their roots, which they maintained were about to undermine the foundations of their houses. For months, the residents had been asking the council to take some kind of remedial action to prevent the roots spreading any farther, or to cut down the trees. The council were refusing to do either.

Normally, Gloria would have ignored such an article. At best she would have given it a casual glance. The reason she not only read it, but took in every word, was that she was one of the Stanmore residents. One of the eighty-foot-high sycamores directly overlooked her back garden. Only a week ago she had added her name to yet another letter from the residents' committee, demanding the council act immediately to protect their homes.

The article ended by saying that the residents' committee had consulted a prominent tree surgeon named Tilda Hasselquist, who said that in her opinion there was no doubt that the sycamore roots were damaging the houses and that the council would be "courting financial disaster if they didn't cut down the trees at once."

Gloria smiled. The council would be mad not to give in. She was about to turn the page and resume her journey towards the births, marriages and deaths when she realized that something about the photograph of the sycamores had disturbed her. She folded back the newspaper, heaved herself out of the armchair and held the article under the standard lamp.

The sycamore which featured most prominently in the photograph was the one backing onto her garden. Gloria was in no doubt about this, because underneath the tree she could clearly see a couple of her Rigby and Peller bras pegged to a rotary washing line. What she couldn't quite make out was who, or what, was crouching in the tree about halfway up, clutching the trunk. It was far too big for a cat. She pushed her glasses onto her head and brought the photograph up close to her eyes, but it made no difference. She couldn't begin to see what the thing could be.

Gloria put the newspaper down on the chair and went into the kitchen, where she had left Harry's tool chest. Among all his bits and pieces there was a Swiss Army knife which she knew had a magnifying glass attachment.

Resuming her position under the standard lamp, she held the magnifying glass over the photograph. Her heart nearly stopped. There was one part of the crouching figure which was slightly less out of focus than the rest. She would recognize that hooter, that grin, those spectacles anywhere.

Gloria was in no doubt. Gerald Brownstein had tunneled out of the Sadie and Manny Lever Home. Not only was he on the run, but he was still stalking her. He had become a tree stalker.

Gloria ran into the kitchen, picked up the phone and dialed 999.

CHAPTER TWENTY-FOUR

ANNA'S ALARM WENT OFF JUST after six. For several seconds she lay rigid with terror while her brain struggled, and failed, to work out who and where she was. When, after another second or two, her memory returned, the misery which had become part of her since Dan left let itself in and made itself at home in her stomach. She wanted to be sick.

She sat up in bed and took a few deep breaths. Her wake-up routine had been the same every day since Dan left. She knew that after a couple of minutes the nausea would pass and that in its place would come anger, desperation and longing. These would be her companions for the rest of the day.

The only vaguely bright spot in Anna's life was that she had made her peace with Brenda. The moment she had got home having run out on Ed, she'd phoned Brenda to tell her about it and to apologize for her behavior when she came to pick up the kids. Brenda had also said sorry for getting on her high horse. It was then that Anna had begged Brenda to go and see Dan to try and persuade him to come home. Brenda, who thought the pair of them needed their heads bashing together and that she should be the one to do the bashing, hadn't taken any persuading. She had driven round to Beany Levine's flat early yesterday evening. The moment she got home, she'd phoned Anna.

"Well, the good news is, he got the result of 'is chest X ray and it was clear. According to Dan the doctor now thinks the cough was nothing more than a stress thing."

"Thank God." Anna almost wept with relief.

"Nevertheless," Brenda went on, "he's still one severely depressed bloke. He's not eating, he hasn't been to work and he doesn't look like 'e's washed for days. I also think he may be hitting the booze big-time. Mind you, that flat doesn't help matters. Talk about a flophouse. Apparently Beany gave up barristering just after his divorce and is trying to make a name for himself doing stand-up comedy. So naturally, he's broke and can't afford a decent place to live—"

"Yes, yes, I know, but what did Dan say?" Anna sounded almost frantic. "Did you tell him that I still love him—that I want him back?"

Brenda went silent.

"Yeah, I told him," she said flatly.

"And?"

"And he says he wants more time on his own. Says he can't bring himself to see a solicitor yet because he still loves you. But he's not sure if he'll ever be able to forgive you."

"And that's it? That's all he said?"

"Pretty much. To be honest, I couldn't get much out of him. I think he'd been drinking all afternoon. He looked half asleep most of the time."

"But didn't he say anything about getting in touch, about seeing the kids?"

"Anna, he really is in a bad way. I blasted in there ready to read 'im the riot act, a bit like I did with you the other night, but he's out of it. He barely knows what time of day it is. I'd only been there twenty minutes and he took himself off to bed. I spent the rest of the evening nattering to Beany. Funny . . ."—her tone lightened suddenly—"I always imagined someone with a name like Beany Levine would be skinny and bald. . . ."

Brenda's voice trailed off. She sounded like she had something important to tell Anna, but had decided this wasn't the right time.

"Anna," she said, getting her thoughts back on track, "I think you've got no option but to do as he asks. You have to back off and give him time to sort his 'ead out. He'll come back. I know it."

As Anna lay in bed, those last words kept echoing inside her brain. She supposed she had to live in hope.

Having allowed her ten minutes' snooze time, the alarm clock went off again. Anna tensed momentarily with surprise, and then reached out to switch it off. She had nearly two hours before she was due at the Channel 6 studio in Hammersmith.

As she had hoped, Bryoney Keen had barely been able to contain her excitement when she'd phoned her and suggested confronting Rachel Stern on live television. The only problem had been Alex. He had immediately agreed to take part, but his heart specialist had decided the strain of doing an interview in the TV studio might be too much for him. It was agreed instead that he would still tell his story live, but from home, rather than in the studio.

Anna stood up and put on her dressing gown. As she tied the belt, it occurred to her that between them, she and Alex could be about to destroy Rachel Stern's career. Sex aside, Anna was the closest she'd been in ages to experiencing a warm glow.

.   .   .

WHILE A MAKEUP GIRL CALLED CINDERS SMEARED FOUNDA-tion over Anna's face with a tiny damp sponge, Brenda came in carrying a tray of tea. She'd insisted on coming with Anna to the studio to hold her hand.

"Christ," she said, addressing Anna's reflection in the brightly lit mirror, "you want to see it out there. They're all running round like tits in a trance. Seems like Stern is stuck in traffic and you're due on in ten minutes."

"She'll be here," Anna said calmly. She refused to be panicked, or to countenance for one minute that her plan to destroy Rachel Stern was about to be scuppered.

Brenda made a space in the clutter of eyeshadow palettes on the melamine ledge under the mirror and put down Anna's cup. Cinders, who wasn't best pleased about her palettes being interfered with, gave Brenda a filthy look. Brenda matched it.

At that moment a very flustered Bryoney Keen appeared. She spoke through a haze of cigarette smoke and coffee breath.

"Thought I'd pop in and explain the running order. Just before half eight we've got the chef doing a gooseberry cobbler. That's followed by a heavyweight interview with a couple of scientists from Imperial College who have isolated the gene which makes women pick their feet in front of the telly and then pile up the dead skin on the arm of the chair, and then it's you. I'll send somebody to fetch you when we're ready. I've just spoken to Rachel Stern on her mobile. She shouldn't be more than a couple of minutes."

Then Bryoney was out of the door. Brenda, who wanted someone to show her where to find the loo, chased after her.

Cinders began taking out the huge heated rollers she'd put in Anna's hair "to give you a bit of volume" and continued with the "less is more" lecture she had been giving before Brenda came in with the tray of tea. This had been precipitated by Anna turning up to the studio wearing her favorite bright-red lipstick, which she thought made her look dynamic as well as sexy. Cinders had tut-tutted as she rubbed at it with cleanser and cotton wool. "Mature women," she had said with twenty-two-year-old cockiness, making it perfectly clear she was refer-ring to Anna, "need to remember that softer, paler colors are more flattering on an aging skin."

As Cinders rabbited on and began back-combing, Anna found herself thinking about Ed and how relieved and grateful she was that he had been able to forgive her for running out on him. When she'd got home after her lunch with Alison, she'd found a huge bouquet of flowers waiting for her on the door-step. The note with them was very brief. It simply said that he understood that she wasn't ready to start a serious relationship, and that his life had taken a sudden and highly unexpected turn for the better. Tilda, his ex, had been invited to join a team of scientists in a biosphere in Arizona. Her brief was to spend two years creating her own rain forest. She had accepted and now, having undergone a complete change of heart, wanted Ed to have the children. Anna had read the last line so often, she knew it off by heart. "Please don't worry about me, I'm happier than I've been in months. I'll miss you and I will always love you. Ed."

Anna dabbed at her eyes with a Kleenex and prayed that the mascara Cinders had used was waterproof.

"Right, that's you done," Cinders said, giving Anna's hair a final spray.

When Anna had finished choking, she took a good look at herself in the mirror. The whole effect was hideous. Her face looked pale and washed-out, and instead of hair, she appeared to be wearing an enormous candy floss hat.

She was about to insist that Cinders redo her face and hair when a young lad in a Channel 6 T-shirt came in to take her onto the set. Ripping off her pink nylon gown, she followed him into the long corridor which led to the studio.

ANNA STOOD JUST INSIDE THE STUDIO DOOR, WATCHING Heather and Tim finish their interview with the scientists from Imperial College. The set, which Bryoney had explained had been designed to look ordinary and unthreatening and to make viewers feel as if they were sitting in their own living room in Croydon, consisted of two sofas with backs shaped like asymmetrical parabolas. One was deep purple, the other lime green. Between these was a vermilion coffee table shaped like a pair of lips. On the floor were two or three huge vases which looked like old-fashioned metal buckets. Each contained two bright-orange bird-of-paradise flowers and a single green leaf.

Heather and Tim, on the other hand, looked genuinely ordinary and unthreatening. Tim, in his M&S slacks and pale-yellow V-necked sweater, gave the impression of being a harmless, avuncular chap who played a lot of golf. Heather, who was wearing calf-length pleats and turquoise jacket, was plump and mumsy-looking.

Heather and Tim shook hands with the scientists and Heather announced a commercial break. While the scientists were having their microphone packs removed, Rachel Stern was brought onto the set. The idea was that Heather and Tim would spend a couple of minutes interviewing Stern about her book and then Anna would be invited to join the discussion. Stern looked stunning in a rust-colored trouser suit which matched her hair. Heather and Tim stood up to greet her. Anna grimaced as she watched Stern give them a haughty stare, flick back her mass of curls and ignore their outstretched hands. Instead she turned towards another lad in a headset and demanded iced Perrier. "And I want it in a glass," she bellowed, "not one of your frigging paper cups." Then, her expression about as warm as Anchorage in December, she wiped over her end of the sofa with a handkerchief and sat down. She was clearly ready to do battle.

Suddenly, Anna was shaking visibly.

"I think these might make you feel better." Anna jumped and swung round. She'd thought Brenda was still in the loo. "I went back into makeup and took them out of your bag." She handed Anna her Denman hairbrush and bright-red lipstick.

· · ·

AS SOON AS THE ADS CAME ON, DAN GOT UP AND MADE HIM-
self another mug of tea. He'd been awake since four. By
six he'd realized he wasn't going to get back to sleep. Wrapped
in his duvet, he'd shuffled into the living room and switched on
the telly. He had followed this pattern every morning since
moving in with Beany. He would begin the day with *At the
Crack* with a pair of gut-churningly chirpy morons called Tim
and Heather. When that finished at ten, he would pour himself
his first glass of Red Label. He would then take the bottle and
the remote back to Beany's filthy, stinking sofa and spend the
rest of the day surfing the satellite sport and movie channels.
The only time he got up was to go to the can.

Dan needed the whiskey because it took the edge off his
pain. Receiving the news from Dr. Harper that he wasn't dying
hadn't eased his misery in the slightest. In a perverse, twisted
way, Dan almost wished he had cancer. The knowledge that he
didn't only put pressure on him to cheer up.

Nothing, not even whiskey, could control the anger he felt
towards Anna. There were moments when he would imagine
she was in the room with him. Then he would shout and swear
and scream the place down. Afterwards he would look round
for something to smash. Even in his misery, he decided,
smashing crockery was a cliché. Besides, Beany only possessed
two dinner plates and a couple of cereal bowls. Without these,
they would have to eat straight from the frying pan. Instead,
when Dan felt himself overcome with rage, he would take it
out on Beany's telephone directories. Last night he had ripped
the pages of the L-to-Z book from their spine. For some reason
he had then taken the last few pages and ripped them to
shreds. Beany had come home to find Dan fast asleep, buried
in Zweigbergs, Zussmans and Zwebners.

He came back into the living room and put his feet up on
what passed as a coffee table. He sipped his tea. Through his
hangover, he was vaguely aware of Heather and Tim interviewing some strident and deeply unpleasant American feminist
about her latest book. He decided he could either cope with
her bellowing voice or his headache, but not both. He picked

up the remote and pointed it at the screen. It was then that he noticed Heather was holding up a copy of that morning's *Daily Mercury*. He took his feet off the table and leaned forward. Anna's huge byline almost leaped out at him from the television screen.

"Now, those of you who have read this morning's *Mercury*," Heather was saying, "will be aware of an article which appears across several pages, and which is deeply critical of the ideas put forward in *The Clitoris-Centered Woman*. The article was written by the journalist Anna Shapiro and she joins us this morning. Anna, welcome. . . ."

Dan could hardly believe what was happening. Hadn't it been enough for Anna to humiliate him in private? Now she was about to inflict even more pain on him by letting the whole world know about her affairs. He sat with his finger hovering over the off button on the remote control. The debate between Anna and the feminist, who he now realized was Rachel Stern, had started to get quite heated.

"I think what you have to realize, Angela," Stern was saying to Anna, "is that in order to become a truly clitoris-centered woman, you have to be determined. You must have balls. . . . Am I allowed to say balls on Briddish television?"

Heather giggled uneasily. "Well, maybe just this once. Oh, and by the way, it's Anna, not Angela," she added.

"Whatever," Stern continued stonily. "You see, my point is that women who have affairs and are found out, or women who have affairs and end up falling in love, are essentially weak and unfocused. Instead of concentrating purely on the sex, they get carried away with the whole romance bit. By now their heads are completely in the clouds and they get careless and—"

Clearly furious, Anna cut across her.

"I don't consider myself to be either weak or unfocused," she spat. "I did my best not to fall for the men I slept with. In the end it was out of my control. I just couldn't help falling for one of them. Then my husband found out."

"Listen to me, Anita, you had your affairs and you screwed up because you didn't obey my rules. Honey, you are simply looking for someone to blame because you can't face taking the blame yourself."

"That is a lie," Anna shouted. Dan could hear tears in her voice. There was no doubt in his mind about why she was in such a rage. She had realized Stern was right and she couldn't bear it.

"The point is," Anna said, going on an all-out attack, "that you are wickedly and cynically conning women into believing they can have a string of affairs without ever falling in love. I believe that eventually even the most 'focused' of women will fall in love and then they have to face the appalling consequences—like I did. Have you even the remotest idea of the pain I am feeling?"

Dan watched as Anna started to cry and Heather reached out to touch her hand and give her a warm and caring look.

"I have lost everything," Anna wept, "my husband who I have never stopped loving, my last lover, and I may even lose my children. I would do anything, absolutely anything, to get my husband back, but because of you it's too late. My life is over."

"Gahd, where did you dredge up this bleeding heart?" Stern sighed.

Anna took a deep breath. "At least," she said with forced calmness, "I have blood in me, and not silicone."

Stern sat back in her chair and laughed.

"I'm sorry, I have no idea what on earth you are talking about."

"Well, let me see if we can make things a little clearer," Tim interjected brightly. "Rachel, you have always been highly critical of women who have cosmetic surgery."

"Ab-so-lutely. Women do it because men are only interested in what they look like, not what they have to say. My message is that women must fight to make themselves heard by men."

"In that case," Tim said slyly, suddenly sounding a bit less bland, and more like a detective superintendent going in for the kill, "perhaps you would like to take this opportunity to explain why you decided to have cosmetic surgery, and why you chose to have it in this country rather than in the States?"

Dan couldn't take his eyes off Rachel Stern. She was twisting in her chair, her eyes darting all over the place. She was clearly desperate for somebody to rescue her. Dan thought she was going to do a runner, but she didn't move.

A moment later a man's head and shoulders appeared on the studio monitor and Tim introduced Alex Pemberton. Very calmly, Alex went through the list of cosmetic procedures he had performed on Stern. Over the last three years, he said, Ms. Stern had received breast implants, a new nose, chin and cheek implants and liposuction on her thighs.

Rachel Stern let Alex finish. Then, her eyes bulging, she began screaming so hard that the speaker on Beany's TV began to distort.

"I know what this is," she yelled at Anna. "This is some kind of plot hatched by the press and the Briddish feminist movement to discredit me. You've always hated me in this country— just like you hate Steinem and Friedan. You mealymouthed Brits can't stand anyone with spunk. You despise anyone who stands up and shouts for what they want. Well, you won't get away with it. I will sue you"—she pointed to Anna—"and you"—she pointed to Alex—"and this entire friggin' TV company. . . ." With that she leaped out of her seat and tore off her microphone. Then she walked over to Anna, drew back an Armani-ed leg and kicked her in the shin. Anna yelped. Her hand darted to the pain. She got out of her seat, picked up the water jug from the lip-shaped table and poured water over Stern's head. Stern, looking like a half-drowned cocker spaniel, suddenly pulled Anna onto the floor, got on top of her and began tugging tufts of hair from her scalp and scratching her face. The camera followed them as they rolled over and over like a couple of boys in a playground bundle. Knocking over a couple of the flower vases on the way, they rolled towards the table where the *At the Crack* chef had left his gooseberry cobbler. Stern, who was on top of Anna, released her grip on her hair and managed to get hold of the Pyrex dish full of cobbler.

Grinning like a demon, she plunged her hand into the pudding and began smearing Anna's face with warm gooseberry mush.

His heart pounding with fear and rage, Dan jumped off the sofa and knelt on the floor, his face inches from the television screen.

"Shit. Why isn't somebody bloody well doing something?" he shouted at the screen as he watched a mixture of blood and stewed fruit running down Anna's face.

Anna had retaliated by ripping open the front of Stern's blouse. The entire nation could now see her maniacally tugging at the front of Stern's skimpy red-lace bra. Dan could tell it was only a matter of seconds before Stern's breasts fell out. He was right. A moment later, the camera zoomed in on them. Dan flinched in disgust. They looked like two particularly large and solid grapefruit halves which had been perched on her chest and covered in taut skin.

Finally two men in headsets and sleeveless black Puffa jackets waded in and managed to pull the two women off each other. As Anna and Rachel Stern were led away kicking and swearing, a tearful and shaking Heather stepped back onto the demolished set. She was accompanied by a grim-faced Tim, who wrapped a paternal arm round her shoulders.

Dabbing at her eyes with a tissue, Heather looked earnestly into the camera and apologized for what she described as a despicable, contemptible and infantile display. She allowed a couple of seconds for a meaningful pause, during which Tim tightened his arm round her shoulders, before breaking into a smile and launching into a chirpy rundown of the program lineup. This included a two-minute featurette on how fifteen million people would be killed by flooding if world governments continued to ignore the dire warnings about the greenhouse effect, and film of her test-driving the latest Japanese hatchback, the Placenta Praevia. This apparently came with oodles of high-tech extras, including a hands-off telephone with a dial-by-voice gadget, which Heather said was particularly useful at traffic lights because it meant you could call up your friends' numbers at the same time as painting your nails.

Dan stood up and stabbed the off button on the TV remote. His pulse was still racing. The only thing he could think about was getting to Channel 6 and rescuing Anna from this mayhem. It was beginning to dawn on him that Anna was genuinely sorry for what she had done, and that he wasn't the only one in pain. From the moment he'd found out about her affairs, he'd understood intellectually that his hypochondria was to blame and that he had been responsible for driving her into the arms of other men.

The difference now, several days later, seeing her anguished face on TV, the sheer bloody wretchedness she was clearly suffering, was that he could actually feel the agony he had caused her, and appreciate for the first time the guilt she was now feeling for cheating on him. All he wanted to do was to hold her, to tell her how much he loved her—and make her understand that he forgave her.

He picked up his wallet and, wearing only his grubby jeans and a white T-shirt, which had been on his back for three days and was covered in Heinz tomato soup stains, ran to the front door. The Channel 6 studios were no more than a few hundred yards away, in King Street. It was only when he stepped onto the pavement that he realized his feet were bare.

As he sprinted to the corner of Beany's road, he felt a few spots of rain on his face. In less than a minute it was teeming down. His hair was soaked, his T-shirt was sticking to his chest and his jeans were covered in the filthy oily spray being shot at him from passing cars. The pavement was becoming slippery under his feet.

After a few more yards he began to feel breathless and he slowed down. A couple of women pushing toddlers in buggies looked at him, assumed he was some kind of schizo nutter on a bender, and gave him a wide berth.

Turning into King Street, he kept hearing Anna's voice saying, "I have lost everything. . . . My life is over. . . . It's too late." "No it's not," he sobbed as he ran. "I'm coming, I'm coming."

The Channel 6 building was on the other side of the road.

The traffic was almost at a standstill. Dan picked his way between bumpers. Gasping for breath, he almost fell into the gray-carpeted reception area. He walked over to the desk and spoke to the uniformed doorman.

"Excuse me, my wife is appearing, that is, she was appearing on . . ."

"Now then, mate, I know it's chucking it down, but you can't come in here. Here's a couple of bob. Go and get yourself a cuppa in McDonald's." He held out a fifty-pence piece towards Dan.

"No, you don't understand. My wife's in the studio being beaten up by some mad American feminist."

"I'm sure she is, mate." The doorman stood up and walked around to the front of the desk. He put his arm round Dan's shoulders. "Look, why don't we have a look and see if your pills are in your pocket. Maybe you forgot to take them today. Shall we see what we can find?" He pushed his hand into Dan's jeans pocket. Dan swore at him and pushed him away.

"Right," the chap said, finally losing his temper, "I've tried being friendly, now it's out you go."

In a second Dan's arm had been thrust up between his shoulder blades and he was being frog-marched towards the exit. The two of them had just reached the automatic doors when an almighty howl came from behind them.

"Please, please don't . . . put him down. Dan, it's me."

The doorman released his grip. He then watched Dan, who looked as if he'd just done a runner from Broadmoor, rush over to a woman who looked as if she'd spent several days sleeping rough under a gooseberry bush and wrap her in his arms. While Dan almost kissed the life out of Anna and told her he loved her over and over again, and Anna told Dan she was sorry over and over again, and Dan said he was sorry too, the doorman began speaking into his walkie-talkie.

"Gordon, it's Vic. I've got a couple of down-and-outs in reception. Both completely bonkers. I'd appreciate a hand."

"Roger, ten four," crackled the response.

Fearing violence from the pair, he then retreated back behind the reception desk.

Dan couldn't take his eyes off Anna, partly because he realized how much he adored her and partly because her face was
still bleeding.

"Anna, look what she's done to you," he said, looking at her
torn, stained clothes and lifting a couple of strands of her hair
out of some congealed blood.

"Don't worry, I'll be fine. The nurse put some Dettol on the
scratches. She says they look worse than they are."

"Come on," Dan said, kissing her wounded face. "Let's get
you home."

"Not yet, I've got to wait for Brenda. She went back for my
handbag."

The next moment Brenda appeared. She took one look at
Anna and Dan with their arms round each other and broke into
a huge grin.

"You pair of smocks," she said, realizing that Dan must have
watched the Shapiro–Stern spectacle and decided to come and
rescue Anna.

"That's *schmocks,* Brenda." Dan laughed.

"Whatever," Brenda replied as she hugged and kissed them
both and handed Anna her bag. "Now I think I'll love you and
leave you. There's somewhere I have to be at twelve and I want
to get changed and put on some makeup."

"Why? Where are you going?" Anna asked.

"Beany's taking me out for lunch," she said merrily as she
walked towards the doors. "And then tonight I'm going to
watch him do his routine at the Comedy Store. See ya." And
she was gone.

Anna looked at Dan and smiled. "I had the feeling the other
night when I spoke to her on the phone that there was something she wasn't telling me. C'mon. Let's go."

"No, wait, look." Dan pointed to one of the TVs which were
mounted on the wall nearest the lift. His attention appeared to
have been taken by a Channel 6 London news bulletin.

"And now we're going over live to the Brent Cross shopping center where our reporter, Kay Armstrong, has the latest on the incident. . . . Kay, perhaps you could recap and tell us exactly what happened. . . ."

"Well, Clive, a sixty-two-year-old woman, who, it appears, had been the victim of a stalker for some weeks, came into John Lewis first thing this morning to buy a roll of plastic carpet protector. The grandmother from Stanmore, whose name hasn't yet been released, had, within the last twenty-four hours, been given police protection. When she arrived at the store, neither the woman nor her police bodyguard, it seems, had any idea the stalker was following them.

"While the policeman went to get a cup of tea, the stalker cornered the woman as she stood at the cash desk. He threatened to swallow a bottle of turps if she tried to move and insisted on serenading her. For over an hour, I'm told, she stood at the cash desk while the elderly man, who is a resident at the Sadie and Manny Lever retirement home nearby, sang 'You Are My Sunshine.'

"Neither the police nor the matron of the retirement home were able to calm the man, and the incident was only brought to an end when the woman knocked him out by hitting him on the head with her roll of carpet protector. He is recovering at the Royal Free Hospital. His injuries are thought to be minor. The hospital is also treating the woman for shock. No one is able to shed any light on how the man escaped, but a spokeswoman for the Sadie and Manny Lever Home has already promised to hold a full inquiry into the home's security procedures."

Moments later Gordon, the doorman, who'd just finished his break, arrived in reception to help eject Dan and Anna. He was too late.

On the pavement outside the Channel 6 studios, a small crowd had gathered in the rain to watch as two hysterical down-and-outs pleaded with a cabbie to take them to the Royal Free Hospital.